ALSO BY ELSIE SILVER

Chestnut Springs
Flawless
Heartless
Powerless
Reckless

Gold Rush Ranch
Off to the Races
A Photo Finish
The Front Runner
A False Start

POWER LESS

ELSIE SILVER

Bloom *books*

Published by Bloom Books, an imprint of Sourcebooks
P.O. Box 4410, Naperville, Illinois 60567-410
(630) 961-3900
sourcebooks.com

Originally self-published in 2023 by Elsie Silver.

Printed and bound in the United States of America.
WOZ 10 9 8 7 6 5 4 3

*For the ones who've spent their lives
being just a little *too* agreeable.
Here's to getting comfortable disappointing
other people to avoid disappointing yourself.*

The truth is we only have control over a finite number of things in life. The rest is a fucking crapshoot.

—KANDI STEINER

Reader Note

This book contains adult material, including childhood trauma, death of a family member, and anxiety. It is my hope that I've handled these topics with the care they deserve.

PROLOGUE

Sloane

THEN...

My car door is open before my parents have put the Bentley in park. My feet hit the gravel driveway before they've even managed to get out of the car. In a whoosh of breath, my arms wrap around my cousin Violet. We almost bowl each other over onto the dirt driveway with the force of our hug.

She smells like green grass, horses, and sweet summer freedom.

"I missed you!" I squeal as Violet pulls away and grins mischievously at me.

"I missed you too."

I catch my mom staring at us, happy and sad all at once. I look like my mom, and Violet looks like hers. Except Violet's mom died, and my mom lost her sister. I always think she likes bringing me out here because she feels close to her sister when she's on the ranch.

It also makes it more convenient for my parents to travel to their favorite spots in Europe. My dad said something about it being good for me to "see how the other half lives." I'm not totally sure what that means, but I saw my mom's lips clamp down on each other when he said it.

Either way, I never complain, because a full month at Wishing Well Ranch with the Eaton family means I get to hang out and have fun with my cousins. The rules are lax. The curfews don't exist. And I get to run wild for four full weeks every summer.

"Robert, Cordelia." Uncle Harvey reaches forward to shake my dad's hand before giving my mom a tight squeeze that leaves her blinking a little too quickly as she peers out over the flat farm fields and jagged mountains behind them. "Nice to see you both."

They start talking about boring adult stuff, but I don't hear them because my other cousins walk out of the big ranch house. Cade, Beau, and Rhett jog down the front stairs, joking and shoving and roaming like a pack.

And then they're followed by one more boy. One I don't recognize. One who immediately has my attention. One with long, lanky limbs, caramel-colored hair, and the bluest eyes I've ever seen.

The *saddest* eyes I've ever seen.

When that boy slides his gaze over to me, there's nothing but curiosity on his face. I jerk my head away all the same, feeling hot splotches pop up on my cheeks.

My mom moves beside me, patting me on the head. "Sloane, you need to remember your sunscreen. You already look too hot, and you spend so much time in the dance studio, your skin isn't used to this exposure."

Her fussing only makes me blush harder. I'm almost eleven, and she's making me seem like a baby in front of everyone.

I give my eyes a petulant roll and mumble, "I know. I will," before taking Violet's hand and storming off.

We go inside and up to my guest room, searching for some privacy while everyone else stands around outside and makes small talk.

Violet flops on the mattress and announces, "Tell me everything."

I giggle and push my hair behind my ears, drawn to the window that overlooks the driveway. "About what?"

"School? The city? What do you wanna do this summer? Just...everything. I'm so happy there's a girl here. This place stinks like boys *all the time*."

Out the window, I see the mystery boy shaking hands with my parents. I note the distaste on my father's face. The pity on my mother's.

"Who's the other guy?" I ask, unable to look away.

"Oh." Violet's voice gets a little quiet. "That's Jasper. He's one of us now."

I turn to her, eyebrow quirked, hands on my hips, trying to play it cool, like I'm not *too* interested, but not really knowing how to achieve that either. "What do you mean?"

She rolls up to sit cross-legged on the bed and shrugs. "He needed a family, so we took him in. I don't know all the details. There was an accident. Beau brought him here one day last fall. I like to think of him as one more stinky brother. You can just think of him like a new cousin."

My head cants as my heart battles with my brain.

My heart wants to stare out the window again because Jasper is *so* cute and staring at him makes it do this weird little skipping thing in my chest.

My brain knows it's stupid because if he's friends with Beau, he must be at least fifteen.

But I can't stop myself.

I look anyway.

What I don't realize is that I'll be fighting the urge to stare at Jasper Gervais for years to come.

1

Jasper

NOW...

SLOANE WINTHROP'S FIANCÉ IS A ROYAL DOUCHEBAG.

I'm familiar with the type. You don't work your way into the NHL without encountering your fair share.

And this guy has the act down pat.

As if the name *Sterling Woodcock* wasn't enough of a giveaway, he's now bragging about the hunting trip he and his dad spent hundreds of thousands of dollars on to kill lions born and bred in captivity, like that will somehow make their dicks bigger.

From the Rolex on his wrist to his manicured nails, he's dripping wealth, and I guess it only makes sense that Sloane might end up with a man like him. After all, the Winthrops are one of the most powerful families in the country, with what is damn near a monopoly on the telecommunications industry.

As Sterling rambles, I glance at Sloane across the table. Her sky-blue eyes are downcast, and she's clearly fiddling with the napkin in her lap. She looks like she'd rather be anywhere but here in this dimly lit, ornate steak house.

And I feel about the same.

Listening to her small-dicked future husband boast to a table full of family and friends I've never met about something that is honestly embarrassing—and sad—isn't how I'd choose to spend a night off.

But I'm here for Sloane, and that's what I keep telling myself.

Because seeing her right now, all downtrodden mere nights before her wedding, it feels like she needs someone here who actually knows her. The rest of the Eaton crew couldn't make it into the city tonight, but I promised her I'd come.

And for Sloane I keep every promise, no matter how badly they hurt.

I expected her to be smiling. Glowing. I expected to be happy for her—but I'm not.

"You hunt, Jasper?" Sterling asks, all poised and pretentious.

The collar of my checkered dress shirt feels like it's strangling me, even though I left the top buttons undone. I clear my throat and roll my shoulders back. "I do."

Sterling picks up the crystal tumbler before him and leans back to assess me with a smug smirk on his perfectly shaved face. "Any big game? You'd enjoy a trip like this." People who don't know me nod and murmur their assent.

"I don't know if—" Sloane starts, but her fiancé steamrolls her attempt at adding to the conversation.

"We all saw what your last contract came in at. Not bad for a goalie. So, provided you've been responsible with your money, it's something you should be able to afford."

Like I said: douchebag.

I bite the inside of my cheek, tempted to say I've been horribly irresponsible with my money and don't have a dollar to my name. But as lowbrow as my upbringing might have been, I have enough class to know that finances aren't polite dinner conversation.

"Nah, man. I only hunt what I can eat, and I'm unfamiliar with how to cook a lion."

A few chuckles break out around the table, including from Sloane. I don't miss the quick moment when Sterling's eyes narrow, when his teeth clamp and his jaw pops.

Sloane jumps in quickly, patting his arm like he's a dog that needs soothing. I can almost feel her slender fingers on my own arm and absently find myself wishing it were me she was touching instead. "I used to hunt with my cousins out in Chestnut Springs too, you know?"

I'm tossed back in time, remembering a young Sloane keeping up with the boys all summer. Sloane with dirt under her nails, scrapes on her knees, sun-bleached hair all tangled and free down her back.

"It's more about the thrill, you know? The power." Sterling ignores Sloane's comment entirely.

He looks at me like an opponent, except we aren't playing hockey right now. If we were, I'd give him a quick blocker shot to the face.

"Did you not hear what Sloane just said?" I'm trying to

be cool, but I hate the way he's treated her through this entire dinner. I don't know how she ended up here. She's my best friend. She's eloquent and smart and funny—does he not see that at all? Does he not see *her*?

Sterling waves a hand and chuckles. "Ah, yes. I'm always hearing about Wishing Well Ranch." He turns to her with a condescending tone and a mocking smirk. "Well, thank goodness you outgrew whatever tomboy phase you went through, babe. You'd have missed your calling as a ballerina."

His shitty response is worsened by my realization that he heard what she said and *chose* to ignore her.

"I can't even imagine you handling a gun, Sloane!" one guy further down the long table exclaims, his nose a deep red from far too much scotch.

"I was good, actually. I think I only hit something alive once." She laughs lightly and shakes her head, bright-blond strands of hair slipping down in front of her face before she pushes them back behind her ears and drops her eyes with a faint blush. "And then I cried inconsolably."

Her lips roll together, and I'm entranced. Instantly imagining things I shouldn't be.

"I remember that day." I glance across the table at her. "You couldn't even eat the venison for dinner that night. We all tried to console you—it didn't work." My head tips at the vivid walk down memory lane.

"And that right there"—Sterling points at Sloane without even sparing her a glance—"is why women don't belong out hunting. Too upsetting."

Sterling's overgrown frat buddies guffaw at his lame comment, which urges him to go all in on his assholery. He holds his glass up high and looks down at the table. "To keeping women in the kitchen!"

There is laughter and a smattering of people offering, "Cheers," and "Hear, hear."

Sloane dabs the white cloth napkin over her full lips with a prim smile but keeps her eyes fixed on the empty place setting before her. Sterling goes back to gloating with the other guests—ignoring the woman sitting beside him.

Ignoring the piece of herself she tried to share with him. Ignoring the way he embarrassed her.

My patience for this night is quickly dwindling. The urge to slink into the background is overwhelming.

Sloane catches my eye across the table and gives me one of her practiced smiles. I know it's fake because I've seen her real smile.

And this isn't it.

It's the same smile she gave me when I told her I couldn't go to prom with her as her date. Taking a twenty-four-year-old NHL player wasn't appropriate for either of us, and I was the asshole who had to tell her that.

I smile back, feeling frustration build inside me over the fact she's about to tie herself to someone who treats her like an accessory, who doesn't listen to her. Or appreciate that she's layered and complex and not just the polished princess she's been molded into by her family.

Our eyes stay locked, and her cheeks start to flush pink. She shimmies her shoulders back, and my gaze drops to her collarbone. Suddenly I see myself trailing my tongue there. Making her squirm.

My eyes snap back up to her face. Like maybe I've been caught. As though she could somehow hear what's in my head. Because we both know I can't be looking at her like that. She might as well be family. And worse, she officially belongs to another man.

Sterling catches the exchange and turns his attention to me once again. It makes my skin crawl. "Sloane tells me you've been friends for a long time. Pardon my confusion, but a rough-around-the-edges hockey player doesn't seem like he'd be friends with a prima ballerina. Of course, I haven't seen you around much since she and I got together. Something keeping you away?" He drapes an arm over her shoulder in a show of possession, and I try not to fixate on the gesture.

"To be fair, I haven't heard much about you either." I say it with enough humor in my tone that anyone missing the way we're glaring might not even pick up on the jab. I lean back, crossing my arms over my chest. "But yeah. I guess I'm not too rough around the edges to be the one who brings over Polysporin and painkillers when my friend's feet are too raw from dancing in pointe shoes to even walk."

"I've told you this." Sloane's voice is placating. "He helped me move into my new condo. Sometimes we grab coffee. Simple things like that."

"Basically, she knows if she needs something, I'll be there," I add without thinking.

Sloane shoots me a look, probably wondering why I'm acting like a territorial asshole. I'm wondering the same thing, to be honest.

"Good thing you've got me for all that now." Sterling is responding to Sloane, but he's staring at me. Then he abruptly places a palm over Sloane's hands, which are now propped on the table. The ones still pulling at her napkin anxiously. But the way he touches her isn't soothing or supportive. It's a swat, a reproach for fidgeting.

It sends fury racing through my veins. I need to get away before I do something I'll really regret.

"Well, I'm going to head out for the night," I announce suddenly, pushing my chair back, desperate for fresh air and a break from the dark walls and velvet drapery pressing in around me.

"Better get a good sleep in, Gervais. You'll need it to get things rolling for the Grizzlies this season. After last season, you're probably on thin ice."

I pull at the cuffs of my shirt and force myself to ignore the jab. "Thank you for inviting me, *Woodcock*. Dinner was delicious."

"Sloane invited you" is his petulant reply, clarifying that he does not like me—or my presence.

I stare down at him blankly and hitch one side of my mouth up. Like I can't quite believe what a raging prick he is. I can feel eyes on us now, other people picking up on whatever unspoken tension is between us. "Well, that's what friends are for."

"Wait, but you're her cousin, right?" The drunk guy's

scotch spills over the rim of his tumbler and onto his hand as he points at me.

I don't know why Sloane and I have always been so adamant that we're friends and not cousins. If someone tried to tell me that Beau or Rhett or Cade wasn't my brother, I'd write them off immediately. Those men *are* my brothers.

But Sloane? She's my friend.

"Actually, he's my friend, *not* my cousin." Sloane tosses her napkin on top of the white linen–covered table with more force than necessary.

The people gathered for her wedding stare.

Her wedding *this weekend*.

My stomach twists.

"Will you be at the stag party tomorrow, Gervais?" the drunk guy continues. He hiccups and grins stupidly, reminding me of the drunk mouse at the Mad Hatter's unbirthday party. "Would love to say I partied with hockey superstar Jasper Gervais."

Color me surprised that the only reason a guy like this wants me around is to boost his reputation.

"Can't. I've got a game." My smile is tight, but my relief is immense as I rise from my chair.

"I'll walk you out," Sloane pipes up, clearly missing the sharp look Sterling slices her way. Or she's just pretending she doesn't notice.

Either way, I hold one hand open and gesture Sloane ahead of me as we weave our way silently across the restaurant.

I go to press my palm against the small of her back to guide her through, but she tenses, and I jerk my hand away at the feel of smooth bare skin burning my fingertips. My eyes find the floor as I shove the tingling hand into my pocket where it belongs.

Because it sure as shit doesn't belong on the bare back of an engaged woman.

Even if she is just my friend.

It's only as we near the front of the restaurant that I glance up again. Sloane's slender frame sways as she strides across the room. Every movement steeped in an inherent grace— one that comes with years of training. Years of practice.

She smiles politely at the maître d' and then walks faster, like she can see freedom through that heavy front door and is desperate for it. Her shoulders drop and her entire body sags, almost in relief, when she rests both hands flat against the dark slab of wood.

I watch her for a moment before I step up behind her, the heat of her body seeping out toward mine. Then I reach one arm above her petite frame and push the door open, ushering us both out into the cool November night.

I jam both hands into the pockets of my slacks now so I don't grab her shoulders and shake her, demanding to know what the hell she's doing marrying a guy who treats her like Sterling Woodcock does. Because it's really none of my business.

Her toned bare back is to me as she faces the busy city street, car lights a blur of white and red just beyond her, misty air puffing over her shoulder like she's trying to catch her breath.

"You okay?"

Her head nods furiously before she turns back around with that weird Stepford-wife smile plastered back on her dainty face.

"You don't look fine." My fingers wrap around the keys in my pocket and jangle them anxiously.

"Shit, thanks, Jas."

"I mean, you look beautiful," I rush out, grimacing when I note her eyes widening. "You always do. You just don't look...happy?"

She blinks slowly, the edges of her mouth turning down into a slight frown. "Is that supposed to be better? Beautiful and unhappy?"

God. I'm really blowing it. I rake a hand through my hair. "Are you happy? Does he make you happy?"

Her mouth pops open in shock, and I know I'm out of line or stepping in it or whatever. But someone needs to ask her, and I doubt anyone has.

I need to hear her say it.

Her pale cheeks flush, and her eyes narrow as she steps up to me, jaw tight. "You're asking me this *now*?"

I huff out a breath and run my top teeth over my bottom lip, eyes totally fixed on her baby blues, so wide and pale and sparking with indignation. "Yeah. Has anyone else asked you?"

She drops my gaze, her hands planting against her cheeks before pushing back through her collarbone-length blond hair. "No one has asked me."

The teeth of my house key dig into the palm of my hand. "How did you meet Sterling?"

"My dad introduced us." Her eyes fixate on the black sky. It's starless, not like at the ranch where you can see every little fleck of light. Everything in the city feels polluted compared to Chestnut Springs. I decide on the spot to drive out to my place in the country tonight rather than spend another night breathing the same air as Sterling Woodcock.

"How does he know him?"

Her eyes meet mine. "Sterling's dad is a new business partner of his. He's focused on making new connections now that he's back in the city."

"And you've known this guy for how long again?"

Her tongue darts out from between her lips. "We met in June."

"*Five months?*" My brow arches, and I rear back. If they seemed madly in love, I could buy it, but…

"Don't judge me, Jasper!" Her eyes flash, and she steps closer again. I may dwarf her in height, but she's not the least bit intimidated. She's spitting mad right now. Mad at me. But I think that's just because she trusts me enough to let her anger out, and I'm okay with letting her. I'm happy to be that person for her.

Her voice shakes when she adds, "You have no idea the pressures I live with."

Without thinking twice, I pull her into my chest and wrap my arms around her narrow shoulders. She's all tense and riled. I swear I can almost feel her vibrating with it. "I'm not judging you, Sunny."

Apparently, this isn't the time for childhood nicknames.

"Don't call me that." Her voice cracks as she presses her

forehead to my chest, like she always has, and I slide my palm down the back of her hair, cupping the base of her skull.

Like I always have.

I absently wonder what Sterling would say if he walked out here right now. There's a petty part of me that *wants* him to.

"I'm simply curious how things happened so fast. I'm curious why I've never met him until now." My voice is quiet, all gravel, almost drowned out by the hush of cars rushing past us.

"Well, it's not like I have a lot of free time with the ballet. And it's not like you've been in touch lately either."

Guilt nips at me, making my chest twist. Our team came off a bad season, and I promised myself I'd train harder than I ever have during the off-season. "I was training and living out in Chestnut Springs." That's not a lie. My brother's fiancée opened a hell of a gym there, and I saw no reason to spend my summer in the city. "And then it was training camp, and I got swept up."

Also true.

The lie is that I was too busy to make time for her. I could have made time for her. But I didn't. Because I knew her dad was back in the city and I avoid him at all costs. And the announcement of her engagement gutted me in a way I never saw coming.

"I should have told you, not sprung it on you the way that I did," she murmurs, and I brush away the memory of Violet blurting out the news of Sloane's engagement at the ranch mere months ago. The way I instantly froze up inside. The way my heart dropped into my stomach with a heavy thud.

I swoop a hand over her head and give her shoulders a squeeze, still trying to avoid that warm bare patch of skin on her back, and reply with "I should have asked. I've just been…busy. I didn't think your life would just…happen this fast." And that part is true.

Her body relaxes in my arms, soft breasts pressing against my ribs as her fingers dig into my back. But only for a moment before she pulls away. The hug went on long enough that it was more of an embrace. It was toeing the line.

But I still want to pull her back in.

"Well, it is." She stares down and brushes at the sleeve of her pale-green dress, silky and shimmering in the shadowy light. "My dad and I agreed it was best to move forward with the wedding in the fall rather than drawing it out."

That comment has my teeth clamping down because the mere mention of Robert Winthrop sets me on edge. And him taking part in her decision to get married has all sorts of alarm bells going off.

"Why?" My brow knits. I should know better. I should walk away. I should let her be happy.

I shouldn't be this bothered. If she actually seemed happy, I wouldn't be.

Or maybe I would.

She waves a hand and glances over her shoulder into the restaurant, exposing her elegant neck as she does. "Multiple factors," she replies with a defeated shrug. It's like she knows her time with me is dwindling. I don't get the sense that

Sterling is going to be the type of husband who's okay with her and me being friends.

"Factors? Like you just can't wait to be Mrs. *Woodcock*? Because no one wants that as a last name. Or is this your dad pressuring you?"

Her blue eyes flare at the mention of her dad because Sloane doesn't see him as a snake. Never has. She's too busy being the perfect daughter—and now a fiancée. One who's good on paper and doesn't go hunting. "And what if he is? I'm twenty-eight. My best dancing years are drawing to a close. I need to settle down, come up with a life plan. He's looking out for me."

I huff out an agitated laugh and shake my head at her. "Where's the wild girl I remember? The girl who danced in the rain and would crawl onto the roof so I didn't have to be alone on the bad nights?"

They've molded that girl into a pawn. And I hate that for her. We've never fought, but suddenly my urge to fight *for* her consumes my better judgment.

"Your dad is an asshole. He cares about himself. His business. *Optics*. Not your happiness. You deserve better."

I could do better. That's what I really want to say. That's what I've realized sitting here tonight.

That I'm thinking things I shouldn't be.

Wanting things I can't have.

Because I'm too late.

She lurches back like I've struck her, lips thinning in anger as she flushes all the way down her chest. "No, Jasper. *Your* dad is as an asshole. Mine loves me. You just don't know what that looks like."

She spins on her heel, yanking the restaurant door open with a level of violence that is unfamiliar coming from her.

But I'd rather she show violence than apathy. That means the wild girl is still in there somewhere.

She hurled words at me that *should* hurt. But I just hurt for her. Because my biological dad *is* an asshole. But the man who really raised me? Harvey Eaton? He's the best of the best. He showed me love, and I can identify it just fine.

Plus, I remember how Sloane looks at a man when she really wants him. And she isn't looking at her fiancé the way she used to look at me.

I'm more pleased about that than I should be.

2

Sloane

Sloane: Are you here?

Jasper: Where else would I be?

Sloane: I thought you might be mad at me. Please don't hate me.

Jasper: I could never hate you, Sunny.

~

I FEEL SICK.

The day I've dreamt of since I was a little girl is finally here, but it's nothing like I imagined.

It's snowing. And I've always wanted a spring wedding.

It's in an ornate church downtown. And I wanted a cozy country affair.

It's a spectacle with hundreds of people in attendance. And all I wanted was something small and intimate.

Worst of all, the man I'm going to walk down the aisle toward isn't the one I see when I close my eyes. He isn't the one I've wanted for the better part of my life.

I've given up so thoroughly that I'm settling for a person I don't love. One who I'm sure I don't even like, and it makes me sick.

No, this day is *nothing* like I imagined.

My cousin Violet fiddles with the bobby pins in my hair while I sit at a stained-wood vanity with my hands clamped around each other in my lap, covering the massive diamond on my ring finger. If I keep them there, squeezing until it hurts, it will prevent me from crying.

Or doing something stupid like running.

"I don't know where it is. I can't see anything with the way they've got it all twisted up."

"It's there. I can feel it pulling. It's too tight. It hurts."

She sighs and catches my eye in the mirror. "You sure it's the hair, Sloane?"

I tip my chin up, lengthening my neck and watching the column of my throat work as I do. "Yes." I force my voice to sound surer than I feel and let my mind go blank, the way it does when I'm performing. When I leap and spin and the lights are bright and the audience is dark, I'm comfortable.

With a heavy sigh and a concerned glance, Violet dutifully goes back to searching for a bobby pin in my hair that she isn't sure exists. She just insinuated that my uncomfortable updo is some parallel for my life.

I can read between the lines.

She hasn't said much about Sterling. No one has—except for Jasper.

Jasper.

I can't even think of his name without a wave of nausea hitting me. The guilt over the words I hurled at him the other evening has eaten away at me. Kept me up at night. And the finality of knowing my already impossible chance with him will end with me marrying someone else never fails to crack my chest open.

Jasper Gervais and I are friends. *Good friends.* He's made that clear a couple times over now. And I'm not enough of a masochist to go for the hat trick.

I'm sure everyone thinks I'm over him, but that's only because I've become an expert at hiding my feelings. He's consumed every corner of me since I first laid eyes on him, and he's never looked at me as more than a little sister.

I grimace when liquid trickles into my hands. I turn them over and peer down. A manic laugh bubbles out of me as I stare down. Blood pools languidly into a perfect, shiny droplet in the middle of my palm, almost like it defies gravity, just by existing.

The puncture from where the pointed claw of my engagement ring dug in taunts me, like the universe knows this marriage will make me bleed in ways that no one else will know or see.

Sterling wouldn't lay a hand on me, but everything else about him—about this life—*drains* me.

"Oh shit! Sloane! You can't get that on your dress." Violet's hands pull away in alarm before she rushes over to the en suite bathroom, black-satin dress swishing against her.

Black. Again, I laugh. I'd never have chosen black dresses for my wedding. I'd choose something light and whimsical. A celebratory color.

But then this isn't really my wedding, and it isn't really a celebration either. Maybe funeral colors make perfect sense.

I haven't been able to muster the energy to complain about the things I don't want. And I realize now, watching the small orb of blood trickle into the center of my palm, that's because I don't want this wedding at all.

"Here." Violet presses a wad of toilet paper against the prophetic cut, looking downright terrified as she stares at me. "Are you okay?"

I huff out a composed breath. "Yeah, yeah. It's not like I lost a limb or something."

The thought of animals chewing off their own limbs to escape a trap pops up in my mind.

Violet's brow crinkles. "Listen. I don't want you to take this the wrong way, but I need to offer it just once or I'll never forgive myself."

My lips quirk at her serious tone. "Okay. I'm listening."

She rolls her shoulders back dramatically as she stares at me. *Really* stares at me. Hard. I'm inclined to glance away, but I don't.

"If you don't want this." Her free hand signals around us. "If you need an out. If you need a getaway car. I'm your girl. I won't say a thing. I won't judge you. But if this isn't right? If you need to run? Like…" She looks away momentarily, lips rolling together as she weighs her next words carefully. "Blink twice or something. Okay?"

I don't blink, but a tear spills out and runs down my cheek.

"Fuck," my cousin breathes. "I made you cry. I'm sorry. I just had to throw it out there."

"I love you, Violet. I'm not sure I've ever told you that. But you? Your family? Those weeks on the ranch every summer are some of the best days of my life."

Her eyes water, and she blinks frantically, cupping my hands in hers. "But today is better, right?"

Her eyes search mine so earnestly, blue on blue. All I can muster is a sad smile. Today should be the happiest day of my life, but it's not, and I don't want to lie to her.

My lips open before I even know what I'll say, but my phone lights up and dings loudly on the vanity counter in front of us. *Saved by the bell.*

Dropping her gaze, I lurch for my phone, relieved by having an out. It's a text from "Private Number," and when I tap at it, the only message attached is Thought you should see this.

Below that is a video. With a preview image that is strikingly familiar.

I hit the play button.

"What the hell?" Violet's hand lands on my knee as she presses forward to get a good view of the screen.

The screen lights up with a grainy video. Loud music thumps. And what's happening front and center should upset me. After all, what looks familiar is my fiancé dressed in the same polo shirt he wore on the night of his stag.

"Violet, can you go get Sterling for me please?"

I should be devastated. But all I can think as I watch a naked woman bounce on Sterling's dick is that I won't have to chew off my own limb after all.

3

Jasper

Jasper: Vi, have you heard from Harvey? I haven't seen him or Beau yet.

Violet: No. But things just went to hell in here.

Jasper: What's wrong?

Violet: Sterling Woodcock is a piece of shit. That's what.

Jasper: What the fuck did he do to her?

~⁀

"WHO INVENTED TIES ANYWAY?" CADE BITES OUT FROM beside me. "They're fucking uncomfortable." He's the oldest of the Eaton boys, the grumpiest, and one of my biggest supporters.

"You look ridiculous in one too." Rhett laughs with a shake of his head, always harassing his older brother.

But it's the middle brother, Beau—who I'm closest

with—who I'm really looking around for. The fact he isn't here yet is making me antsy.

He tried to request his time to line up with the wedding. He's supposed to have a few weeks off at home before he ships back out. But he hasn't shown up yet, and neither has our dad, Harvey.

"Fuck you, Fabio" is Cade's agitated retort as he fiddles with the tie around his neck. Making fun of Rhett's long hair isn't new territory. I've been watching this exchange for years.

"Where are the girls?" I ask, trying to get them both on track. The harpist is playing. People are mingling in front of the imposing church. It's gray and cold and depressing outside. And all I want to do is run away.

"If you call Willa a *girl*, she'll castrate you," Cade grumbles, yanking the tie off and shoving it into his suit-coat pocket.

"She's going to castrate you for not wearing the tie she picked out." Rhett chuckles.

"She'll get over it when I tie her up with it later." Cade inspects the front doors of the church—his radar is that perfectly honed—as Willa pushes the door open, hand slung protectively over the small bump she's sporting. Her eyes search for Cade in the sea of people. She smiles softly when they land on him, but it slips away quickly.

Then Summer, her best friend and Rhett's fiancée, is there too. They move toward us, and both look a little chagrined.

"That was quite the bathroom break," Rhett announces when they get near enough to hear us.

Summer snuggles up under his arm while Willa regards us with a wary expression.

"What's wrong?" I ask, gaze bouncing between the women. Because I can tell something is up and they're not saying it.

"Willa is a nosy little eavesdropper," Summer says. "That's what's wrong."

"Shut up, Sum. It's not eavesdropping when you can hear a person yelling from the other side of a closed door."

"I think that might still technically be called eavesdropping," Cade says as he pulls Willa toward him.

My brain is stuck back on one word. "Sorry. Who is yelling?"

Summer's lips roll together, dark eyes wide and concerned. "It would seem the bride and groom are having a disagreement. And the groom has no volume control."

"He's a slimy little prick," Willa adds simply. "I can tell just by looking at him."

Before anyone says more, I'm in motion through the heavy door, checking left and right to get my bearings, and picking a hallway that appears to have several doorways leading off it. I take long strides in that direction until I can hear the raised voice.

Violet is standing outside the door, doing an excellent imitation of a deer in the headlights, while her massive husband, Cole, towers behind her like he's ready to murder someone. He always looks like that though.

"You'll embarrass yourself more than me," Sterling's scolding tone assaults my ears from the other side of the door.

I peek at Violet and her husband. His lips are flat, and he cants his head at me as if to say, *Are you going in there or am I?*

I'd happily let him put Sterling in his place. But I'd be even happier to do it myself.

"Are you kidding me?" Disbelief resonates in Sloane's voice. "You fuck a stripper nights before our wedding, and *I'm* the embarrassing one?"

Other people in the church appear to be staring—listening—which is why I open the door into whatever maelstrom is taking place. Sloane needs backup. And she needs to know everyone is privy to their dirty laundry right now.

At least I tell myself that's why I'm marching into this room unannounced. It has nothing to do with the fact that Sterling has me seeing red.

"It was my stag party! A last hurrah!" I catch sight of Sterling's back, his arms held out wide as Sloane sits on a dainty antique stool, looking impossibly small, while he stands over her, yelling at her.

Protectiveness courses through me.

"Get out and shut up!" I bark, slamming the door behind me. "Everyone out there can hear you."

Sterling spins on me, eyes narrowing, venom spewing. "Fuck off, Gervais. I don't need a dumb jock's advice. This is between my wife and me."

I cross my arms and stand my ground. I'm officially done being nice to Sterling Woodcock. "She's not your wife. And I'm not going anywhere."

He's not as tall as I am, and the only reason he rivals me in weight is because he's a little thick around the middle.

Soft, like he sits at his desk all day long and drinks too much at night.

"Excuse me?" He's completely turned to me now and taking aggressive steps in my direction. His soft, shaved cheeks are all puffed up and red, contrasting the white and black of his tuxedo.

"I said I'm not leaving. But you need to."

From beyond him, Sloane stares at me wide-eyed. I expected to find her crying, but there isn't a single tear on her immaculately made-up face.

Sterling rushes me, arms outstretched and ready to shove. Like a fucking kid having a temper tantrum. But I press my palm into his damp forehead and straight-arm him before he can lay a finger on me. He lands a few lame blows on my arms, but he's too fucking soft to know what he's doing. Too short. Too weak.

"Raise your voice at that woman one more time and I will drop you like a stone, Woodcock."

"Fuck you! I'd like to see you try." He's really losing his cool now, but I grab him by his silky little bow tie and march him toward the door, wishing—not for the first time—I could give him one swift smack with my blocker. But I tamed this temper long ago and won't let someone as insignificant as *Sterling Woodcock* be the one to bring it back out.

With my left hand, I yank the door open, and with all my strength, I shove him out of the room, waiting a beat to watch him stumble backward before succumbing to gravity and hitting the burgundy rug in the hallway. He lands in an unceremonious pile of limbs, and I commit the image to memory because it's just too damn good to forget.

I close the door and lock it.

Within moments I hear banging and cussing and totally empty death threats, but I ignore them because my attention is on Sloane, who has her elbows propped on her knees, face tipped down into her hands, shoulders shaking.

I take sure steps across the room toward the vanity where she's seated, ready to comfort her, when I hear her gasp.

At first I think it's a sob. But then I realize it's a laugh.

Sloane is laughing uncontrollably, and I don't know what to do other than stand here and stare at how her body is poured into the tight starched satin of her dress. At her hair, slicked back into some painful-looking twist. At the thin crystal-studded straps of her sandals, which I can see digging into her already scarred feet.

Uncomfortable from head to toe.

And now I am too because I just tossed her fiancé out on her wedding day and she can't stop laughing.

"Are you…okay?" I ask, like a total idiot, fingers clenching and releasing at my sides.

"Never better," she wheezes and laughs even harder. "You tossed him out there like a rag doll!" She collapses right down into her lap, head between her knees, trying to suck in breaths as she trails pale-pink manicured nails across the carpeted floor for a moment before sitting up straight.

"He *cheated* on you," I bite out.

"Yeah. There's a video and everything. Someone sent it

to me anonymously. Right in the nick of time." She wipes daintily at the tears in the corners of her eyes.

"Why are you laughing?"

She chuckles again and shrugs before hitting me with a look that's strong, but I recognize the sadness in her eyes. I've seen that look in the mirror. "What else is there to do?"

"You're not marrying him." I swipe a hand over my mouth and gaze around the ornate room. The crown moldings. The over-the-top chandeliers. I feel frantic. I repeat the only thing that's running through my head. "Over my dead body are you marrying him."

She swallows, and I watch the slender column of her throat work. "I'm sorry I said what I said the other night." Her voice is softer, her body language less hysterical and more devastated. "Outside the restaurant."

I wave her off. "It's okay."

"No." She shakes her head and stares down at her feet. "It's not. I was lashing out. And after all the times you've been there for me, you didn't deserve it. I know you were just looking out for me. You were being…" She glances up at me now, a pinch at the corners of her eyes. "You were being a good friend."

I bite the inside of my cheek, hating the look of helplessness on her face. Hating this entire thing for her.

Hating that word.

Friend.

We've been friends for so damn long…

I startle when a small blond head pops out of the window behind me.

"Are you okay?"

It's Beau's little cousin, the same girl who was staring at me out the window this morning. Her eyes are wide, and the expression of concern on her face tugs at my heart. She almost reminds me of Jenny. I'm not okay, but I don't tell her that. "Yeah. Fine."

I turn back to look out over the shadowy ranch. I love sitting up on this rooftop in the quiet, dark night. It's peaceful. Just me and my demons.

"Want some company?"

I sigh and drop my head. I don't want any company. But I don't tell her that either.

She's crawling out before I can even answer, but I offer her a "sure" anyway.

The roof is still dark, but it's no longer quiet. A girl I barely know monologues about her life, and I just listen. She talks so much that even my demons can't compete.

Tonight and every summer night after, she sits with me. I don't invite her. She's just there.

And sitting with her is peaceful…

I clear my throat to push away the emotion clogging it. "If I was going to be a good friend to you right now, what would I do?"

Sloane sighs, relief painting every inch of her body. Like I just posed to her the one question she so desperately needed someone to ask.

"Jas. Get me the fuck out of here. I wanna go to the ranch."

I stare at her for a beat, hands shoved in my pockets, thinking I'd do anything she asked in this moment.

And then I reach my hand out to her with a firm nod. "Let's go, Sunny."

4

Sloane

Jasper: Is there a way out at the other end of the hallway?

Cade: There's an emergency exit.

Rhett: Fuuuuucckk. Are you breaking our cousin out of her shitty, stuffy wedding?

Jasper: Yes. Come up with a distraction and text me when it's safe for us to run.

Rhett: Can I pull the fire alarm?

Cade: I will come up with something.

Rhett: I've always wanted to pull the fire alarm.

Cade: You did. I had to wait for your dumb ass after school while you finished detention for weeks.

Jasper: Guys?

Cade: Willa has a plan. That might actually be worse. But when I say go...go. You need to run.

SUNNY.

I wonder if he knows what that nickname does to me. How it makes my stomach flip.

If he knows, he shows no sign of it. Because, right now, I barely recognize the man before me. Jasper has been in my life for almost two decades, and I've never seen him look so…deadly.

Not even on the ice.

He leads me across the room but stops short at the sound of voices. Sterling. My parents.

God. How many people heard the words exchanged in here today?

With a deep rumble from his chest, he fishes his phone from inside his suit jacket. His lean fingers are flying across the screen.

"What are you doing?" I ask to his back because I haven't gained the courage to get that close to the door yet.

I want to leave, but I don't want to look everyone in the eye. They'll try to convince me to stay, and I just want to go back to where I always felt safest as a little girl. I long for that place and the simplicity of life that came with it. It's a deep pull in my chest I can't ignore.

"Texting my brothers."

"For what?" I step forward and peek over the crest of his bicep, glancing down at the screen. Reading the messages that pop up between him and my cousins raptly.

"Help" is his gruff reply. He turns to me a moment later,

a hint of steel peeking out from beneath his handsome features. "You should lose the shoes."

My face turns down as I lift my skirt. "The shoes?"

"Yeah. Hard to run in."

My toes wiggle, the pink polish glinting under cheap fluorescent lights. I want to tell Jasper that I could easily run in these. I love a good pair of heels, and I'll suffer in them all day. But my almost-future-mother-in-law chose these, and they aren't *me* at all.

The thought of getting out of them is just too tempting.

With a brusque nod, I fist the skirt and pull it up a few inches to bend over. But before I can, Jasper crouches before me. Deft fingers make quick work of the dainty silver buckles while I stand here slack-jawed, watching this man drop to one knee just to take my shoes off, running calloused palms reverently around my ankle as he tugs my feet free.

Without looking up, he hands the sparkly heel to me as he taps the opposite foot. And not for the first time, I'm stuck staring at Jasper Gervais with my heart pounding while he goes about what he's doing like it's the most mundane thing in the world.

"There," he says, glancing up at me with the ankle strap dangling from his outstretched finger.

It's hard not to admire him on his knees, but it's his thumb that makes me gasp. The one pressing into the arch of my foot, like he just can't help but massage me.

"Sore?" His Adam's apple works as he swallows, one knee on the ground while the other is up, making his slacks stretch across his muscular thighs in the most delicious way.

What kind of man stops in the middle of breaking me out of my sham of a wedding to rub my sore feet?

A damn good one.

I shouldn't be salivating over him on what was supposed to be my wedding day. But salivating over Jasper Gervais is part of my personality at this point.

"No, I'm fine," I say quickly, pulling my foot back down to the floor. Feeling more grounded on my bare feet.

I step ahead, rounding Jasper as he pushes to stand, and press my ear against the door. It's hard to make much out besides hushed tones and the deep baritone of what I recognize as my dad's voice.

"Ready, Sloane?" Jasper asks.

"For what?" I whisper, leaning on the door like it might help me catch a few words.

"To run."

My head flips in his direction. "You're going to help me literally become a runaway bride?"

Jasper smiles, and his eyes soften, creases popping up beside them. He's always been my gentle giant. Tall, quiet, and *good* down to the marrow of his bones. "That's what friends are for."

Friends.

That word has haunted me for years. As a child, I felt special when he called me his friend, but as an adult? As a woman? Watching other women prance around on his arm at different events while I get called his friend?

It *kills* me.

And I'm perpetually too chickenshit to do anything

about it. The timing is always off. And I have tucked my tail between my legs since he turned me down for prom and then again in a more joking way.

If we lived together, I wouldn't have to inconvenience you like this.

It was an offhanded remark that rolled off the tip of my tongue far too easily as he helped me mount a TV on the wall in my new condo. He parried it away effortlessly with a deep chuckle as he hefted that flat screen onto the mount, like he was swatting at a mosquito buzzing around his head.

Like that would ever happen.

He said those words to me one year ago, and I took a hint. I decided having Jasper as a friend is better than alienating him altogether. And that's what blurting out my feelings would do. So I let it go. I may be stupidly obsessed with the man, but I have some sense of self-preservation. I like to think I have some dignity. But lately I'm questioning even that.

Realizing I've been staring at him blankly for far too long, I ask, "How are we going to do that?"

He hikes a thumb in the opposite direction from the church entrance. "Emergency exit is that way. Cade and Willa planned a distraction. And then we're just gonna…" He shrugs, looking so damn boyish as he does. "Give 'er."

"Give 'er?"

His laugh is a deep, amused rumble. It pulls me toward him and draws my cheeks up into a grin; it soothes me in a way I can't explain.

He nods, and it's so sure. Decisive. There's something

reassuring about knowing he'll always have my back, that he can take an out-of-control situation and make it feel in control somehow. "Yeah. Like…go hard. Give 'er shit."

I quirk my head. "Is this a hockey saying?"

"Come to think of it, probably. Yes."

"Okay. Let's *give 'er*," I agree with a light laugh.

But a serious expression flashes across his face. "You sure about this, Sunny?"

Sunny. I can't stop myself from flinching this time. I think he notices it because confusion flashes across his chiseled face. And all I can bring myself to do is nod. Decisively.

His phone dings, distracting us both. And then he's reaching for my hand, twining his fingers between mine, and carefully twisting the deadbolt on the door.

Before stepping into the hallway, I hear a pained shout. "Ah! My baby!"

When we peek into the hallway seconds later, all backs are turned to us. Willa is down on all fours in the foyer, grasping at her stomach dramatically while Cade stands by, arms crossed, gruffly asking if she's okay while trying not to roll his eyes.

I'm momentarily confused. Because if I know Cade, he's as protective as they come, and seeing the mother of his child down on the floor in pain would have him wild.

Willa's chin tips up in our direction and she winks before falling into another chorus of loud wails. "Please! I need a doctor!"

I have to press my palm over my mouth to keep from laughing at how ridiculous this plan is. All Jasper does is shake his head, squeeze my hand reassuringly in his, and take off for the back door.

I run barefoot down the carpeted hallway, taking the biggest strides I can muster while desperately trying to control the laughter bubbling in my chest.

It's freeing. It's a relief. And before we hit the door, my fingers loosen around the sparkly heels in my hand.

I drop them like Cinderella and step out into a dull November afternoon, with my palm pressed tight against Jasper's.

~

"How much farther?" I huff, out of breath after running a few blocks in a big heavy dress topped with a hefty dose of adrenaline coursing through my veins.

Jasper slows, giving me a slight grimace. "Sorry. I parked at the stadium. Hadn't planned on being your getaway vehicle." His fingers pulse on mine as he draws me close to his side. And then his tone changes. "Though maybe I should have."

His eyes drop, like he's embarrassed by what he just said, and he lurches to a halt. "Jesus, Sloane. Your feet. I didn't even think beyond getting you out that door." Eyes glued to the ground, I realize he's staring at my feet. My bare feet on a cold winter sidewalk. "Why didn't you say anything? You got something against your feet? I feel like I'm the only one who takes care of them."

"Don't worry about my feet. It's this fucking hairdo that's killing me." I probe at the spot where I can feel tiny hairs tugging against my scalp.

His lips tip down in a surly frown, and then he crouches. "Hop up."

"You want to give me a piggyback ride?"

He shoots me a playful look over his shoulder, one that takes me back to long hot summers spent floating the river, splashing, and staring at Jasper Gervais, who seemed all man to me even at seventeen.

Wish I could go back and warn that Sloane about how he'd grow up to look.

Which is to say, devastating.

"Wouldn't be the first time. Let's go. I don't want *Woodcock* to catch up with us and throw a tantrum."

I can't help the small laugh that erupts from me. Or that my fingers are already gripping at my skirt as I climb Jasper like a tree. Once I get close enough, he hefts me up easily, and I realize I weigh nothing to him.

A tiny ballerina being toted around by a huge hockey player.

In her fucking wedding dress.

Giggles overtake me, and I wrap my arms around Jasper's neck, snuggling into the warmth of his body. I feel the vibrations of his laughter against my chest, and my nipples rasp against the inside of my bodice.

"This is insane." I drop my head to the back of his neck, the tips of his hair brushing against my forehead.

"No." He hikes me up higher on his back as we enter the hockey arena parking lot, and I struggle against the tight dress to keep my legs wrapped around the wide expanse of his back. "Taking Woodcock as a legal name is insane."

"Jasper." I swat at his shoulder. "Be nice."

"No, thanks. I'm over being nice to that guy," he grumbles, still ornery over dinner the other night. Not that I can blame him.

"I was planning to hyphenate?"

"Winthrop-Woodcock is no better, babe."

I snort and am about to pester him back when I hear it. A tearing sound.

Oh my god.

Jasper freezes momentarily. "Was that…"

Silent laughter racks my body. "My dress? Yup."

"Are you…"

"My ass still feels covered. No breeze yet." I reach one hand back to run it over my butt—just in case. "It's still just my hair that hurts," I admit.

He just grumbles, picking up his pace and looking around like he's annoyed by the idea of someone seeing what isn't even showing. Annoyed by my hair being too tight.

I don't know when Jasper got so…overprotective?

"There it is."

The lights flash on a silver Volvo SUV, and I sigh in relief. Sure, those shoes were torture, but running barefoot on cold concrete is a close second in the discomfort department.

He places me down at the passenger's side, but his hands don't leave my body. His palm splays against my hip as he opens the door and lifts me into the seat. He even reaches for the seat belt to buckle me in before he stops himself.

Navy eyes land on mine momentarily and then drop to my lips. He shakes his head, his tall frame backing out of the car away from me.

He's about to slam the door but stops, startling me as he wrenches it back open, steps up close, and bites out, "You know what?" He reaches for my hair, and gentle hands land in my tresses. "This fucking thing needs to go."

I don't know how he manages it, but with one well-placed tug, he pulls the main crystal-encrusted needle from my hair and tosses it on the ground. The tinny clang of it landing against the asphalt sounds loud in an otherwise quiet moment. There's something symbolic about it.

The relief I feel is instant. The spot that hurt doesn't anymore.

My hair tumbles freely around my cheeks, and he watches it sway. For a moment, his eyes heat and shock me when they land back on my lips.

"Is that better?" he rumbles.

My heartbeat thumps heavily in my ears, and I offer a silent nod back. Not sure what to say. Trying to make sense of this version of my friend. Protective and possessive, devotion fortifying every move he makes.

He mirrors my nod wordlessly, then he steps back and slams the door.

Within moments he's settled in the driver's seat, and we pull out of the facility in silence. What felt like relief and freedom before slowly morphs into shock and a steady state of nausea.

A tense moment of *What the fuck was that hair thing?*

A heavy dose of *What have I done?*

I run through the conversations I'll need to have. The contracts we'll need to pay for a wedding that never happened. The move I'll have to make out of Sterling's penthouse.

Dread sinks like a heavy stone into my gut.

"Fuck my life," I mutter, watching the city streets bleed into the freeway that leads out to Chestnut Springs.

"We still good?" I sense Jasper's nervous glances. I know him well enough to recognize he's stressing right now. Worrying. He's always been good at worrying, so his anxiety is probably kicking in something fierce.

"Yeah. I could use a drink though."

He nods, and within minutes we pull into a liquor store.

"I'll get—" he starts, but I hop out of the car and walk toward the store like a thirsty, stunned, barefoot bride-zombie.

With long strides, he rushes ahead to pull the door open for me. As I cross the threshold, I don't make eye contact, but I can feel him regarding me like he thinks I might snap. I think I already have.

Inside, it reeks of stale beer and Pine-Sol.

Jasper turns to peer around the small store. It's more of a wide hallway, packed a little too tight. Kind of like the guy behind the counter, bulging out of his shirt.

"Welcome," he grumbles, scrolling through his phone, not sparing us a glance.

"Do you want…champagne?" Jasper lifts a bottle of the nicest champagne on the shelf, which is not saying much for this dive. "To…celebrate?"

I snort at that. "No." I roll my lips together and keep walking farther back. "I want something fattening and lowbrow. Something Sterling and my dad would never approve of."

I hear Jasper's chuckle behind me as I stalk toward the cold beer section at the back. The way he laughs, all soft and deep, never fails to make me feel like I'm sinking into a warm bath. He's so serious sometimes that when he laughs, it's precious somehow.

The grit on the floor against my bare feet makes me smile. Sterling and my dad would definitely not approve of this, so I press my soles down harder, rolling through my full foot, hoping the bottoms are black by the time I'm done shopping. A completely inconsequential rebellion, but a satisfying one nonetheless.

I stop and take in the cooler shelves. And there it is. Like a glowing beacon before me.

Buddyz Best Beer.

It's really the *Z* that seals the deal for me. It's so unnecessary. So improper. The cans look thin—cheap—with a poorly drawn cartoon basset hound on the front.

"Perfect," I murmur reverently as I reach forward and grab the six-pack.

When I spin around, Jasper is smirking at me. "Buddyz Best is perfect?"

"Yes." I lift the cans to my face and stare at the droopy-faced, sad-looking dog. I feel like a basset hound inside right now. "Buddy is the perfect man for me. Cheap. Alcoholic. And most importantly, not a human male at all."

The grin I give my friend is unhinged at best as I storm to the till and plop the beer down on the counter. Finally, the man lifts his chin from his phone, where he's watching what appears to be competitive bowling.

His eyes assess me before dropping to the beer and glancing back up at Jasper. This guy looks like he's seen some *shit*. I expect him to have questions, but all he says is "Congratulations, you two" as he scans the beer and tells me the total in a bored tone.

I reach for my purse but realize I left it behind when we ran.

A long arm reaches over me, tossing down a ten-dollar bill. "Keep the change," Jasper says. He guides me out of the store with a gentle hand cupping my elbow, eyes fixed on my bare feet. "Sunny, you're gonna need a bath when we get to the ranch."

"Maybe if I drink enough of these"—I lift the six-pack, feeling a little loopy—"I'll invite you to join me."

Jasper just stares back at me, jaw popping like I've pissed him off. Not a single word crests his lips, not a single tug up on his cheeks.

"Just kidding!" is what I fill the awkward silence with before turning and scurrying back to the comfortable SUV. I strap myself in, crack a cheap-ass beer, and take a deep swig in an incredibly sad attempt to drink my problems away and forget the off-color joke I just blurted out.

Jasper and I drive in total silence. I continue to drink, and he makes no comment on that. Instead, he just grips the steering wheel like he's trying to strangle it while keeping intense eyes on the road.

And after my third beer on an empty stomach, I feel a little bit better. Also a little bit drunk.

So I monologue, like I often do with Jasper. "You know I didn't want an ugly fall wedding. I wanted a spring wedding. I wanted a flowy, feminine dress and an outdoor ceremony. No uptight tuxedos and definitely no black bridesmaid dresses." I hold up my hand, staring at the rock about the size of the iceberg that sunk the Titanic. "And I *hate* this ring. I saw one at a little boutique on Sixteenth Avenue—you know that funky area? It was a purple oval sapphire. How cool is a purple sapphire? And they set it sideways in matte yellow gold. Sterling said it was 'weird' and then gave me this ring the next week. I swear he picked the opposite of anything I'd ever want on purpose."

"Romantic," Jasper says, his jaw ticking with tension.

I drink silently, stewing over the fact I pretended I liked this ring when he gave it to me because I didn't want to offend anyone.

When we pull into Wishing Well Ranch, Harvey's truck is in the driveway, even though we thought he and Beau were going to be at the wedding. Jasper and I exchange a confused look, and the second his vehicle is in park, he's skipping steps to get to the front door. I run after him, heart pounding, because something is off.

Inside, Harvey is sitting at the expansive kitchen table with a big glass of bourbon gripped between his palms. An odd shade of green colors his complexion.

Jasper freezes in the doorway, staring at him.

"What's wrong?" I ask instantly because it's one of those moments when you can just *tell*.

The house is too dark, too quiet.

My uncle, who is always all smiles and warm gazes, looks gutted.

Harvey doesn't comment on my bare feet or ask why I'm here. Instead, his eyes latch onto Jasper's, and he says, "Beau is missing."

5

Jasper

I REGISTER THE SOUND OF SLOANE'S BEER CAN HITTING THE hardwood floor, but everything else is just white noise. Blood rushing. Heart sinking.

Harvey's haunted face staring at me from the kitchen table is one sight I'll never forget. It's seared into my memory, right beside the day my little sister died.

"I'm going to need you to say that again." I hear myself talking, but it's out-of-body, like I've stepped out of my skin and am staring down on myself. I see Sloane swaying, her delicate hand pressed against her lips while the other props herself up against the doorframe.

"Beau is missing," he says again.

"What do you mean, *missing*?" It's like I've completely detached from what I didn't want to hear.

He clears his throat and takes another heavy pull of the amber liquid in his glass. Everyone is anxiety drinking tonight. "Come sit down, son."

Anxiety unfurls in my chest, spreading through my veins like wildfire and transforming into blind panic. I feel like a cornered animal.

"I don't want to sit down." My arms hang limp at my sides. My fingers have gone numb. Beau is my best friend. We've been joined at the hip for years. He's the kid who saved me and brought me here—no questions asked. He's my *brother* in every way that counts.

A special forces soldier with a personality the size of his doesn't just go *missing*.

"I want to know what's going on." My voice sounds hollow and robotic to my own ears.

I feel a gentle pulsing around my forearm and the press of Sloane's body inching closer to mine. Her fingers must be squeezing at my arm in a slow, steady rhythm. It almost feels like my heartbeat, the one that has slowed to a dull thud as everything spins around me. Her squeezing is what's keeping it beating at all.

"I got the call last night that he'd missed his scheduled flight, which isn't out of the ordinary with him. But then this morning I got a second call, where I was informed that something went wrong on their mission…and he went missing."

"What do they mean by *missing*?" My words come out harsher than I intend, certainly harsher than Harvey deserves. It's his son who's missing.

Missing. That word is running through my head on repeat to where it's lost all meaning.

Harvey blinks. "You know how that unit works. They

don't tell anyone anything. All they told me is that he was on a mission, something went wrong, and he didn't get on the transport out. They're investigating now."

The air is too thin and my lungs too small. The world is too heavy. Suddenly I'm back there on that day. Hot pavement beneath me, listening to my dad shouting and my mom wailing.

Feeling completely helpless.

"I need water."

Sloane jumps into motion, her dress swishing as she walks across the kitchen and pours another glass of liquor. And I just stand here, staring at the bourbon in Harvey's hand. It reminds me of Beau's eyes, of going out and drinking too much with him, listening to him crack rude jokes and laugh too loud.

"Here." Sloane lifts my arm and curls my fingers around the glass as if I'm a vegetable or something. "Let's go." Her hands are back around my forearm, and she leads me toward the table.

I go, too stunned to know what else to do. She pulls out a chair and sits me down. And then she goes to Harvey.

He forces a smile as he looks up at her. "I'm sorry I missed your wedding, Sloaney."

Her eyes glisten with unshed tears as she drops a small hand onto his shoulder. "You didn't miss a wedding, Uncle Harvey. The wedding didn't happen."

His gaze swivels between us with a small shake of his head. "I guess…I guess that makes sense, since you're here with Jasper and not your husband. The two of you just look so natural together. I…I'm sorry." One broad palm covers his face. "I'm not thinking straight right now."

A choked sob lurches from his chest. Followed by a matching one from Sloane.

And then she's there, wrapping her arms around the man who is my dad. In every way that I needed a father, Harvey was that person to me. He's known so much pain in his life. So much loss and hardship.

Just like me.

And it seems infuriatingly unfair that something like this should happen to us.

Sloane doesn't offer him apologies. She doesn't tell him everything will be okay. "I love you, Uncle Harvey" is all she says as she wraps her arms around his neck and hugs him fiercely, letting him gasp into her shoulder as a stray tear falls down her cheek.

Again.

Sloane has shed too many tears today.

And yet she's here. Drunk. And sad. And lost. She's got dirty feet and is wearing an expensive, ripped wedding dress for a marriage that didn't happen. Her life is in shambles, and she's still here comforting other people.

Sloane is selfless.

She might not look it, but she's strong.

She's a got a huge heart. A gentle soul.

And watching her comfort Harvey right now, I let myself admit that the way I love Sloane might not be how one friend loves another at all.

A fist lands on my shoulder, but I just laugh. This shithead punches like a toddler. And he just left himself open for me.

My knuckles crack when they slam into Tristan's face, and blood sprays from his nose, which seems to function as some sort of signal for all his shark friends to swarm me.

"You're fucking dead, Gervais! I'm gonna go to the back field and burn that filthy car you live in. Put you on the street where you belong."

His words hurt a hell of a lot more than his punches. I glance around, feeling the press of new people around me.

Everyone assumes that hockey players are popular; I'm proof that isn't always true. I've been reduced to town trash in the wake of everything that's happened, and these are the kids at school who've been getting a kick out of reminding me where I belong on their totem pole.

Today I boiled over.

When I glance back at Tristan, it's the boy standing behind him who catches my attention. Beau Eaton. School quarterback, honor roll, basically the town prince who everyone loves. Never took him for the type to join in on something like thi—

"Tristan, fuck off." He gives him a shove and steps up, blocking me from the gathering crowd. "Everyone fuck off! Show's over!" he announces, crossing his arms and glaring back while our fellow students disperse.

Shame hits me. Not only am I the weird homeless kid whose parents left him behind...I'm now the most popular kid's charity case.

Before I can even think about what I'm doing, I turn and run straight for the stand of trees that divide the schoolyard from the scrubby back field. Straight for the old broken-down Honda I've been calling home.

"Hey! Wait up!" I hear Beau call, but I don't look back. Humiliation drives me forward, and within minutes I'm leaned up against the white hunk of metal trying to catch my breath. It's a shit place to live. But it's dry, and it's close to the hockey rink. And that's all I care about.

"Are you really living here?"

I groan. Of course, he had to follow me. "Yeah."

A hush expands between us. I'm too embarrassed to turn around and face him.

"Come to my house." That's what he breaks the tense silence with. That's what has me spinning around to look at this bright, shiny golden boy of a teenager.

"Your house?"

"Yeah." He nods surely, arms crossing over his chest as he tries to look at me and not the squalor I've been living in. "Lots of rooms. Lots of food."

"I—"

"I'm not taking no for an answer. Grab"—he looks behind me now, features pinched—"whatever you need. My brother Cade will drive us once Rhett is out of detention."

"You sure?" A small fragile flame of hope flickers inside me. "What if your family doesn't want me there?"

He just scoffs. "I guarantee my family doesn't want you living here."

And just like that Beau Eaton cements himself as one of the very best things in my life…

"Hi." Sloane's voice is quiet and tentative behind me.

"How'd you know I was here?" I don't turn to look at her head poked out of the window. I'm still frozen, and it has nothing to do with how cold it is out right now.

"Hard to forget our nights out here, to be honest."

She's not wrong. Our nights spent out on the roof were some of the best of my life. They usually started out as the worst nights, but then she'd come join me, and they were instantly better.

"I could also feel the cold air from the hallway."

I grunt, not really in the mood for talking. In fact, I feel completely hollowed out.

"You cold, Jas?"

I shrug, not caring if I'm cold. I'm too busy imagining all the awful things that could have happened to my brother.

He told me he would leave the army soon. Of course, he always said that. And every time I wanted to believe him.

We all hated him deploying—it felt like the statistics weren't stacked in his favor anymore. Like he'd gotten off scot-free too many times. Like he was too sunny and goofy and the universe would take that away from him at some point.

I hear Sloane clambering out the window of her guest room. The room right beside the one I spent my teenage years in.

I'm about to tell her I want to be alone, but when she wraps a blanket around my shoulders and plops down beside me, tucking herself in against me, my body releases a breath I didn't even know I'd been holding. She presses close beside me, all downy and comforting. Her sweet scent wafts to my nostrils. Smells like coconut and icing on a cupcake.

Forcing myself to stay staring at the dark fields, I ignore her presence. Until I see an ugly cartoon basset hound pushed up to my face.

"Drink." It's not a question. It's a command.

I shake my head, feeling more like my traumatized teenage self than I have in years.

"Come on. I'm dehydrated from crying in the shower. Please don't make me drink alone. Beau wouldn't approve."

I snort a laugh, but it's followed by a wounded keening noise. The sound of Sloane sniffing is the only response. We don't look at each other.

"WWBD," she says with a sure nod.

"Pardon?"

"What would Beau do? We both know he'd drink the beer."

I'm sure if I even glance at her, I'll break down, so I crack open the stupid Buddyz Best Beer and take a long pull.

"This tastes like shit."

She drinks, and from my periphery, I see her nod. "Matches the day. Shit is the theme."

I grunt my agreement. "You're not wrong."

Her shoulder bumps into mine, but she doesn't move away. She tucks in closer, pulling the same patchwork quilt we used as kids around us. And just like when we were younger, she doesn't poke and prod. Or try to get me to talk about my feelings like a therapist I never asked for.

She's just *there*.

"Do you think he's dead?" I blurt, trying to cover my fear by chugging more beer. It's the question that's been dancing around in my head for the last couple of hours. The one I didn't want to give voice to, but it leapt from me all the same.

I chance a look at Sloane now to see how she might react to my dark question. But as usual, she doesn't shy away from my darkness—after all, she's my Sunny. She chases away the dark just by being herself.

"I think…" She rolls the can between her hands, creating a loud crinkling sound in the quiet night. "I think that's not the type of energy I want to put out into the universe for him right now."

A strangled chuckle rumbles in my chest, and she jabs an elbow into my ribs. "I'm serious! Do you go into a game thinking you're going to lose it? Or do you envision yourself winning? I obsessively run through a dance in my head before a performance, but I don't let myself see a miss or a trip. And I'm going to treat this the same way."

She nods, small dainty features pressed into a determined expression. "If Beau is out there, he needs our good energy. He's too…" One hand rolls around in front of her as she searches for the word. "I don't know. He's larger than life. He won't go down without a fight. I have faith in him."

Unshed tears prick at my eyes. *Larger than life.* He is that. Determined. Relentless. That fucker doesn't take no for an answer. And wherever he is, I hope he doesn't right now either.

I lean into Sloane, and she rests her head against my shoulder. I don't know how long we sit in a companionable silence, just staring out. No sounds except the intermittent hoots from an owl, the odd huff of air from a cow, and the quiet nicker from a horse.

"I love the moon on nights like this," she murmurs. "It makes everything appear almost silver. It makes everything glow."

Tipping my chin up, I peer at the sky full of creamy-white stars so thick in spots it almost looks like a blanket. It reminds me of when we were in front of the steak house and I couldn't see a single star on a perfectly clear night.

After our argument, I drove out to Chestnut Springs and spent the night in one of the small houses I bought in town. Tonight I'm too fucked-up to go anywhere, but there's this part of me that doesn't want to sleep in my childhood bed.

It feels like too much right now. It feels too real.

Sloane's body heaves a heavy sigh, and I wonder how she's feeling after the shit day she's had too.

"I'm sorry about Sterling," I offer, not meaning it.

"Don't bullshit me, Jas."

A quiet chuckle rolls from my lips. "Okay. I'm sorry about your wedding."

She sighs again, petite shoulders rising and falling with such tiredness. "I'm not."

Her blunt response takes me by surprise.

"No?"

"Nah. Spending my life barefoot in the kitchen as Mrs. Woodcock sounds fucking terrible. I'd rather be barefoot in a dirty liquor store with you."

I want to laugh, but jealousy lances through me. Followed by relief. Relief that she hasn't taken that path.

Relief that she's sitting here with me instead. Because, rack my brain as I might, I can't think of a single other person I'd rather be with in the wake of this news.

I feel her shiver beside me and turn to press a kiss to the crown of her head, but her hair is wet and cold.

"Your hair is wet."

She shrugs. "Yeah. I came straight here after my shower."

An ache hits me in the center of my chest, and I shake my head at myself, not wanting to read more into that than I should. After all, she almost married someone today.

"Let's go, Sunny. You're gonna freeze with wet hair out here." I stand and reach a hand out for hers, small and cool in mine, as I pull her up. I squeeze once and try to let go.

But I can't. I want her close. I just don't know how to go there.

She doesn't suffer from the same confusion though. Without a second thought, she steps into me. My arms fold around her along with the thick blanket that rests over her shoulders as her hands slide over my ribs. Her forehead presses to my chest, and I cup the back of her head.

Maybe it's our height difference. Maybe it's just tradition. But I've always hugged her like this, and she's always let me. There's a comfort in it somehow. A familiarity.

"You'll be here in the morning?" This is what she's always asked me on bad nights. Like she wanted to make sure I wouldn't drop too far into my sadness. So far I wouldn't come back.

"Where else would I be?" is what I've always responded with as my hand slides over her damp hair. Because I will be.

Because she's a tether that has never let go, even when I've wanted her to. Before I joined the Eatons, I felt like no one would miss me if I were gone. But now I know that's not true.

They would. Sloane would. And that's always kept me grounded in a way I needed so desperately as a grieving teenager.

She pulls away with a quiet sniffle and downcast eyes. "Good night, Jas. Just knock if you need me."

"Good night, Sunny." I ruffle her hair and turn away.

We head to our own rooms. The same way we did as kids.

I crouch to fit through my window and curl up on my bed. Then the insistent pressure in my chest cracks and the tears come.

Just like they did when I was a kid.

The difference is, I wish Sloane were still pressed against me, and I never wished for that back then.

6

Sloane

27 missed calls from Sterling

12 missed calls from Dad

Sterling: Where'd you go? Come back. We need to talk about this.

Sterling: Sloane, this is humiliating. Everyone is waiting. Can you have your temper tantrum later?

Sterling: Your dad is furious. We're going to have to cancel all the caterers. Everything. I'm not dealing with this shit.

Sterling: This is fucking bullshit. Get your ass back here and sign the paperwork so we can move on.

Sterling: I'll go to Grand Cayman by myself.

Sloane: Take the stripper. She deserves a vacation after putting up with you for even one night.

I wrench the passenger door of Jasper's SUV open. I *almost* missed him.

"What are you doing?" His eyes widen beneath the brim of his maroon Calgary Grizzlies cap pulled down low.

Ignoring his question, I toss my purse into the back and crawl into the seat beside him. He smells minty and fresh, but the circles beneath his eyes are dark, and his handsome face looks drawn. He looks sad but edible in a pair of torn jeans and a downy plaid jacket. I glance down at my simple gray sweat suit that could fit two of me inside it.

Harvey laid it out on my bed for me while I showered last night. I'm sure it's his, but I'm not about to put my wedding dress back on. So it's good enough.

I reach forward to crank up the warm air coming from the vents. "Fucking freezing out this morning," I mumble, catching sight of myself in the rearview mirror, hair all wavy and disheveled, eyes all puffy.

"Sloane. What are you doing?"

I rub my palms together and blow into my cupped hands before reaching over my shoulder to buckle the seat belt. Strapped in, I have a better chance of not launching across the center console to hug the man beside me. "I'm coming with you, Jas. What does it look like?"

He blinks at me. "I have a game tonight."

"I know you do." I hunker down into the leather. "Does this thing have heated seats?"

He scoffs. "Of course it does." He reaches forward and presses the button that puts the seat to full heat.

"Perfect." I turn wide eyes on him, signaling that he should get going, but he just stares back at me.

"It's six in the morning."

I yawn, holding my hand that is wrapped in the too-long sleeve of the crewneck sweatshirt up to my mouth. "Don't I know it. Can we stop for a coffee?"

He shifts the cushy SUV into drive, even though I can still see the questions dancing in his eyes. The front of his Volvo is lit only by the dash. It's early enough and far enough into the year that it's still fully dark right now, and as the heat from the seat seeps into me, I sigh.

"This is a comfortable car." My eyes flutter shut. "I almost feel like I could fall asleep." Lord knows I didn't sleep a wink last night.

Being a runaway bride who no one could reach stressed me out. And hearing Jasper quietly weep through the thin wall that separated us made me cry too. There were too many things to think about— too much pain to relax—so I lay there, watching the hours tick by on the digital clock. I tried to formulate a plan, visualized my favorite moments onstage, and forced myself to not crawl across the roof and into Jasper's room to hold him.

Because he wouldn't want that. Even listening to him felt like an invasion.

"The safest money can buy," he says, fingers pulsing on the wheel as he looks both ways on the dark country road. Then looks again.

It makes perfect sense he'd choose something incomparably safe.

"You have your purse," he announces as he finally pulls onto the gravel road.

"Yeah. When I went downstairs, it was on the table with a note from Violet informing me that she was heading back home to be with her babies. I get the sense that everyone is retreating to their own corners with the…news."

"Does that mean you're going home? To Sterling?" His voice is thick, and he sounds resigned.

I press my lips together and force myself to stare out the windshield. "No, Jasper. It means I'm coming with you."

The lines of his body stiffen at my response. What I just said feels altogether too vulnerable, so I change the subject. "Can we stop at a Walmart or something so I can get some clothes that fit?"

My question has the corners of his mouth tugging up. "I can just see the headline now"—one broad palm waves across the console in a dramatic swoop—"Canadian telecommunications heir Sloane Winthrop flees wedding and is found shopping at Walmart."

I snort. "Works for me. Sterling will stop blowing my phone up if he sees me shopping with the peasants." My fingers do little air quotes when I say *peasants,* and my eyes roll in time.

Jasper shakes his head but says nothing more.

It strikes me I should be more devastated about my disaster of a wedding day—but I'm not.

I was set to marry someone out of duty, not out of love. I'd dreamed about my wedding since I was a little girl. And I'd given up on that dream enough to agree to spend the rest of my life legally attached to a man who doesn't care about me at all to help my father close a deal.

It sounds archaic. It sounds *insane*.

I love my father. He's always been good to me and doted on his only child, but there's a niggling voice inside me that says if he loved me as much as I love him, he wouldn't have asked me to marry a man to further his financial interests.

It's not something I tell Jasper. He already dislikes my dad, and that gets me feeling defensive—whether or not he deserves my defense.

We drive in silence and stop for coffee at the closest drive-through that's open this early on a Sunday. Closer to the city, we pull into a Walmart, and I tell Jasper I'll just zip in to grab what I need. He ignores me and unfolds himself from the driver's seat, grumbling about not letting me go in alone.

I waddle through the parking lot, hanging back because I have to hold the huge sweatpants up so I don't drop them and flash him. I've always wanted to get naked with Jasper—but not like that.

Coffee in hand, I grab a few simple changes of clothes. Leggings. Jeans. And then I see it. My eyes light, and I speed-waddle through the branded clothing section, straight toward what I need.

"No." Jasper says from behind me as I reach forward.

"Yes," I reply, grinning as I turn back to him, holding up one of his jerseys. Number one emblazoned across the back.

His eyes narrow, and he gives me a flat look from beneath the brim of his hat. "Where are you even going to wear that?"

I roll my eyes at him because I can see the faint blush on the tops of his cheeks, the tips of his ears going just a little red. Jasper has never been comfortable with his fame. It's always made him squirm. "To your game tonight, obviously."

"You're coming to my game?" His head quirks, and he looks so boyish.

"Duh." I add the jersey to the pile of clothes over my arm and head off to the dressing room in the eerily quiet store. It's so early that there isn't even music playing. All I can hear is the hum of the overhead lights that cast a terrible yellow glow over my face as I try on my clothes.

I look exhausted.

I *am* exhausted. The only thing keeping me going is how badly Jasper needs someone to be there for him. And I'm determined to be that someone. Especially after he sprung me from my wedding.

I'm just returning the favor. That's what I tell myself. Because the alternative is that I'm just reveling in spending time alone with him, and I don't want to be that moon-eyed lovesick girl who follows him around anymore. I want to be strong and independent. And a good friend. Because that's what he really needs right now.

"Wow. This jersey looks sooo good on me," I announce from inside the dressing room, pestering him a bit because I know he's leaned up against the opposite wall, all long limbs and navy-blue eyes focused on the door. Somehow even changing with him this close feels intensely personal.

I roll my eyes at myself. But smile when he groans.

"Where are you going to go after the game?" is what he comes back with.

"I mean…" I trail off, assessing myself in the mirror and opting to leave the jersey on. It's big and comfy, and I can tell that underneath all of Jasper's grumbling, he finds it amusing. "I was thinking we'd go back out to the ranch. I guess I should have asked what your plans are. I checked your schedule. You've got a good stretch of home games."

"Yeah. Four."

I fling the door open with a dramatic flourish and strike a pose in my new leggings and jersey. "How do I look?"

He rolls his eyes and folds the brim of his hat. But I don't miss the twitch of his lips or the way his gaze trails to my body and rakes over my legs.

"It might be a late night if we drive all the way back." He holds one arm open to usher me ahead of him, and I go, no longer worried about dropping my pants in front of him.

"That's fine."

"We could always stay at my place in the city." The words are strained.

I stop in my tracks and turn back to him, craning my neck to look him in the eye. "Is that what you want? I don't know what I want, other than to not face reality yet. I'd like to keep my head in the sand for at least one more day. So I'll go wherever you go."

His sapphire eyes drop to my lips for a moment and then drag back up. "No. I'd rather be at the ranch with everyone. Just in case."

Just in case. Just in case there's any news, I assume.

"You could tell the team you need a night off."

He shakes his head and drops a warm hand on my shoulder as he turns us around. "No. It will feel good to play. Normal. Plus, the team needs me."

I nod because I know that feeling. Dancing until my body aches and sweat drips down my back would be a comfort right about now.

"Can I wear these out?" I ask the dressing room attendant as we draw up to the podium.

She eyes me carefully. "Sure, doll. Let me cut the tags off, and then you need to have them scanned at the checkout."

I offer her my best reassuring smile, trying really hard not to appear like a criminal. "Of course. Thank you." She peeks at the jersey and then glances up at Jasper, eyes widening slightly when she puts it together. "Are you Jasper Gervais?" Her silver bob swishes as her head flips between him and the jersey I'm wearing.

"Yes, ma'am." Jasper smiles, always so gracious with his fans. Anyone who doesn't know him wouldn't pick up on his discomfort. The way his neck goes a little tight. The way his thumb presses into the tips of his fingers.

"My grandsons are just the biggest fans. Any chance you'd sign…" She glances around, trying to find something. "Oh gosh. I don't know. Something? A Post-it Note? The boys would love this for Christmas."

I see his body soften as soon as she starts talking about her grandsons. I know Jasper volunteers with at-risk youth sports programs and has a huge soft spot for kids. "Of course.

I'll wait here. Why don't you go grab a couple shirts in their sizes? I'll take the tags and buy them too."

The woman's hands clasp up in front of her chest. "Oh, you are a sweet boy," she gushes, looking at him with hearts in her eyes.

And I can't even blame her. I am too.

"I'll be right back! And I won't tell anyone else and hold you up. But gosh, they'll just love this. Thank you so much!"

Within minutes, she's back with a Sharpie and two tiny little shirts, looking like the happiest woman alive. I watch Jasper's hulking frame bend over the podium as he personalizes each shirt carefully, checking the spelling of their names so he gets them just right. Her words *sweet boy* bounce around in my head. Jasper has always been a sweet boy.

But god, he grew up to be a damn good man.

Moments later, all the tags are cut, and Jasper walks me out into the store, seeming a little calmer than he did before.

"Just a few more things."

He says nothing, which I usually take as his assent. So I walk ahead, veering for the makeup aisle. After seeing myself under those neon lights, I desperately need a little something to cover up the bags and general zombie look I have going on.

Concealer is my first stop. I try to pick a brand but realize I know none of them. I've come to Walmart for laundry detergent, not makeup. Picking one up, I assess it. If it wasn't for the label, it would look exactly like my go-to concealer.

I turn to Jasper. "Do you think what's inside these is really all that different? Like, I usually pay $50 for a tube the same size. Do you think they just slap different labels on them in the same factory and then laugh at the rich people who pay more for the same shit?"

His lips twitch as he watches me closely. "I love the way your brain works, Sunny."

"I'm serious! This is *five* dollars, Jas. That is a ninety percent discount!"

"Well, you can't fault that fancy private school education."

I snort and wag my head. "I'm testing it. This could be life-changing."

"Mm-hmm."

He sounds like he doesn't believe me. "Jas. Have you seen this translucent skin? The nice blue vein that runs under my right eye? Concealer is my best friend."

"I thought I was your best friend." The statement is so simple, and yet it winds me.

I turn back to the wall of alarmingly affordable concealer and scoff. "You can both be. It's mutually beneficial really. You don't want to see me too often without concealer."

"You always look good to me. Concealer, no concealer. Fancy dress, Harvey's sweat suit. Smooth hair"—his hand waves over me with a low chuckle—"whatever *this* is. It doesn't matter. You're you."

I swallow and try my best not to melt onto the floor into a squishy pile of mush. "That's probably what you tell all the girls, Gervais."

"Nah, Sunny. You're my only girl."

A tinny, awkward laugh filters up out of my throat as I reach for what I think will be a close-enough color match.

I do the same with a soft, shimmery pink blush and a plain blackest-black mascara.

Then I hustle out of that aisle, hoping Jasper will follow and leave that uncomfortable exchange behind.

Joke's on me, though, because next stop is underwear, and my wish came true. Jasper followed. Right up behind me.

I stare back at the shelf full of different cuts of black underwear. "Booty short, bikini cut, or thong? Or does your rule of everything looks good on me apply here too?" I blurt out in an attempt at making this less awkward than it is in my head right now.

I fail. Things are officially not less awkward.

Jasper makes a low groaning noise and avoids eye contact. "It applies" is his strangled reply.

When I peek back at him, I don't miss the pink stain on his cheeks, and I laugh, all shrill and forced, really trying to salvage myself after what I just asked him out loud.

Then I swipe a pack of thongs and a matching bra, avoiding Jasper's eyes as I head to the checkout lanes. And within minutes we're paid up, back in his SUV, wordlessly heading toward the city—the place neither of us really wants to be.

~⁓

I watch Jasper skate out of the mouth of a massive fire-breathing bear's head set up in the corner of the rink. He strikes an imposing image, his pads adding bulk to his already towering height.

Under the flashing lights, he glides across the ice toward

his net, every movement somehow matching the beat of the Metallica song blaring from the speakers. His head is down, and the crowd is wild.

The Grizzlies are coming off a bad season. A really bad season. Some players left the team, but not Jasper. He's already got an Olympic gold under his belt, and he's not the type to jump around chasing a championship any way he can get it. He wants to win here.

I doubted Jasper would ever waive his no-movement clause. He locked in a long contract with the goal of staying close to his family—to the ranch—probably until the end of his career.

What little boy doesn't dream of playing for his home-town team?

Between the pipes, he starts at one end of his crease, methodically slicing his blades across the space, scratching up the ice surface to give himself extra grip.

There's something about this moment that always entrances me. He looks so smooth, so rhythmic, so utterly in the zone that I can never bring myself to look away.

I love a lot of things about Jasper, but him being this damn good at something never hurts his appeal.

To me or to other women.

I tamp the envy down as I glance around the family and friends skybox. I've been in here a couple of times but always with my cousins.

Never by myself.

The vibe is fun and lighthearted, but I'm definitely garnering some looks. Especially since I'm decked out in an oversize Gervais jersey and I'm a recognizable-enough face in this city.

"You're here with Jasper?" A perfectly put-together brunette woman appears beside me, bouncing a baby in her arms.

"Yeah." I smile.

She eyes me but not in an unfriendly way. "What's your name?"

"Sloane. You?"

"Callie." She hefts the baby up and sticks one hand out to me.

We shake, and I find myself liking the woman. Her handshake is firm, but she isn't squeezing the hell out of my hand in some weird show of aggression.

"Jasper doesn't usually have anyone up here."

My eyes dart back down to the ice where Jasper is squirting a stream of water into his open mouth through the cage across his face. "No?" I ask quietly, because I've always made a point of not asking about his personal life.

Always felt like it would hurt too much to know.

I've been swallowing the green-eyed monster for decades, but she hasn't stayed down. She leaps up on me unexpectedly.

Potently.

"It's got all the girls talking. His personal life is a real mystery to us all," Callie continues, chucking her chin over her shoulder as the puck drops and the game clock starts.

"Ah." I glance in that direction and see multiple heads flip away quickly, like children caught staring. "If it's any consolation, I've known Jasper since I was ten, and he's still a bit of mystery to me."

"Ten!" Her eyes bulge comically, and then she sighs. "Well, that is just adorable."

I smile, but it's tight. *Adorable.* More like *painful.*

And that pain only grows as the minutes tick on. Because circumstances doomed this game from the start. Jasper is rightfully distracted. His head is certainly not on the pucks heading toward him at blistering speeds.

The opposing team scores first, less than one minute into the game. And it's not a good goal. It's one I know Jasper would want back.

They score again five minutes later.

I nibble at my nails, the pink wedding polish peeling away as I do.

Two minutes later a third shot finds the back of the net.

I groan and bite my bottom lip hard enough that the inside of it bleeds.

And when Jasper lets in a fourth goal before the first twenty minutes of play have elapsed, I have to blink back my tears. Not because they're losing, but because watching him skate off—head low, shoulders slumped—after getting pulled from the game makes my chest ache.

I know he's counting himself responsible.

He looks like the boy I met all those years ago—devastated.

And for the next several games, it doesn't get any better.

7

Jasper

Sloane: Have I told you that you're my favorite
   goaltender in the world?
Jasper: You have bad taste.
Sloane: You're still my fav.
Jasper: You might be the only one tonight.
Sloane: Correction. Favorite hockey player. Number one
   fan right here.
Jasper: Know a lot of hockey players, do you?
Sloane: Only the best one. I'll be at the players' exit.

⁓

A LOSS NEVER FEELS GOOD, BUT SOMEHOW TONIGHT FEELS
worse. I've started four games in a row because this organiza-
tion trusts me. My coach trusts me. And we've lost four games
in a row. This entire home stand straight down the toilet.

It weighs on my shoulders.

I've let my teammates down. My coaches. The entire city, which is so invested in this team's success.

I feel like I let Beau down somehow. Like I couldn't even win it for him. I've also been a miserable asshole to everyone around me. And I let Beau down in that too because that man would plaster on a smile and be kind no matter what.

Then there's the heart-stopping blond who's been up in the skybox every night, supporting me. I spend the games trying to keep myself from looking up at her as I sit on the bench, beating myself up. As though I'd be able to make her out up there anyway.

Tonight I've showered and changed, but I'm disappointed. I'm sad, but I'm also angry. I walk down the back tunnel toward the press gallery. I hate this part of my night after good games, but I don't even think there is a word for how it feels to string together four shit games in a row and then be forced to talk about it on the record.

Torture, maybe.

I know I've played badly. My team knows. The reporters know. And now we're all going to sit down and talk about it publicly. Fucking perfect.

The minute I step onto the stage with a long table on it, I hear the snapping of cameras. A few journalists I recognize say their hellos. I give them a terse nod and fold the brim of my hat. Then I pull out a chair, sit down next to my coach, and take a deep breath.

First question comes from a reporter I've seen before, one who always asks the most obnoxious questions. Like he's intentionally trying to trip us up for a flashy sound bite. "Hi. Mike Holloway from the *Calgary Tribune*. Jasper, why don't you tell us what happened out there tonight?"

I fight the urge to roll my eyes. That's not a question, and he knows what happened out there tonight. He saw it. Making me recount it to him is just a dick move.

"Well, Mike. As you saw, I wasn't my best tonight. Not even close. I know what the team needs from me, and I couldn't deliver. There were a couple goals I'd have liked back; then they had a couple good chances and just got the best of me. Obviously, those are saves I need to be making if we're going to make a run this year."

"Yeah," the slightly round middle-aged man replies. "Thank you. Follow-up to that. It seems this is the new normal for you. Wondering what you're doing to change things up? This year feels do-or-die for the team. Lots of people would love some insight into your training plans to get yourself back into fighting shape."

I roll my lips together and nod, feeling a drop of water roll off the long ends of my hair down the back of my neck. My coach, Roman, glances at me but says nothing. He knows I hate this shit at the best of times, and he's ready to jump in if necessary.

"Specifics are something that stay between me and the training staff. But I assure you I'm working hard. No one wants this more than I do. Definitely putting in the time with the sports psychologist. I'll be refocusing on my mental game in the coming weeks. I can tell you that much."

And it's not a lie. My mental game is trash right now.

I thought playing would provide me a distraction, but I should have listened to Sloane. If I had, I wouldn't have let my team down this way.

"Pardon my saying so, but it almost seems like you might be a little too comfortable in the long contract you just signed."

I blink at the man before me. The one who looks like he hasn't exercised in years, let alone played any sport at an elite level in his entire life.

"Well, then. With your permission, Mike, I'm going to"—I hike a thumb over my shoulder—"take off and get to work on my training. Try to get myself a little more *uncomfortable* for you."

I rise from the plastic folding chair and stand tall, hearing Roman jump in with some comment about keeping questions respectful. But I don't really care. Fuck Mike and fuck this press conference.

I need out.

One quick stop in the dressing room, and I have my bag and car keys. I'm almost out the door without saying anything. I just want to lick my wounds in private, but the guys deserve more. They deserve an explanation.

I turn, gripping the doorframe, eyeing the room. "Guys. I'm sorry. I've been an asshole these last several games," I announce to my teammates still mulling around. I don't talk much, but when I do, they listen. "My brother, the one in the military, went missing in action last week, and my head is fucked-up. You all deserve better from me. And I want you to know that I'm working on it."

Heads snap up around the room. The silence is deafening.

"Jesus, Gervais." With three long strides, Damon is pulling me into a hug, slapping me on the back, and the other guys are crowding in with concern painted on their faces. Damon steps back, hands squeezing my shoulders as he looks me in the eye and gives me a little shake. "You should have told us. Hockey is just a game. Family is family."

"Jasper." I hear my coach's voice behind me and stiffen. He's a good dude. But even good dudes have their limits. And he sounds *pissed*. "Let's talk in the hallway."

His hand lands on my shoulder to turn me away from my teammates, who all look on wide-eyed. I hear a joke about how I've really made Dad mad this time, and my lips twitch.

I shut the locker room door behind us and finally lift my eyes to meet Roman's. They're pinched at the sides, and his thick arms are crossed over his broad chest. Years in the league himself mean Roman King is still fit in his forties. Still a competitor.

Still remembers what it's like.

"I don't know whether to hit you or hug you."

I mirror his position and glare back at him. He's still got bulk, but I've got a few inches on him. "I would hit me if I were you."

"Well, if I were you, I would have told my coach that my personal life was a heaping pile of devastating shit."

I roll my eyes, feeling like a petulant child. "I didn't want to talk about it. I don't want to be treated like I'm fragile."

A broad hand waves in front of me. "Spoiler alert. You *are* fragile."

"Fuck you, Roman."

His jaw ticks. "I'm gonna let that one slide tonight."

"I didn't tell you my shitty life story so you could hold it over me." Roman hasn't only been a coach, he's been a mentor. He knows my childhood shook out poorly. He knows about Jenny. And he knows I'm an anxious control freak and that those character traits are why I continue to put myself in the net every night.

I crave the control the position offers me. It soothes me. No one to blame but myself when a shot goes wrong—which I know isn't true, but it's how I see it.

"I'm not holding your past over you, Jasper. This is me, as your friend, being concerned. As your coach though? I'm pissed you haven't disclosed this. What the hell were you thinking, keeping this under wraps?"

I sigh raggedly, my exhaustion seeping in at the edges of my eyes. It smells like sweat and rubber here, and all I want is to be in the safety of my car, sitting beside a girl who is wearing my jersey and smells like coconut. "I'm sorry. I'll get my head right before the next game. I promise."

His eyes are sad now, and he shakes his head at me. "Jasper, you need to take some time. It's *normal* to take some time."

My nose wrinkles at his implication. "It's normal to take some time when there's been a death in the family. Beau isn't dead."

Pity. It's written clear as day on my coach's face. And I hate being pitied.

"He's not, Roman. And I'm not going to start acting like he is until I know something." Panic leaches into my voice.

I sound frantic even to myself. I can only imagine how I sound to him.

"Jasper—"

"No. I'll be here tomorrow for practice, and I'll be ready to play the next game. I'll be right as rain. Head in the game." The way he shakes his head at me says he doesn't believe me.

"Stop looking at me like I'm a dead deer on the side of the road that you're sad about."

"You're going to take some time off, Jasper. I know you. I know the way your head works. And I know how near and dear your family is to you. Damon was right. Family first, hockey second."

"I don't need—"

"You're suspended," he bites out.

My entire body goes rigid. "Come again?"

"A two-week suspension for not disclosing this to management. We'll call it a leave of absence in the press release."

"You have to be fucking kidding me. The team needs me! The press is going to have a fucking heyday with this!"

The older man just pulls me into a rough hug, ignoring my arguments. "Your family needs you more" is what he grumbles while giving me a tight squeeze. And then he's pulling away, giving me another of those tragic looks. "The press is already having a heyday with you. Hockey will still be here in two weeks. Your head isn't on the ice, and it shouldn't be. Stay in touch."

And then he walks away, dress shoes clacking against the concrete floors like it's just another normal day. Like the world isn't total, utter shit.

Like one of the best people I've ever known hasn't vanished in some secret corner of the world, on some classified mission, where god-knows-what has happened to him.

The reality of the entire situation hits me like a wrecking ball to the chest.

What if he's dead?

What if he needs help?

And the worst possibility of all, what if we just never find him?

Ready to get the fuck away from everything, I march out the doors into the lobby. It's where fans wait for autographs and puck bunnies wait for a shot at a player.

But there's only one person waiting who I want to see.

The beautiful girl wearing my jersey who feels like home. The one who has barely left my side for over a week. We both know she's hiding from the realities of her life, but so am I. We're kindred that way, and we don't pick at each other about it.

Everyone gets ignored as I make my way to her. I don't know who's there or what people are saying. I have tunnel vision, and all I see is Sloane.

I'm grumpy and miserable. The world is dark, but she's like the moon when we sat on the roof. Bright and pure, shedding a silvery light over everything so that I can still see where I'm going.

Her arms clamp around my waist, the look she gives me is pure love and support, and then her head drops to my chest. Comforting me without saying a word. I take a deep pull of her scent and close my eyes to push away the intrusive thoughts threatening to tug me under.

Everything in the world feels wrong.

But standing here with Sloane in my arms feels right.

8

Sloane

Sloane: Just dropping you a line to say hi. Hope you got
home safe. And to remind you that I love you dearly.

Violet: I love you too.

Sloane: I'm sending you the biggest hugs, Vi.

Violet: He'll be okay. He has to be, right?

Sloane: Definitely.

Violet: That game was...oof. Is Jasper okay?

Sloane: No.

Violet: He needs you more than he realizes. Don't leave
him. You're his person.

Sloane: I won't.

THE WAY JASPER CLUTCHES MY HAND AS WE WALK OUT OF THE
arena feels different.

It feels desperate.

We don't talk. He just grips me like I'm a flotation device and he's stranded in a rough sea. The frigid air bites at us as we walk across the parking lot, and I feel ridiculous next to him. I'm in ripped jeans with an oversize jersey, and he looks like sex in a suit, complemented by a stubbled chin and hair a bit longer in the back so it curls along the nape of his neck.

He's a good distraction from the phone that's burning a hole in my purse from the amount of missed calls and texts it's housing. I've opened it occasionally and then promptly put it away.

The mass text I sent letting everyone know I'm safe but decided to get out of town prompted many reactions. Everything from you go girl to grow up and face the music to an utterly charming get your ass back home and stop embarrassing yourself from Sterling.

I responded with an overly sweet go fuck yourself and haven't said another word to him since.

Catch me living in that penthouse again never.

Am I being childish? Hiding from my responsibilities? I mean, yeah. But the more time I have to think about everything that's led me here…about how a real family unit behaves when something bad happens…the more I wonder how the fuck I got to where I am.

How did I agree to marry Sterling in the first place?

And how dare my father think it was appropriate to ask that of me?

It would be good for business, you know? You'd make a handsome couple. Sometimes marriages are more of a business transaction than a love match when you travel in the circles we do. And that's nothing to be ashamed of, Sloane.

Nothing to be ashamed of. It made a cold calculating kind of sense in the moment and felt like an effortless way out of a bleak and uninspiring dating scene. No one was ever up to par for me. They were all just okay. Fine. Passable. And I started to think I was too picky.

The dating scene turned into my own real-life version of one of those Wish.com memes. I kept placing an order for Jasper Gervais, and the universe kept sending me these laughable cheap-ass knockoffs.

So hearing how an arranged marriage wasn't shameful provided me with some sense of…relief. Like I could at least help my family if I wasn't interested in continuing to flail around with online dating or fellow dancers.

It wasn't until I saw that video of another woman bouncing on my fiancé's lap that the shame hit. And not shame because he was cheating on me. Shame because I felt nothing at all. Only a twisted sense of amusement. Like I knew this would happen and couldn't even drum up the emotion to care about it.

And *that* was shameful. That wasn't how I imagined my life playing out. That wasn't what I deserved.

Sure, there was a time when I imagined my life playing out with Jasper—a long-ass time—but the further on we got with our lives, the more I packaged that dream up and pushed it back into a recess of my mind.

That would never happen.

Imagining something happening between us was right

on par with making out with my pillow and pretending it was Justin Timberlake. He was famous, impossibly handsome, and living a completely different life.

But Justin Timberlake isn't the one clutching my hand right now.

I squeeze Jasper's hand absently, the sound of his dress shoes clacking against the pavement echoing through the parking garage.

He squeezes back.

I peek up at my friend and note the way his normally golden skin has paled and taken on a grayish quality. He hasn't been himself this week. He's retreated and become an ornery shell of the man I know.

I hear the jangle of his keys in his opposite pocket and see the lights on his Volvo flash ahead of us. A dry sob heaves up in his chest, and my chin darts up higher to look closely at him.

"What's wrong, Jas?" I squeeze three times in quick succession on his hand, but he doesn't squeeze back this time.

He stops in his tracks, shuttering his eyelids. His nostrils narrow as he desperately sucks air in through them. Then he jerks his hand from mine. Violently enough that I recoil in shock. With long steps, he lurches past me toward a thick pillar and empties his stomach onto the pavement.

I'm just depraved enough to let my eyes snag on his ass as he bends over, the muscled curve of it pressed against his expensive slacks.

It's like I'm trying to give myself things to be ashamed of.

He stands, panting, strong fingers gripping the pillar, as air pulls and pushes in and out through his diaphragm.

I want to ask him if he's okay, but that's a stupid question right now. He's clearly not okay. Figuring the best I can do is make myself useful, I open the back hatch of his SUV and dive into a hockey bag, on the hunt for a bottled water or a wipe or a towel or literally just anything to clean him up.

A plastic Gatorade pull-top sports bottle is the best I can find, along with a towel that smells like something dead.

"Jesus Christ," I mutter, grabbing them and zipping the bag up quickly because the entire thing stinks.

"Sorry," I hear from behind me.

"For what?" I squeeze water onto the towel and walk toward him.

"Getting sick."

My hand lands between his shoulder blades, sliding on the silky fabric of his suit jacket. "No need." I hand the towel to him, and he drops his face into it. "It's your hockey bag you should be sorry for. That towel smells like moldy cheese and not the good kind."

A quiet chuckle shakes his body. Or at least I think it's a laugh. It's hard to tell without being able to see his face.

"Give me the keys, Jasper. I'll drive us."

"Not a chance," he says as he wipes the towel over his face.

"Listen, I know you don't like when other people drive. But I promise I'll be fine."

He shakes his head, peeking at me from over one broad shoulder. "No."

I roll my eyes and sigh dramatically while continuing to rub slow circles on his back. "Control freak."

He stiffens slightly before giving a terse nod. "Yup."

"At least you own it."

He glances at me again as he tosses the towel in a nearby garbage can, but this time there's a look in his eye that wasn't there before. "Yeah" is his faint response.

Then he clamps my hand back in his and walks me to the passenger side, where he opens the door and ushers me into my seat while avoiding eye contact. I don't know if it's the outcome of the game, the fact he just hurled in front of me, or that I called him a control freak, but there's a new tension in the air.

Shame hits me again.

Jasper's having one of the worst weeks of his life, and I'm psychoanalyzing if he's upset with me while he holds my hand and opens a car door for me.

I shake my head at my selfishness as the door slams and he gets in beside me.

"Ranch?" he asks as he slides his long arm over the back of my seat. We've pulled out together in a car a million times, except now the nearness of him feels heavy and unfamiliar.

"Yeah." I sigh and sink back into the plush-leather seat. "Ranch."

We make the same drive we've made several times in the past week. No music plays. All I hear is the white noise of air rushing through the vents as I switch between staring out the darkened window and then back at Jasper's carefully blank face.

"You know the saying, 'There are no stupid questions'?"

His eyes slice my way, and he nods once firmly.

"Would it still be true if I asked you if you're okay?"

His cheek twitches, and I watch his hands twist on the steering wheel.

"Sunny, I am so far from okay, it's not even funny."

My heart twists in my chest, and my tongue darts out over my lower lip as I continue to regard him, racking my brain for what to say next.

"Nothing you say is stupid though," he quickly adds.

I smile flatly and look out over the dash. Leave it to Jasper Gervais to say something like that when I've spent the last five months engaged to someone who constantly made me feel like the things I had to say were dumb.

And I just let him. I put a hand over my throat in a sad attempt to quell the ache there.

This isn't my night to cry.

"Coach suspended me for two weeks."

"What?" I exclaim, turning in my seat to face him. "Why? Every goalie hits rough patches."

"Because I never disclosed what's going on. He knows how I am. He knows my head is somewhere else, and as much as I fuckin' hate to admit it, he's right. I wanna be out there, but I also…" He trails off, broad hands rotating on the wheel in frustration.

He didn't tell them about Beau? God. This man is a vault, locked up so damn tight. He's always been a man of few words, even around me. But at this moment, it's not like he can't find the words. I know he can. It's more like it pains him to wrench them from himself. Like staying quiet and introspective is his best defense mechanism.

I know he's more open with me than he is with most people. Softer, less growly. So I provide cautiously, "You also want to curl up in bed and cry?"

Because if I feel that way right now, he must too.

A curt nod with eyes fixed on the dark road is what he offers back, which is about as much as I expected from him.

A loud vibrating sound echoes against something in my purse, filling the already tense vehicle with another layer of anxiety.

With a deep sense of dread, I pull my phone out and stare at it.

It's my mom. And this is the first time she's called. Her response to my mass text was Take care of yourself. I love you.

I have dozens of missed phone calls from my dad and from Sterling and from countless "friends." I've been referring to them in my head as lookie-loos because if you haven't spoken to me in years, I don't know why I'd chat to you about the implosion of my wedding day.

Over the past week, I've listened to the voicemails from Sterling and my dad, but I didn't delete them. That way, my inbox fills, and they can't leave more. Their messages are angry, frantic, and entitled. Basically the last thing I feel like dealing with.

But my mom? She's another story altogether. She… I swear she looked at me before the wedding like she had something to say. Her lips parted, and her hand stretched out toward me. She was so damn close. Before she could get it out, my dad walked in, told me I made the perfect bride, and whisked her away.

The expression she shot me over her shoulder as he led her out was pleading.

The phone is still vibrating in my hand, and I'm staring at it like a ticking time bomb when Jasper clears his throat and glances over at me.

Swallowing hard, I swipe to answer. "Hi, Mom."

"Sloane." She breathes my name like it's the relief she's been seeking.

"Hi. I'm…"

"I just need to hear your voice. Know that you're somewhere safe." There's a slight tremble in her voice, and suddenly the back of my throat aches with a ferocity that steals my breath. My sweet, supportive mom. The one who learned to put my hair up in a perfect bun. Who drove me to every ballet practice and recital, no matter how early she had to get up.

I'd kill for a hug from my mom right now. Absolutely kill.

Peeking over at Jasper, I reply, "I'm safe." Because how could I feel anything but safe? The man literally broke me out of my wedding, carried me down the street, and never batted an eyelash.

Like he just *knows* I need him, he reaches across the center console and takes my hand. Fingers linking with mine.

I hear a ragged sigh on the other end of the line. "Good. Good. Are you…going away for a while?" Her voice sounds almost hopeful now.

My head quirks at her odd question. I'd expected Mom to grill me about when I was coming back. "Why would you ask me that?"

I look over at Jasper again and catch him watching me. He's listening, and I don't really care. There's only one secret I'm desperate to keep from Jasper—that I've been pathetically in love with him for the better part of my life.

"Because that's what I would do if I were in your position." A tinny laugh follows her statement, and my eyes bug out at her admission.

I know she married into a wealthy family like her own, while her sister married Harvey and lived a quieter life on the ranch. I've often wondered if she's happy in her marriage but never quite worked up the courage to ask.

"Mom, I—"

My phone dies in my hand.

"What happened?" Jasper's voice is all gravel.

"It…it died." I shake my head, running her words of advice through my mind on replay.

"And what did she say?"

"She said if she were me, she'd go away for a while."

"What about the ballet? You must need to go back soon."

I scoff. "I took a leave to plan the wedding. So I'm off through Christmas because I opted out of *The Nutcracker*."

"Why did you take a leave? The wedding is just one day."

Slumping down farther into the seat, I let the back of my head roll back and forth as I confess something that sounds so asinine my stomach curdles just saying it out loud. "Sterling said I needed to be"—I hold my hands up in sarcastic air quotes—"present to plan the wedding and enjoy the honeymoon."

I run a thumb over the small pink scar from where I cut

myself with the massive diamond on my finger. I should really take my ring off. I even *want* to take it off. It's not Sterling who keeps me from doing it. It's that I have this deep sense that once I remove it, *everything* in my life will change. I'll be a new me, and nothing will look the same anymore. My family. My upbringing. Everything I've come to know.

And that scares me.

A muscle in Jasper's jaw pops, and the skin over his knuckles thins under the pressure of him squeezing the steering wheel. "Fucking Woodcock."

I snort a laugh. *Woodcock.*

"So what are you going to do?" The tip of his tongue catches between his straight white teeth, as though he's biting it to keep himself from saying anything more.

"What do you think I should do?"

His mouth twists. "Sunny, the last thing you need in your life is another man telling you what to do."

I sigh and turn away to stare at the dark fields flashing past the passenger window. I'd kill to have Jasper Gervais tell me what to do. The fact he doesn't think he should makes me want it even more.

I need someone to take charge but with my best interests in mind. Not a business. Not perception. *Me. My needs.*

"What would Beau do?" I murmur under my breath.

I don't mean to say it loud enough that Jasper will hear me, which is why I start when Jasper responds with "He'd get the fuck outta dodge and go do something for himself."

9

Jasper

Cade: Why don't you join us for dinner soon?

Rhett: Beers tomorrow?

Roman: If you need to talk, I'm always around. Take care
of yourself.

I CURL UP IN MY CHILDHOOD BED, HUDDLED IN A TIGHT BALL
like I might if I had a hangover. Like if I just lie still and
quiet, I won't hurt.

But then I remember that my brother is missing, and
everything hurts.

I don't even want to think about it. I want to push it into the same corner where I keep my sister Jenny. But it's not working. My mental game is shit right now—something I've proven over and over on the ice lately.

Years of ongoing sports therapy to hone my mind to handle the pressure of my position, and it all crumbles with one swift kick to the foundation. Those vine-like intrusive thoughts creep up and threaten to strangle me.

I tried to do the exercise that's always worked for me. Four seconds is all I give myself to think dark thoughts. I soak in them but only for four seconds. After that I swap to envisioning myself kicking ass, playing my best, and making a highlight reel–worthy save. And then I think about something else entirely.

Just four seconds of fear or sadness or doubt. Four seconds of insanity. That's all I'll allow.

But not anymore. Right now I'm sitting with those dark thoughts like they're an old friend.

I push to sit, pads of my fingers sinking into the too-soft mattress. The house was quiet when we got here. Everyone hiding away in their own corners to deal with this in their own way.

Rhett has Summer.

Cade has Willa.

Violet has Cole.

It seems like every Eaton has someone to lean on. Except me. And Harvey. Which is why I've stayed here for so long. I can't stomach the thought of leaving him all alone in this house after he made sure that I wasn't all alone as a teenager.

Everyone I've cared about in life has left me in some way or another—it's part of my persona now. I can't control who leaves, but I can control everything else to a point where my anxiety doesn't cripple me.

But this? This is ravaging me, and I can't control shit.

"Fuck!" I roar, right as I turn and smash my fist into the wallpapered drywall beside me.

A low sob sound lurches from my lungs as pain lances through my knuckles. I shake my hand and internally berate myself. How fucking old am I? Punching a wall like an angry little teenager.

My door flies open, and Sloane's slender frame is a silhouette in the open doorway. "Jas?" She sounds panicked, a little breathless, like she ran here.

"I'm fine. The wall isn't, but I'll patch it."

"You hit the wall?"

I groan and shake my hand again. "Go to bed, Sloane." I don't feel like talking. And I'm tired of worrying. Right now Sloane is just one more thing I worry about.

Not only because she left her fiancé practically at the altar but because I'm deeply satisfied she did. Too satisfied. The last thing Sloane needs is me crossing that line.

She doesn't make it easy though. Because she flat out ignores what I tell her to do and pads across my room, bare feet on smooth hardwood.

I wish she had ignored other assholes when they told her what to do: Marry some asshole to close a business deal. Leave her job—her passion—to plan a wedding.

It's all such bullshit.

The wild girl I knew would've stuck her tongue out at them and carried on with her life. So I can't help but be a little satisfied when she walks to my en suite bathroom muttering something about "dumb boys" before returning with a warm wet washcloth.

She comes back to stand right between my knees, still wearing my jersey.

My cock thickens at the sight. The silvery moonlight highlights the shimmer on the fabric, and my eyes snag on the hem that falls midthigh.

My fingers twitch like they've got a mind of their own. Like they'd enjoy exploring that hemline. Hike it up gently and see what's beneath. Erasing and ruining years of friendship as they go.

Nonetheless, there's the part of me who wants to erase everywhere that Woodcock asshole got to touch her. Got to *have* her.

He doesn't deserve her.

"Hand out, Gervais." Her voice is soft and soothing. Sleepy and resigned somehow. All it takes is one glance at the digital clock on my bedside table to know she just fell asleep.

If she fell asleep at all.

Jealousy and guilt swirl in my gut. "I'm fine. Go back to bed."

She cocks a hip, making my jersey slip higher on that side. Really not helping my wandering eyes. My hand doesn't even hurt anymore. All I can think about is reaching beneath the fabric and shaping the soft curve of her waist. Tracing the little dimple on either side of her spine just above her hips.

Every part of Sloane is toned and strong. Long and lean. She's like a piece of pale marble that's been sculpted to perfection for years.

"Hand. Now."

I blink, leaning back slightly. I'm too worked up, and neither of us is wearing nearly enough clothing for this interaction. But the expression on her face hedges no room for debate. Grinding my molars, I hold my right hand up to her and hiss when the wet cloth presses against my knuckles.

"Idiot," she mutters, dabbing carefully over every ridge of each finger and holding my wrist with a tenderness that feels unfamiliar in so many ways.

Because, while I do have sex with women, I keep it very private. Separate from every other part of my life. Work and family never cross over. And it's not…personal. I've ensured that it's not. Because getting attached *hurts,* and finding someone to get attached to that I can trust at this point in my career seems downright impossible.

"Wow. Very soothing. You should have become a nurse."

I see a sliver of a smile on her lips as a curtain of blond hair tumbles down over her face. "No, you should have. You were terrific at tending to my feet."

Her feet.

My eyes trail down her legs to the floor, and I remember those days. The blisters. The redness. The swelling.

I kept coming back to help her even when she didn't ask me to. Even though I was told not to. In retrospect, it was one of those nights when I first saw Sloane as a woman and not the little blond girl on the ranch. A cousin. A friend.

It happened while I rubbed her sore feet and trailed a thumb up the arch of her foot. Her head fell back against the pillows on her plush cream-colored couch, and the exposed column of her throat caught the warm glow of the floor lamp behind her in a way that transfixed me. Shadows played across her collarbones. Her cheeks turned a rosy shade.

The moan that spilled from her lips had me shifting uncomfortably in my jeans.

After that I stopped rubbing her feet.

I realized she wasn't a little girl at all. And I wanted what I couldn't have.

She was still young, though, and new to living on her own. She needed a friend. And before long, she had a boyfriend, and the ship had sailed. With our age difference, the close family relation, her dad…there were too many ties, too many complications.

Too much fear that I might lose her.

Not that I would have subjected her to me anyway. But now and then, I'd find myself dreaming. Or her face would pop into my mind while I showered, while my hand wrapped around—

"There. Now lie back and let it dry."

Her palm lands in the middle of my chest and pushes me back into bed, her bare legs pressing against the inside of my knees as she does.

So many people eye me like I'm a Rubik's Cube they can't solve. My colors are all jumbled and on the wrong sides, but Sloane doesn't care that I'm messy. She's never looked at me like I need fixing. She's always looked like she does now. Tender and supportive.

When her eyes drop to my bare torso, tracing the outlines of my dark tattoos, the comfort of the moment turns intimate. Her exhale is harsh in the quiet room before her eyes snag on my boxers and drift to where her bare legs press against the inside of mine. My gaze latches onto her lips, watching them pop open in surprise. Like she was so busy tending to me she failed to notice our mutual state of undress.

I clear my throat, standing quickly and gently guiding her back away from me. Taking the damp rag and tossing it across the room into the hamper. "Thank you." My voice comes out all hoarse and strained. I wonder if she notices, but I can't bring myself to look at her. Instead, I focus on the steady beat of my heart. Grappling blindly in the darkened drawer of my dresser.

"Good night." My voice cracks like I'm a teenager, and I shake my head before I pull on a T-shirt and sit on the bed, as if a shirt and simple duvet will protect me from whatever that moment was we just shared.

I thump my sore fist into the pillow, making a show of getting it just right. It hurts, but I ignore the pain. Or maybe I relish it.

"Jas?" Her tone is soft and uncertain as she stands by watching me, and I hate the thought I might have made her feel uncomfortable with my gruff response.

I hit the pillow harder because I hate a lot of things right now.

"Jas? Talk to me. Tell me what's in your head."

I turn to her, all my restraint snapping under the weight

of the night. "My head? My head, Sunny? My head is a fucking mess. I hate that Beau is missing and my family is hurting. I hate that my team is struggling and I've been sidelined. I especially hate that someone took advantage of you, that he hurt you. Belittled you. *Yelled* at you. You're one of the most important people in my life, and he treated you like shit. And I really fucking *hate* that."

I hiss the last words with venom. Once they've cleared my lips, I pant, breathless over the word vomit I just hurled all over my childhood bedroom at the girl who always listens.

The girl who's always there for me.

The girl I almost lost.

I should be able to let this go, but her arranged relationship with Sterling hurts so intensely that it aches deep in my bones. And I'm not good at letting things go. Every corner of my mind is heavy with regret.

"Jasper, why are you so angry about this?" She looks confused. "I'm fine."

"I'm angry because I want you happy and safe. You weren't. I pulled away when I found out you were engaged." What I don't admit out loud is that my feelings were too jumbled and complicated to face in the wake of that announcement. It winded me in a way I never saw coming. "But you still needed my help, and I wasn't there for you. You came so damn close to being trapped in a life that would have been miserable for you."

This last week has put me into a state where I'm practically frothing at the mouth to protect her, to rescue her—to ensure she never ends up in that position again. And I'm realizing that what I'm feeling is a whole lot more than a brotherly sense of protection.

It's envy. It's *possession*.

"Jasper." Her eyes are like saucers, her hands held wide as she lifts them and drops them back down in an exhausted shrug. She steps closer, eyes roaming my face. "I'm here, aren't I? I'm here. With you." Her fingers slide over my hand still fisted on the pillow, and she locks in on my eyes. "It's just you and me. Together. And I'm safe."

I offer her a terse nod. It's all I can manage right now. My limbs are seized up. Too many emotions. Her body too close.

"Move over."

My head flicks in her direction. "What?"

"Move your ass over."

"Why?"

Those pale-blue irises roll back into her head with so much attitude. It reminds me of her as a teenager. "Because I'm not leaving you alone tonight."

My body goes rigid. "Why?"

"Because I'm concerned for the safety of the walls in this room." The voice she uses is light, but her eyes are just a bit pinched.

Sloane's not worried about the walls. She's worried about *me*. It's why she used to come out on the roof with me too. She's always been a little uncertain if I would take a turn in that direction.

If I'd hurt myself.

Sure, I've contemplated suicide. But mostly in the way everyone has. What it would take. If I could follow through.

In the wake of Jenny's death, I'd toed that ledge, but ever since the Eatons took me in, it was never an option.

I know how it feels to lose someone you love, and I couldn't do that to these people who've become my family. I'll suffer before ever making them do the same.

"Why?" I ask, wanting validation in a moment of weakness. Wanting to hear her say she worries about me or wants to comfort me. It's insecure, and I shouldn't be hoping for something like that from a woman whose relationship dissolved mere days ago.

Her responding sigh is tired. "You're glitching, Gervais. You sound like a scratched record. Move the fuck over."

One cheek twitches at the fact that she resorted to swearing at me. There's something satisfying about proper little Sloane having a sailor's mouth. So I move over, not letting myself think too hard about whether it's a good idea. We're just friends.

My eyes flutter shut at the sound of the sheet rustling, the small mattress dipping under her weight.

Just friends.

A few strands of her hair tangle in the stubble on my cheek as she lies down facing me, but I leave them there, opting to breathe her in instead.

"Well, this bed is tiny."

I chuckle. "It is." The bed usually feels too small for my six-foot-three frame, never mind adding in another person.

The silence stretches out just a little too long. A little too far.

"Am I bugging you? Do you want me to leave?"

My heart slams against the cage I keep it locked in. How could Sloane bug anyone? She has to be the least annoying person in the world.

"No," I husk as I reach down and wrap my hand around her delicate wrist, as though pulling her back from even thinking about leaving.

"Okay," she breathes, sounding relieved.

We fall into silence again, and I let my mind wander to how these last few days must have felt for her. We've been so wrapped up in my life—Beau, hockey, me punching walls like a rage-case teenager—that I've failed to give her the comfort she might need.

"Are you sad, Sloane?"

She shifts, head turning to gaze up at the ceiling, giving me a darkened view of her profile. Her hair slips away, and my fingers twitch on her wrist with the instinct to run them through the silky strands, to rub my cheek along them like I do when we hug.

"I mean, of course. I know Beau isn't my best friend, but he's my cousin. Some of my best memories are of long sweltering summer days spent out here with all of you. I'm… devastated." Her voice breaks a little, and I watch her lashes flutter rapidly.

She's close enough that I could reach out and hold her. But I don't.

"I meant about—" I stop suddenly. His name doesn't belong here in the dark with us. "The wedding."

She hums thoughtfully as she runs two fingers across her lips before firmly pressing on them. Her cheeks go round, and it's like she's trying to push the smile back down. "No."

"Are you trying not to laugh about your big fancy wedding going to shit?" I chuckle quietly, turning on my side to face her.

A grunt-snort noise escapes her, and she's now pressing her entire hand over her mouth. "No!"

"You have always had a fucked-up sense of humor."

Her body shakes with laughter, and she gives me a look of feigned offense. "I have not!"

"You laugh at the most inappropriate times. You know you do." I point at her playfully. "You laughed that time Rhett fell off the llama and broke his arm as a kid."

She laughs harder. "He deserved to be laughed at! He had no business riding that llama! And the way he latched onto its long neck made him look a big dumb koala or something."

She's wheezing now, curling in toward me, and I can't help but laugh with her. He really did look like a big dumb koala.

"And it wasn't even an impressive fall! He just plunked down in the most lackluster way. I've seen him take worse spills off an angry bull and walk away totally fine."

The giggles hit us hard on the walk down memory lane, and I wipe happy tears out of my eyes as I gaze up at the stucco ceiling. God, we had fun as kids out here. It feels good to reminisce. Good to laugh.

Good to lie here with someone who knows about some of the happiest days of my life. We've been in a rut of games and workouts this week. I think Sloane's been dancing for fun in a spare room at Summer's gym and then tending to Harvey. We're all hiding out. Hunkering down. Trying to keep things normal—but failing.

She sighs deeply and carries on, "Anyway. No. I'm not sad about the wedding. I'm…relieved. Isn't that awful? All I feel is intense relief. Am I going to hell for admitting that?"

My thumb brushes over the bone in her wrist. The way I feel about her wedding crumbling into nothing is intense relief too. "Nah. If you're going to hell for that, then I'll definitely be there for all my shit too."

She yawns, and her body softens beside me; she has to be so tired. "Hell might be all right if you were there with me." She stiffens. "I didn't mean—"

Not wanting her to second-guess anything she says, I cut her off. "Hell might actually be all right if we're stuck there together, Sloane."

The sound of her head rustling against the pillow tells me she's nodding in agreement. And then I give in to that little voice in my head. The one that tells me I need her.

I draw her body against mine, my arms wrap her up, and our legs tangle together instantly.

"Good night, Sunny" is all I say as I revel in the comforting heat of her.

A beat of silence passes, and then she sighs. "Good night, Jas."

10

Jasper

Harvey: How's the hand?

Jasper: How do you know?

Harvey: I'm old. Not deaf.

Jasper: It's fine. I'm fine.

Harvey: No, you're not. None of us are. But you know
what will make you feel better?

Jasper: What's that?

Harvey: Fixing my wall. There's spackling and a putty
knife outside your door.

Jasper: Sorry, Harv. I'll fix it. Promise.

Harvey: All good, son. Have you seen Sloane? Her door
was open, and her room was empty. ;)

*"I WAS WONDERING... WELL, I WAS THINKING..." SLOANE PEEKS
up at me from under her lashes, hands twisting in front of her.*

She's stunning. She's grown up so much since last summer I almost can't believe my eyes.

I came out to the ranch for Easter dinner and wasn't expecting her to be here. We still mostly only see each other in the summer, because living in the city, she's busy with dance and high school, and I'm fully immersed in keeping this spot I have on the main roster with the Grizzlies.

I was about to leave when she ran after me to the door.

I drop my voice, resting my hands on her shoulders to look her in the eye. "Is everything okay, Sloane? You're making me nervous. Did something happen? You know you can tell me anything."

"Oh! No!" She laughs shrilly, cheeks turning pink as she pushes her loose blond hair behind her ears.

A pit of dread grows in my stomach. It's the eyelashes. The blushing. The nervous way she's playing with her hair. And the fact that Harvey, Violet, and my brothers are all basically watching from the living room.

I'm not oblivious to the fact Sloane has had a crush on me. But I've pretended I am. Because shit is so much less awkward that way.

"Okay." She smiles up at me nervously, and nerves roil in my stomach. "I'm just going to go ahead and say it." She takes a deep breath. "Will you go to prom with me?"

Now she isn't the only one blushing. I feel like my entire face is on fire. "Oh, Sunny." My fingers pulse on her shoulders, and I get lost in the twinkle of hope in her eyes. Hurting Sloane is enough to make me feel like I might be sick.

I don't want to disappoint her, but fuck…I can't do this

either. *"I'm not the guy you want to go with. I'm…"* I search for a good reason that isn't just I don't want to lead you on. *"I'm twenty-four. Really in the media right now. With you being in high school, I'm just not sure it would be a good look, you know?"*

I try so hard to ignore that her eyes instantly fill. The too-fast way she nods her head. "Oh. Yeah." She steps back from me, my hands falling from her shoulders, and she glances over at the living room. *"Yeah. Of course. That makes perfect sense."*

"Still friends, right?" I reach forward, trying to give her forearm a reassuring squeeze. She tugs her arm back and forces a bright smile onto her face.

"Yeah. Of course. Still friends. Always." With another frantic nod, she turns, but she doesn't head back to the family gathering. She disappears down the hallway that leads to the upstairs bedrooms.

I feel like shit as I wave goodbye to a room full of wide-eyed, awkward-as-fuck family members. I don't know what to say to them. I half expect someone to crack a joke, but no one says a word as I flee the house, and all that does is drive home how brutal that interaction was with Sloane.

Because even if there is a little part of me that thinks it would be kind of cute to go with her, I know I can't.

She needs to go have fun at her prom. Make memories—with someone her own age. She needs to have the very best night, and I'm certain I can't be the one to give her that.

Sloane Winthrop has grown into a woman who is smart, beautiful, and so damn talented. She has an entire life ahead of her with some shiny rich boyfriend she'll fall head over heels for while she pursues her higher education at some fancy private university.

She doesn't need the likes of me holding her back anymore.

I've almost convinced myself I did the right thing by the time I get to my truck. But when I pull away down the driveway, regret niggles at me. I glance up into the rearview mirror, and Sloane is there.

Sitting on that roof all by herself.

Probably realizing what I already know.

That I'm not good enough for her. Never have been. Never will be...

I wake up with Sloane's forehead pressed into the center of my chest. Her hands are rolled into loose fists and clutched under her chin like she's trying to keep herself from touching me in her sleep.

I don't suffer from the same hesitance. I've got my arm slung casually over her petite frame and one leg draped possessively over both of hers.

It borders on too far. Yes, we're friends. But we're also a man and a woman. Alone and barely dressed on a bed that's too small.

And she's still wearing my jersey.

Friend. Friend. Friend.

I slam the word into my brain repeatedly like it might cement it somehow. I imagine it for four seconds, the letters cropping up like they're being typed beside a cursor. Like it might keep me from wondering, "What if we weren't just friends? What if we were more?"

Sure, I shut things down between us when she was practically still a kid. And even not so long ago, she made an offhanded joke that hit a little too close to home as I helped mount her TV on the wall.

I laughed even though I didn't find it funny at all. I told her it would never happen. *Again*. Because how could it?

But she planted a seed that day. One that's grown into a question I'm too scared to ask.

Now I'm lying here wondering…why the fuck can't it happen? There was a time I was convinced I couldn't be the guy to give her what she needs, to make her happy.

She wanted me, and I fucked it up—like I always do.

But that was then. And this is now. I'm not the same scared kid I was back then.

The word *friend* fades the longer I stare at her—the slightly upturned tip of her nose that wiggles a little when she talks. Her high noble cheekbones that go so perfectly round when she laughs. Her lashes that are washed clean of mascara and take on more of a pale-brown color where they're fanned down over her smooth skin.

Her engagement ring, the one she's still wearing, shines blindingly beneath her chin. And it's the dose of reality I need.

Proof that I'm too late. That no matter how hard I work on my reaction time between the pipes, my personal life has always been one big miss. I freeze up. And while I get stuck in my head, the world keeps turning.

Because as I sit around wondering if we could ever be more, nursing all my complicated emotions, the reality is she almost walked down the aisle with another man. Any feelings she once had for me must be long gone.

Truth be told, I can't really tell what she's feeling right now. She can say she's not sad, but I'm familiar with how grief works. I know it comes in waves. I know you can feel fine about something one day and it can fucking cripple you the next.

The anger always comes.

And I know that what she needs right now is Jasper, her friend. Not Jasper who's been too big of a coward to cross that line even though he's been thinking about it for years.

I carefully remove my limbs from her sleeping form, pushing away the swell of regret that hits me when I release her. I force my eyes to the ground, watching my toes against the hardwood floor as I reach for whatever clothes I can find.

And then I leave the room, too weak to keep myself from looking back at her sleeping form one last time. She looks small and frail—too thin. She looks exhausted, and I hope she sleeps. I hope she eats.

The door shuts quietly behind me, and I take long strides down to the kitchen, not sure what I'll be walking into when I get there.

I'll be the first to admit that I don't handle emotional situations well. Trauma? I've got enough, thanks. Feelings? Too many of those too.

I round the corner into the big farmhouse kitchen consisting of wide worn floor planks, dark-wood cabinetry, and hunter-green walls. The entire house is outdated and yet…not. It's like it was transported straight off the set of *Yellowstone.*

Complete with two country boys sitting at the table over a cup of coffee.

"Did you get dressed in the dark?" Cade snipes at me.

Harvey barks out a laugh, and I glance down at myself, realizing I grabbed a neon-pink shirt with a yellow energy drink logo on it and black-and-white stripes on the arms. It truly is atrocious, but it was dark last night. I think it was promotional. I'm positive I've never worn it before. And it really does clash with the pair of army-green joggers I'm wearing.

My lips quirk. "Listen, the day I take fashion advice from someone as old as you who barely leaves this ranch is the day I die."

I see Cade's cheek twitch. Picking on each other is our comfort zone. And damn, it feels good. The days have slowly bled into a depressed normalcy. We've had one awkward family dinner. Harvey didn't make any blow-job jokes, and Beau wasn't there to lighten the mood. It feels like everyone is just going through the motions. Waiting to hear something is the worst.

I go straight for the coffee maker, pour myself a mug, and take a seat at the table with the two other men.

"I think you're just so used to everyone fawning over you that you don't know when you look like a fucking clown anymore."

"Adorable coming from the guy who wears his jeans at least two sizes too small." I give Cade a big cheesy grin, loving the feel of something that isn't just sad.

"Willa likes them tight."

I quirk a brow. "How long does it take her to peel them off you? My money is on at least five minutes."

"Bring your timer. You can watch next time; could probably teach your dumb ass a thing or two."

Harvey's head whips between us, an amused smile on his lips.

"I'll be sure to give you some notice so you can get your Viagra down in time, old boy."

"Oh, nah." Harvey waves a hand dismissively. "The Eatons are a virile bunch. Even I don't need those."

"Jesus Christ." Cade's head drops, and his eyes stare into his coffee cup like he's scrying for answers on how to make his dad stop saying inappropriate things.

I snort because I know that day will never come. And it's a sign of life that I'll take. Harvey's sense of humor is one of my favorite things about him—always has been.

And quiet as I've been through the years, I never can quite resist toeing that line with him. Pushing him a smidge further to see what he'll say.

"You got someone special on the receiving end of all that virility, Harv?"

"A few someones. Hard to pick just one, ya know? Why choose?" He smiles back at me maniacally.

"Make sure you wrap it up" is my casual response. After the death of his wife so long ago, I'm happy he has some company.

Harvey grins. "Talk to Cade about that. Not me."

Cade groans and tips his head back, now staring at the ceiling. "I should have stayed at my house."

I nod, taking a long pull of the coffee in my hand. "Probably. It's early. Wasn't expecting to find you here."

"Well, Harvey and I were about to do rock, paper, scissors to see who would take a road trip out to see Violet in Ruby Creek with a load of hay."

My head quirks. "Sorry?"

Harvey jumps in. "Something about a hay shortage out that way. Hot, dry summer. So she called us, begging for a trailer full to help them get through the winter. She still complains that the hay out there sucks compared to ours." The older man puffs up a little at that compliment from his only daughter.

Cade hits me with a serious look. "But neither of us really wants to leave." He clears his throat. "Just in case."

Harvey nods, eyes shrink-wrapped instantly.

Just in case. I know what they're saying without having to ask for more. Just in case Beau is found. Just in case Beau is gone. Just in case they need to lean on their family when news about their beloved brother comes in.

"I'll go." I don't even need to think twice about it.

Both their heads whip in my direction, surprise written all over their faces.

Harvey smiles at me kindly, the way he has since he took me in, even when he already had too much on his plate. I've never met a man with a bigger heart than what's in Harvey Eaton's chest. "You're a good boy, Jasper. But you've got your season. You can't leave, though it means the world to me you'd offer."

"Yeah, about that… I'm actually on leave now. For at least two weeks."

Harvey's thick brows scrunch on his forehead. "Why?"

"Did you not see his games this week?" Cade tosses in.

I glare in his direction. He just smirks.

"Fucking dick," I mutter with no malice as I turn back

to Harvey. "Because Roman is a domineering asshole who found out I didn't disclose what was going on to management or coaching staff, and then I shit the bed on the ice and lost us a bunch of games. And I guess rather than yelling at me from the bench like he always does, he's decided to be inspiring or some shit and coddle me like a sad toddler."

I'm met with silence and slightly concerned looks because I don't often get that many words out in one breath. In fact, I don't usually get many words out, period. I retreated into myself a long time ago and got really good at listening rather than talking.

"Well…that's quite the story," Harvey provides, like he doesn't quite know what to say.

"You do remind me a bit of a sad toddler," Cade deadpans.

Dick.

"I'll go. You guys stay." I gesture between them. "You need to be here. Cade, you've got Willa and Luke—a baby on the way. Harvey, you've got several girlfriends and also your entire family."

They both chuckle, and I muster a small grin, happy to lighten the mood.

"You're our family too, you know?" Cade is all serious now. It's sometimes hard to differentiate with him because he's got such a dry sense of humor, but this is him being sensitive in his own way.

"I know. But there's no one here who needs me. Let me go. I can support the family by making this trip. You both taught me how to haul. You know I'm capable with the truck and trailer. Plus, it'd be good to see Violet. She could use some distracting as well."

Harvey's fingers drum on the table. "The roads could be bad through the mountains this time of year."

He knows my anxiety about driving, vehicles, and accidents. It's wild how one simple mistake can translate into such widespread anxiety. But for him? For my family?

I can swallow it down and overlook it.

My smile is tense. "I know. I can manage though."

"Yeah." We all jerk, surprised by the soft voice coming from the corner of the kitchen. Like having women in the house is just that unusual these days. "He can manage. And I'll go with him to make sure he has company."

Without even glancing at us, Sloane pours herself a coffee. She's changed into a simple pair of black leggings paired with a gray sweatshirt that swallows her upper body, woolen socks stacked over her ankles.

And when she turns to smile at us, her pale-blond locks a little mussed, I can see the lines on her cheek from where her face was pressed into the sheets of my bed. She looks cozy—a tad dopey. It makes me think of how she felt pressed up against me last night.

She looks different than I've ever seen her. Or maybe it's just the way *I'm* seeing her now.

"Good lord, Gervais. What the hell are you wearing?" she blurts.

Everyone else dissolves into a fit of giggles. Cade murmurs something about he told me so, but I barely hear him.

I'm focused on Sloane. Because I will not tell her what

she can and can't do. So I'm left wondering how I'm going to handle a road trip through the mountains with just the two of us and not go completely insane.

Or do something completely insane.

11

Sloane

Willa: Sloane, can you confirm Jasper is okay? The guys are worried about him but don't know how to talk to him about their feelings. They've requested we ask instead. It's like a game of telephone over here.

Summer: We're all texting. It's nothing like a game of telephone.

Sloane: He's sad. He'll be okay.

Willa: You should bang him.

Summer: Wils, that can't always be your advice.

Willa: Why not? It's solid advice. Worked out for you.

Summer: She just fled her wedding.

Willa: Yeah, but that fucking guy sucked. Jasper has that hot, tortured vibe going for him.

Sloane: He's sad. Not horny, Willa.

Willa: He can be both. Turn that frown upside down, baby girl!

"OKAY, I GOT EVERYTHING I NEED." I SHOULDER MY WAY into the truck with a brand-new duffel bag full of brand-new clothes and toiletries. Harvey took me into town this morning to fill in the gaps in my temporary wardrobe while Cade and Jasper got the truck and trailer set.

Jasper eyes me speculatively. He really hasn't said much to me. I don't know if I scared him off with my comment about how hell would be a jolly good time with him there—talk about cringe—or if he just doesn't want me to come with him.

Maybe forcing my way into his bed was too far.

Maybe he's figuring out that I never really got over him.

It's hard to tell when he doesn't talk. But I'm used to that. He's always been quiet, and I've always just done what I wanted. Talked to him. At him? Practiced my choreography when I ran out of things to say.

And he's always just watched. And listened.

So I guess the way he's staring at me right now isn't new either, but it has the hair on my arms standing on end all the same.

I toss the bag in the back seat, my body rumbling along with the loud truck. The dually is massive, runs loud, and has the power to pull the flatbed that is now loaded with huge round bales of hay.

My palms slap against my thighs as I stare out the windshield at the posts flanking the end of the driveway, the ones joined by an archway that has a wrought-iron Wishing Well

Ranch sign hanging from it. "Okay. Let's get this show on the road." I'm ready for some fresh scenery. I feel like I've been walking on eggshells all week here in Chestnut Springs.

Jasper doesn't put the truck in drive. "You sure?"

"That we should go?" My nose scrunches as I glance over at him, so intent on me.

"No. That you should come with me."

Heat flares on my cheeks like I'm a goddamn teenager. I almost giggle at the turn my thoughts take. *I'd pay good money to come with Jasper Gervais.*

"Yes. Stop asking, Gervais. You're stuck with me."

I chance a glance over at Jasper's handsome face. His stubble a little longer than usual, his hair still damp and combed back. His jaw still just as stupidly square as it's always been.

He quirks a dark brow at me. "Always."

I huff out a small breath and drop his gaze again, trying to figure out what's changed between us in these last several days. Did it all start that night at dinner when he met Sterling for the first time? Or was it when he charged into that room in the church, looking like a fucking superhero in a perfectly tailored suit? Was it when we sat on the roof?

All I know is that *something* is different.

"I can't help but point out that you going on this road trip with me seems an awful lot like you running away from your life."

"My mom said she'd get away, and honestly, nothing has ever sounded more appealing." Jasper is just the cherry on top—but I don't voice that thought. Even I have boundaries when it comes to bleeding all over the place about this unrequited crush.

He gives me a droll look, one that says, *You're full of shit*, before I add, "Oh yeah? And what is it that you're doing, Jasper?"

His Adam's apple bobs just above the neckline of his soft brown fleece as he swallows. "Helping my family."

I guess we both have a story that we're sticking to.

"You gonna try to tell me you don't retreat or isolate yourself when bad shit happens? It's like you forget I've known you for almost two decades."

A muscle in Jasper's jaw flexes with a subtle shake of his head. He reaches forward and shifts the truck into drive. "It's impossible to forget how long I've known you, Sunny" is all he says as we pull away through the gate.

And I spend an absurd amount of time turning that sentence over in my head, wondering just what the hell he means. *Impossible to forget.*

"Do you think about me?" I blurt, watching him still the minute those words leap from my lips. "When we go weeks or months without talking or seeing each other…do you think about me?"

"Why?" His voice is cool and even, giving nothing away.

I twist at my ring nervously and sigh. "I don't know. Here. With you." I gesture between us. "I keep forgetting about everything else in my life. *Everyone* else. But when we're apart, I constantly come back to y—you know what? Never mind. Just ignore me."

The silence that stretches between us is thick, alive, and sparking with the heat and reality of my almost-confession.

A heat that suffuses my entire body when he finally responds with "Every fucking day, Sunny."

~

"Want to play I Spy?" I ask after what has got to be at least an hour of silence.

I can see Jasper retreating into himself. His shoulders curl, his knuckles turn white. I swear I can see into his brain.

And what's in there is a man who is *spinning*.

It makes me want to crawl into his lap and shake him, to bring him back from whatever ledge he's toeing.

The only way I know how to do that is to entertain and engage him. Make him laugh. He has the best laugh, all deep and soft, a little breathy like he's trying to tamp it down and hide it away.

When Jasper laughs, he looks bashful. His eyes drop, and his straight teeth flash. I guess after watching him so closely for so long, I've catalogued his every reaction. The little tics.

It's pathetic if I think too hard about it.

"I Spy?" His brow lifts, and he glances my way.

I reach forward and turn down the Nirvana album that has been the soundtrack to the first stretch of our trip. "Yes. It's a game where—"

He chuckles. "Sloane, I know what I Spy is."

"Well then, keep up. Don't act so confused. You're too old to play dumb. It's not cute."

Amusement touches every feature, and I breathe out a sigh of relief. *There he is.*

"Okay. I'll go first. I spy with my little eye something that is…brown."

He glances down quickly at himself. "My coat."

"No."

"The trees outside."

"No."

"The… Really? Brown?"

I shrug. "Yeah. Brown. What's wrong with brown?"

His eyes roll, and he peers around like he's trying really hard to figure it out. "The grass?"

I scoff. "The grass isn't brown. It's more like yellow."

One of his hands flies up in frustration. His fuse is short right now. He needs a laugh. "I don't know, Sloane. There isn't much that's brown in this truck or out there. What is it?"

"It was a bull in a field that we already passed." It was the darker streaks in his hair. That's how it popped up in my head.

I was lying to him.

He barks out a laugh though, and the lie is immediately worth the deception. "You can't pick things that we've already passed!"

I grin, toeing off my slip-on Vans and crossing my legs on the seat. "Keep up or tap out, Gervais. This isn't baby I Spy. This is the big kids' version."

With a light shake of his head, he glances over at me. "Okay. Fine." His chin dips, and then his eyes are back on the road. They don't shift. They stay fastened to the blacktop that stretches ahead of us. "I spy with my little eye something that is blue."

My lips roll together. "Okay. Blue. The sky?"

"I thought this wasn't the baby version of I Spy."

I huff out a quiet laugh. "All right. The blue snowflake on the A/C button?"

"No."

"The blue stripe on the temperature control?"

"No."

My head whips around as a blue car streaks by. "That blue sedan!"

The corners of his mouth tug up. "No."

"Ugh. Can we play baby I Spy, actually?"

He gives me a sidelong glance. "No."

My eyes roll, and I turn to check the back seat. "My navy bag?"

"It's more of a sky blue."

"Okay, well, I already guessed the sky."

"You did." He nods.

I peer around the vehicle, racking my brain. I should have known he'd trick me after what I just pulled on him. "Did we pass a blue house or a blue barn or something?"

"No. It's in the car. And it's one of my favorite things."

"You're full of shit, Gervais." I flop back, crossing my arms, trying not to pout but failing.

His eyes meet mine again and stare just a beat too long. "No. I'm not."

This time it's my hands that fly up, right as warmth blooms on my cheeks. "Okay. I guess I'll keep things fair and give up. I don't know."

This time when he talks, he doesn't look at me. He stares

at the smooth road like there's something remarkably interesting there. He swallows, and I watch the column of his throat work beneath the stubble. "It's your eyes."

I go very, very still. "My eyes?" I repeat stupidly. I heard him clearly. I just didn't expect that to be his answer. Not even close.

He shrugs like it's nothing. "Yeah. A robin's egg is more accurate. Remember when we were walking to the river that one time and the shell fell out of the tree in front of us? You were so excited about there being baby birds, and I remember picking it up and looking at you, thinking that it matched almost perfectly." He chuckles when he finishes his sentence, like it's just a friendly walk down memory lane. But inside, I'm the one who's spinning now.

I clear my throat and suppress the swirling feelings. "Yeah. Violet and I checked on those robins every day. If we climbed the opposite tree, we could see into the nest."

He smirks. "You two were always climbing trees."

I smile and drop my chin to my chest. "Yeah. We were always trying to spy on you guys. Or eavesdrop. Once, we saw all of you skinny-dipping in the river. Violet wanted to stop after that because she said she'd never recover." I hadn't felt the same, but then I hadn't been looking at my cousins.

My eyes were stuck on a nineteen-year-old Jasper, who was home for the summer from playing junior hockey. A nineteen-year-old Jasper who looked like he spent all his free time working out.

The same man barks out a laugh beside me. "I think she recovered."

"Yeah," I whisper. "I think she did."

"I can't believe you didn't get that one." He's teasing me, oblivious to the effect he has on me—but that's nothing new.

That would never happen.

I scoff and reach across to poke him in the ribs, smiling when he flinches. "How am I supposed to look at my own eyes?"

"Most people use a mirror."

I poke him again, and he snorts.

"Use the mirror, Sunny. What color do you think they are? Tell me that isn't robin's-egg blue."

Pushed toward the center console, I peer into the rearview mirror. They're blue. But so are the circles under my eyes. The vein that no concealer can ever really cover. So is the way I feel inside right now if I really reach down and dig my fingers into that stone at the bottom of my gut. "They're just blue, Jas." I flop back. "And I look *tired*."

"They're not just blue." He says it like it's fact and not his opinion.

My stomach flips.

And then I deflect, not wanting to linger in these memories for longer than necessary. Not wanting to face all the shit I've opted to run away from. Not yet. I launch back in. "I spy with my little eye…"

We play several more rounds.

But we play the baby version, and neither one of us calls the other on it.

12

Jasper

Jasper: Any news?

Harvey: Nothing. If I hear anything, you'll be my first call.

Jasper: Okay.

"I THINK WE SHOULD STOP FOR THE DAY."

We haven't been on the road for long, but I feel the tug of sleep at the center of my forehead like a weight that wants to push my eyes shut. It's only gotten worse since the world's most awkward game of I Spy fizzled out and left us sitting in silence.

All I can hear is the hum of tires against the road. It's a white noise machine at this point.

Robin's-egg blue. What was I thinking? It's just so easy,

so reassuring to fall back into those memories. Sometimes I wish we could go back. It was simple then. I wasn't recognized everywhere I go. Beau wasn't missing. She wasn't running from her life.

But me? I've always been running from mine, trying to escape attention.

"Okay." Sloane looks at me a little too closely, and I raise one hand to bend the brim of my hat, like it might prevent her from seeing me. Because it's always felt like she looks at me in a way I can't hide from, like she sees a little too much. "You all right? Want me to find a good place to stop?"

"Yeah. I'm just… Honestly, Sloane, I'm just really fucking tired. I was all gung ho to leave, and now that I have, I'm exhausted."

"I could drive for a bit?" She says it lightly, but we both know she knows the answer. She's the only one who knows that whole story, every dirty detail. Everyone else has bits and pieces, but with Sloane, I laid it all out. She was too young to really understand, which I think meant she was too young to judge me.

I sometimes wonder if she judges me now.

I keep my eyes peeled on the rocky rises of the surrounding mountains, so tall and ominous you can see them from the city. We're well in their midst now, traveling through the rolling yellowed foothills and into the jutting peaks capped with pristine snow. "No. Not with the load we're hauling. You don't have any experience with that."

Her eyes narrow, and I feel it more than see it. "And you do?"

One of my shoulders pops up. "Not recently. But yeah, I hauled plenty of loads of hay in the summer when I was younger. You don't live at Wishing Well Ranch and not become a full-blown country boy."

She doesn't respond. Instead, she pulls her phone out, thumbs flying across it. I see a call come in, and the screen flashes. Sterling. She quickly declines it and keeps searching.

"You ever gonna talk to him?"

"There is a town called Rose Hill coming up that has a hotel by a lake. Looks pretty."

I nod. "I know it."

"Yeah?"

"Yeah. We had a dry land training camp there once. Beautiful spot. How far does it say?"

"Thirty minutes. Turn off at Junction 91."

"Okay. I just need you to keep talking to me."

She straightens in her seat. "Okay. What do you want to talk about? Should we trash-talk your coach for forcing you on leave?"

I grumble out a laugh. "No. I already asked you a question."

Her head swivels away from me to glance out the window, and she taps one thoughtful finger on the tip of her nose. "I forget what it was."

My lips flatten, and my palms tighten on the steering wheel. She's lying, but that's okay. We both have secrets we keep. "I asked if you were ever going to talk to him."

"Who?" Wide turquoise eyes turn in my direction, and I give her a droll look.

"You tapping your nose to keep it from growing, Pinocchio?"

"I don't want to talk about it with you." I ignore the ache in my chest, realizing how we've grown apart this past year with Sterling on the scene. Who pulled away first? When did it happen? Could she tell I was looking at her differently?

"Well, there's no one else here, and I know the way your head works. You talk things out. And I'm good at listening. So spill."

Her responding laugh is soft and quiet. I know she must be thinking of the way she'd talk *at* me as a child while I sat around and brooded.

Hilariously, the more things change, the more they stay the same.

"I don't know if he deserves my words really" is how she starts, and I swear it sucks all the air out of the cab. "The more I think about it, the angrier I am—at myself more than anyone. I went along with it and let him talk to me the way he did, belittle me the way he did. And I just never really cared. I was going through the motions, I think. Focusing on the ballet company. Focusing on my parents. Focusing on everyone other than me, and now I look at myself and I…I don't like what I see. I don't like the choices I've made. And I think ignoring him—petty as it might be—is a choice I actually like right now. I don't even know what I have to say to him, you know? I'm clinging to what little sanity I have, and I don't want to share it with him. He can't have it."

I nod and twist my hands on the wheel, resisting the urge to reach out and touch her, to tell her how proud I am of her. To tell her she could be mine instead. Because I told her I'd listen, and she doesn't need me complicating her already complicated feelings. And she definitely doesn't need my stamp of approval on them.

That's not how feelings work—they just are, no matter what anyone else thinks of them.

I've been told repeatedly I'm not responsible for what happened on that highway, but it doesn't change the way I feel.

I feel responsible.

"I feel sick over my dad."

Icy tendrils slide down my spine. As far as I'm concerned, her dad is a colossal piece of shit, but I'm not going to be the one to tell her. I'm not sure she'd ever forgive me if I did. "But I'm so angry at him too. The messages he's left me…" Her top teeth clamp down hard on her pillowy bottom lip like hurting herself will make the pain of her father's betrayal sting less somehow.

"He's being a real piece of shit. You know that?" Her voice is harsher now; it clashes with the soft femininity of her. It's a fascinating dichotomy. "Like I could just…I don't know, throw a tantrum and stomp on his foot or something equally childish. I'm so *disappointed*."

"What did he say to you?" I ask tersely, already wishing I hadn't, already knowing it will make me hate the man more than I already do. Knowing it will pull the scab off an old wound.

"He included Sterling in the text and told me to do my wifely duty and come home immediately." She snorts, and

I silently rage. His face pops up in my mind, and I imagine driving my blocker into it. "I responded with the only thing I've said directly to either of them since you broke me out of that church."

I arch a brow, hoping she'll share her response.

"I told him I'm no one's wife and I don't owe either of them shit." A strangled laugh bursts from my lips, and she smiles at me, looking mighty satisfied with herself. "They can both mull that over while I continue to ignore them."

No, Sloane doesn't need my approval. But goddamn, she has it anyway.

***

"King-size bed or two twins? Or separate rooms?" The woman behind the counter eyes me in a way I've encountered a million times. Like she recognizes me and…like she wants me.

I'm not especially comfortable with either of those looks. It's why I keep my cap on and try to blend into the scenery, which is hard to accomplish at six foot three in a small hotel lobby with no one else around.

Glancing down at Sloane beside me, I fold the brim of my hat, wondering when it might snap from the repeated pressure.

Sloane is outright glaring at the woman. She did this when she was younger, when she had the most blatant childhood crush on me. Beau made fun of me about it, and I'd have to tell him to shut his big mouth so he wouldn't embarrass her.

"We'll take—"

"Two twins," Sloane supplies while still staring at the woman with a blank look on her face. She peeks up at me from behind dark lashes, blond tendrils slipping down around her temple, and gives me a shy smile and a shrug. "More fun that way."

Fun. I wonder for whom because the more time I spend one-on-one with her, the more it seems like torture. Like a video reel of missed opportunities. Of me being oblivious. Of me being too big of a coward to pursue her when I had an inkling of something more.

But being paralyzed by indecision isn't new for me. The only place I don't feel that is usually on the ice, between those pipes.

That's when I feel in control of my life. I feel safe there.

Spending another night in the same room as Sloane feels a lot less safe than facing flying pieces of frozen rubber somehow.

For four seconds, I flash images in my mind of her and me tangled up together. Skin sliding on skin. Her moaning my name. I think about bending her over the back of the lobby couch and peeling those leggings down her firm thighs, telling her exactly what to do while I watch.

And then I force myself to stop.

"Okay. Here are your room keys." She slides a small envelope across the desk, and I can hear the woman talking about Wi-Fi passwords and where to eat, but I turn away to stare at the crystalline glacier lake out the windows. I'm too tired to focus on anything other than how the water is the exact color of Sloane's eyes.

I was wrong about the sky. I was wrong about the eggshell.

It's the glacier lake.

I see her everywhere.

A gentle hand at the center of my back returns my focus to the charming lobby of the small boutique hotel. "Ready?"

With one of our bags in each hand, I nod and let Sloane lead the way. Her lean figure pulls ahead of me to walk down the hallway. "Apparently, there are only main floor rooms right now."

"I just need somewhere to sleep for a bit. I was going to get you your own room."

Her hand flicks over her shoulder, dismissing the comment. "Saves us money this way."

I almost laugh. Neither of us needs to be concerned with saving money. I know—like I did when I was younger—Sloane keeps me close because she worries about me.

She stops abruptly, glancing between the envelope in her hand and the number on the door. "Here we go." She swipes the key card, and with a soft beep, the door unlocks.

We enter the room, and it's nicer than I expected, spacious with a sliding-glass patio door that opens onto a small courtyard facing the aquamarine lake. Best of all, the beds look so damn good.

Without saying a word, I walk across the room, kick off my shoes, drop my coat and hat on the floor, and flop down onto the bed closest to the windows.

I drift off staring at the crystal-blue water. Daydreaming about the girl with crystal-blue eyes.

13

Jasper

MY DAD AND I ARE USUALLY THE ONES WHO TAKE THE QUADS OUT, but yesterday he won at the casino. So today, he bought two more so we can go adventuring as a family. We live in a double-wide and eat an awful lot of mac 'n' cheese by the end of the month, but Dad loves his toys and never hesitates to spend on them.

We're squeezing in a quick maiden ride after our typical Sunday family dinner. We may not have a lot of spare cash, but we're happy.

And it's fun.

The light is golden, and so are the leaves falling from the trees above the ditch. Fall is in the air, but it's warm tonight, almost hunting season, and I can't wait to do that with my dad too.

We clear a covered culvert, and I catch a little air—grinning. I can hear my little sister, Jenny, laughing wildly behind me and can almost envision the way her light-brown hair is whipping out the back of her helmet as she gets more comfortable adding speed.

Her new unit is smaller, lighter—easier to handle than what Dad and I are driving. Mom's looks like some sort of Barbie quad with its neon-pink paint job.

With a glance back, I see my parents moseying behind Jenny while I lead the way, serpentining up and down the ditch walls.

My parents are bickering because Mom doesn't know how to handle the vehicle properly, but she also doesn't want Dad telling her what to do.

It makes me smile.

I know the spot we're coming up to. Dad and I have ridden it a million times. He's put the fear of God into me with this crossing. Two highways intersect near a bend in the road, and a copse of trees can mess with perception coming out of the ditch.

We've practiced it, over and over again.

"I'm going!" I call back.

My dad's hand shoots up, offering me a thumbs-up. "Pay attention! Let us know how it looks from the other side" is his response.

I guess now that I'm fourteen, he believes I know what I'm doing out here. Pride blooms in my chest as I climb the incline onto the shoulder and carefully check both ways.

I look, I listen, and when I deem it safe, I rev my engine and shoot forward across the highway safely.

I stop and turn on the other side to catch a view of the bend in the road. A large semi with a trailer is coming, and I can see the rest of my family on the other side. All together. Smiling and laughing—even through the bickering.

Again, I feel proud that my dad trusted me to be the first across. I feel capable. I feel grown-up.

We've spent years practicing safety protocol, so I know all the signals. I lift my hand straight above my head, the sign we use for "stop" anytime we go out on the quads and, in the winter, the snowmobiles.

Except Jenny doesn't know these hand signals, and she must mistake it for a wave or me ushering her over. Or maybe it's because the sun is low and in her eyes.

Either way, I see her grinning at me from the other side of the highway as her wrist twists the throttle.

I scream at her to stop. Dad lurches forward as though he can grab her and stop her.

But it's too late.

And I'll never stop feeling responsible.

$\sim$

I wake, nauseous and unsettled. That dream always does it to me. I keep my eyes closed, trying to think of something happy for four seconds. But everything is shit right now, and the only thing that pops up is the shy smile Sloane hits me with sometimes. The one she gives right before she tucks her hair behind her ears and drops her eyes.

She's the only person I've told about the hand signal, about how I'm responsible for Jenny's death. Other people know the Coles Notes version of the day my life went to shit but have no idea I can still make my shoulder ache from wishing I hadn't lifted my arm to show off that I knew those hand signals that day.

When my eyes crack open, I take a brief inventory of my body, noting the aches and pains in certain spots that grow more persistent with age.

My vision gains some focus, and then my eyes catch a figure down at the edge of the lake. Sloane is standing there in a terry bathrobe, staring at the water. Her hair is pulled up in a tight bun, the elegant lines of her neck silhouetted against the setting sun. Water that was blue now reflects the dramatic sky, all purples and pinks and golds, dark clouds streaking across a perfectly still lake.

I bet it would be a good lake to play hockey on when it freezes. But I'm the one who freezes as the robe drops from her shoulders. And then her thong-clad ass, tight waist, toned back, and black bra straps are all I see.

Her fingers curl into her palms, and her shoulders scrunch up. It's like I'm watching her give herself a mental pep talk.

I smile at the sight.

Round ass cheeks fold in equal turn as she walks slowly toward the water. She dips one toe in daintily and snaps it back with a shiver that racks her entire body.

I see the deep breath she takes before she charges into the water. A little wild, a lot brave. *There she is.*

I swear I can hear her squeal as she dives into the water, fully submerging herself under the still surface for a few beats that seem to last a lifetime. Her head breaks out several feet from shore, rivulets of water streaming off her bare face as her hands come up to push the wetness away from her closed eyes.

She treads water and turns away to look at the mountains, just black silhouettes against the fiery sky.

I sit up and stare. It could be a painting. A photograph. A beautiful woman in a beautiful lake.

It's peaceful. Serene. So unlike how I feel inside. It makes me wonder what view Beau's looking at right now.

I find myself up and walking out the sliding door, needing fresh air, wanting to touch this view somehow. Commit it to memory. Like running my fingers over the mounds of oil paint. It almost doesn't seem real. I need to prove to myself that it is.

My socked feet grow cold as I walk over grass that is just a little too firm. It has a slight crunch when my weight presses into it, evening frost already descending over the picturesque mountain valley.

When I get to the water's edge, I feel the finest grains of sand slipping through the fabric, lending a gritty texture to the bottoms of my feet. But I don't care. I'm still entirely focused on Sloane.

My *friend* Sloane, who is still treading in place gracefully like this is just another dance for her. I wonder what she's thinking about. I wonder if she feels as shredded as I do—as tattered and torn.

Almost in slow motion, she glances over her shoulder, the tip of her nose wiggling just once as she turns to face me. "Hi."

It's one simple word, and somehow it still tugs at my chest. I'm so at peace in her presence. I always have been.

"Hi." I shove my hands in my pockets, pressing my

thumbs against each fingertip in turn to calm my nerves. Trying not to think about my friend's bare ass and all the things I'd do to it.

And then I give in. But only for four seconds. I give myself four seconds of chaos before I rein it in and pack it down—before I force myself back into control.

Sloane's head quirks. "What are you doing?"

"Counting to four."

"Is that a dumb jock joke?"

I huff out a laugh. "Really nice, Sunny."

She gives me a perfectly innocent look, all doe-eyed. "Ya'll aren't famous for your brains." She's teasing me, but I don't bite.

"It's a thing I do to help with feeling out of control. So when an opposing player scores a goal or something, I give myself four seconds of frustration before I get my head back in the game."

Our eyes shift and then lock in the wake of my explanation.

"Are you feeling out of control right now?"

"No." My reply comes a little too quickly.

She nods, teeth pressing into her bottom lip. Her eyes spark with a challenge. And then she says, "Come in."

"No, thank you. I bet it's freezing."

"Didn't know they grew 'em so soft out at Wishing Well Ranch," she taunts, sliding her arms away and pushing herself farther back.

"Don't go too far" leaps from my mouth before I can stop it.

"What are you gonna do?" Her legs kick under the water, pushing her farther away. "You're too scared to come in here."

I press my thumbs into the pads of my fingers and count to four again.

"What would Beau do?"

I stop and stare at her blankly. Only she would have the balls to throw that in my face right now. Everyone else has been walking on eggshells, but her constant stream of consciousness won't allow it.

It's refreshing.

I reach my right hand over my shoulders and pull my T-shirt off from the back of my neck. It falls to the sand, and I catch Sloane's eyes tracing my torso before she forces herself to look away quickly at the peaks surrounding us.

The silence is almost deafening. All I can hear is the soft swish of water lapping at the sandy shore and the quiet hum of highway traffic in the distance. I make quick work of my jeans and socks before pulling one arm across my chest into a stretch, hoping she doesn't watch me too closely.

"What would Beau do?" Her head flips in my direction at the sound of my voice, and I grin at her, feeling instantly lighter somehow. "He'd run in there and dunk your snarky little ass."

And that's exactly what I do. I charge into the glacier lake and dive in, going straight for her, ignoring the way the icy water sucks the air from my lungs.

She tries to swim, but I catch up to her in no time. My hands slip through the water and over her smooth skin as I grab her, heft her up, and toss her through the air.

Her playful squeals take me back, and when she hits the water with a loud slap, I bark out a laugh that echoes around us, bouncing off the mountains. I don't know where Beau is, but I do know he'd approve of this. And somehow that brings me comfort.

She surfaces, sputtering and wiping at her face. "Jasper Gervais! You did not just do that to me!"

"I did. And you squealed like a pig."

She gasps in faux offense. "Take that back!"

"Okay, fine. You squealed like a piglet. Far more high-pitched and ladylike than a plain old hog."

"You dick!" She's laughing breathlessly as she launches herself at me. Her strong thighs wrap around my rib cage, and she brings her hands onto the top of my head, trying to push me under.

The position puts her breasts right at my eye level. And god. I try to be a good friend and not stare, but the bra pushes them up in the most distracting way. The cool air and even colder water has goose bumps dotting the tops of them. Nipples straining against the flimsy fabric.

"You're going down, Gervais!" She keeps pushing on me, giggling and wiggling and trying her hardest. She's strong but not strong enough, and her words are so open to misinterpretation, I can't even handle it.

"Oh, I'll go down, Winthrop. But I'm taking you with me."

And with that warning, I flop back, plunging us both down into the icy depths. For a few beats, it's silent and dark.

She grabs at me, and I give myself four seconds of insanity in our private bubble beneath the lake.

Our hands roam frantically over one another's bodies, sluicing through the water. My hand, her thigh. Her hand, my ribs.

Are we playing? Wrestling like when we were kids?

Or are we taking liberties we'd never take above water?

On the fourth second, I push up and away, and we both crest the water, panting and staring at each other. Her tongue darts out over her lips, tasting the glacier water clinging there, and her eyes drop to my mouth as I mirror the motion.

The water between us doesn't feel so cold anymore. I let myself stare at her for another four seconds. The tension expands in my chest, pushing until it feels like it might burst.

"Reminds me of playing in the river when we were kids. Jumping off the bridge on the back quarter."

She blinks, like I've just shaken her awake, and plasters a flat smile on her face. "Yeah. I never did quite get the nerve up to jump off that bridge."

"Next summer," I offer, letting myself float away from her so I don't do something colossally stupid like let myself get all handsy with her again.

"Yeah." Her teeth chatter as the word passes between her lips, and I nod toward the shore.

"Let's go. Get you warmed up. Track down some food."

"I could really use a drink," she says.

Fucking same, I think to myself.

We swim until we can stand. The tiny pebbles dig into the bottoms of my feet, and I work to keep my focus on where I'm going rather than letting my eyes wander over Sloane's body in the departing light.

She's too tempting, and I'm too confused.

Her eyes stay on the ground too.

On the shore, she dries off with her robe and tries to hand it to me to use as a towel, clutching her arms over her mostly naked body. But it's her wide eyes that catch my attention. I can't place the look in them, but I know I'm not letting her walk back to the room uncovered and cold.

I smile and shake my head, pulling the robe from her hand and wrapping it around her shoulders.

"But you'll be cold," she says while I give a brisk rub up and down her arms a few times once the garment is in place.

I grab her hand and start walking back to our room. "You don't need to worry about me, Sunny."

I don't look back when I hear her soft response.

"I always worry about you, Jas."

14

Sloane

Sloane: This waitress is a fan.

Jasper: Sloane.

Sloane: What? She looks like she's going to gobble you up.

Jasper: Don't.

Sloane: Are you blushing?

Jasper: She's a stranger. Doing her job. She isn't looking at me like anything.

Jasper: Don't make that face.

Sloane: If you need space, just leave a sock on the hotel room door.

Jasper: Sunny, shut up. I'd never do that to you.

~~

THE WAITRESS SEATS US NEXT TO ONE OF THE ENORMOUS windows overlooking the lake. We didn't know what to expect at Rose Hill Reach, only that it was right next door to the hotel. It's a lovely spot though. All windows face the lake, and one door opens to a long dock with a wide landing that I'm assuming could function as a patio in the summer.

Inside it's all vaulted ceilings and dark wood. River-stone fireplaces and butcher-block tables. In one corner, there are even pool tables and dartboards.

It's cozy. I almost feel like I'm at a ski lodge as I remove my jacket and scoot down into the rounded wooden chair, gazing out over the water. The water where Jasper and I just… Well, I don't know what we were doing.

I glance back at Jasper and watch him fold his tall powerful frame into a chair that's too small for him.

He reaches up to take one of the burgundy leather-bound menus the waitress is now holding out to us. Her eyes widen when the tips of his fingers brush against her hand. Even hidden beneath the brim of his hat, he's recognizable— especially only four hours away from Calgary.

"Oh my god. Hi," she breathes out, looking like a kid on Christmas. "You're Jasper Gervais." One of her hands falls across her chest, and I have to resist the urge to roll my eyes.

Jasper gives her a kind smile and a gracious little dip of his head. "Hi" is all he says back, turning his small smile down to the menu. In typical Jasper fashion, he's friendly but not *that* friendly.

Friendly enough that no one can say he's rude, but not friendly enough to invite more conversation.

Not that it's ever stopped me.

"I, uh…" The girl's brown eyes flash between us, trying

to read the situation before she points a finger like she's come up with a great idea. "I'll give you a minute with the menus!" She's chipper, and I can't help but notice the way her cheeks pink when her eyes land on Jasper again.

She's starstruck, and it's honestly cute.

Jasper doesn't notice though or, at the very least, doesn't comment. He hunches over his menu and stares at his options. It strikes me that he isn't an easy man to get to know, that he must seem closed off to most people he meets. Two-dimensional even. But I know better. I know his humor. I know how fiercely he loves his family, and I know he has social anxiety that makes him seem standoffish to most.

He keeps so much locked up inside that he never talks about.

"What are you going to have?"

My eyes snap up and back down at the menu filled with standard pub fare. "A salad."

Jasper's head tips up, and he stares at me, expression carefully blank before his eyes roam over me, catching on my shoulder, which peeks out of the neckline of the thick-knit navy-blue sweater I recently purchased.

I wonder if he's about to say something about my meal choice. I know I'm thin. Too thin. But after years of fighting my way to the top of our ballet company and then being told I need to look a certain way for our wedding, it's hard to change my mindset. Besides, with everything that's happened since the wedding, my appetite has been almost nonexistent.

He shrugs and drops his gaze back down. "Okay."

I keep reading the plastic pages before me. "Oooh. They have Buddyz Best on tap!"

Amusement sparks on his handsome face. "You can get something better, you know."

I laugh. "Of course, I know. But I've developed a taste for it."

Jasper flips his menu shut and leans back in his chair, crossing his arms. His biceps bulge against the soft gray waffle-knit Henley he's wearing.

I try not to stare.

"You sure you aren't just ordering it to be contrary?"

I lean back and mirror his position. His midnight eyes drop for a split second to my shoulder again before resting back on my face. "Nope. I *love* it. I bet it tastes different on tap. Better even."

His grin widens. "Yes. I'm certain the quality is really affected."

I nod. "I wonder if it's available in bottles."

He snorts.

"I'll have to try all three to really pass judgment."

He leans across the table with a spark in his eye and a small smirk on his shapely lips. His fresh scent—spearmint and something earthy, like one of those dried eucalyptus sprigs—drifts my way as his long fingers tap on the table twice. "New goal for this road trip: try Buddyz Best absolutely everywhere we can. Become true connoisseurs."

I laugh, wagging my head as I lean forward. Gravity pulls me toward him, and our eyes lock. They lock so hard that I can't pull mine away. His dark blues are like a vacuum. They suck me straight in, and for a split second, everything around us gets lost in the rush of blood in my ears.

"All right! You two ready?" The server pops up next to us.

We both start and sit up straight.

With a quick coughing noise, Jasper recovers. "Yeah. Sloane, go ahead."

I tuck my hair behind my ears and smile at the girl whose cheeks have gone pink again. "I'll have a green salad with vinaigrette, please." I hand back the menu, face flipping in Jasper's direction when he says he'll have the same.

He doesn't pay me any mind though. "But I'll also have an order of the battered cod bites and popcorn chicken."

She nods, smiling so broadly my cheeks almost hurt for her.

"I'll also have a pint of Buddyz Best," I say.

Jasper holds his menu out. "Let's make that a pitcher."

She reads our order back to us and scampers away. I can feel the other staff looking over at us, but I don't pay them any mind. Because the way Jasper is staring at me right now has my stomach twisting and thighs clenching.

I return to gazing out the window at the black lake and try to gather my thoughts.

Because I've been staring at Jasper Gervais since I was ten years old, and suddenly…he's staring back.

~

"I think the popcorn chicken pairs better." I lean back in my seat and pat my stomach. Once we had our salads, Jasper made the excellent point that beer doesn't pair all that well with lettuce. He explained how we wouldn't be giving the flavor profile a fair shake if we didn't taste it with something appropriately greasy and salty.

Which is how I found myself scarfing back deep-fried meats and considering their merits while enjoying a second pitcher of cheap beer that doesn't taste that great no matter what I pair with it.

What it tastes like, though, is rebellion. And for right now, that's good enough for me.

Jasper nods, assessing the plates before us. "I think you're right. But I love fish and chips with vinegar."

Yeah, we ordered fries too. According to Jasper, just saying "fish" and not "fish and chips" is weird. Through all the gluttony, he hasn't said a word about my weight or mentioned how much or how little I eat. He's just put food in front of me and involved me in the fun of trying it all out with him.

Even with everything so fucked up, I can't remember the last time I felt this relaxed.

Tonight I'm basking in being myself, and it feels good not worrying about calories or how everyone around me is perceiving my every move.

"Fair. That was amazing too. Plus, those fries are totally homemade."

He tosses another one in his mouth, chewing and nodding appreciatively. "I think you're right. Wanna play a game of pool before we go back and pass out?"

He juts his chin just past me, eyes catching on my shoulder. Again. As I turn to look at the pool table, I sneak a peek down at it to see if I spilled something there or have sprouted a long hair out of a mole or something.

Seeing that my skin is clear, I hum contemplatively as I catch sight of the pool table. It isn't overly busy, but it's not empty either. There are people milling around, so that means witnesses to how bad I am at pool.

And I hate being bad at things. Hate failing. Hate losing. I'm competitive to my core.

"I don't really know how."

"Well, I'll just have to show you." Jasper pushes to stand and, with two steps, has rounded the table and hovers over me with one outstretched hand. He looks relaxed. The way his hair curls out of the back of his hat makes the tips of my fingers itch.

"I'm good. I'll just watch you."

He scoffs playfully. "Come on, Sunny. WWBD?"

"Huh?" My head tips to the side, and I eye his wide warm palm skeptically.

"What would Beau do? WWBD."

"I actually think that's more of a tongue twister than just saying the sentence."

His hand bounces in front of me. "Stop stalling. Let's go. Beau would play pool even if he sucked at it. And he'd have fun sucking."

I quirk a suggestive brow at Jasper. I'm sure that's not how he meant it, but after several pints of shitty beer, it's where my head goes.

His usually serious face immediately breaks out in a breathtaking smile as he glances across the room with a laugh. White teeth. Dimples hiding under his stubble. It's impossible to look at Jasper smiling and not smile too.

Laughter bubbles in my throat, and I slap my palm into his as he pulls me up to standing. "Fine. But I'm going to suck."

His tongue slides out over his lips almost suggestively, head shaking like I'm in trouble. Something about the combination makes an ache unfurl behind my hips. He is effortlessly sexy. Totally distracting.

"But you're going to have fun doing it." He points at me as he drops my hand and reaches for our beers before turning toward the empty pool table in the corner.

We're toeing the line of this joke, even for us, but the alcohol coursing through my veins has me feeling bolder than usual.

"I always do!" I say cheerily to his broad back, which presses rhythmically against the gray fabric of his shirt as he walks away, knowing I'll follow because he has my beer and a killer ass.

I watch his head tip back at my words. A small prayer for patience, I'm sure. "Jesus Christ, Sunny."

After setting our drinks on a tall table, he grabs two cues and turns toward me with a challenging glint in his eye. My heart flutters in my chest, and relief hits me like a tidal wave. I've been so damn worried about him. When he retreats into himself, he scares me. I worry if he goes too far back—if he slips into those dark cracks—that he won't come back out.

Or he won't come back out the same. Broody and shy but sweet. Jasper Gervais is so damn sweet under his standoffish exterior that it almost makes my teeth ache.

That's another side of him few people get to see. And I think I like that about him too. He doesn't give his attention away willy-nilly. He doesn't absently hum along to what you're saying while scrolling on his phone. If you have Jasper Gervais's attention, you've got it all, and that's because he wants you to have it.

He doesn't just listen to me. He *hears* me. He *sees* me.

And there's something precious about that, the way he can look at someone and make them feel like the only person in the room. He's not showy, he's not the life of the party, but he knows how to make a person feel special, feel loved and cared for.

I've never known a soul more truly *present*.

The way he is? It speaks to me. It always has. He's like a warm blanket that I want to wrap myself up in. And when his eyes are bright and his smile is soft like right now?

Forget it. He's breathtaking.

"Ready to play?"

"Let's do it." My eyes widen. God. What is wrong with me? "Pool. Let's do the pool." I hold a hand up. "Play pool. Not do the pool. Ha." I quickly reach for my beer and take a deep swig while Jasper chuckles at me.

Handsome fucking brain-cell-killing jerk.

"Do I need to cut you off?"

"Shut up, Gervais. Let's play."

Fire blazes in his eyes, and he stares back at me. "Okay, Sloane. Let's play."

15

Sloane

Jasper: Why are you taking so long in there?

Sloane: Giving myself a drunk pep talk.

Jasper: What is that?

Sloane: It's where I splash water on my face and stare at myself in the mirror. Then I tell me to pull my shit together and be cool.

Jasper: You're talking to yourself in the women's bathroom to be...cool?

Sloane: Exactly.

Jasper: Sunny. Be less cool. Come save me. The waitress keeps trying to talk to me.

Sloane: So talk to her.

Jasper: I don't like talking to people.

Sloane: You talk to me.

Jasper: You're not people.

Sloane: Lmao. What am I then?

Jasper: My person.

"Stop it. I'm already dead."

He barks out a laugh as he rounds the table and leans over it. Is pool supposed to be sexy? Because Jasper makes it look sexy.

His hard body leans against the green felt top. His veined hands wrap lightly around the cue. His eyes narrow like this is a Stanley Cup final or something.

The way that boyish smile lights up his face when I complain about him kicking my ass. I hate losing…and yet, to see him smile like that, I'd lose over and over again. I'd sit on a cold roof. I'd dance in the rain. I'd go on a road trip and drink shitty beer and eat greasy foods.

For Jasper, I'd do anything. Except actually tell him that.

Because when he turns me down, I'll break. A million little pieces of me scattered into the wind.

It doesn't matter that my love for him is pathetic and tragically unrequited.

It just is. The sky is blue. The grass is green. And I've loved Jasper Gervais from the first day I laid eyes on him.

With a few too many pints of cheap beer, it's easy to admit to myself because my mental walls have evaporated entirely. I'm a twenty-eight-year-old woman with a soul-consuming, one-sided childhood crush. It's hilarious if I think about it.

A drunk, girlish laugh bubbles out of me, and I'm not laughing with me—I'm definitely laughing *at* me.

"See? You just made a joke about being dead. You laugh

at the most morbid shit." Jasper grins at me from beneath his cap, leaned on the vertical pool cue.

I shake my head with a smile and take another sip. I really do laugh at inappropriate stuff. *If he only knew*.

"I really am atrocious at this. I hate myself a little bit for it too," I reply, but I'm chuckling as I say it.

His chin tips out at me before he moves in my direction from the opposite side of the table. "Here. Let me show you. You're holding it too tight."

Jasper racks his cue on the wall and steps up behind me, his fresh, minty scent a vivid reminder of listening to him take a shower in the same hotel room as me. The smell of his soap wafted out on the rush of steam that escaped when he emerged with a towel wrapped around his waist and dark tattoos tracing every hard line of muscle. I didn't get a good look at them all because I didn't want to gawk.

I forced myself to stare at the e-reader on my lap. Pure torture. I stared at the same page of the same book for the entire ten minutes, like my ability to read grew wings and flew out of my head at the mere thought of him naked and soapy.

Sure, we've lived at the ranch house for the past week, but there were so many other people in and out of the place that it never felt like we were truly alone, other than the nights we spent sitting on the roof.

Now? On the road together? It's like we're completely isolated.

"Like this." His pecs bump into the blades of my shoulders as he stands behind me, arms dropping down around my torso like a cage. My body seizes up, and he doesn't help matters when he softly says, "Relax, Sloane. Bend over the table."

My cheeks flame dark like a cherry, and I swallow before doing as he says. I hinge at the hips, sliding my left hand up the shaft of the cue and lining it up with the white ball.

I'm already bad at pool, and having Jasper imitating fucking me from behind in public definitely isn't going to make me any better. All the balls are just a blur of color before me because my body is entirely homed in on his. The feel. The smell. The way my chest vibrates from the butterflies crashing around in there.

I laugh. "I think I saw this in a Hallmark movie once."

His right hand cups my elbow, and his left hand slides down my arm as he gently adjusts my position.

My biggest worry is that I'm going to grind my ass back into him like a cat in heat. The beer goggles are real. As real as the shame spiral will be tomorrow.

Be cool.

Be cool.

Be cool.

Even my inner voice slurs as I give myself another internal pep talk.

"This isn't a Hallmark movie, Sunny." His warm breath caresses the side of my neck and breezes through my hair. I suck in a quick breath and my nipples pebble instantly as his hips line up with mine.

"What is it?" My voice comes out as a hoarse whisper.

His left hand moves up, his thumb brushing once over the bone in my wrist before he slides his fingers out over mine. "Relax." He gently shimmies my wrist. I think trying to indicate my hand is too tense. And then I watch raptly as the pads of his fingers dust over the massive diamond ring that still adorns my finger.

"This is a friend teaching another friend how to hold a pool cue properly."

"Right." It feels like sinking into that freezing-cold lake all over again. A cold dose of reality.

He pulls my cue back as he helps line up the shot and then pushes it back through the crook of my thumb. When the chalk-covered tip hits the ball, we freeze in place. His body on mine. My body flush against his.

For that moment, we press into each other.

The clank of the balls crashing into each other and the pounding of my heart are all I hear. We watch together, breathing in the air that the other breathes out, as the solid purple ball drops into the pocket.

And then he pulls away. Like he always does. And I'm still leaning over the table, overthinking a perfectly innocent interaction.

Like I always do.

The voice I hear next sounds like twisting chalk on the felt tip of my pool cue. "Oh my god! Are you Jasper Gervais?"

I don't even need to look to know that Jasper offered an uncomfortable smile and his signature head nod to elicit the girlish squealing that now assaults my ears.

Pushing up to stand, I walk over to the rack without a backward glance. I press the stick into the claws that suspend it on the wall before turning and taking in the scene.

I permit myself one deep, desperate, centering breath before I plaster a smile on my face and make my way back over to the beer waiting for me.

Two girls are fawning over Jasper. I see them but not really. As usual, I just see Jasper. The way his body tenses, the light-peachy stain that creeps out from under his stubble across his cheeks, his hands obsessively folding at the brim of his cap.

I slide up beside him, reaching for my beer and watching one girl's eyes catch on my ring. "Oh shit. Are y'all together?" Her finger lazily flicks back and forth between us.

Jasper's head swivels in my direction, eyes boring into mine like I might save him. But save him how? I'm just not sure. Especially not after he told me in the plainest terms possible that I'm his friend as he bent me over a pool table.

If that felt platonic for him, well, fuck me sideways, I must be totally hammered.

"No. We're friends."

The girl smiles and sighs in relief. "Well, congratulations on the engagement." Everyone's eyes drop to my hand, and I lift my head slowly, offering her a wan smile in return. "Thanks."

"Will you sign the back of my shirt?" Her friend asks as she tugs her coat down and pulls her hair over one shoulder, exposing her back and bare neck to my stupid-hot friend-cousin who just takes the pen the other girl holds out to him.

When his hand wraps over her shoulder to hold her shirt in place, I walk away and order another beer that I do not need because I cannot stomach the sight of his hand on another woman.

I feel like there's hot coal burning in my gut.

I swivel my hand in a *let's fucking go* motion to the bartender, and he smirks at me. He can probably tell I'm wobbly on my feet or that my eyes are glassy. But you know what? I don't care. I've been dutiful beyond compare to my family. I've been a professional in my career. And I've had a few shit weeks. If I want to watch my life circle the toilet, I can at least throw back a few delicious Buddyz Bests while I do.

I peek over my shoulder at Jasper. His hands still rests on the random girl's back as he crouches to sign her plain white shirt.

If making yourself sick with jealousy were an art form, I'd be a master at my craft. Over the years, I've tortured myself by watching the NHL Awards. I've watched him year after year with a different woman, each one more stunning than the last. I'd watch them all dolled up, walking the red carpet, smiling for the cameras, and when it was over, I'd crawl into bed and imagine what they were doing at that very moment.

I'd envision them clinking crystal flutes filled with fancy champagne, surrounded by other players at some ritzy club, followed by a quiet hotel room, where Jasper would peel off her slinky, sparkly dress. Because they're always slinky and sparkly.

His lips.

His hands.

Her moans.

Imagining is easier to take than seeing it up close.

I wrap my hands around the slippery pint glasses that appear in front of me and walk back to our table.

"I want you to sign my tits" is the first sentence I hear, and it makes me slam the pint glasses down with more force than I meant to. Drunkenness collides with anger and makes the golden liquid slosh over onto my hands.

"I only sign paper, clothes, and merch" is Jasper's simple response. I'm sure he's heard this titty request many times.

I turn, wiping my hands on my jeans, not caring about the wet spots they leave.

The girl sidles closer and rolls her eyes like what he's said doesn't matter. "Come on. There's barely anyone here." Her lips tip up in a smirk, and she pulls the neckline of her already deep V-neck down even lower. "Right here."

"I'm sorry, no."

He's apologizing to her? His eyes fall to mine, and to his credit, he doesn't even glance at her cleavage, which now shows the trim of her red lace bra.

"Would you rather do it in the bathroom so no one can see?"

His eyes are tight and searching. He looks like a dog staring up at me through the bars at a shelter, desperate for someone to save him, to shield him. I think he's always needed that in some way.

Holding his navy-blue gaze, I take a deep swig, and goddamn, the more Buddyz Best I drink, the better it tastes.

"Girl, stop. You're embarrassing yourself," I blurt, flicking my eyes over to the woman who is holding her tits out to him like she's the deal of the day at a fast-food restaurant.

I'm cringing for Jasper, but I'm also cringing for her.

Hilariously, I'm cringing for me too.

Cringing all around.

Her eyes narrow, and her shoulders shimmy. "He's just playing hard to get." She turns to Jasper with a slow feline smile stretching at her lips. "But I'm patient. And I like to play."

I snort in the most unladylike way, my alcohol consumption really coming out to play. But it's like I'm watching myself from above. Little Sloane taking her toboggan down a slippery slope with no way to stop.

"Play what? Sexual harassment?"

The girl crosses her arms under her breasts, pushing them up again. And god, they really are big. I'll readily admit I'm a little envious. "Rich coming from the girl who was just all pressed up against a man who isn't her fiancé. Bet your real fiancé would love to know that you're here whoring it up with an NHL player."

One loud laugh erupts from my throat, and everyone looks at me, stunned. "Whoring it up?"

It's funny. Sterling would absolutely use the term *whoring it up*.

I laugh again, and the girls stare at me like I'm fucked in the head.

And they're not wrong.

The thought of Sterling knowing I'm on the road with Jasper, that we're sharing a hotel room, playing pool, and having fun is suddenly deeply satisfying.

And hilarious.

I can vividly imagine the vein in his forehead throbbing and his meaty fingers curling in on themselves while he stomps his foot and demands I come home. Suddenly Sterling Woodcock is nothing more than a badly behaved, red-faced toddler in my head, and the image sends me right over the edge.

Laughter bubbles up slowly, and before I know it, I'm laughing hard enough that tears prick at my eyes.

Jasper shakes his head at me, but the amusement on his face is clear. He moves in and slings a long arm over my shoulders. "Time to go, Winthrop." He turns to guide us away, the girls clearly confused as all get-out.

"No! I need to finish my Buddyz Best so I can round out my training as a connoisseur. And you need to sign that girl's jugs so she can continue to pretend she wants your autograph when she just wants you to fondle her melons."

The sound of a scoff and the sight of the girls turning to leave draw my attention momentarily. "I really hope she tracks Sterling down and tells him about this."

Jasper's laugh rumbles against me as he leads me to our coats, and it just makes me laugh harder. So satisfying. Even if I am making an ass of myself. I'm just past the point of caring. The point of caring was two beers ago.

"Sunny, you're cut off, and all melons are going to remain in the produce section."

"They were big, Jas. And so round." I hold my hands up in front of me and mimic squeezing a set of breasts. "I'm a little jealous if I'm being honest. I'd kill for melons like that. Do you know which grocer carries them? I'd pay good money."

He covers me in my coat and slings his over his arm

before tossing cash on the table. Then I'm tucked up against him again, and we're walking out into the dark frosty night. "You're perfect the way you are, Sloane. Don't let anyone tell you otherwise."

Usually I'd preen and overthink that sentence, but right now I just giggle.

"Are you saying my melons are nice?" I press my chest out and cup them.

"You're gonna get me in trouble one of these days" is how he responds.

"Would you sign my melons if I wanted you to?"

"I need to get you some water."

"Don't be such a stick in the mud, Gervais. Answer the question!"

"I don't know, Sloane." His breath puffs out in front of him as we walk the short path back to our hotel room. "It's hard to imagine you ever asking me to do that because you know me so well. Really proved you understand how much I hate that shit by shooting from the hip like a total nut."

My head whirls, and I lean on his sturdy form. "Or!" I hold one finger up triumphantly. "Shooting from the tits!"

"Lord, help me," he groans.

"Like the ladies on *Austin Powers*! You know the ones. The bullet bras? Sooo cool."

"Thanks for looking out for me, Sunny" is all he responds with as he gives me a squeeze.

I rest my head against the edge of his shoulder. "Always, Jas. Plus, I think those girls really liked me."

16

Jasper

Harvey: You kids got somewhere safe to spend the night?

Jasper: Yeah. Hotel in Rose Hill.

Harvey: Two rooms or one? ;)

Jasper: Don't be weird. One room, two beds.

Harvey: I'm not weird. You're the one with a crush on your cousin.

Jasper: She's not my cousin.

Harvey: Ha! But you didn't deny the crush.

～～

SLOANE IS DRUNK.

Hilariously hammered. Totally unfiltered. And leaning on me way harder than I ever imagined someone her size could.

Her soft giggles accompany the low hum of the yellow-ish neon lights above us in the hotel hallway, and she keeps stepping on my feet.

"You're a ballerina. Aren't you supposed to be graceful?"

She ignores me, tilting her head up in my direction. "Have you noticed that you have a zit right…" She pokes a spot right near my hairline that curves around my temple.

I snort. "No, Sloane. I haven't been concerned with my skin of late."

"It's annoying. I bet you wash your face with shampoo, never moisturize, and only put sunscreen on when you're on vacation. And you still look like that." Her hand waves over the length of my body.

I reach into my pocket and pull out our room key, giving it a quick swipe before pressing into the room. "I wash my face with bodywash."

She groans and tosses her head back dramatically, staring at the ceiling. "You can't do that."

"Why? My face is part of my body."

"It doesn't have the right stuff in it." She sways as she pulls at her shoes, and I stifle a laugh. "Even if it smells heavenly, like mint and whatever else."

"Mint and eucalyptus. Same bodywash I've used for years. What stuff does my face need?"

A shoe flies past us and hits the wall. "Whoa!" Her eyes widen, and she giggles again. I count my blessings that she's a happy drunk. I don't think I could handle her being sad right now. "Vitamin C. Peptides. Exfoliating acids. You're not getting any younger. You should consider a retinol, but then you need to put sunscreen on every day. Oh my god!" The next shoe follows suit, and she swaggers into the bathroom. "I have the best idea."

"Sunny, I'm not sure this is the moment where you'll come up with your best ideas."

"You calling me drunk, Gervais?" she hollers from the small room. I hear shuffling in there as I peel off my shoes and straighten hers by the door.

"Never. You are perfectly sober. But I'm going to grab you a bottle of water, and you're going to drink it, all right?"

"Are there any of those small bottles of Grand Marnier or whatever? Hotels are always stocked with alcohol that nobody drinks. I mean, who drinks Grand Marnier?"

I huff out a quiet laugh and pad over to the fridge. There are two bottles of water. "I don't think this is a Grand Marnier type of hotel."

She pops out from the bathroom doorway as soon as I straighten with one plastic bottle in each hand. But she has some bottles of her own that she's holding out.

"Facials!" she squeals.

"What?" I blink once, staring at her soft blond hair and happy eyes.

She holds up a purple squeeze bottle and a green glass tub of something and shakes them at me like I'm stupid. "I'll drink your water if you give me a facial."

Gotta say, the first place my head goes is not to beauty products.

"Don't worry. I'll give you one too."

The image of Sloane straddling my face, my hands on

her ass while she stares down into my eyes, flashes into my mind.

It's not the first time. Usually I push the thought away, but tonight I'm feeling just loose enough to let it linger. To watch her move. To think about the sounds she might make.

"Buck up, Gervais!" She hops onto the bed, drops the skin-care products on the mattress, and gestures me toward her, fingers folding down onto her palm.

Seriously not helping. All the blood in my body rushes south, and I cover by tossing her a bottled water. "Drink this first," I say as it flies.

But her reflexes are slow tonight, and the bottle hits her in the face.

Square in the nose.

The guys and I toss each other water bottles on the bench all the time. It's second nature. She flinches hard, and I gasp as I take long strides over to the bed to check on her. Her hands are clasped over her face, and her fingers move to check herself over.

I feel *awful*. I feel *sick*. The thought of anyone hurting Sloane—even me—has fire coursing through my veins.

When I reach for her shoulder, she peers up at me, and she…

Bursts out laughing.

"Jas! You just threw that at my face, you awkward motherfucker!"

"I didn't!" I'm shaking my head in denial. "I didn't mean to! I'm so sorry! Are you okay?"

She laughs harder. "I'm fine! I'm fine. Totally fine." Her words wheeze out around her laughter.

My palms squeeze her shoulders in time, which draws her attention up to my face. "Sunny, you are crazed right now. You need to drink some water."

Her lips roll inward as she fights to hold it together. "Okay." She nods and opens the water bottle beside her. She lifts it almost to her lips and stops, looks away, and bursts out laughing again. "I can't believe you smoked me in the face like that!"

I scrub at my stubble, trying not to laugh, but it's infectious. "I didn't mean to."

"I know. But it's still funny."

I cross my arms now, trying to convey how serious I am to her. "It's not funny."

"That's only because you didn't see your face." She contorts her features into a very exaggerated expression of horrified shock.

And then belly laughs some more.

I groan and toss my hat down on the desk. "Bet you used to get kicked out of class for getting the giggles."

Her index finger flips out from around the plastic bottle and points at me while she takes a deep swig of water. "Facts."

I can't help but chuckle. I can totally see it. The bed sags a little when I sit down on the edge, not too close to Sloane. She continues to sip her water as her laughter subsides, and I pick up the two products she brought out of the bathroom.

"Okay, fine. I'll give you a facial."

This time when she laughs, water sprays out toward the front of the room.

"Good god." I flop back on the bed and toss an arm

over my face, feeling my body vibrate as I laugh with her. She's always had this effect on me. Her sunshiny persona is infectious. Sometimes I fight it, and right now for the life of me, I can't figure out why.

She claps one hand over her mouth and from behind it says, "I'm sorry. You can't trust me right now."

"Okay. More water. Then you can put whatever fancy voodoo-skin-shit this is on me."

"Way to avoid saying *facial*." She's sitting on her knees now, looking down on me while she carefully sips her water.

"Please don't spit water on my face" is my reply as I stare back up at her, our eyes latching on to one another and not letting go. Without the brim of my hat, I feel exposed, laid bare, but for her I'm not sure I mind so much.

People looking too closely makes me nervous, makes my skin itch. But with Sloane's eyes on me, all I feel is warmth.

When the silent eye contact seems like it's gone on for too long, I lift the purple tube and read the instructions while she polishes off the entire bottle of water. Once it's empty, she tosses it over her shoulder. With a smirk, she reaches for the tube and flips the cap open, squeezing white clay onto the tips of her fingers.

"It says you're supposed to wash your face with warm water first."

Sloane rolls her eyes at me. "Rich coming from the guy who cleanses his face with bodywash."

And then she's slathering it onto my forehead. Down my nose. Up my cheekbones. Her eyes take on this slightly faraway look as her gentle fingers glide over the skin of my face. Her brow furrows in concentration, and her glacier irises move around every corner of my face as she meticulously spreads the clay. She catches me staring at her, and I drop her gaze, closing my eyes like that might help.

Except behind the privacy of my own lids, her touch sends electricity sparking across my skin, and the darkness transforms into the image of her bent over that pool table in front of me. I can still feel her slender body beneath mine, still feel the way my dick twitched before I had to force myself not to grind against her.

Because friends don't grind their cocks on their friends' perfect asses. It's just not done.

Despite that friend rule, I feel the familiar swelling sensation all the same, and it has me lurching up and away from her touch. "Okay. That's good," I grumble, the thick clay substance tingling and tugging on my face. "Your turn."

She nods, looking a little wide-eyed now. I'm not sure what went on in her head while she rubbed that into my face, but there's immediate tension between us now. The playful notes are gone. Like in the lake. Like over that fucking pool table.

I take the tube and squeeze a dollop of the clay onto my fingertips. As I reach toward her face, I stare at her mouth rather than her eyes, thinking that will be less distracting.

I'm wrong.

Everything about Sloane Winthrop is fucking distracting. And I've been trying really damn hard for a really long time not to notice.

When I brush my fingers over her cheekbone, she sucks

in a sharp breath. Both our gazes move to my hand, the one that shakes subtly under the scrutiny.

I just swallow and forge ahead, forcing myself to stare at my fingers and where I'm spreading the clay rather than her baby blues. I have to be careful with her. I don't want to get it in her hair. Or her eyes. I'd like my low point for the night to remain hitting her in the face with a water bottle.

When I smudge the material over her jaw and swipe it over her chin, the tips of my fingers slide over her bottom lip. I watch it happen in slow motion. Chalky white over plush pink. My fingers. Her lip. The way it flattens and presses to the side with the lightest pressure. Everything about her is so soft and malleable.

She gasps again, her mouth popping open, and this time my eyes snap to hers. They're wide and glowing, all the shades of blue. A kaleidoscope of colors. A prairie sky. A robin's egg. A glacier lake. Streaks of something darker, making all those pale colors pop.

And that fucking gasp is a shot of lightning to my groin.

"You know what?" Her lashes fall down like a curtain, and she pulls away, unfolding herself from the bed. "I'll just finish this myself. Won't make you do it."

Before I can say anything, she's in the bathroom, and the sink is running. By the time I get there, she's scrubbing at her face and avoiding making eye contact with me.

She eventually gives me a flat smile while casting a furtive glance my way through the mirror, eyes lingering on my face that's covered in what looks like drying white paint. It clings to my stubble and is cracking in spots.

It reminds me of myself in a way. A fragile shell. One little crack and the entire thing is liable to burst open.

"You okay?"

"Yup," she says a little too brightly while drying her face. "Just realizing I should go to bed if I don't want to feel like total shit tomorrow."

When she leaves, I let out a heavy breath and drop my palms onto the counter before me.

I'm not sure what's going on with us today, but we're both going to feel like total shit tomorrow, regardless of alcohol intake.

Because Sloane is going to be hungover. And I'm going to be tired from staying up all night fighting off thoughts about all the filthy things I want to do to her and those soft, puffy lips.

17

Sloane

Sloane: Send help.

Summer: Help with what? Are you guys okay?

Sloane: I'm so hungover. I want to die.

Willa: Nice. Shame spiral. Did you bang him?

Sloane: No. We gave each other facials and passed out awkwardly.

Willa: High five. I love it when Cade gives me a facial.

Summer: Good god.

Sloane: That is...not what I meant.

I REALLY NAILED IT WHEN I SAID I WAS GOING TO FEEL LIKE total shit in the morning.

It's like I had a premonition or something. Because my head is pounding, there's a heavy weight that reminds me an awful lot of shame pressing down on my chest, and the silence in the truck is fucking *deafening*.

Jasper and I exchanged good mornings. He asked how my nose was, and I rolled my eyes at him. He's acting like he hit me with a fastball, not lobbed a flimsy bottle of water at me that sort of rolled down my face.

Because yes, I remember everything about last night in excruciatingly clear detail. I was just drunk enough to not give a fuck about anything but not drunk enough to forget it.

Most times I would say getting hammered and not blacking out was a win. But I'd be happy if I'd blacked out last night. It would have prevented me from running that tape in my head on repeat.

The sky above us is dark gray, and snow falls in big fat flakes, landing in loud wet slaps against the windshield. The windshield, where we both keep our gazes fixed.

Because shit is awkward this morning, and it's probably because I went all green-eyed on fans of his and then dragged him back to our hotel room where I asked if he'd sign my melons and give me a facial.

What can I say? We all have our breaking points, and it would seem I've hit mine.

I glance over at the speedometer, and we're going a good chunk below the speed limit.

You live near the mountains long enough, and you know what heavy snowfall looks like before it hits. And this is that.

I know it. And Jasper knows it.

And I know Jasper well enough to know that inside his

head right now, he's agonizing over our safety. That's his default mode.

"You must think I'm an idiot" is how I open our conversation.

His head flips my way so sharply that I wonder if it hurt his neck. His face softens when his eyes land on me, and my heart skips a beat. Within seconds, that chiseled face turns back to the road, knuckles white on the steering wheel.

"I absolutely do not think you're an idiot."

"My life is in shambles, and I'm ignoring it by choice. And I was definitely an idiot last night," I joke, turning to stare out the passenger window at the rocks and trees crowding the mountain pass so tightly, it feels like I could open my window and touch that dark craggy stone. Icicles cling to the sharp edges from the hard frost that hit overnight.

"No. You deserved to let loose. You were funny. I needed it. I had fun. *We* had fun."

"Hmm." I let his words bounce around in my head. *We had fun.*

"I'm sorry if I embarrassed you."

"How could you have embarrassed me?" He sounds genuinely confused.

"With those girls. I was a major cockblocker."

He chuckles quietly now. "And I appreciate the blocking."

"You're just saying that. Let's not pretend you don't enjoy female company."

He shocks me when he responds bluntly, "I like sex. The rest is too much."

I try to swallow and end up choking on my saliva—like

the winner I am right now. He's always so damn quiet. I didn't expect the word *sex* to crest his lips so effortlessly. Let alone the part about him liking it.

I recover with "I've seen you out with women at those fancy awards and stuff. So nice try."

He shrugs, and his thick biceps rise and fall with the motion. "Looks can be deceiving. Sometimes it's just a friend of a friend. Usually it's someone I only see now and then. Who gets what I want and doesn't ask for more."

"Like a fuck buddy?" I almost want to say friends with benefits. But somehow the thought of him actually being friends with some other woman is worse. Sex is sex. Friendship though? With Jasper, friendship is love.

He clears his throat. "Basically."

That's such a fucking Jasper thing to say. Elusive and secretive.

"Whatever that means." I roll my eyes and stare back out at the mountains. I don't know how to handle this newfound tension between us. Before, it was just me in my head. Now his eyes linger a little too long, and so does his touch. Fingers twined with mine. Hand on the small of my back.

"It means meeting someone who actually likes me for *who* I am and not *what* I am feels downright impossible at this point in my career. It means I can spend surface-level time with people, but it always comes back to what I do for work or how much money I make or how famous I am. It means I can never just meet a person without that notoriety hovering over me, and that means I question everything and everyone."

My tongue swipes over my bottom lip, and my chest tightens as I unravel everything he just admitted.

"Even my mom pops up when I'm in the news or if she sees me on TV."

I still. Jasper *never* talks about his parents.

"She does?" My voice is small, and I regard him carefully.

"Always."

"Just to…say hi?"

He scoffs, and one corner of his lips tips up. But it's not in amusement. It's more of a wry twist, a cover for a deep hurt. "No, Sunny. For money."

"I'm sorry. Do you know where she is?" It's not enough. It's not nearly enough. But I don't know what else to say to him. I'm out of my depth with his accident and everything that came in its wake.

It strikes me as unfair that so many terrible things can happen to one person. That one human can defy the odds so thoroughly. That the universe couldn't have sprinkled a little of Jasper's pain over more people to make his burden just a little bit lighter.

His sister.

His mom.

His dad.

Now Beau.

It's cruel, and it makes my heart ache for him—it always has. Those sad fucking eyes, which I drowned in on that first summer day. A dark-blue abyss. Sometimes I feel like I sank to the bottom of that deep ocean and just took up residence.

I got lost in Jasper's eyes and never left.

"She comes and goes. You know how she is. In the wake of Jenny's death, she started self-medicating. And within a year, she was another person, living another life. One that took her from flophouse to flophouse. From prison to rehab. To…I don't even know anymore." He pauses, and all I can think is she became a person who broke her son more thoroughly than he already was. "It's my fault."

His words strike a heavy blow.

I've lived such a pretty and privileged life, one tied up with a shiny satin bow. I've never even been hit. Never lost a family member. Never experienced physical pain that wasn't my doing. Sure, my parents have their quirks, but they've never set out to hurt me or cared so little about me, they would do something that might cause me pain.

But I imagine this is how it feels.

"It is *not* your fault."

"It is. And I send her the money to atone for that."

A quiet groaning sound aches in my throat. Nausea roils in my stomach, and I can't be sure if it's the hangover or the topic of conversation. "You have nothing to atone for."

"I d—"

"No," I snap at him, clapping my hands firmly to cut him off. "Nothing. Nothing at all. I've told you before, and I'll keep telling you until the day I die. You were a child, she was a child, and it was an accident."

His breathing sounds heavy, almost labored, as we both stare out the front window.

"I still remember the night I told you what happened. I remember you crying, which was even worse than saying it all out loud. Watching you cry…so young and naive…"

I did. I sobbed. I broke for him, wanting to take some of his pain and make it my own. If the universe wouldn't help him share the burden, I decided that I would do it myself.

That night, with only the moon as his witness, a devastated boy divulged his deepest darkest secrets to the most inconsequential person he could find. A girl who never looked at him with pity, only adoration.

And he shredded his heart for her. Left all the jagged, torn pieces at her feet.

And I became the keeper of those pieces. I didn't balk at the rawness of the moment. I don't think I even really understood it, but I picked up every little scrap and stowed them all away in my heart for safekeeping.

With time, I made sense of his story. I mulled it over. I became a part of it, inserted myself somehow. And those pieces became seeds. Seeds that I watered and tended and kept safe for him.

But seeds grow, and now the roots of him and that night are wrapped so tightly around my heart that I'll never be able to extricate myself from Jasper Gervais.

There isn't a soul in the world who can remove those roots and the stranglehold they have on me.

"I learned with my parents that no matter how fiercely I love someone it isn't enough to make them stay. But you? I told you every dirty little detail, and you could have hated me. But you stayed. You danced."

"I could never hate you, Jas." Tears prick at my eyes.

I did the only thing I knew how to do. Under the light of the moon, in a field of lush green grass, I got up and let the movements flow through my body. The classical tune played in my head. The only real music was the hush of a suffocatingly warm summer night on the prairies.

And the only person in the audience was a beautiful boy with haunted eyes who watched my every movement and told me it was beautiful when I finished. Then he left. And I could only hope that he'd sleep. That he felt a little lighter.

He might have been an abandoned teenager, and I might have been some naive little kid, but that night we were just two souls with one secret. And after that, unlikely friends.

"I'm surprised you didn't laugh when I told you." He chuckles darkly.

I turn and punch his arm, feeling a little irritated with him for still being so goddamn hard on himself. "Shut up."

"What are you gonna do about it?"

"Probably throw a water bottle at your face."

A relieved laugh escapes him, and I watch his hands twist on the steering wheel, eyes still fixed on the road. "I didn't throw it at your face. Not my fault your hand-eye coordination is trash."

"Tell my nose that." I rub it dramatically, even though it doesn't hurt at all.

"The huge new bump on it suits you. Adds some character to that otherwise perfect face."

He's trying to divert back into playful, friendly banter. The kind we do so well. The type that cropped up between us once everything was out on the table. After that night, I never hesitated to tell Jasper anything. Of course, as we got older, things changed, but we had this foundation of raw honesty I could always fall back on.

I trust him, and I think he trusts me. I don't know why he trusted me that night. Perhaps he just needed to unload and I was the puppy-love-riddled girl who was already up watching him, who just "happened" to be out for a walk.

Either way, it connected us. For life, it would seem. Because I don't think he's told another soul the entire details of that day. That he held his hand up in that signal. That his family fell to shambles in the wake of it. That he feels responsible. That Beau found him living in a car in a field behind the school because his mom was missing and his shithead dad had started a fresh life and failed to keep coming home for him at all.

The mention of *perfect face* brings a hush back through the cab, and with all the quiet, my mind wanders.

My curiosity gets the best of me when I ask, "You hear from him at all?"

He knows I mean his dad without even saying it. Harvey has filled that void for Jasper the best he can, but there's no getting over a parent who leaves you by choice. A parent who blames you for the worst day of your life.

He clears his throat, glancing at me from under the brim of his cap. "No."

I nod, tamping down the rage that his biological dad always stirs up in me.

"I drove there once, you know. Just to see. Parked on the street and watched his house for an entire day. His wife. His kids. A fucking cat. I always wanted a cat, and he wouldn't let me get one."

"Did he see you?"

"Eventually."

"What did he say?"

His throat works in tandem with his hands on the wheel, and he shrugs.

"I could kill him," I mutter, rubbing my hand over my lips as though I can press back in the words I want to spew about this "man" who abandoned his only surviving child to start fresh without him. Grief twists us all in unusual ways, and I wish I could bring myself to be more forgiving considering what he went through.

But I just can't. All I see is Jasper and what it did to him.

I know my dad can be a domineering dick, but he cares about me in his own way.

Jasper chuckles sadly. "That's the thing, Sunny. He said nothing at all. He saw me. We made eye contact. And he just closed the door and flicked off the porch light. Went to bed."

"I'm sorry." My voice cracks when I offer the apology, and I reach out to wrap my fingers around his shoulder, fingertips dusting the curls that trace the back of his neck.

He inclines his head toward me, and the pads of my fingers rasp over the bone at the top of his spine. I rub a slow circle there and feel his body relax under my touch.

It strikes me again that it isn't enough to heal his wounds. But it's what I've got.

I can be a person who really knows *who* he is rather than *what* he is. I can listen.

When he talks, I'll always listen.

"Shit happens to the best of us, Sunny, and I am not the best of us."

"To me you are" is what I tell him.

My eyes catch on the diamond that sits on my finger, and I recoil at the sight. I need to take it off, but I'm stalling. And not because I miss Sterling.

It's because I worry that if I take this ring off, I'll do something stupid and desperate where Jasper is concerned. It's like a mental seat belt for me at this point—one of the few things keeping me safe from myself and an impulsive decision.

But I reach out, take his nearest hand off the wheel, and link my fingers tightly with his over the center console.

And the ring doesn't stop me.

18

Sloane

Dad: Sloane, it's time for you to answer my calls. I raised
you better than this. I know you can be highly
emotional, but this is too far. Pull yourself together
and behave like a Winthrop.

———— ✑

Harvey: How are you kids holding up?
Sloane: Good. Spent the night in Rose Hill. Should be in
Ruby Creek this afternoon. Will keep you posted.
Harvey: How's my boy?
Sloane: Good. Fine.
Harvey: And how are you?
Sloane: Hungover.
Harvey: He driving you to drink?
Sloane: Pretty much.

I TURN MY HEAD BACK TO THE WINDOW AS WE CREST THE top of the mountain pass. Visibility has gotten worse. I can see the red taillights of the few vehicles around us and feel the truck straining to chug its way up the steep incline. In the side mirror, I can see the big round bales strapped to the flatbed, two layers fit together like puzzle pieces and covered with tied-down tarps to keep them from getting wet.

My ears pop as we hit the top altitude and start our descent, the front end of the truck pointing downward suddenly. A soft grunt comes from Jasper, and I turn to look at him. His thick brows are furrowed as he glances between the dash and the road.

"Turn the music down, Sloane."

It's already quiet, but I do it anyway because the tone of his voice is jarring. There's a note of anxiety, a note of authority that has my hair standing on end.

We're picking up speed now, and when I shift to peek at the speedometer, it creeps up incrementally second by second. A hazard light glows red just beside it.

"Jas," I breathe out. "What's wrong?" My chest is tight, and without even knowing what's going on, my right hand reaches up to grab the roof handle.

"You're buckled in, right, Sunny?" Jasper bites out, not once looking my way.

My eyes drop to both of our seat belts. "Yes." Fear bleeds into my voice.

"Sloane. Relax. I'm going to keep you safe, okay? Tell me you understand that."

I'm nodding rapidly at him, but no words spring from my lips. They're clamped shut too tightly.

"Talk to me, Sunny. Who found you that night when you got lost in the woods playing capture the flag?"

We're just going faster and faster.

"You did."

"Who bandaged your feet?"

"You," I whimper, watching the speedometer creep up.

"Who broke you out of that fucking sham of a wedding?" he growls, tone dropping, like this is the time to be mad about that. When we're both about to die.

"You, Jas. You. Always you." My hand grips the front of the seat so hard I feel like I might rip the leather.

"The brakes that connect to the trailer are malfunctioning. I can only slow us down so much."

I gasp. But Jasper is stoic. Pale but stoic. Eyes fixed on the road.

He lays hard on the horn when we come up too fast behind a car, urging them to move over. A harsh breath escapes him when they signal and switch lanes.

"There's a runaway lane up ahead that I'm going to use, but it's going to be bumpy. I want you to hang on as hard as you can and just breathe—trust me. You're brave. You've got this." I can't tell if he's talking to me or himself. "You got that? Do you trust me?" His voice is loud now, sharp, so unlike the soft mumbled tones I'm used to from him.

"Yes, of course. I trust you."

He looks my way quickly and nods.

The next few moments pass in the heaviest silence of white knuckles and held breath. There's an almost ethereal quality to the moment. Like I'm watching a slow-motion video of us cruising to our deaths.

When the lane appears through the heavy snowfall, jutting sharply up the side of the mountain, I bite down on the inside of my cheek.

It's *so* steep.

I know that's the point, but it doesn't stop the abject terror from blooming in my chest.

My eyes clamp shut when we ram into the gravel roadway. The impact jolts the truck and jostles my body as Jasper maneuvers us to safety. Or at least I hope he does. I can't look, but I haven't felt us flip or crash, so that's a win.

Within seconds we aren't moving anymore. The truck stops on the sharp incline, and with one steady hand, Jasper jams the emergency brake into place before wrapping it back around the wheel in a death grip.

The entire episode lasted mere moments, but it felt like hours. My entire body is vibrating, my chest thumping so hard with the heavy beat of my heart that it feels like it actually rattles my vision.

"Jesus fucking Christ. Holy shit. You okay?" I whisper-shout all my favorite bad words, letting go of the handle and laying a shaking hand flat on my chest.

After a few seconds, no response comes, so I turn to peer at Jasper. His hands are squeezed tight, and his entire body looks made of stone. He's a statue, so still I can barely see him breathe.

"Jasper?"

His strong nose is pointed straight forward, and his skin is the color of crisp white printer paper, like all the blood has left his body.

"Jas." I touch him tentatively and squeeze his shoulder, but he doesn't respond. Suddenly I'm less scared about our situation and more scared for him. "You're freaking me out."

His jaw flexes and he swallows, but his eyes stay trained out the windshield, the wind howling as the tall dark pines sway and white snow swirls around us.

He's in shock, that much I can gather. And while I'm no psychologist, I imagine this event was a little too close to the day we were just talking about.

The day it all fell apart.

Because the man beside me looks traumatized.

Without thinking, I unbuckle myself and make a few quick moves. I pry his hand from the wheel and crawl onto his lap, straddling his legs and trying to get him to look at me rather than at the windshield like he's frozen in time— another time.

My hands flatten on his shoulders, and I give him a little shake. "Jasper. Look at me."

His eyes don't move, and panic nips at all my edges. I gently remove his hat, tossing it onto the passenger seat. It's too hard to see him from beneath the brim, and deep down, I know that's the whole point of why he always wears it.

He's constantly trying to blend into the background, but even when he's hiding, I see him.

I slide my palms over the tops of his shoulders and up

the sides of his sturdy neck until my fingers weave themselves into the hair at the back of his skull. Spearmint and eucalyptus. The scent bowls me over every time. It's a shot of electricity to my senses. I realize that if he's washing his face with that bodywash, he probably uses it as shampoo too.

The tips of my fingers move of their own accord, massaging the base of his skull. Am I taking freedoms I might not usually? Definitely. But desperate times call for desperate measures, and this whole petrified-wood-on-the-side-of-a-mountain act has got me stressed.

I press my forehead against his, trying to force his line of sight up to my own. "Jas. I'm right here. You kept us safe. Everything is okay. You did so good. Thank you for always looking out for me."

He blinks once, and it's like he pulls away a layer of dark shadow that covered his irises. Where they bordered on black just moments ago, they're back to the soft navy I know so well—soft like velvet, highlighted with streaks of denim and little sparks of brightness where the light reflects.

"Sloane." He sighs, and warm breath hits my throat. He doesn't move his forehead, but he does move his hands. They shape my waist, and I feel them tremble.

All I do is continue to rub at the back of his head, soothing him in the only way I know how.

"Are you okay?" His voice is gritty and wavers slightly on *okay*.

I nod, rolling my forehead against his. "I'm good. I'm all good."

He pulls back, and as if he doesn't believe me, his hands

take inventory of my body. They roam down, squeezing at my hip bones through my thin leggings. They slide over the tops of my thighs, and he watches raptly, like he needs to see it and feel it to believe it.

Me telling him isn't enough.

His breathing turns ragged, and the tremors that started in his fingers take over his arms as well. When he looks into my eyes, I nod my head, trying to reassure him. But it doesn't stop him. His fingers start back up my legs, and his hands splay on my back, big enough that they cover it entirely.

"Nothing hurts?"

"Nothing hurts," I confirm, staying deathly still, not wanting to break whatever moment this is right now.

He needs this, and so do I. But in two very different ways.

When the heat of his touch rounds over my shoulders, I give in to my body and let my lashes flutter shut for one brief moment. I bask in his gentle hands, gliding up my arms in unison, checking every spot like I'm the most precious glass doll.

"You're safe." I'm not sure if he says it to me or to himself.

But I affirm it anyway. "I'm safe."

When he gets to my wrists that sit on either side of his neck, he grips them and finds my gaze again. He breathes in for four seconds. And out for four seconds.

And we just exist in each other's eyes.

Locked. Loaded.

"Are you sure your nose doesn't hurt?" He asks about my nose, but he's looking at my lips. My tongue darts over them as I try to calm my rioting nerves. This moment feels intensely intimate.

I've had a lifetime of intimate moments with Jasper, but none have felt like this, with the air around us thick, heavy, and hot.

Pushing us together somehow.

His finger dusts down the bridge of my nose. It's barely a touch. It's a whisper. "Does it hurt, Sloane?"

I watch his lips press together and come apart to form the words. And god, I want to kiss him. I want him to kiss me. I want this moment to never end. I want to live in this truck, in the snow, at the top of a mountain with him and never leave.

My lashes flutter, and I tip my chin down incrementally to keep our lips from being lined up, to keep myself from doing something that will embarrass me—or, worse, ruin us.

We're so damn close. Close enough that he…presses a soft kiss to the tip of my nose and steals my breath in the process.

My eyes snap to his. Wide. Shocked.

"I'm sorry I threw that at you."

All I can manage is a nod. My mouth is dry. I hear ringing in my ears. My eyes are sucked into his midnight sky.

He leans forward again and kisses my forehead. My fingers grip his hair, and I move in closer. I tilt my head as though I could nuzzle into him, as though I could crawl into him and curl up in his chest. I want him to be as connected to me as I am to him.

He inclines his head, eyes searching. A silent question.

And I nod my response.

Then his lips are on my cheek. His hand slides around to the back of my head, and he cups my skull.

We're so close. So latched onto one another. Like neither of us wants the other to pull away.

Jasper drags his lips along the top of my cheekbone, his stubble rasping over my skin, dotting it in tiny fires that I never want to put out.

He kisses the corner of my jaw, and when the tip of his tongue flicks out, I moan. Shamelessly. Desperately.

He tugs me closer. His strong arm wraps around my waist, and he clamps me to him.

"Jasper," I whisper.

In response, he fists my hair and tugs my head to the side, dragging his hot mouth down and then back up my neck. I squeeze my legs tighter on him, hearing only the pounding of my heart in my ears and the deep groaning sound that vibrates from his chest.

"I can't ever lose you," he growls.

"You won't," I reply quietly, right as the tip of his nose traces the shell of my ear.

"I might."

"Nev—"

Before I can say *never*, he cuts me off with "Because I think I'm about to fuck everything up between us."

And then he kisses me.

His lips mold to mine and his fingers weave into my hair as his grip turns soft.

I go still with shock—utter disbelief—and when I do, he

stops, pulling away as his warm palm slides down over my throat to look me in the eye.

"I'm sor—"

I cut him off by launching myself back at him. And he doesn't miss a fucking beat.

He doesn't kiss me like a friend. He kisses me back with equal fervor. He kisses me like he wants to consume me.

And he does.

His hands are hot brands on my body, touching and squeezing in places I'll never forget. His lips are warm and firm. He's gentle, but he commands me. He tilts my head the way he wants it. He sets the pace for our languid kisses until he takes on a more demanding pace.

Until his tongue slides into my mouth and his teeth nip at my bottom lip.

And me? I turn to putty in his arms. I've been lost to him for years, but today in a quiet truck, in the middle of a snowstorm, I let myself get lost *in* him.

He takes and I give.

I take and he gives.

I roll my hips against his, and he groans out, "Sloane."

The hand in my hair tightens, and I feel the dull burn of him tugging against my scalp. His opposite hand moves lazily down my rib cage, coming to rest at my hip, long fingers splayed casually over the curve of my ass, his thumb rubbing against the outline of my thong.

Everything is slow. Achingly slow. So representative of us in so many ways. But there's also an edge of desperation in us both.

A hard bite to every movement.

My nipples pebble. My heart pounds. My body is alight. My hips roll again.

This time the hard length of him presses back. I whimper, aroused and relieved all at once. I've spent years thinking Jasper Gervais couldn't want me, but right now his body tells another story.

And so do his words.

"Sunny, you're gonna make me lose my mind."

"Good," I murmur against his mouth. "We'll be insane together. I'm so tired of doing it alone."

I'm ready to tear his clothes off and impale myself on him, here and now. I'm crazed. I feel more drunk than I did last night.

I kiss him again, pouring all the frustration and longing into him. And he gives it back tenfold. He bowls me over and steals the air right from my lungs.

And then he pulls me away. With one hand tight in my hair, he angles my head up to him and peers down at me. His eyes flit around every corner of my face as he assesses me.

He reads me like a fucking book and then tells me something I've longed to hear.

"You're not alone. I'm right there with you."

I let out a breath so big that my body sags when it leaves me.

"But this isn't the time or place. It's not safe. And you are too fucking precious to take chances with."

Fuck my safety. If I died riding Jasper Gervais in the driver's seat of this truck, I might be fine with that. What a way to go. Out with a bang, so to speak.

"When is the time and place?" I breathe out instead.

He ghosts a kiss over my damp, puffy lips and guides my ear to his mouth. "When I say so," he rasps.

A shiver wracks my entire body. When I pull back, his eyes are dark again, and they land on my lips, then my breasts, before roaming back up to my face.

He cups my head softly. "I'll be right back. I need to check the brake attachment so I can get us back down this hill. Buckle up, just in case."

I nod, and he lifts me, depositing me in the passenger seat effortlessly.

He's out the door and into the blowing snow without another word.

And I sit here, dumbstruck, hoping he's okay. And taking an inventory of all the things it did to my body when he said, *"When I say so."*

19

Jasper

Jasper: Bad roads. Brake issues. Spending the night in a town called Blisswater Springs.

Harvey: Do you win a prize for using as few words as possible? You guys okay? Can you elaborate?

Jasper: I'll call you from the hotel. We're all good. Safe. You don't need to worry.

Harvey: Come on. Give me something. One bed or two?

Jasper: Talk to you later.

THE TIPS OF MY FINGERS ARE TINGLING AS INTENSELY AS THE rest of my body. Sloane is silent and introspective beside me. When I got back into the truck, she stared at me with comically wide eyes, pressing her lips together either to hide a smile or to keep from saying something.

We're safely back on the highway. The wiring is firmly in place with the connector, and I'm finding it easier to breathe—unless I think too hard about Sloane writhing in my lap, her ass grinding against my cock.

I'm still stopping at the closest mechanic to have the brake connector checked because that shouldn't have come loose at all. According to Google, that means we're spending some time in a town called Blisswater Springs.

"Are we just not going to talk anymore?" Sloane blurts, cutting the silence. "Like, I know you're generally not a big talker. But can we not be awkward about the…" Her hand flaps around in front of her.

"About the kiss?"

"Yeah. It was a stressful moment. A moment of insanity. We can be cool about it."

I've thought about kissing Sloane for a long time now, whether or not I've wanted to admit it to myself.

In fact, she almost took the last name Woodcock for the rest of her life because I've spent so long thinking rather than doing anything about it.

This might not be the perfect moment for me to figure out my shit where Sloane Winthrop is concerned, but it is *a* moment. And if I've figured out anything in this Shakespearean tragedy of a life, it's that life is just moments all strung together like multicolor Christmas lights. You always end up liking some colors better than others.

Joyful, tragic, peaceful, funny. Unforgettable moments and moments we wish we could forget.

And kissing Sloane in this truck is not one of those. It's a moment I fully intend to hang on to. In the past, I was told to stay away from her. In the past, I cared about that warning.

In this moment though? I don't give a fuck.

"It wasn't a moment of insanity," I say matter-of-factly.

"Sorry?" She sounds incredulous.

"I definitely meant to kiss you."

She scoffs, crossing her arms and turning beet red. "You were barely responsive mere seconds beforehand. You were in shock, so you'll forgive me if I don't believe you."

"I don't need you to believe me for it to be true."

I don't know why after years of keeping my mouth shut, I'm now blurting this all out. Most likely, it's because I saw our lives flash before my eyes back there. When I looked over at Sloane beside me and saw her beautiful blue eyes clamped shut, fingers gripping the seat, shoulders scrunched up to her ears, I realized it could be my last moment with her.

My last moment and she would never know what she is to me. How much she is to me. That she's *it* for me. And that's just fucking insane. Like a waste. Like for a man who knows loss so intimately, why would I ever set myself up to lose something so precious?

I think that's the realization that hit me at the dinner where I watched Sloane sit beside a man who talked over her every chance he got. She was about to marry a piece of human chauvinist garbage, but she could have had me—if she wanted me.

If I'd just told her.

And she didn't know because I was too stuck in my own

head to tell her. Too paralyzed by my fear of losing people I care about. Of losing *her*.

But, fuck, losing someone and having them not know that you care about them? Wishing you could go back and tell them?

That's a special hell. One I have no intention of living in because I've given my demons enough of myself already—they can't have her too.

"I just almost married someone else."

I nod brusquely, glancing over at her. She looks *pissed*, which is not the reaction I expected. But then so am I. Because the mere mention of her marrying someone sends me into a hot, simmering rage so unlike me I don't even know what to do with it.

"Yeah. That would have been a shame because he really fucking sucks."

"Ha! Un-fucking-believable." Her jaw pops, and she stares out the passenger window. "I've known you for what? Eighteen years? Almost half your life? And this…this *feeling* is just occurring to you now?"

A humorless laugh bubbles up out of her, and she shakes her head. "Someone else came to play in your sandbox and you got all territorial after years of not giving me a second look? *Love* that for me. I'm not a fire hydrant for you to piss on, Jasper." Her hands shoot up beside her head. "Like…I'm supposed to buy that you've just had some sort of awakening and your childhood friend is suddenly hella kissable these days? God. That's hilarious. If I didn't like you so much, I'd kick you in the balls for this."

I should be worried, but all I can think is *There she is.* The firecracker girl. The prima ballerina who trains her ass off and drinks cheap beer like it's fine wine.

I tell her the truth, eyes on the road. "It's not just occurring to me now."

She rolls her eyes, shimmying her shoulders up taller, as if straightening in her seat might make her feel less vulnerable.

"It's true." I wish the roads were better so I could give her my full attention and look her in the eye. Wipe that petulant expression off her face and kiss her again. Make her believe me. Because I know I haven't been imagining these moments between us. The ones where the air grows so heavy that it feels like more than I can bear.

"I don't believe you," she repeats, but this time her voice is a little hoarse.

"You kissed me back," I say right as I'm hit with the sickening thought that maybe I'm out to lunch. Maybe this is all very one-sided and I've gone horribly off track. After all, my experience with women in any capacity beyond sex is nonexistent.

Except for Sunny. She's the girl I tell everything. The girl who was always there on my worst days and darkest nights. Not because I asked her to be, but just because that's what we are to each other.

It doesn't matter how many years have passed. We'll always be that to each other.

"No shit." She's crossed her arms over her ribs again, and my eyes trail over the way it props her breasts up. The tingle in my fingers is now an itch to explore every inch of her body, to show her all the ways I want her.

Fuck, I want her.

Sloane is soothing. She's the eye of the storm. True north. Somehow our compasses always bring us back to each other.

When we stop at the first red light in Blisswater Springs, I turn in my seat and ask, "What's that supposed to mean, Sloane? I was there. Felt your thighs go all tight on me when I tugged your hair. Heard you moan when I kissed you. Are we going to sit here and keep pretending that things don't feel different between us now?"

"They've always felt this way for me!" she explodes, arms flung wide, eyes shining with emotion. "And you've *never* noticed. But *now* you do? What am I supposed to do? Jump for joy and say thank you for blessing me with your interest?"

I pale, hands going clammy on the wheel. I respond in a stream of consciousness, trying to explain myself in the wake of what she's just said. "I mean…we all knew you had a childhood crush. I was a teenager. But you were just a kid. And then you outgrew it. You had boyfriends and ballet. I had hockey and endless training. We became friends in the city. You got *engaged*."

Her pale-pink lips part like she's about to say something but quickly press back together. She turns back to the windshield, eyes forced ahead so hard it almost looks painful. The seconds stretch out, and I'm certain she's not going to respond to me. And, shit, that's what I deserve for everything I just dumped on her.

But right as the light turns green, her sad voice hits me like a punch to the fucking gut.

"I never outgrew it, Jas."

⁓

When I kissed her, I counted to four in my head. I told myself I'd give it four seconds, but she took more.

It was a moment of insanity.

Or maybe all the moments where I tried to deny what I was feeling for her have been moments of insanity all strung together. Lights of all one color.

Does regret have a color?

"Check again," Sloane says to the woman behind the front desk at the small resort-style hotel. "There has to be something."

Listening to Sloane explain that we need separate rooms feels like her own moment of insanity. But I'll let her have it.

Because I *know* Sloane. I know how she processes things.

What I didn't know is her childhood crush never left. I should feel bad for never noticing. I should feel like an idiot. But I feel...relieved.

I see a chance. A glimmer of hope.

"Something with two beds at least? How about a rollaway cot? I'm almost child sized." She gestures down at herself.

I stifle a chuckle and look out the window toward the parking lot, where snow is still falling heavily.

"We can have a cot sent up, of course." The woman at the desk smiles patiently, eyes bouncing between us curiously like she can't quite figure out what's going on.

"That will be fine," Sloane forces out, a practiced smile on her face. Cool mask perfectly in place. Her bun is pulled up tight the way she likes it when she's ready for a performance—or for battle.

That's what she resorted to doing in the truck. She tugged down the visor and used the mirror to obsessively pull her hair back. It was never flat enough or smooth enough, so she'd pull it out and do it all over again.

She did it five times. I know because I counted. There wasn't much else to do once she settled into ignoring me. I was also struggling to peel my eyes away from her after her crush revelation.

This woman has been my friend for eighteen years.

How did I miss it?

Either she got good at hiding it or I wasn't looking. It was probably a combination of both.

Defiant stray blond hairs catch the light in the dated hotel lobby. I almost want to point them out just to rile her up.

Because when she's riled, the truth comes out.

"Thank you for your help," she tells the woman as she turns to me, holding up two key cards. The smile on her face has moved from forced to kind of insane looking. "Let's go," she singsongs a little too loudly before storming away, clearly expecting I'll follow.

Within a few strides, I'm standing right beside her, staring at the elevator door.

"Fourth floor," she says rigidly.

"Okay."

"One king-size bed."

"That's fine."

"No. I'll sleep on a rollaway cot. They're going to bring it up."

"Sunny, that's really not necessary. It's just a bed. We slept together the other night."

She hikes her bag higher on her shoulder and tips her nose up. "Yes, well, that was before I embarrassed myself and decided I was pissed at you. So I'll take the cot."

I resist the urge to roll my eyes. I'm glad she's not being the doormat she was with that dickhead, but I'm also not accustomed to her being angry with me.

When the elevator dings, I gesture her ahead of me, letting my eyes drop to her ass as she walks inside. Only a day ago, I watched her walk into the lake in her underwear, but it feels like it's been weeks.

I guess it's been years.

"You heard from your dad?" I ask as the doors slide shut.

"No. I mean, well, yes. He's messaged. And called. And emailed. But frankly, I'm not a fan of his tone, so I'm ignoring him too. At least until he asks me how I am or if I'm safe rather than just demanding I come back."

"Fair."

I hear her teeth clank together over the soft elevator music. "Come to think of it, I'm kind of done with men in general right now." One hand waves up and down in my direction. "The whole lot of you."

"Also fair."

She spins toward me now. "Why do you have to be so fucking agreeable, Jasper?"

"Because I'm your friend, Sunny. Nothing will ever change that. If you need to bitch about something, even if that something is me, I'll be that person for you."

"What if I go back to Sterling?"

My entire body stills. *Not a fucking chance.* I know she's goading me. And it's working. "No."

"You think you can just waltz in, tell me you're"—her hands form sarcastic air quotes as she carries on—"kind of interested mere weeks after I was meant to get married, and I'm going to take your hand and skip off into the sunset? After these past couple of weeks, I must seem really stupid to you, but I'm not *that* stupid."

The door opens, and she surges out of the elevator and down the carpeted hallway, irritation wafting off of her. She laughs. Actually laughs.

Because of course she does. Only she would laugh at a moment like this.

"This is insane," she mutters as she turns the corner and finds our room. One swipe of the key and she's into the space, tossing her bag onto a chair. She storms toward the windows, where she stands with her hands on her hips, silhouetted by the whiteout on the opposite side of the glass.

"You're not going back to him."

She shrugs nonchalantly. "Maybe I will. You don't tell me what to do, Jasper."

Not yet. But I will.

"You're not."

She spins, her voice cutting across the room like she's thrown a dart right at my chest. "And why not?"

"Because he sucks the life out of you!" She rears back, clearly shocked by the volume of my voice. "And I want to breathe it back in."

Her laugh this time is not at all amused. "Years, Jasper. *Years.* For years I have been the little cousin, the little sister, the good friend. For years I have *seen* you. Waited for you every summer. Watched you go on dates with women who weren't me—who would *never* be me. I was *sick* over you. And then I came to terms with what we were. I accepted I would always want you and you would never want me back. I convinced myself that sometimes the greatest loves of our lives will be our closest friends. And I was okay with that."

My stomach drops, my chest seizes, and nausea roils.

"I got really fucking comfortable in my head where I could want you that way but had the safety of knowing you didn't want me back. And now? You just change your mind? Willy-nilly? When emotions are already running high for us both? This is insane."

"I didn't just change my mind." I dread what I'm about to tell her. She's already angry with her dad, and I loathe the thought of being the one to make her hate him. Because hearing what she's just told me, I know this will hurt her.

"Make this make sense for me then!"

My voice drops, and so do my eyes. "It was your dad."

"What?"

I pry at the edges of my cap, pulling the brim down to shield myself. "It was the fall you got a spot with your company. Finally went pro. Got a role in *The Nutcracker*. I came to help you move into your new condo downtown. You were eighteen, and I was twenty-four."

"I remember." Her voice is quiet, hollowed-out sounding.

"We had fun setting everything up."

She nods. "We did."

"I had secured a spot on the Grizzlies. Clawed my way up off the farm team."

"I remember," she repeats.

"Everything was going so well for both of us. I was so happy for you. So excited to see you onstage. To have a friend from back home in the city with me."

Her eyes are shiny now.

"But your dad found me leaving your place." I swallow, staring down at my hands, arms limp at my sides before crossing them and slipping them beneath each other like a shield. "He threatened to pull strings with his friend who owns the team and have me cut from the roster if I ever crossed that line with you. He told me to stay far away from you. That he never wanted to see me in your presence alone again."

She still says nothing. Her baby blues bore into me with unnerving intensity.

"You were still a kid to me back then. I really didn't think of our relationship that way, but he scared me all the same. Sloane, you have to understand, I had *nothing* to my name except being good at hockey. Being *really* fucking good at hockey. Good enough to pull myself out of the gutter I got left in. And your dad? He's just powerful and connected enough to follow through on his threats."

Her bottom lip wobbles, and her eyes blink. "But why would he want you to stay away from me?"

My face scrunches, and I wipe a hand over my stubble, hearing the rasp in my ears. "You really can't guess, Sloane? It's because I'm not one of you. I'm from, I believe he called it, 'the wrong side of the tracks.' I don't take six-figure trips to hunt lions or drive a Maybach. I came from nothing and made something of myself by working my ass off and putting on a show for the masses. I'm beholden to men like your father, but I'll never be one of them. I'm an Eaton at heart. A small-town boy. And I always will be, no matter how many zeros are on my paycheck. And to be frank, I'm happy with that."

"But I don't care about your paycheck. I never have." Her voice is so small, so brittle.

I sigh and reach up to squeeze at my brim, wanting to comfort her but not wanting to overstep either. "I know you don't. But this is what I've been trying to tell you all along. *He* doesn't care about *you*. He doesn't care that Sterling is a shit match for you. He doesn't care about what you want. He cares about what he needs. He couldn't risk me or you ruining his plans or his reputation with my dirty upbringing and fucked-up family dynamic. And I was too young and too desperate to defy him. I missed your first professional ballet on the big stage because I was scared. I kept you in the friend zone for years after because I was scared."

She stays perfectly still. The shiny veneer she's assigned to her father all these years has cracked, and a tear spills down her cheek. A perfect droplet rolling over her pale skin, the reality of his manipulations seeping out in a slow, devastated trickle.

That frustration surges up in me at the sight, and I say what I've been wanting to say to her for god knows how long. "Times have changed, Sloane. I'm not scared anymore. You're not my fucking friend. You're just *mine*."

20

Sloane

Dad: Sloane. Answer this fucking phone. NOW.
You're done disrespecting me. And if you're off
gallivanting with that homeless orphan, there will
be consequences.

———⁓———

I DIP MY FACE INTO THE WARM WATER, HOPING IT WILL MAKE
the tears on my cheeks blend in. The steam from Blisswater hot
spring wafts up around me while fat white snowflakes fall down.

I sit on the tiled bench, submerged, and I watch. The
instant they make contact with the top of the water, they
melt away into nothing.

I feel alarmingly kindred with them. Everything I
thought I knew about my life has melted away into nothing
in the span of a five-minute conversation.

Worst of all, I'm angry with myself for not seeing it. Because the more I think about it, the more I think I've been willfully ignorant concerning my father.

What little girl wants to think her dad wouldn't have her best interests at heart? I wasn't subtle about my crush in the early days. He and my mom would have known; they'd have seen it.

And he moved us all around like chess pieces. For what? For optics? To close a deal?

To benefit himself.

Try as I might, that's the only thing I can come up with. Having me connected with Jasper wasn't beneficial to him, so he made sure it would never happen.

It crushed me when Jasper didn't show up to my first performance. He texted me and said he got caught up reviewing game tape. Sent flowers instead.

I should have been happy I'd finally made it. That he sent flowers. But instead, I cried in the dressing room while wiping off copious amounts of makeup.

I dip my face in the water again, washing away the fresh tears that have tumbled down.

When I pull my head back and turn my face up to the cool night air, someone sits beside me.

I don't even need to look to know who it is. I know his smell. I know his size. I know how my body reacts when he draws near.

I know him so well. And yet I didn't know *this*.

Letting my head tip back against the tiled edge of the pool, I allow my body to relax and sink into the water.

We don't talk. What is there to say? So much and so little all at once. His arm brushes against me, and then his pinky finger wraps around mine.

I don't know how long we sit there like this. Snow falling. Fingers latched together. Steam billowing up around us. Light instrumental music plays through the speakers, and I can hear the joyful squealing of children jumping into the cold pool on the other side of the deck.

Tears continue to leak silently from my eyes. I wish I could make them stop, but I can't. The ache in my chest is insistent, and the what-ifs and could-have-beens consume me.

What if my dad hadn't run into him that night?

What if their elevators had passed each other? One going up while the other went down.

What if I hadn't forced myself to hide my feelings and move on to other relationships?

What could have been if I'd just blurted it all out to Jasper?

What could we have been if he'd done the same?

Would we be together?

Would my parents support it?

Would I even care? Or would I throw it all away for a shot at something with Jasper?

The questions don't stop, suffocating me under their weight. They say comparison is the thief of joy, and comparing how different my life might look if one tiny interaction hadn't happened is definitely doing that.

It's like imagining winning the lottery. Fun to dream about until you get depressed about the fact that it will never happen.

One hot tear streaks down the side of my face, and the water swishes beside me, followed by the calloused pads of Jasper's fingers brushing over the apple of my cheek. A breath hiccups out of me at his touch.

I still don't open my eyes. Instead, I just let myself feel him. Jasper has wiped many of my tears away over a broken heart, over frustration, impostor syndrome, raw feet.

But never like this. Never over being the one to make me realize I've been a puppet. Everyone in my life has treated me like the tiny ballerina inside a jewelry box. Nice to look at and cute to listen to when you're in the mood but easily shut away when you have something else to do.

I'm furious with myself for smiling and spinning every time someone opened that box. I'm angry at myself for not flipping them the finger and refusing to twirl around mindlessly. I'm not angry at anyone else.

It's all directed at myself.

And somehow I'm harder to forgive. I think deep down I expected better of myself.

I wonder if this is how Jasper feels too. Fuck, that must be a heavy burden to bear.

His broad hand slides over my cheek, his thumb and forefinger gripping my chin to turn my head his way. "Sunny, look at me."

The authority in his voice sends a shiver down my spine even though I'm sitting in perfectly hot water. My eyes open and immediately latch on to his.

I'm transported to that first day I saw him, all tall, lanky, and boyish. Even then he moved like an athlete. His gait, his mannerisms. Everything about him screamed strength and agility. It still does, but it's tenfold.

Looking at him is almost unbearable right now.

His irises are dark sapphires under the night sky as they trace my face. Eyes. Mouth. Throat. Then lower.

A cold snowflake lands on the tip of my nose right as he asks, "Tell me how to make you feel better."

My heart accelerates in my chest, like a car going from zero to sixty. It's his voice. It's his hands. His nearness. It's the open-ended question he just asked.

I could tell him to carry me up to our room and fuck me, ruin me so thoroughly that all I can think about is him and where he's touching me, and he'd do it.

I open my mouth to say it, but then I rein it back in, feeling so far out of my depth. Like I have whiplash. Like I need to gather my thoughts before I say or do something stupid.

Like completely ruin this friendship.

"I'm going to go take a shower," I rasp, holding his gaze and watching his chin dip in a subtle nod.

And then I move across the pool, the water caressing my body like silk running over my skin. The sensation of his eyes roaming my back and my ass as I take the shallow steps up onto the pool deck is heady.

My body screams at me to go back to him. But I don't want to be that ballerina in a jewelry box with him. I don't want him to feel like he needs to save me.

I want to save myself.

I emerge from the bathroom in a puff of warm steam. My skin is pink and raw from how hot I had the water, from how hard I scrubbed my skin.

I feel like I scalded an entire layer of myself away in there. Found a little kernel of strength hiding underneath and latched on to it. Decided I won't be the girl who goes along with what everyone else around her wants.

I'm going to speak up.

I'm going to get comfortable disappointing other people to avoid disappointing myself.

I won't apologize for doing things the way I want to do them.

I'm ready to be unapologetically me and let go of the people in my life who don't approve of the person I am now.

Jasper's head snaps up, eyes dragging down my body and the small white towel I have wrapped around my torso. He doesn't bother dropping my gaze or hiding the intense look of want that paints his features.

And I decide to revel in that. The petty part of me hopes it hurts. I hope he feels a fraction of the longing I've felt for him while he sat around, not telling me why he's stayed so close and so far away all at once.

"Shower's all yours. Bathroom lock doesn't work." I hike a thumb over my shoulder and walk straight toward my duffel bag, which is beside the atrocious little cot I've told myself I'm going to sleep on.

I'm not sure what point I was trying to prove. The new me would make Jasper sleep on it, but one look at him and his hulking frame tells me that isn't an option.

I love him too much to do that to him. And he likes me too much to say no.

God. We're so fucked.

"Thanks." I hear him move across the room, the floorboards beneath the tightly woven carpet creaking as he lumbers past.

I try to force myself not to turn and check him out as he goes.

But I fail.

Miserably.

I let my eyes wander over his broad toned shoulders, the way his muscles ripple in his back as he walks. The indent down the column of his spine. The grayscale tattoos that wrap around his arms, and a lone one that peeks out on his ribs. I can only see it because he lifts one arm and runs a hand through his hair, but it looks an awful lot like...

No.

I shake my head and turn back to my bag. When I hear the click of the bathroom door closing, I drop my towel and quickly slide into a pair of black Calvin Klein sleep shorts and a tight black tank top. No bra. My breasts aren't big enough for it to matter. This stretchy material presses them into place without issue.

I sit on the cot, and a spring pokes my ass through the flimsy mattress. It's fine. I didn't torture myself in pointe shoes for years to be put off by a minor discomfort.

As I lie back on the squeaky cot, the glimpse of Jasper's tattoo keeps popping up in my head. I've always known Jasper has a lot of tattoos. What started out as one grew into many. They cover his biceps, twist over his shoulders, and crawl down his forearms. They're all black, the older ones more faded than the newer ones.

For me, they just add to his appeal. Men like Sterling don't get tattoos. They get facials. Jasper isn't "one of us," as my dad would say—a comment that rings a lot more offensive now that I've removed my blinders.

Jasper is nothing like the men I grew up around. He's raw and dirty and loves so hard he hurts himself in the process.

And I want to know what that fucking tattoo is.

I stand, storm across the room, and toss the bathroom door open, stepping into the space.

One strong hand props Jasper's hulking form up against the shower wall while the other grips his cock, pumping up and down slowly.

His head turns to me.

Wet caramel hair frames his face, and the spray from the shower lashes his spine before streaming down in rivulets over his tightly muscled back and perfectly round ass.

I always knew Jasper's body was great, that he spent long hours training and working out and taking care of himself, but he's…magazine worthy. His body looks cut from stone.

Right along with his cock.

"I'm sorry," I say instantly, frozen on the spot, staring at his well-proportioned body. He's a big man, and so is his…

"No, you're not." His eyes hold a wicked glint as they fixate on me. He straightens, but his hand keeps twisting languidly, casually, like it's perfectly normal for him to jerk off while I watch.

"I didn't mean to barge in here."

"Yes, you did." He smirks at me now, and my knees go a little weak.

He knows me too well to pull off playing stupid. Plus, I promised myself I'd stop apologizing for being myself.

And myself *really* wants to see Jasper naked.

I stand here, mouth popping open and closed like a fish out of water, not sure what to do now because…his hand is still moving. The muscles and veins in his forearms ripple as he pumps.

"Sloane, close the door and sit on the counter."

Pump.

"Pardon me?" My heart thrashes wildly in my chest.

"Shut the door."

Pump.

"And put that tight little ass up on the counter."

Pump.

My cheeks flame.

"We both know you want to watch."

I want to deny it, tell him he's crazy and out to lunch. That we're friends and I don't want to ruin our relationship.

The truth is, though, I want to ruin it. Badly.

My brain might be in bitch mode, but my heart? My heart is in slut mode.

I take a couple of steps and lift my *tight little ass* onto the counter.

Pump.

"Good girl," the toned Adonis in the shower praises me,

and my fingers tighten around the edge of the counter hard enough to snap a nail.

He's so brazen, so unlike the quiet, broody man I know. His eyes lick over my skin like fire, and he never stops jerking himself as he incinerates me. Every muscle in his body is held taut, every line defined. His pecs. His abs. Those sharp V-lines that trail down to where all the action is taking place.

A prim voice inside me tells me the polite thing to do is look away.

But tonight I'm not being the polite woman I've been told I should be.

So I stare. I take it all in. The round smooth head. The thick girth. The smattering of hair that leads to his toned stomach.

I absently lick my lips, and he groans. My gaze snaps up to those navy eyes I know so well. They hold me captive. They're simmering with a heat I've never seen. He's done a good job of looking at me like I'm a friend, but he isn't right now.

He's looking at me like I'm *his*.

"Sloane," he rasps as his fingers curl into the vinyl wall. "Look at me. Talk to me."

I lick my lips again, shifting and feeling how slick I am from watching him. If I slid a hand into my shorts, I could make myself come in seconds. "Keep going" is all I say back, squeezing my thighs together as I revel in the wet slapping sounds of his increased pace.

"You wearing anything under those shorts, honey?" I didn't think his voice could get any lower, but it does.

"No." My heads shakes rapidly, and I swallow.

Jasper's responding groan is pure masculinity. "I could so easily pull them to the side and see it all." His words vibrate through my body, hitting my core with an almost painful pang of longing. For *that*. Exactly what he's describing.

His gaze drops, and I squirm under the weight of it. He stares hard at the apex of my thighs, where my shorts are wedged up just a little too tightly. Then his heated stare snags on my hard nipples, the frantic rise and fall of my chest, before he dives back into my eyes.

The eye contact is unnerving.

It's erotic. He looks wild and undone.

"Fuck," he curses before murmuring, "Sloane," again. His body grows rigid, every hard edge of him strung tight as he tugs at his cock savagely.

And then the first shot of his cum sprays onto the glass wall in front of him. A moan erupts from my throat at the sight. Another surge. And another.

It feels messy and animalistic, and my body is a fiery ball of nerves as I watch him fall apart in front of me with my name on his lips.

I've never felt more important to someone, and the man hasn't even touched me.

His chin drops to his chest, and I watch him pant, his body heaving. I'm in the same boat. It's like I just went through an entire choreography at full intensity.

My eyes bounce between his body and the cum slipping down the glass.

He shifts the showerhead, muscles flexing as he rinses

the glass before turning the shower off and stepping out of the water. He doesn't bother covering himself. There isn't an ounce of self-consciousness in him.

In fact, when he sees me staring, he *smirks*.

Droplets of water hug his skin in a way that makes me irrationally jealous. Then he reaches for a towel, and I see it again.

The tattoo.

"I came in here because I wanted to see that." One shaky hand points at his rib cage.

He towels himself off. "You wanted to watch me fuck my hand while I pretended it was you in those tiny shorts? That's why you barged in here?"

My core clenches, and goose bumps break out along the back of my neck, cool sweat on my temples. I swallow and push ahead. "I'm talking about the tattoo, Jas."

He glances up now, seeing where I'm pointing, and lifts his left arm. I get a full view of the tiny ballerina inked on his skin. It looks like the ones inside a jewelry box I'd been thinking about earlier.

"Oh." He sighs. "That."

"Yeah. That."

Jasper drops the towel and closes the space between us, stark naked and confident, cock still full, looking fucking delicious. He puts one hand on each of my knees and pries them open. Keeping my legs clamped together was dulling the ache in my core, and I whimper before biting down on my bottom lip to shut myself up. I'm soaked, and I'm sure he knows it.

He steps between my spread legs like he knows he belongs there and lifts his left arm to give me a close-up view of the tattoo.

She's dainty and has a serene doll-like expression on her face, hands held up in perfect pirouette position. The ribbons from her pointe shoes wrap around her ankles as she spins, and little dots texture the lace of her tutu.

I reach out and trail the tips of my fingers over the inked tulle as if the texture might be real. But all I'm met with is smooth skin, firm muscle, and a sharp intake of breath from the beautiful man who stands before me. Jasper watches my fingers as I slide them over every detail of the small ballerina tucked safely under his arm.

"What…?" I shake my head, trying to put my words together in coherent order. "What is this?"

"I thought it would look familiar to you," he quips, just letting me soak it in as his hips bump against the inside of my thighs. His thick cock so damn close.

My head tilts, and I peek up at him. "Why?"

He knows I mean why does he have a ballerina inked on him when the rest are patterns—scales, lines, and geometric shapes that remind me of a kaleidoscope.

His Adam's apple bobs. "Because I missed your first professional dance." He clears his throat, staring at my hands and avoiding my eyes. "I wanted to be there so badly after all the times you'd been there for me, so I went and did something that night to commemorate it in my own way."

I blink my lashes rapidly to clear my eyes. "You said you were reviewing game tape."

His right hand squeezes my knee and slides up my thigh, fingers sneaking under the hemline of my shorts, dusting up farther than ever before. "You really think I'd miss your big night to review game tape?"

"I…" I trail off because, no. If I really think about it, I know he wouldn't. He's always been there for me, and that night was an outlier. Looking back, it doesn't make sense for him to miss it at all. "But you've come since then."

"I started coming when I figured your dad wouldn't be there to catch me. Your debut night was too risky. I saw the show though. I came a few weeks into the run and sat in the nosebleeds by myself."

I flatten my palm on his ribs and turn my face up to his, his breath fanning out across my wet lips. "Why?"

His pupils shift between my eyes before he sighs and says, "It took me a while to figure that out. Years, in fact, to sort through my feelings, to make sense of them, figure out where they came from and where they were going. I thought you were just a friend. But him telling me to stay away? Him telling me I couldn't have you? It broke something inside me. Telling me I wasn't good enough for you? All that did was make me want to be good enough for you."

I groan. "You have always been good enough for me."

He grips my chin and regards me carefully under the bright lights. "I never felt like I was. But I do now."

My head swims with his admission. Excitement quarrels with frustration. Desire wars with self-preservation.

"I need a minute" is what I come back with as I gently push him away.

And walk out of the bathroom.

After years of longing for Jasper Gervais, I'm in shock. And I can't think straight with his naked body against me.

I feel wrung out. I feel sad. I feel angry.

I feel so fucking horny I could burst.

21

Sloane

I CRAWL INTO MY CREAKY COT, FEELING IT WOBBLE AS I berate myself for being so stubborn that I thought this rickety little kid's bed—that's probably seen some nighttime accidents—was a better idea than sleeping in the same bed as Jasper.

The thump of his feet across the room actually shakes the cot. I've got my back turned to him and my eyes squeezed shut, so my auditory sense is heightened. I can hear him putting on clothes. The zipper on his bag. The wispy popping noise of his big stupid head coming through the neckhole of his shirt.

The head that pops up every time I close my eyes lately. How could he have seen me this way for so long and said nothing? Watched me date other men? Almost marry one?

I guess I should ask myself the same question. Maybe I have a small stupid head. Maybe we were both so good at hiding it and convincing ourselves that the other could never feel the same that we've spent years staring at each other from a distance.

The entire thing is profoundly stupid.

Suddenly I'm aware of the heat of his body behind mine, his soft exhale at the back of my neck as he drops to his knees beside the cot. "What do you think you're doing?"

His nearness. His voice. It's too much. A shiver races down my spine, and I clamp my lips tight against each other to stifle whatever desperate little noise would leap from them.

"Going to sleep. You should too. Been a long day," I whisper back huskily.

"Do you really think that I'm going to let you sleep on this joke of a cot? Or just walk away after that?"

"I don't need—"

"Come to bed," he urges, not backing down.

"I am in bed," I grumble back stubbornly.

"The big bed, Sloane."

"Seriously, get fucked, Gervais. Go snuggle with your secrets, you exhausting, broody asshole. I'm not leaving this mattress. I'm putting my foot down."

I peek at him over my shoulder, and he gives me a little smirk. "There she is."

"Yes," I huff, turning away and hearing the mattress creak. "Here I am."

Hands reach between the thin mattress and the metal coils beneath it. I go rigid as Jasper drops his mouth to the shell of my ear. "I told you that you aren't sleeping here. And I fucking meant it."

When he lifts me, I squeal. The mattress is so shitty it curls up around me, making me into a little Sloane taco.

"What the hell do you think you're doing?" I shout at him, not wanting to squirm too hard in my precarious position.

He turns with me and the mattress and all the bedding in his strong hold and takes three long strides toward the bed before gently plopping me down on the king-size bed.

I sit up, glaring at him, but he takes no notice. In fact, he turns around, grabs the cot frame, drags it to the door, and tosses it out into the hallway with a loud metal clang. Then he locks the door and struts back to the bed.

Looking all fucking smug and satisfied.

"Did you hear me, Gervais? I asked you what the hell you think you're doing."

He flips the covers back on his side of the bed, a few inches lower than where I'm lying beside him, and flops onto the bed.

"Are you smiling?" My voice is shrill now.

"You told me you weren't leaving that mattress, Sunny. I'm just trying to respect your wishes."

I punch him in the bicep, and he *laughs*.

"Your mood swings are out of control. Do you know that?" I drop back down, turning away from him. I punch my pillow, agitation lining every movement. "Everyone talks about women being too emotional. Too hormonal. I'm inclined to think men are the problem. We women would be just fine without all of you fucking us up."

I hear him struggling to contain his laughter as I lie on

my side, staring at the wall. Silence stretches between us until I wonder if he's fallen asleep.

"You're right," he finally responds.

"I am? About what?" My brain isn't firing because we've talked about so many things today, bickered over so many bygones. I don't even know what I'm right about anymore. Or if I even care about being right.

"Everything."

I don't respond. I lie beside him in the dark room and think. And think. And think. Which leads to a lot of uncomfortable tossing and turning. Because what I'm thinking about is his cum dripping down the glass shower encasement. The way his body flexed. The way my name sounded on his lips.

What I'm thinking about has me unsettled and wishing I weren't lying right next to him. He's too close, and I've seen too much. I wish I could un-turn myself on. But I don't know how.

"Sloane, are you planning on sleeping tonight?" His voice cuts through the quiet room. "Are you uncomfortable? Do I need to get rid of that shitty mattress for you?" I can hear the taunt in his voice.

"I'm extremely comfortable. Thank you very much."

What I mean is, *I'm painfully horny thanks to your little show, but I'm also angry right now.*

He chuckles, a deep, soft rumble in the dark. I feel him move closer. "Are you all wound up, Sunny?" I start when the pad of his finger touches the top of my ear. He traces the outer edge down to the lobe.

When his touch moves to the side of my neck, light and reverent, I shiver.

I shake my head no.

His finger moves down and explores the ridge of my collarbone. "Do you need me to lend you a hand?"

I'm about to say no out loud, but his fingers jump to my mouth, pressing on my lips and silencing me.

He drops his head to my ear. "I saw you in there watching me, Sunny. I saw you squeezing your thighs together. So fucking needy." His fingers leave my lips and move to toy with the thin spaghetti strap that's strung over my shoulder. "Now that I've seen it, I can't unsee it. It's game on for me now. So I'm going to ask you one more time. Do you need me to lend you a hand?"

I sigh, dreaming of letting myself give in, even just for a minute. I want to give in, and I told myself I'd start taking what I want.

"I'm upset. I'm confused. I'm angry about the state of my life. But I… Yes, I want that."

He slides the strap down and presses a kiss to the top of my shoulder. "I know you are." I shiver. "But we can be angry together. Because I can't stand seeing his ring on your finger."

I glance at my flattened hand on the pillow and reach for the ring, suddenly desperate to take it off, but Jasper's opposite hand pushes my arm back down before slipping under the black fabric of my tank top.

He palms my breast, tweaking my nipple. I buck against the sheet covering my body and moan. "I'm going to make you come, with *his* ring on, as one final fuck you to that asshole. And then you can go back to being mad at the world. I don't blame you one bit. And when you're done with having your moment, we'll talk."

I scoff, but it holds no bite. "What does that even mean? *We'll talk?*"

His teeth graze my shoulder. "It means I want you, Sloane. But I'm complicated. The things I like, the things I want, the way my head works. You're so light and shiny. I don't want to tarnish you. I don't want to hurt you." His teeth sink into my shoulder, and I buck back against him, gasping. "More than anything, I don't want to lose you."

"You won't. I promise you won't," I breathe out, gasping as he twists my nipple hard enough to jut up against the edge of being painful.

Jasper chuckles, a dark chuckle that holds so much promise. "Don't make promises you can't keep, Sloane. I have a special knack for pushing people away. They always take off. And they're never all that sad to leave me behind."

Is that really what he thinks? My heart cracks wide open for him. Like it always has.

He glides his hand from under my tank top and lazily trails it down the side of my body, pulling away the flimsy sheet as he goes. So cool and confident.

So practiced.

My knees are tucked up in front of me, so he tugs the hem of my shorts up, exposing the curve of my ass and palming it gently before squeezing with a quiet groan.

And then he's touching me, stroking my core, spreading the wetness he knew was there. He slips it all over my pussy, painting me with my arousal like he's proving some sort of point.

His forehead drops against my shoulder, and he groans so deep, it sounds like it physically pains him to touch me. "So fucking wet for me," he says as his lips drag up my shoulder and he dots slow kisses up my neck toward my ear.

His fingers swirl and press down on my clit as he cups me firmly, making me whimper. Making me sound so fucking needy.

He sucks on my neck, hard enough I know it will leave a mark.

I'm about to protest, but he steals my breath instantly as he pushes two fingers inside me. My body arches to accommodate him.

"Have you been pretending other people were me all these years? Just like me? I bet you have."

"Oh god." I moan and push back on his fingers. He eases them out and twists them back in, painfully slow. I savor the pure longing in every motion.

It's delicious torture. And that's what I like.

"You might be wearing his ring, but we both know it was my cock you were riding in your head," he husks across my skin.

Embarrassment swirls with arousal. He's not wrong. Well, not entirely. He's wrong about Sterling and me having much sex at all. During the short time we were together, I managed to get an awful lot of migraines or be stuck training at the studio until late.

His fingers work me, and I feel myself leaking, growing

more aroused the more he touches me. The more he talks to me.

He pushes up onto one elbow so that he's staring down over me. "Look at me, Sloane."

I've kept my eyes fixed on the darkened wall ahead of me until now. Looking at him feels like…a lot. Like laying myself bare for him when I've told him so much and he's given me so little.

I decide to stay facing the wall, protect what little shreds of my heart and dignity might still be mine. Because Jasper Gervais consumes every other part of me.

He pulls his fingers out, and I roll onto my back, ready to demand he keep going, but as soon as my eyes meet his, his hands are back on me.

"I don't like to ask twice" is all he says before plunging his fingers into my pussy. I clench and moan, relieved to have him back inside me. "Eyes on me, honey."

All I can do is stare at his dark-blue eyes fixed so tightly on me. His body expertly works mine, and that exquisite pressure builds, twisting itself up from every corner of my body.

I'm mad at him for all the things he hasn't told me.

But I'm also attached to him.

Probably already forgiven him.

Most likely irretrievably in love with him.

"When you're fucking someone else, who are you thinking about?" he rasps. "I want to hear you say it."

"Why? Are you jealous?" I prod him, trying to avoid the inevitable, trying to get him to give me some shred of feeling when he's always locked up so damn tight.

He doesn't hesitate. "Jealous is only the tip of the iceberg. You have no idea how many times I've wished I was the man touching you." His hand takes a tour of my curves as he talks. "The man palming these pretty tits. The man with his head between these thighs making you scream. The man filling up this tight little pussy every night."

My breathing goes ragged.

"Tell me, Sloane."

This is one of those things I keep in the dark recesses of my mind, away from the light of day. And now he's asking me to just admit it?

He adds a third finger and strums my clit with his thumb, making me buck wildly.

"You. It's always been you." I spit the words out with force. It's the only way to get them past the logical part of my brain telling me to keep these secrets locked up tight.

"Of course it has," he growls. "And now I'm going to remind you why."

And then his lips crash down on mine, claiming me like I've always dreamed he would.

We pour ourselves into this kiss. The good. The bad. The longing. The hurt. The love.

His body softens, and he drapes himself over me, one hand tangling in my hair while the other works between my legs. I adjust, spreading myself and giving him better access. I give myself to him, and he gives a little piece of himself to me.

After all, he's Jasper. The boy with sad eyes and a heart of gold.

I've always trusted him, and I always will.

The thought of him, of us wraps around the magical way his fingers touch me, and I careen toward that edge. My vision goes spotty, my lips feel numb, and an ache unfurls behind my hip bones.

"Jasper," I whisper between soft, searching kisses. "Oh god. Oh shit. Oh, oh—"

And then I free-fall. My body thrashes as a powerful release washes over me. My vision goes fuzzy at the edges while I luxuriate in the most intense orgasm of my life. And Jasper just keeps holding me tight, watching every little move I make with rapt fascination.

With adoration.

Then his lips move down to dot kisses over my entire face. My fingers tangle in his wet hair, and my body softens when he says, "See, Sloane? You can wear someone else's ring, but we both know you've always been mine."

22

Jasper

I TOLD MYSELF I WOULD ONLY TOUCH HER FOR FOUR SEC-
onds.

I told myself I would only kiss her for four seconds.

I told myself I would only be mad about seeing that sparkly fucking ring dusting over *my* tattoo for four fucking seconds.

And it turns out I'm a big fucking liar.

I'm still touching her. I've still got my fingers stuffed in her tight pussy. My lips are still dragging all over her soft fucking skin.

And I'm still furious that she's wearing that gaudy ring.

Mine.

Why the hell did I tell her that? Why the hell have I gotten so damn possessive since the second I found out she was engaged? Why have I always considered her mine and never felt threatened about it until *him*?

I am one hundred percent out of control, and I *hate* this feeling. Intrusive thoughts rapid-fire into my head, and my walls crumble.

Ruining our friendship.

Her leaving me.

Her hating me.

I let myself think about those things for four seconds. Then I put them in a box and stash them away with all the other thoughts that eat me alive, including the ones I've kept locked up tight about Sloane.

I withdraw from her soft, warm body because I did what I promised—took what I wanted, what she *needed*—and now we're going to sleep.

We'll talk about everything with level heads in the morning, when anger and years of pent-up sexual frustration don't rule us.

From both sides. Because I'm not an idiot. Sloane Winthrop has been turning heads for years, and I'm sure as shit not immune. Her face. Her body. Everything about her is outwardly appealing.

Fucking distracting.

But it's what's inside her that's so special. Her heart. Her brain. Her capacity for empathy.

She's unusual. She's too damn prone to do what people tell her so she doesn't ruffle any feathers. Whether or not she realizes it, she doesn't need another man in her life controlling her.

And my need to take control is a beast I keep locked inside, away from the girl I've put up on a pedestal. I'm not keen to test that shit with the only girl I've ever cared about while we're both feeling so raw.

Because what if I do and she leaves me?

I wouldn't survive it.

With one last kiss to her warm cheek, I pull back, trying to wrap my head around what the fuck I've done in my several seconds of insanity. If four seconds were the goalpost, I blew right the fuck past it.

"More," she murmurs, voice thick with arousal.

My head tips back, and I stare at the ceiling praying for…something. My body riots. I want to give her more. Taste her. Roll her over and cover her body with mine. Watch her come apart over and over again.

Her hands reach for me, and my chest aches as I fight off the urge to reach back.

"That's it tonight, Sunny," I say, my voice soft yet firm. "Come here." I open my arms, ready to shove that nasty mattress onto the floor and hold her all night long.

"What do you mean, that's it?" She turns to face me.

"I mean, that's it. For tonight." I trail a hand through my hair, tugging hard as anxiety lances through me.

You've already fucked this up, you horny fucking idiot.

"I'm not doing more while you're angry at me. I don't want to hurt you."

"You would never hurt me."

A breath hisses out of me. Hearing her say that physically pains me. It undermines all the guilt I like to walk around with because she's right. I would *never* hurt her. "It's complicated" is my stupid response.

She sighs. "Things with you always are." Her hand trails up my forearm. "Tell me what's wrong, Jas. I can see you freaking out in there." Her chin gestures toward my head. She's always known when I'm freaking out. It's like she has a sixth sense for it.

"I just… I like…" *Fuck.* I have no problem telling a random woman what I like sexually. It's power. It's control. It's watching her do exactly what I say. It isn't just sex; it's proving to myself that when I tell someone what to do, the outcome is good. I can make it so damn good for them.

"You like what?" Her eyes are wide, her face so perfect, her tone so accepting.

I'd hate for her to see me differently. I want her, but I'm scared of changing *us* in the process.

"We'll talk tomorrow. Let's sleep." My body hums. I may have lent her a hand, but all I've done is work myself up all over again in the process.

Her gaze searches my face for a few moments. A frustrated laugh bursts from her lips, her head shaking on the pillow as she reaches down to pull the sheet over her body. "Well, at least you're consistent with being terrible at talking about your feelings." She turns over in a huff, muttering, "Boys are so fucking dumb. Thanks for the orgasm."

"It was a good one, wasn't it?" She doesn't need to confirm it. I know it was. I felt it too.

I'm met with a few seconds of silence and then a frustrated "Ugh" before she hunkers down and gives me the silent treatment.

I smile. At least she's beside me. Pissed off and on a

child-sized mattress over the top of the perfectly spacious king is better than across the room and uncomfortable.

I lie here thinking about how this entire night is quintessentially *us*. Highs and lows, pleasure and pain, happiness and sadness. Secrets and truths.

With Sloane, the rest of the shit in the world doesn't matter because when I'm beside her, it always feels right. It soothes me. She soothes me. She always has.

She's that person for me.

I'm out of my depth with her, but this is Sloane. *My Sloane.* No matter what, we're there for each other.

My Sloane.

I think it again, and god, it feels good.

~ ૭

I wake up with Sloane's body draped over mine. Her junky little mattress hangs off the edge of the bed because she clearly pushed it away in the middle of the night.

Last time I woke up like this with her, I snuck out with my tail between my legs. No such inclination hits me today though.

Instead, I lie here and bask in the warm press of her body, her soft breasts pushed up against my chest, and her fingers splayed out over the tattoo I had done to remind me of her.

It's my favorite tattoo.

For my favorite person.

I can still feel the way her body clenched around my fingers last night. The way she got wetter when I made her admit she thought about me while she was with someone else.

There's definitely a part of me that got off on that too. Watching her come apart with his ring on her finger was satisfying.

Fucked up.

And satisfying.

A quiet chuckle rumbles in my chest, and Sloane stirs. I swear I watch awareness overtake her, every limb coming back to life, her hand jerking out from under my shirt.

"Ugh" is the first thing she says as she pulls away from me.

I can't help but laugh. "Nice to see you too, Sunny."

"You and your multiple personalities are already giving me a headache, Gervais." She shoots me a look that might make some men wither, but I just… I don't think there's anything she could do that would scare me off.

"I hear orgasms can help with those," I volley back, refusing to be discouraged by her mood.

She scoffs. Or maybe it's a laugh. I'm not sure because she's already getting up and walking away to the bathroom. My eyes trail over her tight torso and the black cotton shorts that were so easily pulled to the side last night.

My cock thickens as I watch her round ass walk away.

This morning I'm feeling every year of our pent-up frustration and wondering why I bother resisting when everything about us feels so damn inevitable.

23

Jasper

Jasper: Any news?
Harvey: Still nothing.

～～

SHE DOESN'T TALK TO ME AS WE PACK OUR THINGS. SHE doesn't talk to me in the car. She doesn't talk to me the entire way out of the mountains to Violet's farm in Ruby Creek.

Sloane turns the radio up and stares out the window. Right now I can see her doing the same thing in her head she always says she can see me doing. She's freaking out, and I can't blame her. I laid a lot on her.

Her dad being a piece of shit.

Me hiding my feelings for her.

Then I made her come on my fingers while having her admit she thought about me while she fucked her fiancé.

I might have gone too far with that part, but I'm irrationally pleased about it.

My jealous side came out to play, and I didn't hold him back at all. I let him dig his claws in, and now I'm worried I might have embarrassed her in the process.

She told me so much, and I gave her so little in return.

Like I always do.

When we turn onto the road that leads to Gold Rush Ranch, I catch her checking her phone since neither of us had reception coming down the connector.

I want to peek over and see who's texting her. Woodcock hasn't stopped, and her dad hasn't either. But she's playing mad at me right now, so I don't ask.

As we pull up to the sprawling fancy racehorse training facility, I chance another look at her. All the blood has drained from her face, and her eyes are stuck to the screen, finger suspended above it, shaking.

I glance back at the perfectly paved circular driveway, careful to turn wide enough that I don't catch a corner with the trailer. This place looks expensive to fix.

Where Wishing Well Ranch is all wood posts, dirt roads, and rustic finishings, this place is glass, white-vinyl fence posts, modern touches all over the place.

There's a fucking chandelier hung over the entryway to the barn.

And below it is Violet.

Smiling.

And sobbing.

As soon as I put the vehicle in park, she runs to the

truck, blotchy face popping up beside me as she wrenches the door open.

I've barely put my Blundstones onto the asphalt when the words burst from her lips. "They found him! He's safe!" *Safe* comes out as a sob, and she launches her tiny body at me, arms tight on my neck as I lift her off the ground.

They found him. He's safe.
They found him. He's safe.
They found him. He's safe.

The words echo in my brain. If I repeat them enough times, they might actually sink in.

I feel the wetness from Violet's tears. The little sister I still have. My chest cracks open. Because I've been so focused on how Beau's disappearance felt to me, I forgot to think about everyone else.

I've been selfish. So fucking selfish.

"They got him. They got him, Jas."

My arms lock around her as she cries into my shoulder, my own eyes filling. "Where? How?" I murmur against her hair.

"I don't know. We've all been trying to call you, but it goes to voicemail. No reception, I'm guessing. All I know is they found him and he's getting medical attention. I'm sure Dad will hear more."

We both sigh, and I slowly drop her to the ground. She's so small but somehow looks even tinier right now.

Her head turns, and she sees Sloane standing at the front of the truck, watching us, tears streaming down her face. "He's okay?" Her voice breaks, and her hand flies over mouth to hold back the sob.

Violet nods, holding her arms open to her cousin for a hug. Sloane flies toward her, the two women holding each other and crying.

I wipe my nose and tip my head up to the sky, hoping the tears welling might leak back into wherever they came from.

The sky is perfectly fucking blue, like Sloane's eyes. Not a cloud as far as the eye can see. Not for the first time, I wonder what Beau is looking at right now. Bright hospital lights? An aircraft carrier of some sort? The back of his eyelids?

I see Cole, Violet's husband, approaching us. Appearing all dark and foreboding—but he isn't. Well, unless you're the dumb sucker who slighted his wife—then he has the same switch Beau does as a military member.

The switch that flips, and they turn into the man who can kill you with their bare hands.

He gives me a nod as his hand slides over the back of Violet's head, and I itch to touch Sloane with the same comfort, the same possession.

When his wife turns into him and disappears into the cage of his arms, it's Sloane who turns to look up at me.

"He's okay," she says again.

I nod, feeling my throat go thick and the bridge of my nose sting.

She reaches for me at the same time I reach for her. All the tension between us is washed away by how desperately we need each other. One of her hands grips my shirt while her right one slides inside my jacket and flattens over the tattoo. I squeeze her tight, and when her forehead presses to my chest, I drop my lips to the crown of her hair.

Like always.

"We're all okay," I reply roughly against her hair.

Pure relief courses through my veins.

She nuzzles against me, and I nuzzle against her. We latch on to each other like we have for the better part of our lives.

Because no matter what else is going on in the world, everything is better with her in my arms.

24

Sloane

Sloane: Give your boys hugs from me. And yourselves. I can't believe it. <3

Summer: I can't stop crying. I'm so relieved. We're sending hugs back to you.

Willa: I'll hug Cade for you if you bang Jasper for me.

Sloane: When I bang Jasper, I'm banging him for myself.

Summer: Ooooooo!

Willa: Possessive. I like it.

Willa: Wait. Did you say WHEN?!

I'm HAPPY AND WRUNG OUT ALL AT ONCE. I'M BACK IN A HUGE truck, but this time, Violet is behind the wheel. I'm sitting in the front passenger seat, and all three of her closest friends are in the back.

Billie, who has a knack for making us all laugh, proclaimed that unloading hay is a "boy" job and we should all go get wine to drink straight from the bottle. She's a bit scary if I'm being honest.

She's like Willa.

On crack.

Then there's Mira with her black hair, keen eyes, and knowing smirk. I feel like she knows all my deepest darkest secrets just by glancing at me.

And Nadia, who's a little younger, is so beautiful I can't stop staring at her. It's like she strutted right off a Victoria's Secret runway and onto the farm.

They chatter happily in the back while Violet and I sit in a companionable but stunned silence up front. It's like I didn't realize how much tension I was carrying over Beau until the weight lifted.

Now I'm hit with a full-body exhaustion that stretches from the tips of my fingers to the ends of my toes. I could sleep for a week.

"You okay?" Violet glances at me, high ponytail flipping over her shoulder as she does.

"Yeah." I sigh. "Just so, so tired."

"You guys had a long journey."

"That we did."

Long doesn't even begin to cover it.

A smile tugs at the corner of her lips. "I always wondered when you two would notice the other."

My head flips to her. "Pardon?"

"You and Jasper. You've both been so in love with each

other for so long. I saw that hug. Plus, I saw the look on his face that day when I first spilled the beans about your engagement. And on your wedding day?" She snorts. "I think he was looking for a reason to barge in there and break you out. Poor emotionally stunted idiot that he is."

I just blink, mind whirring. "He's not emotionally stunted." I always jump to defend Jasper, no matter what.

Violet hits me with a sidelong glance. "Yeah, he is. I married one of those, so I know them when I see them."

"Wait," Nadia says. "Aren't you guys cousins?"

Mira's finger waves back and forth. "No. He's the adopted brother."

I see Nadia's smile in the rearview mirror. "Fuck. That's hot."

I groan but don't get a word in edgewise before Billie pipes up. "You should fuck him."

I can't help but laugh. My body shakes with it because this scenario is just too much. Emotions are too high. I'm delirious.

Violet laughs too. "Billie, that's always your advice."

"I tried," I say from behind my hands because hiding while I admit this feels easier. "He said we needed to talk first."

"But something happened?" Violet can't hide her curiosity. She always was the chatty girl-talk type.

"Yes." I lower my hands, staring at the roof of the truck. "Something happened."

Billie hums thoughtfully from behind me. Like she's about to offer profound advice. "You should demand he fuck you."

I snort, and a different type of tears well in my eyes. They're the good kind that come from laughing and trying to hold it back. I glance over my shoulder into the back seat.

"It worked for me," Mira says with a feline smile on her lips.

"Ew. Don't tell me these things about my brother, please." Nadia turns away and stares out the window, a look of exaggerated disgust on her face. "You could do what I did and just drive him insane until he snaps."

Billie pipes up again. "No. Pull a Violet. Just send him nudes."

Violet doesn't shy away from Billie's statement like she might have when she was younger. Instead, a proud smile touches her face as she drives down the snowy road until we pull up to Neighbor's Pub, the most run-down bar and liquor store I've ever seen. A flashing sign advertises, "COLD BEER AND WINE!!!"

Exclamation marks and all.

It feels suitably dingy for the updated version of me I'm working on.

I like it already.

"Or just do what I did and make him so jealous he loses his mind, bangs on your door, and then bangs you on the kitchen counter," Billie adds.

I laugh harder, so does everyone else, and warmth flickers in my chest. I'd love friendships like this in my life. I think I could have them with Willa and Summer.

When we pile out of the truck, moods lighter from

cracking jokes about my hot mess of a personal life and flaming dumpster fire of a friendship/relationship/lifelong crush turned who-the-fuck-knows-what, I ask, "Do you think they sell Buddyz Best Beer here?"

"Fuck yes, they do," Billie calls over her shoulder as she heaves the wooden door open.

Suddenly I don't feel so bad about everything anymore. Everyone I love is safe and content. Violet has a happy little crew here. They found Beau. Things between Jasper and me are messy right now, but…it's us.

We always end up back together somehow.

We just need to stop fighting it.

Mira's husband, Stefan, cooks us a massive gourmet meal. Over dinner everyone in Billie and Vaughn's expansive house clearly shares my feeling of relief.

Vaughn cracks jokes that lighten the mood considerably. Cole and Griffin are quiet but friendly. The sense of family between all the friends warms my heart. Wine flows easily, and so does the conversation.

The dining-room windows look out over the pristine farm, and all the kids have crashed out in the enormous sunken living room while a Disney movie still rolls on the screen.

It's cozy and comforting, and I can tell this group of people gets together like this often. There's a level of comfort between them I want to curl up in, but I still feel slightly removed from it all. I'm still an interloper here.

It just isn't Chestnut Springs.

I keep peeking at Jasper across the table from me, wanting to see him smile, wanting to see him looking relieved and happy after weeks of seeing him look devastated.

He's not wearing a cap tonight, and it makes it so easy to see every expression that touches his face. I want to know he's okay, but I still quickly glance away when his eyes lock on mine.

My cheeks heat and my spine tingles, and my brain plunges me back into last night when he slid his fingers between my legs and made me come harder than I ever have.

I told him so much, and he told me so little. He still held back, and that stung. I've always felt like I'm his person, his safe place to let it all out, but in the past couple of days, it's come to my attention that he still keeps so much locked up tight.

He hasn't told me everything, and that shouldn't matter. We all have those secrets, I guess.

But it does. I want to know. I always want to be the person who knows the most about him. That's always been the one thing I've had with him that no other woman can claim.

I might not know his body. I might not have memorized all his tattoos. But I know his heart. I'm intimately familiar with all the pieces of it he's given to me over the years.

But they aren't enough.

I want the rest of it too.

When a lull in the conversation hits, I stifle a yawn.

Violet, sitting beside me, pats my knee. "Tired?"

I nod. "Yeah. Think I'm going to pack it in for the night."

"Okay. I took your bags to the little A-frame cottage near the creek. That way the kids won't wake you at like five in the morning."

"Perfect."

Billie leans over and whispers in my ear, "That cottage has become known as the Love Shack around here."

Violet gives her an unimpressed look. "That's what we called it when you and Vaughn lived there."

Billie holds her hands up in surrender. "Right. I'm just saying there's good 'fuck me' juju in there."

I push to stand, smiling at their antics, but freeze and glance down at the sassy brunette. "Wait. Is this the kitchen counter place?"

She shrugs with a knowing grin. "I'm a clean freak. Don't worry. I sanitized it."

I roll my lips together to keep from barking out a laugh, but Jasper draws my attention from across the table. "I'll go with you." He nods to the men at the other end of the table. "Thank you for dinner. It was excellent."

There are hugs and "Good nights," but they all blend into the heavy pounding of my heart because within minutes it's just Jasper and me walking on a quiet farm under the dark night sky.

We've been here before.

In the dark together.

But it's never felt quite like this.

Jasper enters the code into the lock on the door. The tension between us is so thick right now that neither of us even laughs about that code being 6969. I'm tired and wound up all at once.

We step inside, and I toe my shoes off, keeping my eyes trained on the floor. I showered and changed at the main house when we arrived but haven't been into this cottage yet.

It's a cozy open concept with exposed wood beams. I assume the flight of stairs leads to a bedroom. Or bedrooms? I'm not sure because it doesn't seem like there's enough space for more than one.

But no one even asked us about that. So either there are definitely two beds or my cousin and her friends are playing matchmaker in the fucking Love Shack.

"Cute cottage," I say absently as I look around.

Jasper's tightly corded back strains against the navy T-shirt he's wearing as he pours himself a glass of water from the dispenser on the fridge. I take a moment to ogle the broad expanse of his shoulders, his posture always so immaculate, and the way it tapers down to his waist.

To that round hockey-boy butt.

I tip my head up and stare at the ceiling, all wooden planks and cross beams. Industrial wrought-iron light fixtures and a fan hang above me, a funky contrast to the Persian rug beneath my feet. Cushy leather couches face the tall A-frame windows.

"You must be feeling relieved about Beau," I say right as Jasper turns and leans against the kitchen counter. I absently wonder if it's *that* counter but decide against bringing it up right now.

"Yeah. Will be good to see him. Hopefully, we'll get more information from Harvey once he gets there."

I nod. We found out later in the day Harvey was flying out east to a military hospital where they had transferred Beau so he could be with him.

"Are we going to stick around here at all? Or head straight back?"

His head tilts, and the expression he gets when he's heading out on the ice paints his features. The focus. The edge. The narrowed gaze.

"I don't know, Sloane. What do you want?"

I sigh heavily, rolling my shoulders back and holding my head high where I stand near the front door. "For once, I would like you to tell me what's going on in your head. I'm tired, Jasper. Tired of guessing, tired of tiptoeing around everyone else's feelings, tired of giving so much and getting so little back. And not just from you, from everyone. Can you just tell me something real for once? What are you feeling? What is our plan? Are we staying here? Or are we driving back? It's really not complicated. And since you're the one on a timeline with the team, I'm going to assume that you have a plan. Because you always do."

He glares at me, so I keep going. "You just, *as usual*, don't feel the need to talk about it." I wave a hand in front of me, frustration bleeding into my tone. "Or anything, for that matter. I guess it's much better for you to keep everything locked inside and then blindside me with all of your shit at once. So, like, can I have a heads-up or something?"

I watch his jaw pop, fingers clenched around the glass

of water, forearm rippling as he squeezes it. We stare each other down, and I dive into those eyes I know so well, willing him to say *something*. I've spent years monologuing while he listens, but I'm done with playing that role for him now. Frustration simmers in my chest before leaping out.

"Oh my god, Jasper! Fucking say something!"

"I feel like I could crumble under the weight of not wanting to disappoint you. I'm paralyzed by my fear of losing you."

His words suck all the air out of the room. Like a punch straight to the gut. I remember falling off the tire swing on the ranch as a child and gasping for breath.

He was there…rubbing my back and telling me to stay calm.

I open my mouth to respond, but he cuts me off.

"The thought of needing you this badly and letting you down." He drops my gaze, shaking his head. "It fucking kills me."

"You're never going to lose me," I whisper back, itching to rush forward and touch him but wanting to give him space. I don't want to corner him or smother him.

"I almost did lose you." He takes a couple of steps forward, and I think he's going to come to me. But he places the glass of water on the marble island before propping his hands there, like that island is the only thing keeping him from moving across the room toward me again.

As though he's fighting to keep himself away from me.

"On that mountain runaway lane. To your dad's maneuvering. To *him*," he adds, eyes dropping to the ring on my finger, the one that clearly did not prevent me from crossing that line with Jasper at all.

"Then fucking take me back already! I've been dreaming of you for literal years and never knew you saw me as anything other than a friend." He flinches, but I'm done holding back. "I've been licking those wounds for so damn long, Jasper. And you've been too chickenshit to say anything. So say it already. Tell me what you want!"

He groans and drops his head for a beat before leveling me with his midnight stare. "That's what I want. That's what I get off on. Telling you what to do and having you listen. Control." His cheeks flush bright under his stubble. "I've tried not to. But with everything that's happened in my life, it's just become…" He runs an agitated hand through his hair. "Part of me. But I don't want you to do something that makes you uncomfortable just to give me that. That's not what you need. It's not what I want for you. I see you. I see what you've been through. I've seen these men in your life telling you what to do, using you as a pawn. And I don't want to be another asshole telling you what to do."

Arousal unfurls in my gut, heat leaching out into the tip of every limb. "Don't you get it, Jas? I've seen all the darkest parts of you, and I'm still here. I still want more. Stop trying to scare me away. It isn't going to work."

He looks pained now. "I don't want to be another man who—"

My hand slashes out in front of me, and I cut him off. "You talk about not telling me what to do, that you don't want to let me down, but I'm sick of being treated like I'm too fragile or too pristine. I don't want to be a damsel in distress! So stop treating me like one. I'm not a trophy. You aren't *telling* me to do anything! I'm telling you I want you to take me, and you're sitting here, patting my head like I'm stupid, telling me I don't know what I want. If I don't like something, I will fucking tell you. But for the love of god, stop deciding what I like or don't like. What I can or cannot endure. What feels good or doesn't. Stop holding back with me."

My breathing is labored by the time I finish. Saying what's on my mind feels *good*. I feel empowered and frustrated and…alive.

"How many times do I need to tell you for you to believe me? Before I get to hear it back?" I shake my head in disbelief at this man I know so damn well yet not at all. "It's always been you, Jasper. It will always be you."

I sigh heavily. "Please tell me what to do with that."

25

Jasper

I listen to Sloane, all fierce and determined, laying into me and being so damn right.

She's telling me to take what I want, taking what she wants, and there's nothing holding me back. They've found Beau. I'll be able to get back to the team. The only thing left unfinished is Sloane and me.

The restraint inside me snaps as I stare back at her. Chest heaving. Cheeks flushed. It's like a shoelace tugged too fucking tight. I've been pulling back so hard that my steady hand flies back with the weight of my resistance.

Fair, unfair. Appropriate, inappropriate. It all fades away under the simmering rage and arousal of so many missed years with this woman. We came close to missing so much more.

I don't want to miss another second. And she *told* me to stop holding back.

My voice comes out harsh and gravelly when I say, "Take your clothes off, Sloane."

She startles ever so slightly, but her top teeth sink into her bottom lip, and I know she wants this just as badly as I do.

I push myself back into the countertop behind me so that I have a better view across the open living space, feeling the bite of the edge against my palms. If this is what she wants, I plan to take my time.

I plan to savor her.

If Sloane says she can handle me, then she's right. Who am I to tell her she can't?

She flicks open the top of her baggy jeans and drops them around her slender ankles before stepping out of them. Those crystal-blue eyes don't leave mine for a single second. Holding my gaze, she unbuttons the soft flannel shirt she's wearing, light pink and cream plaid falling open to expose the unpadded pink-lace bralette hugging her breasts.

I rake my eyes over her long lean limbs. Pink scraps of nothing cover the places where I plan to spend the entire night.

When the shirt clears her wrists and falls to the floor behind her, a smirk touches her lips. She stands there not looking the least bit self-conscious.

In fact, the way her tongue slides over her lips tells me she's nothing short of eager.

There's an alluring blush to her pale cheeks, and her skin, lit only by the floor lamp in the corner, has a golden glow.

"All of them." I gesture a hand down her body, watching

the flush creep over her collarbones and toward her nipples that are pushing against the delicate fabric.

When she removes the bralette, I don't bother pretending I'm not staring at her body. Her breasts are perfect, small and perky, with pale, dusky nipples pointing straight at me. Begging for my attention.

I groan at the sight and watch her thighs clamp together. Her stomach clenches.

"I bet you're fucking soaked," I murmur, watching her thumbs hook into the waistband of the matching panties.

She tilts her head and gives me a coy shrug. My dick twitches.

When her panties are down around her ankles where they belong, I peruse my way back up her legs, pausing on her pussy and the glimmer of wetness between her soft lips. "You're perfect."

"Thank you," she whispers back, breathless.

I lick my lips and adjust myself in my pants. This is pure torture, but I think we both like it. We're both about the anticipation. The ten feet that still separate us practically hum with it.

"Use one finger—only one—and show me how wet you are, Sloane."

Her chest rises and falls while her eyes remain latched onto my face. Arousal is written all over her, and the little voice in my head that told me she might hate me if I revealed this domineering side of myself stays blissfully quiet.

I see a sparkle in her eye. No hesitation. Instead, a challenge.

Her hand slides down her stomach, and with a quiet moan, she pushes one slender finger into her pussy.

It slips right in, confirming what I already knew. Seconds later she holds one trembling hand up, index finger soaked with her arousal.

"Are you nervous?"

"No. God no" is her response.

"Good. Now put that finger in your mouth and clean it off."

A light, disbelieving chuckle escapes her, and I can't help but crack a smile. Only she would laugh right now. As she turns her palm toward her face, showing me the back of her hand, the smile melts from my face. Because my eyes catch on a flash of light attached to her finger as she slides it between her lips.

My fingers grip the counter behind me, to the point of pain, while I try to hold back the green-eyed monster.

But I fail.

"Sloane."

"Mm-hmm," she hums, still sucking on her finger, giving me blue doe eyes.

I want to ask her how it tastes.

Instead, I snap.

I point at the floor beneath my feet and say, "Lose that fucking ring and crawl."

Her mouth pops open, hand falling down, and her lashes flutter a few times as she processes what I just said.

But she doesn't hesitate. She *smirks*.

She yanks the ring off her finger and tosses it across the

room before dropping to her knees. I thought she'd falter. I think there's a part of me that thought I could prove to myself I was right and she'd hate me for this. That I could push her too far and she'd tell me to fuck off.

But her hands come to the floor, and she crawls for me. The small house is dead silent as her body moves with such inherent grace, like there's music playing in her head.

"Like this?" Her heart-shaped lips curve up seductively as toned arms stretch out before her, and I have to blink a few times to believe what I'm seeing. She's feline in her movements, not shy at all. But she's spent years performing onstage.

Soft and quiet doesn't have to mean shy.

And my girl doesn't look shy at fucking all right now.

"Yes," I growl, my body coiling tighter at the sight. When she gets close enough to kneel at my feet, my entire body shakes with restraint.

And for what?

She's still looking up at me like I hung the moon.

Like she always has.

"Fuck, Sloane." The sight of her stripped bare below me feels so good it's almost unbearable. I let go of the counter and drop to a crouch, gripping her chin and searching her eyes for any glimpses of discomfort, but all I see is need.

My opposite hand slips between her thighs, fingers pushing through her wet folds gently. She's soaked.

She whimpers but doesn't drop my gaze, so I continue playing with her cunt. I don't push in, just tease. I watch her squirm, her hips trying to buck against my hand.

But she plays the game so perfectly. She just stays there and lets me explore.

"Did you like crawling for me?" I ask.

She smiles, but there's a flash of sadness in her eyes. An instant shot to my chest. "Jasper, it feels like I've been crawling after you for years. This is nothing new for me."

Her words strike a blow I didn't see coming.

My fingers stop moving, and I cup her head, whispering the words "I'm sorry" in a cracked voice. I press my lips to hers, falling to my knees for her. "God. I'm so fucking sorry."

I take her mouth, clutching her naked body to me, wishing I could go back in time and tell her everything when I first started feeling it. But I'll settle for right now since it's the best I've got.

The kiss starts off with us clamping our mouths together, needing to be joined, but quickly turns frantic. It takes on an edge of frustration as her teeth nip at my bottom lip and her hands grapple with the hem of my shirt.

It's pulled off and discarded within seconds. And then I'm standing, lifting her small body with me and taking a couple of steps across the kitchen.

With one swipe of my arm, everything on the island flies onto the floor with a loud clatter. Fruit. A bowl. A magazine. My glass of water lands on the opposite side of the room and shatters into a thousand tiny pieces against the hardwood floor. The perfectly clean cottage turned upside down in mere seconds.

None of that shit matters because legs wrap around my waist. Lips pepper kisses all over my face, down my neck.

Fingers tug at my hair. She's attacking me with a fervor I've never experienced.

One I've never felt inclined to match until her.

Sex has always been a game. Another event for me to control. But there's nothing in control about us right now.

And I don't even care.

I lie her back on the island, wanting to explore her. She hisses, and her back arches away from the cold marble, pushing her perfect tits up in the process.

I don't know where to look first, but like always, it's her eyes that catch my attention. All those blues. My gaze travels down the slender line of her neck and detours to the stray strands of soft blond hair that are plastered to her wet, puffy lips.

My hands slide over her waist, shaping it, and I revel in how big my hands look wrapped around her. I cup her breasts, the perfect size to grip.

I squeeze and flick a thumb over her pointed nipples, noting the way her back arches again when I do. "You like that?"

"Yesss," she hisses, eyes closed now, tongue darting out over her lips in the most distracting way. I can't wait to see how they look wrapped around my cock.

But first, I keep sliding my hands up her body, noting the way gooseflesh crops up in my wake. When I get to her shoulders, I trace fingers over the line of her collarbone while the other hand continues moving up and wraps around that pretty, slender throat. The way she carries herself is always so regal.

I've dreamed about wrapping a hand here.

So I do.

I squeeze, but not too hard, leaning down over her, giving the lobe of her ear a quick nip before asking, "What about that, Sloane? Do you like that?"

"Yes."

Her sure response is a shot of electricity straight to my cock. My fingers press a bit harder, and I watch her cheeks turn a soft red. Her legs clamp tighter around my waist. I ease off and drop my lips to hers, stroking her neck softly before I kiss my way back down to her breasts. Her nails slide up my back, over my shoulders, and down my arms reverently.

I start soft with one nipple, licking and kissing, getting off on the way she moans and squirms. The way her nails dig into my skin—just a little bit feral.

And then I give it one hard pull, grazing my teeth as I go. It's the way she gasps and bucks that really gets me.

"So sensitive," I murmur, moving to the other side and giving her the same treatment. I get her comfortable and then lay in with a little pressure. A little bite.

Her nails tangle in my hair and scratch at my scalp.

Then I'm licking my way down her stomach. She squirms as I slide my tongue just beneath the line of her hip bone, so I spend extra time exploring. When I drag my teeth there, she makes a whining noise.

I plant a palm in the middle of her chest and press her down. "Lie still, Sloane. Let me enjoy myself."

"Fuck you, Jasper," she huffs and wiggles harder.

I chuckle and move my hand back around her neck. "You will be, Sunny. Just not until I say so."

26

Sloane

I MAKE THAT SAME DAMN NOISE WHEN HE MOVES TO THE opposite hip. I never knew this was a sensitive spot for me, but Jasper homed in on it instantly. My pulse thumps under the palm of his hand. It speeds up when his teeth drag over my hip bone, and his grip around my throat tightens every time I move.

Heat suffuses every limb. My pulse thrums everywhere. I've never focused entirely on one thing except for when I'm dancing. But I am now. My mind doesn't wander to my to-do list or the next episode of my favorite show. It stays on Jasper and the way he's playing my body like an instrument he's known his entire life. Like a virtuoso.

As much time as I've spent having sex with Jasper in my head, I didn't expect him to do things to me I've only read about or watched but never had the nerve to ask for. Not sure the boys I dated would have indulged me anyway.

But Jasper isn't a boy. He's a man.

His hand moves away from my throat, and I almost want to beg him to put it back. He trails it down the center of my body and then taps on my hip bone and says, "Now spread these pretty thighs for me."

My heart rate ratchets up when I catch his eye in the softly lit kitchen.

He's not brooding Jasper right now, and he's not sweet Jasper either.

He's… I don't know. I don't recognize this look, but I like it. I love it. I especially love being on the receiving end of it.

Without another thought, I unlatch my legs from around his waist. I'd been holding him to me for fear he might pull away again, but it feels like we've moved past that phase tonight.

It feels like he's seeing me in a different light.

I push away any shreds of shyness and open my legs, baring myself to him. Panting and dripping.

I'm ready to beg him to touch me when his big warm palms land on my inner thighs, smoothing up the insides toward my knees and pushing me farther open.

"So fucking flexible." His thumbs brush against my skin, and I swear I could come just from him running his hands all over me.

I'm ready to explode, and we've barely done anything.

"So fucking pretty." His dark-blue eyes drag over my body like fingertips, their smoldering weight grazing over my skin as he pulls me up to sitting. "Are you on birth control,

Sloane?" He holds my thighs open, staring between them. Making me squirm.

"Yes," I hiss. "Yes. IUD." Apparently, I'm monosyllabic right now.

"Anything else you need to tell me?" I know what he's asking. He's trying to ask it delicately. He's being responsible, but it hits a nerve all the same.

I sit up. "I don't know, Jasper. Why don't you tell me? You're the one who's always traipsing around with different women."

His fingers pulse on my legs, and his eyes snap to mine. A knowing grin touches his lips. "I like you with your claws out, Sloane." He picks my hands up from where they're planted against the counter and places one on each of my knees. "Is this uncomfortable? Sitting here?"

Uncomfortable? Is he kidding me? I don't even know what comfort is anymore. All I can think about is coming with his hands on me. "No."

"Good." He licks his lips as he stares down at me, biting down on his bottom lip to stifle a grin. "Stay like that."

And then he turns and...walks away.

I flip my head to watch him. Ready to snap at him. "What the—"

"I was about to tell you I've never had sex without a condom, Sloane." He bends down and picks the bowl up off the floor. "I was about to tell you the only way you'd look prettier was with my cum in that tight little cunt."

"Jesus," I mutter, feeling a blush overtake my entire body.

He casually picks up a banana and puts it in the bowl,

followed by a couple of apples that must be bruised to shit now. "But you had to make that snarky little remark. A jealous little dig. So now you can wait."

He shakes his head, and my hands tremble on my knees. Who knew sitting here exposed—waiting for him to fuck me—could actually make me hotter.

I start to pant, and he picks up a broom and dustpan from the corner, carefully sweeping up the bits of glass behind where I'm seated.

"What the hell are you doing?" I ask, almost laughing at how insane this is.

"Can't have my girl stepping on glass, can I?" He swoops down and sucks on my neck while heading to the garbage. Hard enough I know it will leave a mark.

I thought my heart was racing before. But now? Now it may have stopped altogether.

He washes his hands in the kitchen sink before he comes back, towering over me, all shreds of playfulness gone.

He bends down and kisses the top of my shoulder. "I've spent a long time thinking I don't deserve you," he whispers. Bending farther, his lips move to the top of my hand that's still clasped over my knee. "That you're too good for someone like me."

"Jasper." I reach out and cup his cheek with my hand, one leg hooking him back to me as he stands up straight. When he's saying things like this, I want to see his eyes. I don't really give a fuck about following his orders.

There's no reproach though. Instead, he tilts his head into my touch, and his big warm body folds around mine.

"I don't think I suffer from that way of thinking anymore. Suddenly I don't really care about deserving you when it's so damn clear you belong to me and always have."

He turns his head and presses a kiss into the center of my palm and moves back down my body as he methodically lays me flat on the cool counter again. My rock-hard nipples rise and fall as I breathe hard. He leans down in front of my spread pussy, pushing me farther across the counter as he pulls each of my legs over his shoulders.

Dark blues still on baby blues.

"But Sloane?"

"Yeah?" I reply instantly, pushing up onto my elbows to better see him.

"I'm done sharing."

Then his head drops to my pussy, and he makes me see stars with every perfectly placed lick, every growl vibrating through my body. Even the pads of his fingers digging into my thighs make me wild. His hands never stop moving, exploring—driving me insanc.

I thrash against the hard marble when he sucks my clit into his mouth firmly. His tongue working softly and then flicking sharply. Sliding straight into me as he fucks me with it. He adds two fingers, curling them up into a spot I've only reached with a toy. But Jasper? He finds it on the first try, shoving me toward release. Just a steam train barreling down a track to ecstasy.

The rush of it all flushes through my body.

"Jasper, I'm going to—"

He pulls away. Mouth gone. Hand gone. Body *aching*.

"What are you doing?" I whine, tipping my head back in frustration.

He smirks at me, licking his lips purposefully as he pushes to stand above me. His hands are at the button on his jeans, casually popping it open and dropping the zipper. I see what looks like a painful erection, ready to bust through the dark denim.

"Making you wait," he responds as he shucks them off and rubs his cock through the fabric of his boxers.

I clench and release at the gravel in his tone, and his gaze drops between my legs.

"Why?" My voice is breathy when I reach down to touch myself. His eyes flare as I circle my clit shamelessly.

He allows me to get away with it for a few seconds before he lifts my hand and sucks that naughty finger into his mouth. With a loud pop, he pulls it out. "Because I like to watch you squirm. I like to make you wait."

He tugs his boxers off, and…my eyes are stuck…latched onto his long hard length.

I wish I had something cool and sexy to say after everything he's told me tonight. But his dick has quite literally rendered me speechless.

"Something you wanna tell me, Sunny?"

"You're so fucking hot" is what I blurt.

Only Jasper Gervais would have a body like a titan, a face like a model, and a cock like a porn star.

With a deep chuckle, he runs the fat head up and down my slit, taking a few extra seconds to press hard against my clit. I bite down on my lip to keep from moaning, from sounding too desperate.

I watch him run his cock all over my pussy. Fisting it firmly. Teasing me with the tip. Pushing it in, watching my body stretch for him, and pulling it back out.

"You want me to fuck you, Sloane?"

"Yesss," I hiss out.

He lifts his thick cock up and slaps it back down lewdly on my wet core. "Ask politely."

"You've got some nerve, Gervais," I say, going hot all over.

He quirks a brow as if to say, *Go on.* And I didn't make it this far to back down now, so without hesitation, I say, "Yes, *please.*"

My entire body is one huge heartbeat. Just a pulse covered by desperate flesh. I've never felt so wanton, and I've never felt so desired.

Like we're two opposite ends of a magnet, there's no resisting the pull. There are forces beyond us at work now, and we're at their mercy.

Maybe it's science.

Maybe it's fate.

But when Jasper slides himself inside me and murmurs with a playful smile, "Such a polite girl," all I know is that it's *right.*

We're right.

My lashes flutter down as I struggle to accommodate his size. My legs shake as they wrap around his waist and latch together over his firm ass.

His hands start on my thighs and slide sensually up over every curve while he's seated inside me. Fingers pulse over my breasts, and his hips shove forward even though he's as far in as he can get. His arms wrap around my rib cage, and he pulls me up to him, hands splaying possessively over my back as the fullness inside me shifts.

"Jasper, it's too much," I murmur, dropping my forehead against his chest.

He plants a kiss against my hair and pulls out, like he's going to grant me some reprieve. His head drops beside my ear, and he whispers, "You can take it," right before driving back in.

"Oh god!" I call out as he works himself in and out. Not too fast, but not too slow. Every movement is measured—controlled—and, with him, *of course* it is.

His career.

His mental game.

His protective streak.

His trauma.

It all makes so much sense.

"Fuck, Jasper!" I gasp as he works me over. He kisses me hard. He brings me to the edge and pulls us both back. I let him take care of me the way he needs to, and I revel in it. I trust him so implicitly. It comes so easily.

I bask in his attention, in the way his hands move over my skin, the way his lips fit so perfectly against mine, the way he chants my name in my ear as he moves against me. Hips slamming roughly, making a slapping noise against my ass for several seconds before easing off and rendering me senseless with slow, deep strokes that keep the pressure in my core building in the most delicious way.

"You're so fucking perfect," he murmurs. "So fucking tight."

It feels like I'm riding waves in the ocean, my body soft and relaxed, the white noise of water tumbling in my ears accompanied by his deep rumblings of worship.

My body feels more his than mine, and I'm entirely at peace with that notion.

I can feel every ridge, every vein, every pulse of him inside me. And it makes me wild. I scratch at him, my nails raking against his back. Urging him to give me more. I bite at him. I'm downright feral with my need for him.

"Closer. Deeper. More," I beg, and he gives me everything I ask for and more. Eyes always coming back to mine, watching me so damn closely. Cataloguing every little motion, every gasp of pleasure.

Learning me as I learn him.

"Jasper…" I moan as he carefully lays me back down on the chilly marble, hands roaming reverently, fluttering over my throat for a moment before shifting down to my hips. "Please don't stop. I'm so close."

My hands wrap around his veined forearms, and my eyes sweep over his perfectly defined torso. It's dotted with perspiration and goes taut every time his hips flex forward into me.

He glances down at my left hand before hitting me with that intense eye contact of his again. "Tell me you're mine, Sloane." His thrusts slow, and the look he gives me shows a flash of insecurity.

One that doesn't need to be there.

Without hesitation, I say the words. "I'm yours, Jasper. I always have been."

Satisfaction flares in his dark irises, and he unleashes on me, one hand slipping down to rub my clit while he fucks me hard enough to make my body slide and stick against the marble.

"And you always will be," he grunts out as we combust, each of us belonging more to the other than to ourselves as I feel him jerk and spill himself inside me.

27

Jasper

I DROP BACK DOWN OVER HER PERFECT FUCKING BODY, dragging soft, messy kisses over her sweat-slicked chest. I work to get my vision straight, blinking and willing my heart rate to even out.

All my hottest sexual fantasies have featured Sloane.

And none of them were as hot as the real thing.

Her fingers comb through the back of my hair. "It's a shame that I've peaked at only twenty-eight," she breathes out raggedly. "I'm sure every sexual experience will be downhill after that."

I chuckle against her, and it vibrates through her body. I love feeling this connected to her right now. Like I could send her subliminal messages and she'd just *know*.

"Sunny, we're only getting started." I pull away, and my cock slips from her heat. A rush of cum follows, spilling out. Holding her gaze for a beat, I reach down and use one finger to slide it back in. My cock hardens as I work her, practically ready to go again when she whimpers and clenches around me.

I stand, wanting to see her right now. Not just being mine, but really looking like mine.

My eyes rake over her body, all splayed out for me. My stubble burn on her chest. My cum inside her. And I smirk, feeling incredibly satisfied with the mess we've made.

"Fuck," she huffs out, eyes fluttering shut, as I continue to slide my finger in and out of her.

"Is that a request, Sloane?"

Her lips quirk up, her mesmerizing blue eyes taking on a dreamy, faraway look that I want to get lost in. "No, Jasper. It's a demand."

I immediately reach for her, pull her into me, and lift her up in my arms. "Whatever my girl wants," I rumble against her hair as I carry her into the living room.

Then I drop her to the couch, put her on all fours, and drag her ass up into position before giving in to all of her demands.

Repeatedly.

I expected to wake up with Sloane's head pressed to my chest. Instead, I wake up with her naked and straddling me, running her hands all over my chest, her perfect tits with this alluring little C-shape beneath them.

"Eyes up here, Gervais." Her fingers pinch and give a little tug to the hair on my chest, drawing my attention to her face.

"Wasn't trying to find your eyes, Winthrop." I shoot her a wicked grin, one that doesn't come out to play much.

It dawns on me that I don't smile much, period. Don't usually feel inclined. But with Sloane, they crop up out of nowhere. There's a special power in being able to make a person smile just by existing.

"Pig," she huffs, dropping her chin shyly and going back to tracing the lines of my tattoos with her fingers.

"I've spent years getting lost in your eyes, Sloane. The rest of you though? It's all new. I imagine this is what going to Disneyland for the first time is like. Overstimulating."

"My boobs are—"

"Perfect," I cut her off, catching the self-deprecating look she shoots down at herself.

Sloane rolls her eyes and pauses. "Wait, you've never been to Disneyland?" One hand shoots up to cover her mouth, and her eyes go wide, like she spoke before thinking about how my childhood played out. Even before that day, expensive family vacations weren't in the cards for us. "Shit, I'm sorry."

"Don't be. I much prefer this version of Disneyland. No waiting in line. The ride is all mine." I reach up, gently palming her breasts before sliding one hand under the sheets and landing a slap on her ass. "Does Cinderella have an ass like this? Because unless she does, I'm not interested."

A shy smile graces her lips, and her soft hair brushes her collarbones as she stares down at me. Sun blazes in from the skylight above her, making her glow.

Not for the first time, I'm struck by the feeling that everything feels different between us. And yet the same somehow. There's no awkwardness. There's not that sensation that usually hits where I want to be alone.

I'd rather just lie here and stare at her.

"Hi, Sunny." My hands land on her hips, holding her gently, fingers trailing over the dips at the base of her spine.

"Hi, Jas." Her fingers splay over the ballerina tattoo on my ribs, and we stare at each other for a few beats. "What are we going to do today?"

"Whatever you want." My hands pulse, and her cheeks turn pink as my cock hardens beneath her.

"Are we leaving this cottage?" Her head tilts when she asks me the question.

"Would probably be most polite if we did."

"Since when do you care about being polite? You usually sit in the corner with the brim of your cap pulled low so no one talks to you."

"Yeah, but it doesn't work. You talk at me anyway."

She slaps my chest playfully. "Okay, fine. We'll go see everyone…" Her eyes drop to my chest, fingers moving to land a quick pinch on my nipple. "But not yet."

I hum, taking my hands off her and putting them behind my head like I'm lying on a beach somewhere. "Definitely not yet."

Her eyes snap to mine, and she searches my face. "Tell me what to do."

"Yeah?"

She bites her lip, trying to keep from beaming at me. "Yeah."

"Are you sore?"

"Have you seen your dick?"

"Answer the question, Sloane."

She scoffs and rolls her eyes, looking all bratty as she does. "Yeah. I mean, I'm a bit sore—"

"Good. Get up here and sit on my face."

When I shoot forward and grab her, she squeals.

And when I make her come, she calls out my name.

~

"This isn't fair!" Sloane calls from the opposite side of the pond, warm breath puffing out in little clouds in front of her. "You guys have a literal NHL player on your team!"

Vaughn, Billie's husband, hollers back from our end, "To be fair, his team doesn't belong in the NHL this year!"

Cole groans and rolls his eyes.

Griffin, Nadia's husband, who I recognize as a retired football player, punches him in the shoulder with a grumbled, "Dick."

"Sorry, man." Vaughn chuckles. "Lifelong Vancouver Titans fan. Nothing personal."

I tap my stick against the ice and offer him a smirk. "It's all right. I get it. There's no accounting for taste when someone is a Titans fan."

A chorus of *ooooh*s sound around us.

Everyone agreed a day off was in the cards. A game of shinny on the frozen pond is what they decided on doing, and I'm not mad at it.

With the weight of Beau missing off my shoulders, I'm craving getting back on the ice. But instead of top-rate gear, dull skates on bumpy ice and work gloves with an old heavy stick and antique pads are what I've got.

"Okay, enough shit-talking." Stefan, the most refined looking of the bunch, skates over and gestures all the men toward him.

"What are you? The captain now? Just because you're the evil mastermind of the group?" Vaughn rolls his eyes, clearly the playful one.

"It's the turtleneck." Griffin points at the perfectly polished man's sweater. "Only a man with big enough balls to be a captain would be caught dead wearing one."

"You guys!" Stefan laughs. "My neck is warm, so leave me alone. Worry about Mira." He angles his chin over my shoulder to where the woman with long black hair flowing out from under a cream hat is grinning at him. "She's got that crazy competitive look on her face. We know these women. They are insane."

"Hear, hear!" Vaughn nods enthusiastically.

"They can't be trusted."

Cole straightens. "Watch your fucking mouth, Dalca."

"Whatever, G.I. Joe." He waves him off and continues, "We need to win. Or risk the women completely emasculating us." Stefan can't even get that last part of his ridiculous pep talk out without chuckling.

"You're already wearing a turtleneck." Griffin shakes his head.

"You little bitch babies ready?" Billie calls from the other end of the pond. "Or are you all just gonna stand around in a circle talking about your feelings while we wait?"

"Baby, you're dead!" Vaughn shouts back at her.

She smiles and gives him a wink.

The shit-talking continues as they make their way to center ice to drop the puck. But I'm not watching that.

I'm watching Sloane.

Sloane, who just took her coat off and is wearing *my* jersey. The gold highlights on the maroon base match her hair, and the big grizzly on the front makes her appear more vicious than she is.

Somehow she takes an oversize jersey and makes it look so damn good. Too damn good.

And when she turns around with GERVAIS written across her back? I smile behind the cage of my helmet.

My name looks good on her too.

The game is amateur enough that I could stop everyone's shots in my sleep, but I let some in…just to keep things exciting.

It's the joking and camaraderie that I enjoy the most.

It's watching Sloane dart around on the ice wearing my jersey that gives me a semi the entire game.

And it's when she skates up to me and whispers in my ear, "Jas, when we get back in that cottage, I want you to shove me on my knees and show me exactly how you like your cock sucked," that Mira slips around me and my one-track mind to score the game-winning goal.

"Got yaaaaaaaa!" Sloane's hands fly up over her head as she cheers with the other women, celebrating their win of what Billie coined "The Kindergarten Cup" because "*only a bunch of man-children could come up with a game that's boys against girls.*"

Sloane laughs. She's light and bright. She's Sunny. She makes me smile so hard my cheeks hurt.

I can't take my eyes off her.

28

Sloane

Willa: Looping Violet in on this chat to get the full picture. What's the over-under on sweet little Sloane and moody hockey boy hooking up before they get back to Chestnut Springs?

Summer: Why are you so invested in this?

Willa: No one deserves the last name Woodcock. He'd have to look like Henry Cavill and fuck like Peter North for me to overlook that.

Violet: Ew. Have you seen Peter North? So tanned. So greasy.

Willa: That's why I said he'd have to look like Henry Cavill.

Summer: Hold, please. Googling Peter North.

Violet: Lmao. Careful.

Summer: Well, he does seem...talented. I'm not mad at it.

Willa: I'm only mad at Sloane for not responding.

Violet: Based on the way she and Jasper have been
   staring at each other, I think she might be busy.

Sloane: Y'all are a bunch of nosy, dirty bitches.

Summer: Where's the lie?

Willa: Just tell us! On a scale of one to Peter North, how
   big is Jasper's D?

~e

I STEP OUT OF THE SHOWER FOR WHAT FEELS LIKE THE HUN-dredth time since Jasper and I started fucking. It would seem that making a mess of me is his new favorite pastime. And I'm definitely not complaining.

"Get on the bed," I hear from behind me.

A shiver runs down my spine before I even turn to face him. The bite in his voice has my core twisting with anticipation, and when I turn to look at him, I get wet instantly.

He is mouthwatering in boxers and an open flannel shirt. I can see *my* tattoo peeking out over his ribs, and I'm hit with a blinding flash of jealousy, one that scratches painfully at the back of my throat as I wonder how many women have run their hands over that tattoo.

"Am I the only one?" I blurt, ignoring his order to get on the bed.

His head tilts, and he appears almost predatory now. "The only one what?" I can tell he's not in the mood for this conversation. I can tell when he's let his head wander some-where it shouldn't have—and this look is that.

Jasper is on edge, probably about the drive home, and I'm pushing him anyway.

"In your life. That you're with." I clutch the plain white towel tighter around me like it might keep me safe from this very unsafe conversation I started.

"Get on the bed," he repeats. "Now."

I want to demand he answer me, but I also want to pretend I never mentioned this at all. I walk toward the bed and sit down on the edge, probably looking as pouty as I'm suddenly feeling.

Maybe it's because our stay here is already over after two short days. This morning we packed, and he hooked the truck back up to an empty trailer.

Maybe it's because I had to say goodbye to Violet and everyone else this morning before they got back to work. I miss seeing my cousin. She's my closest and most constant female friend.

Or maybe it's just the hot fucking mess of these last couple of weeks piling up and making me feel a little emotionally wrung out.

"Lie down. But turn. I want your head at the side of the bed."

I do as he says. The thrill of the way he commands me edging away the doubt in my mind. He's still Jasper. *My Jasper*. The boy with the sad eyes and the heart of gold who I've trusted for years.

Lying here waiting, I hear him walk over. Within seconds he's in my line of vision, towering above me. Eyes serious, jaw clenched.

He bends down and kisses me, tugging my wet hair to angle my head. This kiss isn't soft or searching—it's claiming.

When he decides it's done, he pulls away and growls in my ear, "You're the only one, Sloane. Don't ever doubt that."

His tone hedges no debate, but I blurt out, "I know there have been—"

He cuts me off with a dismissive shake of his head. "We're both adults, Sloane. Let's not pretend we haven't lived our lives. We've both been with other people. But the real question is…"

His thumb strokes my jawline as he tugs the towel away, exposing my body to him while his eyes devour every inch.

"The real question is, do any of those other people matter when I only ever see you? When I only ever think about you? When I've done nothing but become more and more obsessed with you since I was told to stay away from you?"

I whimper. Or moan. Or make some sort of noise like someone has punched me in the gut.

"Do they, Sloane? Do they matter? Does any of that seem like it matters in the face of what you and I have happening right now? In the face of eighteen years of friendship? In the face of wanting each other for so long? Is a single other person even a factor? Even a blip on the radar?"

"No," I whisper instantly. When he puts it like that, no. *No. No. No. No. No.*

"None of it matters."

"That's right." His fingers trail over my lips. "The answer is no. None of that shit matters. Because we're me and you. We're us. Unlikely and inevitable all at once. We're forever."

I nod, willing away the sudden sting in my eyes.

Because Jasper isn't an overly emotional man, and that might be the first time I've *really* heard him admit what this all means to him.

What I mean to him.

With a quick squeeze to my throat, he murmurs against my hair, "Now hang your head off the edge of this bed and open your mouth."

I watch in rapt fascination as his impressive cock bobs over me, his boxers discarded. Last night he shoved me to my knees and told me how to suck his cock, just like I asked him to. I came from his dirty words and the pressure of my thighs squeezing together while I sucked him off. It was definitely the first time anyone *talked* me into an orgasm.

I lick my lips as he drops his cock to my face and gently adjusts my positioning. Then he's propped over my body, hands braced on the bed on either side of me.

The panels of his button-down shirt fall like curtains on either side of my face. I open my mouth eagerly, and his smooth length slides between my lips. His fresh and earthy scent swirls around me. It's a heady combination.

"Play with your tits, Sloane. I wanna watch you while I take your mouth."

I moan on his length and start plumping my breasts. Tweaking my nipples. Losing my mind as he sets a slow rhythm between my lips.

This angle is new for me, and my eyes water from how far back he's able to push, but he's always careful with me. Careful not to push too hard or too far. Careful not to hurt me or alarm me.

And yet he pushes me further than anyone ever has, which I love. At school I pushed myself harder. With ballet too.

"So fucking good. This hot little mouth, Sloane. Sucking dick like you were born for it. You have no idea how good you feel wrapped around my cock. It's fucking addicting."

He thrusts in hard, and I make a light gagging noise, tears blurring my vision as I pinch my nipples. "That too far, honey?"

I shake my head vigorously and hum on his length, squeezing my legs together and feeling the wetness between them slip. I mean, it is too far—logistically speaking.

But I'm into it. Really, really into it.

He chuckles, hand shaping my waist. "So fucking hungry." His fingers rap lightly on the top of my thigh. "Open for me."

His hand presses to the inside of my thigh, guiding it back to the bed so that I'm completely exposed to him as he steadily fucks my mouth. Far, but not so far that I gag again.

"Whose pussy is this, Sloane?"

He slaps it, and I can hear how wet I am over my moans. I offer a muffled Yours from around his cock since he doesn't pull back to offer me a reprieve.

"That's right." His voice is so low I almost don't hear him. There's too much. I feel too much.

He's too much.

His expert fingers run through my core, and my hips buck toward him, lifting from the bed. I'm ready to come, ready to let him pull me apart piece by piece and watch it happen.

Powerless

If I've learned anything in the last couple of days, it's that Jasper enjoys telling me what to do and watching me do it.

That alone can get him hard. That alone can get me wet. So I guess it works for us. Just like this position does.

His cock is in my mouth and he's matching that rhythm between my legs with only one finger. It's not enough. I want more. I want that fullness when I explode. And I'm so damn close.

My body must give me away, the arousal dripping down my legs a perfect match for the saliva on my cheek.

"Do you love me stuffing you full, Sloane? It seems like you do." He leans forward, pressing his wicked mouth to the top of my bare pussy. "Seems like you've been spoiled though."

His scruff hits all the right nerves as he dusts his mouth over my lower stomach and makes me writhe beneath him. "A spoiled little princess who needs to learn some patience."

With one last kiss to my navel, he withdraws from my body.

From the bed, from my space, from my mouth.

He leaves me empty, throbbing, and so fucking needy.

"Jasper!" I whimper his name. "Are you kidding me right now?"

I hear the rustling of clothes behind me before he says, "Let's go, Sunny. We need to hit the road."

"I just need—"

"Sloane." The cool tone in his voice stops my hand from sliding farther down my body. "I know I don't need to tell you that you're only allowed to touch *my* pussy when I say so."

I can't help it. I laugh and throw my hands over my face in exasperation. "Lord help me, Gervais. I wish I could go back and tell my teenage self what she's in for ten years down the line. She'd have keeled over on the spot."

I hear his deep chuckle, the one that warms me to my bones. The one that reminds me of the adolescent, bashful version of him. The one that's still a facet of the complicated man he is today.

"If you go back, make sure you tell her she's got drool on her face and that it's time to get her fine ass out of bed."

"I hate you," I laugh back at him.

But I always laugh at the wrong moment. And right now I laugh because I don't hate Jasper at all.

I love him. I love him like that girl ten years ago never could have imagined.

"Are you missing dancing?"

Our conversation started off stilted on our long drive home because all I could think about was holding Jasper down and riding his cock until I got this pesky, consuming orgasm out of the way. Eventually his erection subsided and his jeans became less strained. Sadly for me, I think my underwear might not be salvageable.

But then we started talking about hockey, and I got interested in something besides the ache between my legs. He told me about his plans for when he gets back to Calgary. The training. The sports therapy. He eats specific types of meals, which sound like an awful lot of turkey and salmon.

His excitement is infectious. It's so easy to get caught up in him when he's animated and carefree like he is right now.

The sun is shining, and the roads are perfect.

I cherish these moments with him.

"Not like I thought I might. Or, well, I should say that I *was*, but I think I was only missing it because I would have rather been running through the same mindless choreography repeatedly while getting yelled at in Russian than planning a wedding to someone I didn't want to marry."

Oof. I really know how to kill a relaxed moment, don't I? Jasper's hands constrict momentarily on the steering wheel, and the silence is thick. I try to keep myself from laughing at how I just waltzed in and dropped an A-bomb on our happy drive without even trying.

But an amused little giggle slips out all the same.

"Good lord, Sunny." Jasper's lips quirk, and his head shakes.

I laugh into my hands for a minute before regaining my composure. "Anyway, for the last couple of weeks, I haven't missed it the same way. I've been sad but not stressed, if that makes any sense? I wanted to dance to get all the anxiety out of my body, to tire myself out enough that I wouldn't think too hard. But dancing in Summer's gym was...relaxing somehow. No one watched. I played whatever music *I* wanted. I did whatever choreography *I* wanted. I just got to be myself, and that was therapeutic, I think. No one telling me what I can and can't do."

"Until I rolled around," Jasper grumbles darkly.

I laugh lightly and reach over the console, hoping I can pass off accidentally rubbing his dick as a reassuring pat on the leg.

My hand lands on his muscled quad, sliding inward. "Yeah, but the difference is I like it when you do it. I want it when you do it. I told you to do it."

His cheek twitches under the strain of hiding a smile. My fingers inch farther down between his legs, my pinky shifting out to trail down his impressive length.

"Sunny."

I peek up at him, plastering an expression of faux innocence on my face. "Yeah, Jas?"

"What do you think you're doing?"

"Patting your leg?" I roll my lips together, keeping my eyes as wide as possible.

"This innocent look on your face is adorable when only a few hours ago I hung your head off that four-poster bed and watched you choke on my cock."

Warm splotches crop up on my face immediately. Placing one hand over my chest, I lean away from him dramatically. "I am scandalized."

"Yeah." He chuckles, peeking up to the rearview mirror. "You're about to be. Get back in your seat and lose the pants."

My heartbeat thrums in my ears. "What about you?"

"What about me? I'm driving."

"Aren't you uncomfortable?"

"I've been fighting off getting hard around you for years. I'll be fine. Pants off. I'm already tired of waiting."

I blink once. *Years*. How did I not notice? Did I convince

myself so thoroughly he would never be interested in me that I stopped really looking at him?

The answer is yes. It got to the point where it almost hurt to look at him that closely. To think about things that specifically.

"Sloane." His voice is authoritative, and that's "The Daddy" voice, I decide. There's a switch that gets flicked and he goes from quiet, aloof Jasper to *that.*

Whatever the voice is, it catapults me into action. My boots are already off, and I pull away the soft thermal socks, dropping them in the footwell before lifting my heavy wool sweater's hem and peeling the black leggings from my body. His eyes stay on the road, but when I go to discard my panties, he says, "No, those stay."

"But they're—"

"An uncomfortable reminder of how desperate you are?"

"Ha." A laugh bursts from my lips. "Yeah, that's one way to put it."

A smug smirk graces his lips as he peeks over at me briefly. "Good."

I groan and tip my head back against the seat, bare thighs squeezed together while I wait. When no further directions come, I glance at him. "What now?"

"Now, you sit there and tell me about what you plan to do when we get back to the city."

"But...that's not hot."

He laughs. "No. But it's a necessary conversation."

"Why did I need to take my pants off for it?"

He shrugs as he casually looks over his shoulder to swap lanes. "Just like to watch you squirm. Tell me your plan."

With a heavy sigh, I pluck at my lip and turn to stare out the passenger-side window. "Well, I'm due to go to Sterling's penthouse and pack up the stuff I kept there."

Jasper is deathly still beside me. "I'll go with you."

"Yeah." I snort. "That should go over really well. I can manage."

"I know you can manage. But I'm still coming."

I breathe out slowly, letting that go for now.

"And I'm going to have to call my dad. Face the music on that front."

"He should be apologizing to you."

I nod solemnly. "That might be true. But Robert Winthrop isn't big on apologizing, so I won't hold my breath. Most of the stuff I moved out of my condo when my lease was up at the end of August is at my parents' place in boxes. So I'll have to figure out what I'm going to do. Where I'm going to go."

"My place."

"Do you think moving straight in together is the best idea?"

God. I really hate this conversation.

"Why not? Now spread your legs. Pull your panties to the side with one hand and rub slow circles on your clit with the other."

I bark out a disbelieving laugh. "Are you joking right now?"

"No, Sloane. You look tense. Take the edge off."

I'm shaking my head at him while I do as he instructed. He left me seriously riled up this morning, and as much as

I secretly like playing this game, I will not turn down an orgasm to help with that.

Plus, he's not wrong. I go from tense to buzzing with anticipation instantly. With two fingers, I hook the wet fabric out of the way and find my swollen clit.

I press down firmly before circling, biting down on my lip to keep quiet.

"I have houses in Chestnut Springs," he says, like carrying this conversation on while I play with myself is perfectly normal. I have to bite back my smile. I never saw this side of Jasper coming, and I am fucking living for it. He likes being in control, and choosing this with him makes me feel like I'm taking back part of myself I never indulged either. My own control. "Multiple. You'd have to commute. Or you can spend the next few months dancing at Summer's gym. But you can have one."

"Multiple houses?"

He nods, clearing his throat. "Keep rubbing, Sloane. I bought an entire block. A row of businesses on one side—including Summer's gym—and houses set on the other. I figured I'd need something to do when I eventually retire, and fixing up a bunch of old bungalows in a town I love would be a fun passion project. Something to keep my hands busy."

At that mention, he glances down at my hand. His jaw pops before he looks back up at my eyes. "Plus, I found out your dad wanted to buy that block and put in a stupid mall or something. Ruin the town with his shiny cookie-cutter bullshit. So I fucked him in the process by going to the real estate agent personally. That's the thing about small towns. They trust and like who they know. And she knew me."

I'm a little floored by what he's just told me, but I'm not thinking straight with my fingers between my legs. Plus, he's pushed the sleeves of his sweatshirt up, giving me a sexy view of the veins that run from his hands into his tattooed forearms. "But you could have spent all that money on hunting lions," I quip, watching the muscles under that black ink flex.

"Put one finger in," he bites out instantly.

And I do.

"Now two."

I moan and easily slide a second finger into myself, pressing in and out a few times.

"Feet up on the dashboard," he clips, reaching down to adjust his cock in his jeans.

"Oh my god," I murmur. The blush from my cheeks instantly blazes out over my chest, my breasts, my stomach. My entire body is on fire for him.

I move my feet up onto the dash, making the fit that much tighter. I moan at the sensation.

"You love this. I know." He juts his chin at me. "Knees open so I can see."

"You sure this is safe?" I tease breathily.

"There's nothing safe about how badly I want you, Sloane. Never has been. Now add a third finger. I wanna watch you work for it."

His head flips back to the road. It's a straight, quiet stretch on a perfectly sunny weekday afternoon. Jasper would never take unnecessary risks.

As I slide a third finger in and feel the bite of my body stretching, I decide this risk is very necessary. Coming is very necessary. And following his orders like this sets my body buzzing like I've never felt.

"How does that feel, Sloane?"

I close my eyes, imagine his body over mine, and moan. "So good."

"You pretending it's me stuffed between your legs rather than your fingers right now?"

My eyes snap open, and I glare over at him.

"Fuck your fingers and answer my question."

My hand moves in and out slowly, feeling so fucking good. It's dirty and kinky and so unlike the reserved version of me. I became someone else under the thumb of all the shit around me, so I let myself luxuriate in feeling dirty and free to take what I want.

"Yes. I was thinking about you. I'm always thinking about you."

A soft, satisfied smile touches his lips. Everything about him is so hypermasculine, hard and domineering but doting all at once. Jasper always makes me feel like he'll catch me when I fall. He always has.

"Do you want to come?"

"Yes," I pant out, still working my fingers wantonly into myself.

"Too bad." He chuckles. He fucking *chuckles*. "Put your pants back on and wait."

A loud groan erupts from my throat as I bang my head against the seat, instantly crossing my legs to ease the swell of pleasure coiling in my core.

Like I might strangle it. Snuff it out.

But it doesn't work. Every nerve ending is firing. Everything I see is Jasper.

I've never been so fucking worked up in my life.

"That is just cruel. Aren't you so uncomfortable?"

He shrugs, looking altogether too pleased with himself. "Yeah. It's not worse than watching you date losers for years though."

I scoff at that. "You're a masochist."

He doesn't even flinch. "I believe a therapist suggested that once."

"Or you just secretly hate me." With a shaking hand, I reach for my leggings, which I so badly do not want to put on. Even running fabric over my skin is going to drive me insane. It's just going to make me hornier.

"Trust me, Sunny. I don't hate a single thing about you. But I do hate you talking about *him* while you're touching yourself."

"I didn't—oh. The lion hunting."

He gives me a wink. A playful, handsome, fucking *infuriating* wink.

"I hate you."

He clicks his tongue and gives his head this little dip that makes his thick hair flop. No hat today. "You mentioned that this morning. Somehow I'm not all that worried about it. You'll take it back when I make you come so hard you can't even walk."

I sigh, wanting to push away the reminder that I did, in fact, already say that today. I said it and immediately thought it wasn't true.

That I loved him instead.

I know I love him.

But I'm still having a tough time believing he'll ever be able to love me back in quite the same way.

⁓

"It's dark. Let's stop here again for the night." Jasper flicks the signal light to turn into Rose Hill, his voice bleeding exhaustion. We're only a few hours from home, but he's right. It's dark, and our conversation has fallen into a quiet, tired lull after ten hours of driving.

All I can think about is sex.

How I went from dancing so rigorously and working such long hours that it barely ever crossed my mind to being feral for it is really a wonder to behold.

I decide I will now refer to this phenomenon as the "Jasper Gervais Effect."

He'll edge you for a day and turn you into a happy, desperate ho! That could be his tagline.

I'm living, squirming, tense proof of that at this point.

When we pull back into the Rose Hill Inn, we park along the tree-lined side of the parking lot to accommodate the empty trailer behind us.

Suddenly I'm desperate for fresh air. The truck smells too much like mint and eucalyptus bodywash. I'm also jittery and agitated and—

"Where do you think you're going?" Jasper's voice cuts me off as I reach for the door handle to escape the suffocating sexual tension between us.

I startle and look back at him. "Out." I hike a thumb over my shoulder.

"Not a chance. I think we've waited long enough." He crooks a finger at me and then fists my sweater, gently tugging me toward him. With a heavy sigh, I scramble over the center console and straddle his lap, just like that day on the runaway lane.

His fingers stroke up the sides of my face, over my cheekbones, hooking into my hair and pushing it back behind my ears. "You have no idea how lovely you are. How distracting you are. How much I've loved watching you follow my directions all day," he murmurs, eyes tracing my every feature while his rock-hard cock drives up into my ass. "I want to try this again. No rush. Nowhere to be. No near-miss car crash. Just you and me." His voice is so soft, his hands so tender.

"Just you and me," I whisper back.

"I want your eyes on mine when you come in my lap." He cups my head delicately, and I drop my lips to his hungrily. His steely arms wrapping me up. Somehow fitting around me so perfectly. Making me feel so safe. So cherished.

I melt against him. My hands roam his chest, his throat, his hair. Touching him freely is such a pleasure.

When he pulls away, he removes my pants, one leg at a time. Followed by my underwear. He undresses me and soaks in the sight, lit only by the glow of the headlights. Every brush of his fingers is reverent, every look is loaded.

He kisses me first, and my chest aches with the sweetness of it. His lips are firm and soft all at once.

As he reclines his seat, I help him get rid of his pants, rubbing his cock and cupping his balls, making sure I sneak a hand under his shirt to run my fingers over the ballerina he got just for me.

"I don't know how I went so long without you," he murmurs, pushing my hair behind my ear and cradling my skull. "I never want to go without you again," he adds, fisting himself and swiping the thick head of his cock through my core.

"You'll never have to," I whisper as I kiss him back, trying to match his rawness with my own.

"Promise me." His eyes bore into my mine, and I nod. "I promise."

Then he notches himself inside me, pushing in just an inch, and still my back bows toward him. My body bends so willingly under his touch as he holds me in position, and when I slowly push myself down his steely girth, feeling every inch of him, he whispers, "Sloane," with a hitch in his voice.

Our bodies meld to each other in the dark truck. We start out lazily. Lovingly. But soon our hands and kisses become frenzied. My body feels ready to burst.

"Jasper, I'm going to—"

He grips my chin and pulls my face a hairbreadth apart from his. "Rub your clit, honey. Come for me."

When he exhales, I inhale his breath. He's inside me in so many ways. I don't even know if he realizes.

His cock hits that spot, I brush my fingers over my

swollen bundle of nerves, and I shatter, eyes locked on his. "Ah! Fuck. Jasper."

"Sloane," he growls, right as his hand drops to my throat and he kisses me fiercely.

My name is on his lips as he spills himself inside me, sounding just a little bit undone.

Just a little bit out of control.

And it gives me just a little bit of hope that Jasper Gervais might love me the way I love him too.

29

Jasper

Jasper: We're home safe. How is Beau?

Harvey: Oh, good. Relieved you two are back. Beau is in good spirits, all things considered. He wants to call you. He's sleeping right now though.

Jasper: We're here. Anytime. When will he come home?

Harvey: It might be awhile. He's in good hands here.

THE FIRST THING I DID WHEN WE GOT BACK TO THE BIG empty house at Wishing Well Ranch was drag Sloane up to my teenage bedroom and fuck her while she wore my jersey.

It's all I've thought about since she waltzed out of that dressing room wearing it with a teasing little grin. Harder for her to grin with my dick in her mouth. Major fan of the satisfied smile she shot me after though.

Then we passed out, limbs tangled in the tiny bed. Dead to the world. It seems like it has been months since her almost-wedding day.

Now we're unpacking our bags and enjoying a nice cold Buddyz Best, Sloane is downstairs starting the laundry, and I'm feeling really fucking domestic and happy about the entire situation as I fold the basket she just brought up.

I can see us doing this forever. Taking trips together. Napping together. Doing chores together. Me walking up and pressing a soft kiss to her cheek, just because I can, and then carrying on with my shit. Even doing boring stuff is infinitely less boring with Sloane by my side.

"Jas! Harvey is FaceTiming! Can I answer?" she calls from downstairs.

I freeze midway through folding the ugly T-shirt Cade gave me shit for wearing.

"Yes!" I call back before dropping the shirt and striding out of the room, covering as much ground as possible without running. We've gotten the odd text update from Harvey but not a lot of information. I know he's trying not to worry us, but the less-is-more strategy really isn't reassuring with the way my brain works.

"Hiiiii!" I hear Sloane's sunny voice coming from the kitchen as I approach her from behind. "Look at you, Beau! God, it's good to see you."

When I get close enough to see the screen, my chest cracks wide open. Harvey is sitting beside Beau, and they're both grinning back at Sloane.

The closer I get, I can see how thin Beau looks, that his

expression is a bit drawn. But he's there. Breathing. Talking. *Alive.*

"Oh! There he is!" Sloane can see me in the little rectangle at the top of the screen as I approach. I push up close behind her, and without even thinking, I wrap one arm around her stomach and take my friend—my brother—in.

He and I are tight, but we aren't sappy. Beau isn't a sappy guy. Sometimes I think he's just as dark as I am and just hides it better. Aka, he isn't a sullen dick when he has a bad day.

But I'm me, so I open with "Hey, asshole. You look like shit."

Beau chuckles, a wry grin twisting his mouth. "When I get home, I'm gonna kick your ass, Gervais. No helmets and pads allowed though."

"If that's what it takes to get you home, I'll allow it. Missed you, man."

He forces a smile now, his eyes a familiar brand of haunted. "Missed you too."

Sloane glances over her shoulder at my face, like what she sees reflected on the screen just isn't enough. Our eyes catch for a moment. She smiles at what she sees there, and just as she turns back to the phone screen, Harvey lets out a loud whistle.

"Well, I'll be…" His head shakes.

Beau snorts.

"What?" I ask, stepping away and crossing my arms over my chest. Because I'm not stupid. I know what they just saw.

Harvey's grin is just a little too wide when he says, "Y'all went and made that kissing cousins saying a real-life thing."

My eyes close, and I take a deep breath. I've never had immunity from Harvey and his bad jokes, but I've always flown under the radar enough to not be his prime target. I momentarily wonder if this is how Cade feels.

Sloane gasps. "We're not cousins!"

Beau elbows his dad, playing off him like he always does. "I think they might be doing more than kissing. Look how red she is."

I glance up at the corner of the phone to see her face, and sure enough, Sloane's doing her best tomato imitation.

"We're not cousins." I back her up, but my lips twitch. We're going to get this joke for a long-ass time; we might as well roll with the punches.

"I mean...sure. Not the type that'll make a baby with a tail or something," Harvey starts in, gaining momentum the more we all react. He's like an overgrown child. "But still cousin-y if you ask me."

"Literally no one asked you, Harv."

"Hey, Dad." Beau's head inclines toward Harvey, and he reaches out to palm the back of his son's neck. Harvey looks both exhausted and relieved. I twitch my nose a little to chase away the sting that crops up there.

"Yes, son?"

"On a scale of one to tail-baby cousins, where would you put Jasper and Sloane?"

"Oh my god." Sloane collapses onto the counter, holding the phone over her head, shaking it like I should take it from her.

"Like a five, probably."

"Beau," I cut them off with an amused shake of my head, taking the phone from Sloane's hand. "How badly injured are you? Because I'm gonna make you pay for that joke."

I meant it in a teasing way, but I can tell my comment sobers them both. I have a real knack for being a buzzkill. Sloane stands back up and leans her shoulder into my chest to appear back on the screen.

Beau clears his throat. "Some minor burns." He gestures to his legs. "I might need a few months. Then I'll be able to take you."

I notice the IV line that disappears at the top of his hand. "What's the deal?"

"Gotta stay here for a bit. Then they'll be able to transfer me home. All you complainers will be happy to know that my days moonlighting as James Bond have ended."

Sloane's head nods in understanding. He doesn't seem keen to disclose more, and I'm not one to push when someone wants to keep things under wraps, so I don't. I default to our regular friendship.

"Yeah, but Bond gets pussy."

Beau barks out a laugh, and I smile at the sound. Fuck, it's good to see him and hear him laugh.

"Dude, you're hooking up with your cousin. Don't even talk to me about that."

Sloane pushes up on her tiptoes in front of me, like a fiery little dragon, all protective and shit. "Beau Eaton! Never mind Jasper. *I'm* gonna kick your ass when I see you. Right after I hug the hell out of you and tell you how much I love you."

Beau smiles, more natural than I've seen on his face for this entire conversation, but I can see he's getting tired. "I'd like to see you try, Sloaney. But I'll take the hug."

Harvey must notice the way Beau is fading too because he cuts in,. "Okay, we're gonna give Cade and Willa a call next, so I'm gonna jump in here. You two lovebirds have fun. It's about dang time you two figured it out. Jasper's been creeping on ya from under the brim of that dang hat for years. So just be safe. Know that Grandpa Harvey will love the baby, tail and all."

"Harvey! Are you—"

Beau is laughing when Harvey cuts me off. "We love you two hooligans! Bye!"

And then the image cuts out with a monotone whoosh.

When I glance down, Sloane is laughing hard enough that tears are gathering in her eyes as she wipes them away with the back of her hand. "Goddamn. Harvey is a beast."

"Never mind Beau. Harvey is dead," I joke, knowing I'll never follow through on it.

"Hey, Jas?"

"Yeah?" I tip my head and look down at the woman who has rotated to press her body against mine.

"Have you really been creeping on me from under that hat?"

I shrug and pull her head against my chest. In the same spot I always do—pressing her to my heart and dusting my lips over her hair. "I mean, Sunny…have you seen your ass?"

312

"You're not supposed to be here, Gervais. Hasn't been two weeks. I'm gonna pretend I didn't see you." Roman drops his attention back down to the papers in his hands as he tries to edge past me down the back hallway of our practice facility.

"Well, I am. And you need me, Coach."

"Don't tell me what I need, Jasper. That's not your job."

"We've been on a losing streak." Like he doesn't know. He's the one who sits on the bench, watching it all happen. For me, I haven't been able to bring myself to watch. Too hard. Too maddening.

"Yup." He pops the *p,* still not giving me his attention. "And we were losing when you were playing too."

"I need to play. You need me to play—"

The older man stops right in front of me, his brow quirking speculatively as he cuts me off. "No, I need the *better* version of you, who has his head screwed on straight. And you need these last few days on your time-out to do it."

"Time-out? What am I? A seven-year-old?"

Roman shakes his head, glancing back down at whatever super interesting shit must be on the paper in front of him. "Sometimes it feels like all of you are just a bunch of seven-year-olds."

I almost laugh.

"They found him. He's alive."

At that, Coach's head snaps up. "Yeah?"

"Yeah." I can't stop the bashful grin that twists my lips.

"Well, heck yes, Jasper." Roman smiles, crinkling the skin at the corners of his eyes. "That's the best fucking news I've heard in ages."

He claps my shoulder once. Twice. And tugs me in for a gruff hug before pulling away, one hand on each shoulder to really look me in the eye.

"I want to play."

He nods. "You been training?"

I doubt Roman would consider a boys-versus-girls game of shinny—plus a record amount of fucking—training, but exercise is exercise, so I say, "Yeah."

He eyes me speculatively, and I train my face to not give anything away. It's not the first time I've bent the truth with management.

They tell me not to ride horses in my contract too. Doesn't stop me from getting up and helping with the branding every summer and working cattle for the family reunion in the fall though.

I'm not as good as Rhett or Cade—or Violet—but I'm still a country boy at heart. I can saddle a horse and herd a cow.

"All right. You come to practice and training for the next three days. Show me your focus is back and I'll let you play."

"Yes, Coach." I steel my features, trying not to give away that I really wanted to play tonight. Right now, if possible. I had hockey pushed out of my mind. Didn't feel like I needed it, didn't miss it, because my brain was too full of grief and self-pity. But now? Now my fingers itch with it.

With a nod, I turn to walk back out the doors to where Sloane is waiting safely in my SUV.

"Hey, Gervais?"

Roman's words turn me around right as I near the metal push bar on the exit door. "Yeah?"

He gestures at his head. "Where's your hat?"

I blink once, putting his question together. I reach up and run a palm over my hair to check for it. Wearing my team hat has been a part of my identity for the better part of my life.

"I don't know. I guess I forgot to put it on."

The man quirks his head at me and smiles before walking away.

I told him the truth that time. When we got ready, I didn't even think about putting my hat on this morning.

I guess I didn't feel like I needed it.

30

Jasper

Cade: Want to come over for a delicious home-cooked
meal tonight? Would love to see you!
Jasper: Why are you talking all weird like that?
Cade: Like what?
Jasper: Never mind. I'll ask Sloane.
Cade: Are you guys banging yet?
Jasper: Jesus, Willa. Give Cade his phone back.

⁓

"No." I cross my arms over my chest and glare at
Sloane from the driver's seat of my Volvo.

"Yes." She tips her chin up.

"I'm not staying in the fucking car like a little kid, Sloane."

"Listen, you got to deal with your shit. I need to be the
one to deal with mine."

I groan and run a hand over my face. "You're making me sound like some sort of domineering asshole."

"If the shoe fits," she says and flattens her lips, giving me a little shrug.

I tip my head back. "I just want you to be safe. I don't like Woodcock. I don't trust him."

"He's probably not even home." She glances out the passenger window at the tall glass building over her shoulder. "It's the middle of the afternoon, and he's a workaholic."

"And if he is?"

"And if he is, then that's a conversation I'll have with him. I don't need you standing there snorting like an angry bull behind me."

"I'll wait outside," I concede.

"Outside the building?"

"No." I unbuckle my seat belt and round the vehicle to open her door. "I'll be outside the door of his unit."

When I look down into the car, Sloane sighs. But I see her lips twitch. I'd never forgive myself if he laid a hand on her, and I don't trust the fucker as far as I can throw him.

"Fine," she huffs out, taking my hand as she steps out.

Without letting go of her hand, I open the back door and pull out the cardboard box we brought with us. We enter the ritzy building and head straight for the elevator. As the doors close, I catch sight of us in the mirrored wall of the small space and read Sloane's body language. The way she's tucked herself tight beside me, the way her long bangs have swept down over her face, the way her teeth are scraping over her bottom lip repeatedly.

The woman can dance onstage in front of thousands of people with all the confidence in the world, but this has her nervous. These people who were supposed to care about her—supposed to love her—have beaten her down.

They make her feel insecure.

And I hate them for it.

I pulse my hand around hers reassuringly, and her head snaps up.

She catches my gaze in the mirror. "Hi, Jas," she whispers.

"Come here, Sunny." I tug her gently into me, turning her into my chest where I can feel her breath on my shirt, feel her heartbeat against my ribs.

It almost doesn't seem real how we slipped so effortlessly into this new relationship. It feels like we've been together all along, and I guess in some ways we have.

"I'll feel better once I get all my stuff out."

"You should let me—"

"Jasper, stop. I need to do this for myself. Reclaim my life on my own. You get the hallway. Deal with it."

I squeeze her head again, resting my cheek against her hair. I watch us again in the mirror.

Her bright blond, my warm brown, her porcelain skin, mine tanner. The way she fits against me and complements me. It just doesn't seem like it can be a coincidence.

It seems like something so much bigger than us.

"You're gonna deal with me peeling those jeans off and eating your pussy in this elevator on the way back down," I mutter against her head.

She laughs as she rolls her forehead across the dark-gray

T-shirt that stretches over my chest. "You're such a caveman sometimes."

She tenses when the elevator dings and comes to a slow stop at the thirty-first floor. The doors slide open to reveal a small foyer. There are no other doors off it, just the big sleek one before us.

A security camera resides in the upper corner, the red light blinking at me like a dare.

I toss the box toward the stately entrance and cup Sloane's head, pushing her up against the wall, crushing my mouth against hers.

The first noise she makes sounds surprised; the second is a moan. Her hands rake up my chest, nails scraping when she drags them back down. Her lips go soft, and her jaw relaxes in my grip.

I have never been able to scare her off. She's relentless and loyal.

No matter how many people leave me, she never does.

It doesn't matter what I say or what I do—what I like. She just rises up to meet me. Turns to putty in my hands while I kiss her senseless before sending her into the penthouse she shared with her ex mere weeks ago.

~~~

I've stood out here for thirty minutes, too tense to even scroll through my phone. Instead, I listen at the door like a total creep, trying to make out whether I can hear voices. I can hear shuffling, possibly even humming, coming from the unit.

I'm assuming if Woodcock were in there, I'd hear a lot of bitching and moaning.

Keeping myself from barging in there is a Herculean feat. And it's not even jealousy at this point or concern for her safety, because I'm almost positive she's alone in there.

It's that I'm finding I don't like being away from her at all. I don't know if it's the need to make up for lost time or if I'm just being a clingy bastard, but I'd rather be in there helping pack her stuff than standing out here overthinking every small particle of my life.

And hers.

I hear the knob jostle, and her petite form pops out through the door. She's struggling under the weight of the box and still manages to look lighter somehow. "Hi!" Her voice is bright, a little breathy.

Rushing forward, I snag the box out of her arms and press a quick kiss to her lips, feeling desperate for her. Relieved. I want to whisk her away, back into the bubble that was just the two of us on the road.

Yeah, everything in our personal lives was shit at the time. But it was us, alone. Not all this other stuff to deal with.

"All okay?" I ask.

"Yeah."

"He wasn't there?"

"No." She shakes her head briskly, reaching forward to press the elevator button. "Just me, burning through there to find my stuff. It's funny…" She glances over her shoulder at the door.

"What?"

"I just… I thought I was going back there to get my stuff. That I needed my stuff. But as soon as I walked in there, I wanted to be back out here. With you. Hell, I didn't want to be here at all today, and I told myself I'd only grab the things that were important. The things that meant something to me. So I walked around looking for them but…I didn't find them."

"Did that asshole do something to your stuff?"

"No, no. It's just…nothing in there means anything to me. I've lived there for a few months, and I'm attached to *nothing*. There was nothing…important. Not a single memory of my time with him that I wanted. People say I'm overly sentimental, but I couldn't find a single thing in there to feel sentimental about."

Fuck, that's sad. I don't like Sterling, but Sloane is a different story. And to hear she was living a life that held so little meaning to her fucking hurts. I slide my spare hand over the small of her back reassuringly. "So what am I holding in this box?"

"Oh, that? Yeah. I ended up getting every single thing that was mine and cramming it in there."

I snort. "I thought none of it mattered?"

She lifts her face, looking like royalty as she tips her chin all high and regal. "It doesn't, but I'm not leaving a single piece of myself in there. Not my favorite chips. Not a toothbrush. I want to disappear from his life. Just poof"—she snaps her fingers—"gone, like I never existed in that penthouse. For a while, I felt like he deserved an explanation. But

I don't think he does anymore. That was the only closure I needed."

She takes a small step closer to me, which is all the confirmation I need. Deep down I know it was never really a choice between the two of us.

But it feels good to be chosen all the same.

It also feels good when I slide my hand down and take a big handful of her Levi's-clad ass while winking over my shoulder at that red blinking light. Because I know Sterling Woodcock will check these tapes.

31

Sloane

Jasper: How's my girl? I'll be back tonight. Meet you at the ranch?

Sloane: Yes. Really good. Especially when you call me that.

Jasper: My girl?

Sloane: Yeah. Haha. Never thought I'd hear that.

Jasper: Sunny, you've always been my girl.

~ ~

SWEAT TRICKLES DOWN MY BACK IN THE QUIET STUDIO. There's no barre, and the floors are too soft for pointe shoes.

And I can't remember a time when I loved dancing so much.

Possibly as a child, before it got competitive and came with criticisms about my body. Before it made my feet so sore I could barely walk.

For over a month, I've danced how I want to dance, ignoring every single responsibility and enjoying every moment of independence.

I stand in the skybox and watch every single one of Jasper's games.

I wait at the exit and feel my heart race when his tall broad form appears in the doorway.

I revel in the way he comes straight for me, kisses me, and squeezes me against his chest.

I make love to him whenever I want.

I dance when I want.

I eat what I want.

I only take the phone calls I want.

I sleep in until whenever I want.

I spend my hard-earned money the way I want.

I'm finally living for myself and feeling empowered about it.

I feel reborn.

Jasper and I have holed up in the house at the end of the block he owns. It's right behind Summer's gym, so I can easily have social time and get my dancing in too.

When Jasper heads out for away games, I have girls' nights with Willa and Summer, or I have dinner with Harvey, or I help Cade check all the electric waterers on the ranch. Or I stay up too late putting fresh coats of paint in the bungalows Jasper owns.

I've watched YouTube videos on how to install new faucets, and Jasper never tells me I can't or I shouldn't or that it's something a man should do.

No one does.

Instead, he walks in, gives the house a little smirk with his hands slung casually in his pockets, and tells me how fabulous it looks. What a great job I've done. How capable I am.

He makes me believe in myself.

Then he bosses me around in bed—but I like that part.

The rest of it makes me realize how powerless I've been trained to be my entire life. It stirs an unfamiliar rage inside me, one that keeps me from answering any of my dad's phone calls.

I miss him, and yet I'm furious with him. I miss who I thought he was—the relationship I thought we had—and yet this new perspective I've gained makes me loathe him at the same time.

I've had the time and space to reflect on the controlling way he treats my mom, the way he's always treated her. The way he talks to serving staff, the way he walks all over anyone he deems beneath him.

Which is alarmingly similar to how he's treated me. The only difference is that with me he uses a sugary voice and calls me "darling" while he pushes me into the places he wants me. The places that benefit him the most while sucking the soul right out of me.

Without this distance, I'm not sure I'd have even noticed. I'd still be a pretty little mannequin, born and bred to make appearances in his world.

But that era has ended. I do plan to face him at some point, to demand the respect he's never given me. And every day I get closer. Every day I grow stronger.

Distance has brought perspective, but also an all-new pride in my capability, in my intelligence. Women like Summer and Willa surrounding me bolster my inner fortitude.

And the support of men like Jasper, Harvey, Rhett, and Cade makes me feel less self-conscious about this new version of myself. The one who does weird dances in the back room of a gym and drinks coffee at 11 p.m. so she can rip out vomit-green shag rug until two in the morning and admire the hardwood floors beneath.

I feel…found. I enjoy helping Cade and Harvey at the ranch. I enjoy doing odd jobs. I still love dancing, but I've reclaimed it for myself. My body doesn't riot when I dance now; it sings with it.

I don't know how this all looks for me long-term, but I am tentatively happy. Tentatively optimistic.

I sit on the floor and fold myself over my legs, sinking into the stretch. My body is all warm and buttery, and I feel a deep sense of accomplishment, like I've flattened another little corner of my scrunched-up life map in my head while I danced around today.

Jasper is heading back from an away game, and we're doing a holiday dinner at Wishing Well Ranch. Christmas is a week away, but there's a vibe at the ranch that always makes it seem like Christmas.

Warm. Cozy. Family.

A wholesome movie-style Christmas, not a ball gown or caviar canapé in sight.

I wrap my fingers around the arches of my feet and press my breasts down into my legs, my sit bones into the floor.

When my phone buzzes across the room, I ignore it. It buzzed while I was dancing, cutting off the music in my earbuds, but I didn't feel like stopping. Whoever it is doesn't give up this time. It just starts up again. With a sigh, I decide I've done enough with my workout that I can abandon it. I sit back up, walk to the table in the corner with the big stereo system, and pick the phone up.

Royal Alberta Ballet Co. flashes across the screen. They're probably wondering if the prima ballerina they've dumped years of development and money into is done fucking around. I haven't gotten back to them about spring season. I saw the email, and I just…didn't feel like responding.

I slide the green phone symbol across the bottom of the screen and take the call.

Everyone was jealous of the hockey game Jasper and I recounted when we returned from Ruby Creek, so I spent the afternoon helping Rhett clear off a shallow and very frozen section of the creek near Beau's still-empty house for a few Christmas games of shinny.

From what I gather, Beau won't be back until the new year. He told us "minor burns," but since Harvey's return, it's become clear that *minor* might be an understatement.

All I know is that he's going to be okay and he's coming home. Jasper is itching to see him. I'm just not sure the man he'll see now will be the same as before he deployed.

Rhett dropped me off at the main house ten minutes ago. It's snowy out, but the bench beside the wishing well is cleared off. The sky is so full of stars that I stake a seat in all my snow gear, tip my head back, and stare up at the chips of bright light as I wait for Jasper to arrive.

Constellations. Planets. Satellites.

Everything is clearer out in Chestnut Springs. Not just the stars.

I remember Jasper sitting in this exact spot on a rainy summer night. It was the night he told me everything. It was the night I danced for him because I didn't know what to say. It was the night we became irrevocably tied to one another.

I hear the brittle crunching of tires against the packed snow on the main gravel road followed by the soft rolling sound of them hitting the asphalt driveway up to the main house. When bright-white lights turn toward the house, my heart pitches in my chest.

Eighteen years I've known Jasper Gervais and I still get excited when I'm about to see him. Still look forward to him coming home every day. Still smile when a text comes in.

I'll never tire of him. Of that I'm sure.

His SUV rolls right up in front of me, and he grins at me through the window.

He looks happy.

Happier than I've ever seen him. And I can't help but hope I'm playing a part in his happiness.

That *we* make him happy. Because we make me so fucking happy.

He jumps out, dressed all classy in a camel-brown peacoat over a charcoal suit. Brown dress shoes on his feet. He is pure sex.

"I came straight from the airport," he says as he rounds the front of his vehicle, eyes raking over me like I'm his first meal in days.

I shiver under the intensity of his stare. His irises are a perfect match for the navy winter sky lying like a blanket over us. His long legs eat up the ground, dress shoes crunching on the packed snow.

"I can see that. You look all shmancy, Gervais." I smirk and twirl a finger. "Do a spin. Let me see that ass."

He chuckles, a low rumble that I swear vibrates the air between us before he scoops me up and switches places with me. "I'd rather be grabbing yours," he breathes, pressing a chaste kiss to my lips as he easily flips me onto his lap.

My legs straddle his, and his broad palms firmly grab each ass cheek as he gazes up into my face and whispers, "I missed you, Sunny."

I roll my eyes. "It was only two days."

"Too long," he grumbles, giving me his signature broody look.

"All you did was fly out, play hockey, and then fly back."

"Yeah, but I like it when you're at my games."

"You *have* played better since you and I…" I wiggle my eyebrows suggestively, and his fingers pulse on my ass.

"You trying to take credit for our wins?"

"It's science, Gervais. You can't argue with it. You were sucking, and now you're not. Your winning streak is going to break records at this rate. My pussy is good luck. The kingmaker. No…" I hold a hand up. "The Stanley Cup Maker."

Jasper gives me a flat expression. "I'm not calling your pussy the Stanley Cup Maker, Sunny."

I giggle, feeling all girlish and giddy sitting in my childhood crush's lap, in the snow, under a starlit sky, like it's the most normal thing in the world. And then I drop my head down to kiss him, the cold tips of our noses brushing together. The stubble on his cheeks pokes through the thin knit of my gloves, scratching against my palms as I hold his handsome face.

When I practiced my choreography out here as a child, I dreamed of kissing him, his hands on me, his warm sure body under mine.

I thought I loved him then, but I'm not so sure I did. I was infatuated with him. This? Now?

It's different. We're different.

"I missed you too, Jas," I whisper against his lips as I pull away to run my hands over his hair, trying to remember the last time he's worn a cap. Maybe when he works out? Or when we work on the house together. His cap functions more as a way to keep his hair out of his face now than to hide behind.

It seems like maybe he's done hiding.

Maybe we both are.

"I got a call today," I continue, taking in his heavy brows and the fine lines across his forehead.

"Yeah?" His hands rub firm circles over the globes of my butt cheeks, warming me better than my thermal leggings.

Light snow falls, and I watch a crystalline flake land on his dark lashes, suspended there for a moment until he blinks.

Powerless

"Yeah. The backup dancer for the Sugar Plum Fairy in *The Nutcracker* is out with the flu, and the principal dancer for the role has Achilles tendinitis that needs a rest. They asked me to step in tomorrow for the final show before Christmas since I danced the part last year."

"And? Are you happy about that?"

The person I'm with asking how I feel about something shouldn't seem like a big deal. But it strikes me here and now that no one has ever really asked me this.

This is new for me. He doesn't jump to tell me whether I should or shouldn't be happy about something. He just asks me how I feel. Like what's going on inside my head—inside my heart—is worthy of his notice and respect.

And I think I love him even more for that.

"Yeah," I whisper, going all mushy as I stare at him. "I think I am."

A soft smile touches Jasper's lips, still glistening with my lip gloss from the sloppy, happy welcome-home kisses I planted on him. His dimples peek out from behind his stubble, and I almost swoon on the spot.

The way he's looking at me right now makes my cheeks heat despite the chilly air. Unable to withstand the saccharine sweetness of the moment, I drop my face into his chest. I suck in his signature scent and nuzzle against him as he wraps his arms around me.

We sit like this until we hear cars roll down the driveway. I turn my head at the lights that crop up as they draw near. The vehicle in front is a pearl-white Audi sedan, and behind it is a massive silver truck with chunky winter tires and a loud engine.

The Audi screeches to a halt at the top of the roundabout driveway, and a tiny blond woman flies out of the driver's side with her finger pointed at the truck, key chain jangling beneath her hand. She has her keys shoved between her fingers like claws. Like she's ready for a fight.

"Are you fucking insane?" she yells.

Jasper sits up tall beneath me, clutching me protectively against his chest. I can feel every limb go taut, like he's ready to spring into action. After cutting the engine, a handsome dark-haired man hops out of the huge loud truck. And not regular handsome, the kind that would turn heads when he walks down the street.

The patio lights illuminate the grin on his face, and when Jasper catches sight of him, his body relaxes.

"Easy, Tink," the man says good-naturedly but a little teasingly. "You're gonna pop a blood vessel stomping around like that."

"Tink?" she shouts, pulling up about six feet from him, not at all affected by his good looks.

He waves a hand over her casually. "Yeah. You've got this whole angry little Tinkerbell vibe happening. I dig it." His eyes rake over her body appreciatively but not lewdly.

"You're fucking nuts, you know that? You drive like an asshole behind me for a solid ten minutes, and now you follow me here? To...to...check me out and compare me to a Disney pixie?" The woman continues reaming him out, her doll-like features twisted in a furious mask. "That was dangerous. You could kill someone."

My head whips between them as they volley back and forth.

"I think she's actually a fairy. And for the record, driving twenty below the speed limit is also dangerous and could kill someone. Mostly me. From boredom," he quips, leaning a hip against the truck and crossing his arms over his chest, not looking the least bit concerned.

"It's dark and snowy! I don't know the area. There could be wildlife! Driving slowly is safe so long as a back-forty hillbilly isn't riding my ass in his small-dick truck, flashing his high beams at me."

Jasper's body shakes with laughter, and I toss a hand over my mouth to cover the snort-laugh that's ready to burst out. "Who is she? I think I love her."

"That's Summer's older sister, Winter."

My eyes shift back to the interaction near the front door. We're obscured by Jasper's SUV but still have a good vantage point for the unusual but superior holiday entertainment.

"Ohh. *That* Winter?"

"Yeah. That Winter."

The man's dark brows shoot up on his forehead, and I can tell he's trying not to laugh. "I hear that if you want your ass ridden, a small dick is the way to go. So maybe I'm your guy."

Winter's mouth drops open comically wide, and I cover my entire face with my hands to smother my giggles. "And who is he?"

Jasper wheezes a laugh, clearly enjoying this exchange just as much as I am. "That's Theo."

"I don't think I know him." I peek back over at the clean-shaven man. His eyes sparkle like polished onyx, eyelashes so dark and long they make me jealous. "He's cute."

Jasper pinches my butt. Hard. And I squeal into his chest.

"Theo Silva. Bull rider. Rhett's been his mentor for a while now."

Winter holds up her left hand and cocks a hip. "I'm married, you fucking pig. Now leave."

Theo shrugs and smiles. "Married for now, maybe."

Rhett's voice draws my attention to the front door. I don't know how long he's been standing there watching. "Yeah, don't worry, Winter. We're definitely gonna free you from that husband and bury him in the back field. It'll be like that Dixie Chicks song. Rob is the new Earl."

Winter presses her fingers to her temples. "You're lucky you make my little sister so happy, Eaton." Rhett chuckles, and suddenly Winter looks exhausted and very wrung out. She looks like she could crumple. I want to march across the driveway and hug her, but I also don't want to out our eavesdropping position.

"Theo's just a baby though. You can't corrupt him, Winter." Rhett carries on while Winter shoots him an exasperated glare, sighing heavily.

Theo rolls his eyes. "I'm not a baby. I'm twenty-six."

Rhett scoffs. "No, you aren't. You're twenty-two."

"Dude. I was twenty-two when I first met you on the circuit. I've gotten older. You're doing the thing my mom does with her pets. They hit a certain age, and then she says they're that same age until one day they just die."

Rhett chuckles. "Well, I'll be. You're like that store with the skimpy dresses. Forever 22."

"Yeah. You're definitely getting old. That store is called Forever 21."

Rhett swipes a hand through the air as though batting away a fly. "Whatever. I only know about the skimpy dresses."

"Are you two done? I need a drink if I'm going to stay here all night." Winter's arms cross over her stomach protectively. From what I know, she and Summer have been mostly estranged all their lives, and for good reason. But in recent months, they've been trying to mend that bridge.

"Ah, yes, Winter, meet my protégé Theo Silva. Theo, meet Doctor Winter Hamilton, my future sister-in-la—"

"Winter Valentine," she corrects stiffly.

"For now," Theo reiterates and winks at her. She rolls her eyes dramatically, which makes Theo smile bigger as he sticks his hand out to shake hers.

She walks past Theo's outstretched hand without a second glance, and he rolls with it by swiping his palm through his hair, joking like he wasn't trying to shake her hand at all.

"Call your dog off, Eaton," she mutters as she passes Rhett and enters the log ranch house.

"Woof!" Theo makes a deep barking sound into the snowy night air, and Rhett laughs at him as Winter disappears.

"You're an idiot, Theo."

"Dude. I think I'm in love with your sister-in-law. She's so fiery."

Rhett shakes his head as he turns to go back into the house, Theo on his heels. "Like I said, man, you're an idiot."

Elsie Silver

The door closes, and Jasper and I snuggle up into each other on the quiet bench again.

"Well," he starts, arms swiping up over my back. "Should we go in? I don't want to miss this dinner. It's gonna be a good one. I can tell already."

"Yeah." I chuckle, kissing his bristly cheek. "Let's go."

I go to extricate myself from his lap, but his hands clamp down on me, keeping me where I am.

"First, can I come to *The Nutcracker*? I wanna see you dance. I wanna be there. Front row. Big bouquet of roses. The whole thing."

"You better be there, Gervais." I grin at him, heart swelling in my chest. Having the people I love in the audience is the best part, and suddenly my heart twangs at the loss I feel where my parents are concerned.

They might not be there, and I'll be spending Christmas without them for the first time in twenty-eight years.

My birthday is this week too. I absently wonder if I'll miss that with them as well.

But as we stand, Jasper squeezes my hand and draws me close. And nothing in the world has ever felt more right.

I can't have them, but I have him. And the more time I spend living my own life, the more I think that's an okay trade to make.

Jasper is worth it.

32

Jasper

Beau: Dad just told me you paid four times face value for a front-row ticket to see Sloane dance. They pay y'all too much to run around on ice wearing sharp blades.

Jasper: It's an investment.

Beau: In what?

Jasper: Us.

Beau: Oh, dude. You're so far gone.

Jasper: You're such a dork.

Beau: Only you would have waited this long. I almost feel bad she had to fall for someone as slow to process as you. Do they give Olympic medals for patience? You could give her yours.

Jasper: You know what her dickhead of a dad said to me.

Beau: Yeah. But that was then. That guy ain't shit

now. You're Jasper fucking Gervais. Olympic gold

medalist. Future Stanley Cup champion. Sports

Illustrated cover model material. Cousin fucker.

Jasper: I am really glad you're alive. But I also hate you.

Beau: Hate you too, bro. <3

~

SLOANE IS INCREDIBLE. SHE WEAVES MAGIC ONSTAGE.

I've come to know her body well over the last couple of months, but I'm still in awe of the way she moves, the attention to detail. From the tips of her toes to the very ends of her fingers, she's in perfect control of every movement without even trying.

She's stepped into this role and made it look effortless beyond compare. She leaps across the stage and lands so softly, and from the front row, I feel like I'm right there with her.

In the moment…oblivious to the ornate theater and every person around me.

But she's always had this effect on me. The ability to pull me out of my head just by chatting or dancing or resting a hand on my shoulder.

It's like she and I are tethered together, but she's the strong one. The pillar. And when troubled waters wash me downstream, all I have to do is follow the rope that ties me back to her.

It always leads me back to her.

Getting to watch her do something she loves from the

front row rather than back in the nosebleeds is something special. The spot where her tattoo sits itches, and I press my arm against it.

I missed her first one, but I wouldn't miss the rest if I could help it, even if it means a grown-ass man sitting by himself in the front row at the ballet.

Seems like the least I could endure for her.

Because I love having her at my games and I know she must feel the same. When the dancers line up to take their final bows, her eyes find mine, and a heart-stopping grin spreads out over her captivating face.

And I realize it then... I'd do anything to see this girl smile.

The minute the velvet curtain closes, I'm up, striding left toward a side door that leads backstage where she told me to wait for her. Except I don't wait.

I can't wait.

I push right through that swinging door, fingers itching to touch her, chest aching to have her head rest against it, and cock swelling after so long stuck watching her tight fucking body glide around onstage.

It's a good thing I didn't watch her dance much when she first joined this company. I wouldn't have been able to keep my hands off her, and now I just don't care.

Now I know my hands belong on her.

"Can you tell me where Sloane Winthrop is?" I ask a woman walking down the dim hallway with a clipboard in her hand, glasses shoved up on the top of her head.

She looks me up and down with a blank expression on her face. "Who's asking?"

I hesitate but only for a minute. "Her boyfriend."

She looks me over again, this time more slowly, but with a little twist to her lips. "Huh. Well, good for her. She's down that way." The woman turns and points to the area from which she came. "Left when you hit the end and then all the way down that hallway. Last door on the right."

I offer her a chagrined smile, knowing there must have been talk while Sloane and I were away. They announced her wedding to Sterling in the newspaper. Her colleagues would have known—maybe they even know him.

"Thanks." I nod my head and pass the woman, sensing her gaze on me as I head down the hallway. Backstage is a flurry of activity. Dancers are everywhere in the hallways, laughing and chatting. I hear the pop of a champagne bottle as they unwind for a Christmas break.

Turning left, I feel the tug. The pull to Sloane. After years of denying myself the pleasure of her proximity, my body has lost all patience with me and desperately wants to be close to her.

My knuckles rap against the door labeled SUGAR PLUM FAIRY.

"Just a second!" Sloane's voice only ratchets up the tension in my body, and when she finally swings the door open, I'm on her.

My hand lands on her throat, my lips crashing against hers as I tower over her. She tenses momentarily, clearly caught by surprise, but it doesn't take her long to catch up. Her hands slide up the arms of my suit jacket as I walk her backward into the dressing room, kicking the door shut behind us.

I turn her instantly, shoving her up against the wall beside the door. Because we're just not getting any farther than this right now.

She looked too good. There were too many eyes on her. More than just mine. And I'm feeling a little untethered and a lot territorial.

"Hi, Jas," she huffs out playfully against my lips, but all I offer back is a low growl as I take her mouth again. My hands slide into the thin cotton robe she has wrapped around her slender body. After a few well-placed tugs, it's gone, pooling at her feet on the floor where it belongs.

"You were perfect," I breathe, gaze raking over her. Wide eyes and heaving chest. Flimsy bodysuit over tights. Slippers off. Ornate costume gone.

"Yeah?"

"Yes." I thumb the thin strap of her bodysuit before tugging it down, letting it hang off her toned arm. "You stole the show. Every eye in the house was on you."

She laughs, and my thumb shoots up to press against her lips, silencing her. "I'm not joking. Everyone was staring at what's mine."

Her mouth pops open under the pad of my thumb. I smile and tilt my head into her neck, running the tip of my nose up the sloping curve. "And now I want to take it back. Remind you who you belong to."

She lets out a small gasp as I drop to my knees in front of her, jerk the bodysuit to the side, and use my fingers to rip a hole in the flimsy tights.

I push a finger in, and her pussy clenches in surprise.

She's not ready yet, but she will be.

I tear the hole open wider and then tug one leg up over my shoulder, watching her spread for me as she whimpers and drops her fingers into my hair. I dive in with one long slow lick. She squirms against my tongue.

"Who does this belong to, Sloane?"

"You, you, you," she chants breathlessly, and when I glance up, she's tossed her head back in ecstasy. Already so fucking gone for me.

Me.

I lift her opposite leg to my shoulder so she's straddling my face as I push her into the wall—one hand splayed across her stomach to hold her in place and the other wrapped around her right thigh, fingers digging in hard.

I make a feast of her against that wall. I start off slowly, licking her up each side and then straight through her center. Hitting everywhere except her clit. Getting off on teasing her and feeling her writhe against me as she desperately tries to shift her hips so I hit that spot.

But I don't give in. I taste her arousal building, feel the tension in the way her legs clamp around my body. I drag my hand down and slide two fingers into her. They go so fucking easy now. I've got a front-row seat for the second time tonight. Her tight little pussy parts and squeezes around my digits as I scissor them inside her under the bright lights of her dressing room.

Wetness leaks out, making a fucking mess of us.

"Jasper." She moans. "More. Please."

"So fucking polite," I murmur back, glancing up to see

her watching me with shiny, heavy eyes. My fingers brush over her clit, and she jolts around me. "So tight and ready and needy for me. And you danced so fucking pretty for everyone. I think you deserve more tonight, don't you?"

She nods, top teeth pressing into her pillowy bottom lip. How desperate she looks right now makes me grin.

Just as desperate for me as I am for her.

So I reward her for that.

I slide two fingers back into her and drop my mouth all at once. My teeth graze her clit as my fingers work her, and she lets out a little shriek. I latch on, sucking her into my mouth, still working my fingers and tongue, getting off on the way her shriek morphs into a loud moan.

A moan that ends with "Oh god. Jasper. I'm going to come."

My fingers take on a twisting motion, and I don't let up. She thrashes around me, legs shaking and fingers yanking almost painfully in my hair as she comes apart above me.

And not quietly either. She calls out my name, louder than she should, but I don't care. I get off on people knowing what we're doing in here.

After years of keeping it a secret, it feels good to let it out.

When her limbs soften, I glance up, fingers still stuffed inside her.

Her eyes shine down at me. "Well, that was unexpected. Better than going for another tattoo?" She quirks a brow, and I match the expression as I withdraw from her warm body.

"So much better and I'm not even done." I push to stand, taking her body with me, sliding her up the wall as my free hand grapples with my pants.

Belt. Button. Shirt. Boxers.

I rip through it all and shove into her as her legs wrap around my waist. "Fucking the fancy prima ballerina up against the wall like the filthy girl she really is? Much, much better than getting another tattoo."

My hips flex as I buck into her again.

"Fuck." Her eyes flash and flutter shut as her head rolls against the wall. She's so gone right now, and we're past the point of pretending our bodies don't drive the other one absolutely insane.

"Eyes on me, Sloane." My fingers find her throat and give her a warning squeeze.

Lashes flick open, and she looks me straight in the eye. No hesitation. No shyness. I'm sure I've fucked all the shyness out of her in the past several weeks.

"Harder," she urges.

"Which one?" I push my hips forward hard, slamming her into the wall. "Pussy?" Then pulse my hand around her neck, "Or throat?"

Heat simmers in her aqua eyes; they burn so fucking hot when she tips her chin at me in challenge. "Both."

I snap.

I feel like I unleash a lifetime of pent-up tension.

I feel unhinged as I fuck her into the wall without mercy, spurred on by her loud cries and nails digging in against the back of my neck. My hand squeezing just a little bit harder at the slender column of her throat—just how she likes it.

She's small, easy to maneuver how I want, but there's

nothing fragile about Sloane. She takes everything I have to give and meets me with equal fervor.

The wet slapping of our bodies mingles with the rattle of the painting on the wall every time I drive into her body.

I'm hard and unrelenting.

But added to our soundtrack is her demanding, "More," and "Harder," and I don't hold back. There's nothing tender or sweet about us right now, but we have lots of moments like that together. We reach for each other in the middle of the night, slowly moving together. We're playful in the mornings, my stubble against her inner thighs making her giggle and gasp.

But right now?

This is therapeutic. Like we're punishing each other for so many years and moments missed.

If she wants *more* and *harder*, I'll give it.

I'll give her anything she wants at this point.

"Jasper, I need more." Her eyes lock with mine. My wildness reflects right back into hers. I drop a rough kiss to her mouth and pull out, flipping her. I'm manhandling her and thriving on the way she moves the way I want her to.

"Hands flat on the wall, Sloane. Bend over. Spread your legs." She obeys and I reach down, further ripping the wet hole in her tights and tugging the bodysuit way off to the side.

She tilts her ass out in offering, and I step close. "You want me to fill you up, Sloane?"

"Yes," she moans, pressing herself back into me.

"Say it," I palm her firm ass cheeks, spreading her and teasing her entrance with the head of my cock.

"I want you to fill me up, please."

I smirk and lean next to her ear. "Of course you do. You're fucking desperate for it, aren't you?"

It's her turn to smirk over her shoulder at me. "Yeah, but so are you."

Her hips swivel in a taunt, and I grab them hard, shoving into her. She barely lasts bent over before I've forced her right up against the wall as my dick drives in and out of her, hitting that spot I know she loves so much.

I know because of the noises she makes. The way she pushes back on me. The way she cries out.

She keeps her hands on the wall like I instructed but is still looking over her shoulder at me with so much fucking love in her eyes. More love than I've ever seen. More love than I deserve or know what to do with.

The kind of love I've been known to sully.

I grip her chin and kiss her. I kiss her hard and full of all the feelings I'm too fucked-up to put a title on.

And then we topple over the edge together, into something I'm trying not to let panic me.

I fight to stay in the moment, with her pressed tightly against me.

We're so in tune.

So perfect together.

So perfect together that icy tendrils slink down my spine. Because I'm me. And any time something is perfect, it always goes to shit.

The knock on the door is proof of that.

33

Jasper

"JUST A SECOND!" SLOANE MELTS AGAINST ME.

We're plastered against each other, breathing heavily when there's another hard knock at the door.

I smirk, running my nose along the back of her neck, damp with sweat and little flyaways loose from the tight bun in her hair. "Someone probably heard you screaming and wants to check if you're all right."

Her shoulders shake with laughter as I pepper kisses over them. "I'm not alright. You made a mess of me, and my legs are going to give out if you let me go."

With a deep laugh, I swoop into a crouch, picking her robe up off the floor, knowing it will be the quickest, easiest way to cover her up. With me holding it wide, she slides her arms into the loose sleeves while I settle it around her shoulders.

I spin her to face me, press a quick kiss to her ravaged

lips, and step back to fix my own pants. I don't bother tucking my dress shirt in. I just make sure I'm clothed and shove my dick back into hiding.

Sloane's deft fingers make quick work of the belt around her waist, and after a once-over of me, she nods. And blushes, pushing those little flyaways back with a disbelieving shake of her head.

She gives me that look a lot, like she can't believe we're here, doing this. Sometimes I feel the same. Like it's all just a dream.

When she swings the door open, that dream freezes in place. We wake up from it abruptly, like we've fallen right out of bed.

Robert and Cordelia Winthrop are standing in the hallway. Robert is red, almost vibrating with fury. Sloane's mom is standing a few feet behind him, eyes dropped to her shoes with an embarrassed blush on her cheeks.

"What the fuck do *you* think you're doing here?" Robert asks.

Sloane's arms cross, and she goes instantly rigid. "I could ask you the same thing, Dad."

"I wasn't talking to you, Sloane. The ballet company announced in the newspaper you were filling in, and we would never miss our little girl onstage. I'm talking to *you*." His meaty pointer finger jabs in my direction. "What the fuck are *you* doing in here with *my* little girl?"

What I want to say is, *I think you heard exactly what I was doing to your little girl*, but I have more respect for Sloane than to go there.

I hit him with a blank look and push my hands into my pockets, which just draws his gaze to my untucked shirt. "What I should have done a long time ago."

Robert's hand trembles as he thrusts his finger my way with force, right over Sloane's shoulder, like she isn't even there. "I told you to stay the hell away from her." His loose jowls jiggle with the force of his anger.

"It seems you failed to inform me of that." Sloane's hand props against the door as though she's blocking her father from getting at me. Protecting me like always.

To her own detriment.

"Sloane, move aside like a good girl. This doesn't concern you. We'll have plenty to discuss once I have taken the trash out."

Good girl? Is he out of his fucking mind talking to her like she's a dog?

Sloane gasps. I've always known he's a piece of shit, but I think this might be the first time she's really seeing it.

With two long strides, I'm at her side, entirely blocking the doorway.

"Talk to her like that again and see how it ends for you." The angry, fucked-up teenager in me flares to life. I've worked hard to get control of myself over the years, and Robert fucking Winthrop just undid it all with one well-placed tug on a loose string.

"You forget what I told you, boy? You want that career? You want that paycheck? I can still ruin you. I can take it all away in a second." He snaps his fingers for emphasis.

The logical part of me doesn't want to believe him. The

logical part of me knows I'm a household name. A national sensation, as the headlines would say. Indispensable to my team—at least when I'm playing well.

Sloane steps up to her dad, dwarfed by his size but holding her head high like she doesn't notice at all. Her dainty finger points at her father, steady and strong. "Talk to *him* like that again and see how it ends for *you*."

"Sloane, let the men talk." He waves her off like she's completely inconsequential to him.

She rears back as though he's struck her. And I guess in a way he has.

He also talked to her like that again when I told him not to.

With one gentle hand, I usher her behind my body, protectiveness pouring out of me. "Get out."

"I'll ruin you, Gervais. You're not in the plan for her. You're an orphan who works in the entertainment industry. She's practically Canadian royalty."

My head tilts, and Robert Winthrop might as well be a puck. Because all I can think is that I need to stop him. Stop his forward motion into this room. And stop his stupid mouth from running.

"I think Sloane will be the judge of that. I think we're all going to step away from telling Sloane who she is and what she needs to do. I think Sloane is very smart and very capable of knowing what she wants for herself."

My gaze flits over his shoulder to Cordelia, whose eyes are boring into mine. She looks angry but not at me. It's the type of anger that could brim over into hot, quiet tears.

I know that anger. I know those tears. They taste like regret, and that's what's written all over her face.

She looks so much like her daughter, it's hard not to see the parallels between them. It's hard not to see her as living the life that Sloane could be years from now. Having to watch her own daughter get pawned off like chattel.

I shake my head. What fucking year is it? I guess I really must be from the wrong side of the tracks because these business transaction marriages are just not a part of my world.

"Is that so, Sloaney?" Robert peers around me, bending down condescendingly, looking far too amused by his daughter's distress.

I want to deck him in the face and watch him crumple to the floor. But despite my lowbrow upbringing and being "an orphan who works in the entertainment industry," I'm not dumb. He's the type of asshole who will waltz into his fancy lawyer's office and fucking cry about it.

Sloane's fingers link with mine as she steps close to me, holding her chin up, refusing to cower. "You need to leave. When I'm ready to speak to you, I will. And my name is Sloane. Not Sloaney."

Robert blinks once as he straightens. He expected her to roll over and show him her belly, not curl her lip at him.

I'm proud of her. Of how much she's grown in the last couple of months.

The beefy man tugs at the lapels of his jacket. "I've made us a dinner reservation for your birthday on Wednesday. If you deign to grace us with your presence, it would be lovely to have the birthday girl there."

He slips into being a condescending asshole so easily. My teeth grind, and my fingers curl tightly around hers while the opposite hand balls easily into a fist.

"Jasper has a game that night," she says matter-of-factly.

Robert smiles. "That's fine. He isn't invited. Not if he wants to keep that gig."

Sloane's chin dips, and her shoulders roll inward. Disappointment paints every crevice of her body, but she doesn't offer a response.

He's almost out the door when he turns back and delivers his killing blow. "Think hard, *Sloane*. If you're going to be master of your own destiny or whatever this new phase is, you have to consider some things. Do you want to be the reason Jasper Gervais goes back to where he came from? That's a long way for a man like him to fall."

With that, he raps his fingers against the doorframe and strides away like he owns the fucking place.

Cordelia's haunted eyes are a shot straight to the chest. The look of pleading she hits me with is heavy and uncomfortable.

Almost as uncomfortable as the silence that descends over Sloane and me in the aftermath of that conversation.

I want to tell her that I love her. The words practically scorch the tip of my tongue as I hold them back. But it's not enough. Or maybe it's too much.

Of course, I love her. I always have. But this? Now? I love her so much differently than I've loved a single other person in my life.

A truck, a hotel, a snow-covered runaway lane, it doesn't matter—she's home.

She's the air I breathe, and that fucking terrifies me.

Because no matter how fiercely I love someone, I know they always leave.

34

Sloane

Dad: 7 p.m. Wednesday at The Frontier. Make the smart choice.

Sloane: Smart for me? Or smart for you?

WE DRIVE IN TENSE SILENCE, CLUTCHING ONE ANOTHER'S hands. I don't think I've let Jasper's hand go for longer than a few seconds here and there.

And he's been the one to reach for me. Every time.

After years of reaching for him, he's reaching back. I just don't know if taking his hand is the smart move anymore.

I went from elated and horny, bursting with all the mushy feelings, to worrying my love might ruin this man's life.

My dad pulled the rug out from under me with such force that I'm toppling. I'm Alice down the fucking rabbit hole into Wonderland where absolutely nothing makes sense.

Except nothing about this situation is charming or quirky.

We pull up in front of the little bungalow I've worked the hardest on updating. The one we've been playing house in. The one he bought just to give my dad a solid *fuck you*. And now I'm seeing why.

I sit stunned, seeing the house in a new light. It felt like we were building a home here. We've made a point to make love in every room. I've put a wreath on the front door and twisted Christmas lights around the patio banisters.

My dad has managed to tarnish even this for me. Chestnut Springs. Jasper. My love life. I'm once again plunged into that ice bath of realizing I've been the perfect little pawn and haven't been smart enough to notice.

"I have to go back into the city early for practice in the morning," Jasper says.

I nod. When he asked me where I wanted to be, I said, "Take me to Chestnut Springs."

I had zero desire to stay in the same city as my dad.

"You okay?" His warm fingers squeeze mine, pulsing like a heartbeat.

Jasper has always been my heartbeat, and I still wonder if I'm his. If he feels this as intensely as I do.

If he loves me.

He hasn't said the words, and neither have I. In a way, we've felt tenuous, too unsettled. Fragile, like a stack of blocks that's slightly askew. One brief rumble and it could all go toppling. We both have shit we haven't been brave enough to face. We've had our heads in the sand.

Could he love me if it meant losing his career, his passion? It's the one thing he's worked so hard to achieve. He overcame everything for it.

"No," I whisper. "I'm not."

"I'm sorry, Sunny."

"Yeah." I sigh raggedly, finally turning to look at Jasper. His keen midnight eyes analyze me under furrowed brows. He is so damn handsome in his expensive suit. He's a man of contradictions. Rugged and polished. Hot and cold. Soft and hard. Happy and sad. Broken and mended.

A patchwork quilt that I love to snuggle with.

Just staring at him cracks my fucking chest open. I could give him the freedom to keep everything he's worked so hard for. Even though it would rip me apart to do it.

But I'd rather hurt.

I'd rather have a Jasper-shaped hole in my chest than drag him off the little chunk of happiness he's carved out for himself just so I can keep him. This life has been so unfair to him in so many ways. Over and over again.

I don't want to be another thing that's unfair to him by taking more than he can reasonably give someone.

"Sunny…" He turns in his seat, brushing calloused fingers over my cheek. "Why are you crying?"

My free hand wobbles up to my face and comes away wet. I didn't even realize I was crying. I stare at the glistening water on my hand, and it takes me back to my almost-wedding day, watching that little droplet of blood bead on my hand.

Jasper's hand cups my cheek, the pads of his fingers trailing over the back of my neck. "I don't want to be the reason you're estranged from your family. I don't want to make you choose. Because I know how badly it hurts to lose your family, no matter how terrible they might be. I don't want to tell you what to do. This isn't about me. I just want you to be happy. Go to the dinner. Mend your fences, burn your bridges. Whatever you need to do. I'll go to my game. It doesn't matter to me." His thumb rasps across my cheek, and his voice cracks. "Just tell me how to make you happy."

"I don't want him to ruin your career." I sniff, clearing my throat as I look up into the eyes that have held me captive for eighteen years.

He wags his head. "He won't."

"He said he would."

"He can't."

"You don't know that!" My whispers turn to an agitated shout. "You don't know the pull he has. The connections. I've seen it my entire life and somehow never judged the way he wields that power. I've been so stupid. So blind."

"He can't. And you are many things, but stupid is not one of them. You're going to stop saying that now because I'm not living in fear of him anymore, Sunny. And you should stop living in fear too. I spent years losing sleep over that threat. And I'm done. Blind, maybe? But I can relate. We're often blind to the people we love the most."

The expression on Jasper's face right now is one of pure focus and determination. Pure *love*.

But I push past that. Bat it away. Clamp my heart shut. Sometimes loving means losing, and I love him enough to do that. If he needs me to, I will.

"But what if he can? What if he can cut you off at the knees and make it all disappear? It's not out of the realm of possibility where Robert Winthrop is concerned. Then what would you do?"

Jasper blinks at me, going still in the quiet SUV.

My hand clenches his as I put it all on the table. The question I know will either make or break my heart. "Are you willing to take that gamble?"

I roll my lips together, willing Jasper to say *of course* he'll take that gamble. But also willing him to say no. I want him to keep what he's worked so hard for, not throw it all away over some lovesick girl.

The seconds stretch out, and Jasper says absolutely nothing. His expression is stricken, and his eyes stare off into some faraway place.

I can imagine where. To a day a long, long time ago. One that still haunts his every decision, one I don't know that he'll ever be free of.

Jasper feels that his decision that day lost him everyone he loved.

Now I worry that he'll be forced to make a decision that will put him back there all over again.

But he says nothing. He doesn't tell me what I want to hear. And he doesn't tell me what I don't want to hear.

He just freezes. Like that day on the runaway lane.

And somehow that hurts worse. My heart feels flayed in

my chest, like it's trying to crawl up my throat to escape the pain of being in my body.

My head understands his indecision, but my heart wanted him to say, "Yes! I'm willing to take that gamble."

My heart *needed* him to say that.

I squeeze his hand one more time, swallowing hard to force myself into a state of cool composure. If I can dance on bloody toes, I can make it out of this vehicle without crumbling.

"It's okay. I understand. But I think you should go back to your place in the city tonight. Make sure you're ready for your games this week. Take the time and space. We both need it. I'll call you."

I'll call you. I almost laugh at how cliché I sound. What could be worse? *It's not you, it's me?*

When he doesn't respond, I peek at his face. A familiar frozen expression gracing his features.

"I know you're crumbling right now. I can see you falling apart right before my eyes, Jas. But I also know you need to be the one to put yourself back together. If it's me, I'll constantly be the one mending you when you break. Pulling you back from that ledge. And I can't be responsible for that for the rest of our lives. That needs to come from you." My voice cracks. "I can barely put myself back together these days."

And with that, I pat his hand and pull away, leaving the warmth of his vehicle, turning with my head held high to walk to the front door. In an even but forced tempo, I breathe in through my nose and out through my mouth.

I lean on my years of training, walking gracefully with my shoulders rolled back and head held high.

It's not until I've safely closed the front door that the engine revs and wheels crunch on the snow-packed street and I let my composure slip.

Then I crumble too.

35

Sloane

Summer: I think we need to do a boozy brunch.

Willa: I'm. Pregnant.

Summer: It's not always about you, Willa.

Willa: Who else would it be about?

Summer: Winter just showed up and asked if we could get coffee. I really want to talk to her. But…I don't know what to talk to her about. I need people to run interference.

Willa: You can talk about what a piece of shit her husband is? How cute Theo is?

Summer: Not touching any of that with a ten-foot pole. Also, Sloane might be dead. She's just lying on the floor of my gym staring at the ceiling.

Willa: Sloane. Pick up your phone. Death isn't an option. You're too young and hot. And I still haven't found out how big Jasper's dick is.

Sloane: Why don't you just ask him?

Summer: Lmao. Yeah, Wils. Just drop him a casual line.

Willa: You're alive! He's so tall! His hands are so BIG.

Please confirm the size.

Sloane: His feet are big too.

THE NEON LIGHTS ABOVE ME FLICKER, AND I WATCH ONE long bulb burn out entirely. Little spots crop up in front of my eyes from staring at them for so long.

I was hot when I finished dancing, but now the sweat on my skin has cooled, and discomfort seeps into my pores. I still don't move.

Discomfort is my new default.

I've been in this studio for hours now, dancing until I can't think anymore. I don't want to think. I lay in bed awake all night thinking.

I even thought about responding to Jasper's text message this morning. And then I didn't because I don't know what to say.

Good morning.

Actually, no. It's not a good morning. It's a shit morning. And I love him so much I could easily slip into hating him. I could say something cruel. I could make him feel bad.

It might make me feel better for a minute to lash out. To make him hurt as intensely as I am.

But deep down I know he already is. I *know* him. I know he's panicking. He's locked up. Frozen solid like on the steep runaway lane.

I know he's suffering, and that fucking kills me.

What's worse is I pushed him away. I thought it might be better for him this way. Now I'm not so sure that's true. I'm not sure of anything—myself included.

For years I wanted to get into Jasper's head. Until now. Now, I think it's best to not know what's going on inside his head.

It hurts less that way.

"Okay, you've been lying here far too long. My sister is a doctor, so she's going to come check on you."

My head rolls across the floor to peer at Summer in the doorway to the back studio of the gym. She's leaning against the frame while her equally adorable blond sister stands beside her, looking notably uncomfortable in her scrubs and puffy down jacket.

She gives me an awkward wave and a tight smile, not nearly as homicidal as the night I first saw her.

I lift a hand back in their direction. "I'm perfectly fine. No cause for alarm. But you do need to replace a light bulb in here." I gesture up to the ceiling. "Actually, if we're offering doctor advice…is staring at light bulbs bad for my eyes?"

Winter shrugs. "Probably isn't ideal."

"Okay." I sigh. "I'll close them. Doctor's orders."

Winter lets out a dry chuckle, but Summer doesn't. Her footsteps approach, and when she nudges my foot with the toe of her sneaker, I peek up at her.

"Let's go," she says. "I know what you need."

I nod, letting my eyes drift shut. "Yeah. A time machine."

"No. A boozy brunch."

"Summer, it's a Monday!" Winter sounds alarmed, and it makes me laugh.

"So? You just finished a long shift, and I'm done with my clients for the day. Willa is bored and blowing up my phone about penis sizes. And Sloane looks half-dead. We all got somewhere to be? Important things to do? You eager to head back to the city?"

Winter's lips purse tightly as she shakes her head.

I point at her, already feeling a little tipsy. Lack of sleep will do that to a girl. "Girl, same. Let's just hole up in Chestnut Springs with a hot country boy and never go back to the city. The city fucking sucks, and so does everyone who lives there."

A small smile plays across Winter's impassive face, and she shrugs, crossed arms rising and falling as she does. "I suppose I could drink to that."

"Heck yeah!" Summer whoops. "I'll give Wils a call, and we can meet her at Le Pamplemousse."

"Here, have another one." Willa pushes a mimosa across the table toward me in the charming sunlit Parisian-style cafe, drawing my attention off Rosewood Street, the main thoroughfare in Chestnut Springs.

"I already have one." I tip my champagne flute at her.

She points to my opposite hand. "Yeah, but that hand is empty. And I'm not going to drink it. I'm pregnant." She rolls her eyes like I'm dumb and places the glass so it brushes up against the tips of my fingers.

"Why did you order it then?" I don't fight it. I curl my fingers around the stem of the glass and bring it closer.

Willa shrugs with a light laugh. "I dunno, wanted to be part of the boozy brunch."

Winter arches a brow from beside her. "You're literally *here*. At boozy brunch. What more do you need?"

Willa stares longingly at my double-fisted mimosas. "Booze. Obviously."

"What about some orange juice in a champagne flute?" Summer offers sweetly.

Willa makes a groaning noise. "That's just offensive."

My eyes bounce between the three women, and I realize I'm already feeling more human. Smiling isn't the Herculean effort it felt like earlier.

Winter takes a deep swig. "This drink tastes fantastic. I should do this more often."

Willa's elbow nudges her side. "Fuck yeah, you should."

Summer nods before shyly adding, "I like having you out here, Winter."

I lift my glass across the table. "I'll cheers to that. I could use a little Winter inspiration. I watched you dress Theo down the other night, and I need to channel that with the men in my life."

She clinks her glass against mine, but her head tilts. "I'm not sure I'm someone to aspire to in the man department." I quirk a brow, eyes dropping to the ring on her finger. She notices and just says, "Yeah. That."

"When is that ending?" Willa asks it so casually, like ending a marriage is cut-and-dried. I don't know all the dirty details of Winter's marriage, but I know it's complicated as hell. I also know that she and Summer are on fragile footing and spending time together like this is new for them.

They all came out for me, but it's clear that having Willa and me here gives some extra padding between the sisters.

Winter takes another deep slug, draining the flute. "Who fucking knows? I think dragging it out makes him hard or something." Summer coughs like her mimosa went down the wrong tube. Winter doesn't seem to notice though. The alcohol must have her feeling loose already. She tips her head in my direction. "Sloane's idea of hiding out in Chestnut Springs is sounding really, *really* appealing. Where do I sign up for this?"

I push my spare mimosa across the table to her, and she takes it without saying a single word. The closer I look at Winter, the more I think she might need the drinks more than I do.

I feel wrung out, but she seems profoundly tired, like my one sleepless night is her norm.

"Wanna rent a house here?" I ask. "I'm in the process of updating a few across the road from Summer's gym."

That lights Winter's face up. "Yeah?"

"Yeah. I can show you after this boozy brunch."

"Jasper's houses, huh?" Summer asks curiously.

"Yeah, why don't you tell us more about that?" Willa urges.

I tuck a stray piece of hair behind my ear and drop my eyes. "Well, he actually owns the entire block. I've been painting and—"

Willa waves a hand. "No, no, no. Tell us about Jasper."

"Yeah!" Winter holds up her glass. "Tell us why you were lying on the floor for like an hour."

Summer reaches under the table and gives my knee a squeeze, always so sweet.

"I don't even know where to start."

"Can you at least tell us if Jasper has a huge dick?" Willa leans across the table.

I nod.

Winter snorts.

Summer gasps.

"I knew it!"

Summer gives Willa a chiding look, widening her eyes at her best friend. "Why don't you start at the beginning, Sloane?"

I flop back in my chair and stare at the three women sitting with me. "Well, I'd have to go back to the very first time I laid eyes on him when I was ten years old."

A communal whoosh of air leaves everyone's lungs. I lift my glass. "Yeah. Cheers to that, right? A decades-long unrequited crush. Except I recently found out it wasn't so unrequited."

Willa's hand rolls in the air. "Hence the whole runaway-bride-shacking-up-with-her-friend thing, yeah?"

My head tips back and forth. "I mean, yeah. It's a little more complicated than that."

"What's the issue?" Willa seems confused.

"Yeah, what'd he do?" Bitterness bleeds into Winter's voice.

"He didn't do anything. That's the problem. He just froze. He had this perfect moment to tell me everything. And he just froze. He's so broken. Locked up so damn tight. And I know the reasons why. I don't even really blame him. I just… I wanted to be enough for him to push past it."

I blink rapidly, taking a huge swig. "Everything he does for me says he cares. But I need"—I click my tongue and give my head a sharp bob—"I don't fucking know. I guess after years of believing he doesn't want me, I need more than just him falling into a happy, simple little rhythm with me. I want to feel like he can't live without me. Like he'd do anything to have me. If he can't find the words to tell me, I want actions. Just…*something*."

Heads nod, and I feel spurred on by the reassurance, the lack of sleep, and the champagne on an empty stomach.

"At the risk of sounding petty, I want him to be just as lovesick as I am. I've wanted him for so damn long. I'm almost angry he never noticed. I want him to prove he notices now."

"So are you guys…broken up?" Summer asks, her voice small and tentative.

"No. I don't know." A dark laugh bubbles up in me as I shrug. "I think we're both just traumatized by our upbringings. Adulting is hard when your parents fuck you up, ya know?"

Summer and Winter give each other a loaded look before Winter says, "Yeah. I think we can relate."

"Deep down I know Jasper will never leave me. Not even at my worst. That's the thing about us. We can both be on our shittiest behavior, and we'll never hold it against each other for long."

"Ugh. I love that." Willa sniffs.

"I want him to make me feel secure. But I haven't told him anything to make him feel secure either, and I know he needs that. Basically, I have no plan because...I really don't know what to do with myself." I sigh, looking up at the lights above me, feeling a little responsible for pushing him away. "I need to face my dad so that I can properly move on. Start fresh. I need to find my own security first. I just hope I'm not too late. But then the thought of him losing hockey? His career? His passion? All for me? I'm worried I can't stack up against that."

"Have you not seen the way that man looks at you?" Winter is grinning at me even though it's an odd time to be grinning.

"I guess not."

"I only just met you two at dinner the other night, but he hangs on every word. Traces every movement. I'm not sure he even knew what else was going on in that room. It made me...it made me, well, it made me feel bitter if I'm being honest. It almost hurt to watch. But, ha, that's a me thing." She glances out the window. "At any rate, I'm giving him and his big dick my vote of confidence. Trust me. You stack up. I think he'll come around."

"But what if he doesn't?"

Winter shrugs, and the other two continue to stare at me all wide-eyed. I doubt they know what to say. Jasper is a mystery wrapped up in an enigma to most people.

"Then you move on."

Move on.

I take a deep swallow of my mimosa. It sounds so simple. So easy. So…obvious.

And yet so impossible.

If moving on from Jasper Gervais was an option, I'd have done it by now.

36

Jasper

Willa: Hi. It's Willa.

Jasper: Hi, Willa. It's Jasper.

Willa: I was going to message you and ask how big your dick is, but I don't think Cade would love that.

Jasper: I wonder why.

Willa: Instead, I thought I would tell you that now is your chance to *prove* how big your dick is.

Jasper: Thanks for the advice.

Willa: That wasn't advice. It was motivation.

Willa: Also, you'll never do better than her. I don't care how famous you arc.

"SO SHE ASKED IF YOU'D GAMBLE YOUR CAREER FOR A SHOT with her and you didn't say anything?" Harvey is glaring at me over the rim of his steaming coffee mug like I might be the stupidest thing he's ever seen.

"I went straight to Roman's house and we called team management to sort things out. Explained it all."

"Did you tell her that?"

I just glare back at Harvey. "Maybe I should have, but I wanted to go to her with a plan. *Proof.* I wanted to be able to assure her that my career was safe. That *we* were safe."

Harvey must think my plan sucks because he says, "All you boys are idiots."

I called Sloane on Monday. She ignored the call but texted me to say she was out with Summer and Willa. Didn't stop me from sleeping on an air mattress in the empty house next door just to be close to her.

I went to our house on Tuesday after I'd finished at the rink, but when I went to the front door, I saw Sloane and Winter with a six-pack of Buddyz Best Beer and Chinese take-out boxes sprawled out between them. They were lying on the floor, staring at the ceiling, laughing uncontrollably. It seemed like a dumb moment to knock and interrupt.

I also just plain chickened out. Got stuck in my head and let all the self-loathing get the best of me. I walked away, settling for laying my eyes on her to get a fix. Slept next door again.

Today is Wednesday, and I should be in the city getting ready for my game tonight, but I'm going out of my mind. Sloane has dinner with her dad tonight, and I have a divisional game with two points on the line that we desperately need.

But I'm here, talking to the only man I'd ever come to for

real advice. Because while I never met his late wife, Isabelle, I know he was an excellent husband. He has to know a thing or two about relationships, where I don't know anything. Haven't exactly seen great examples in my life.

"I froze. I panicked." Like I always do.

"Jasper." My name is a sad sigh on his lips.

"I'm trying to be respectful of her wishes," I explain.

"Son, I'm going to tell you something that I'd only say to a man as good as you." He pauses, eyes scanning my face. "In this instance, you're being *too* respectful."

"Thanks for the words of wisdom." I huff out a disbelieving laugh as I flop back on the couch, scrubbing at my face.

But every time I close my eyes, I see Sloane.

She's dancing or carefully rubbing a clay facial on my face. Sometimes I see Sloane scaring other girls away from me in a random bar. Other times she's swimming in a mountain lake. I see Sloane onstage.

The color of the lines on the ice? Remind me of her eyes.

When I put too much cream in my coffee the other morning? Her hair.

When I use my favorite bodywash? The way she leans into me and sucks in a huge breath.

Sloane is *everywhere.*

"So are you two broken up then? Family reunions are gonna be awkward now. Violet is gonna kill you."

"We're not broken up," I snap.

Harvey arches a brow at me as if to say, *Watch your tone, idiot.* "How do you know you're not broken up? Did you talk about it?"

"Because…"

"Or better question: How does Sloane know you're not broken up? Oh boy, did she even know you were together?"

I groan and stare up at the ceiling. Anxiety swirls in my chest. I rub at it as though I can ease it away, but it doesn't help. "Yeah. She knows."

"How?"

"I don't know. You don't just break us up. We're… I dunno. We're bigger than that."

"I mean, if y'all can overlook tail babies, I'm not sure what could really keep you apart."

I shake my head. "Dick."

"So you're like"—his hand waves around—"soulmates on a break. Yeah, yeah. Makes perfect sense."

Soulmates. That feels heavy.

But it doesn't feel wrong.

"Do you love her?"

I stare at Harvey, trying to work it all out in my head like I have been for days. "Of course I love her. I've always loved her."

"Did you tell her that?"

A stone drops in my stomach. "No."

"Why not?"

I shrug noncommittally, feeling like a child getting a scolding.

"You know why. You know this. Say it out loud."

My voice is strained when I finally say the thing that's been holding me back. "Because the people I love either die or leave me."

Harvey sighs, creaking back into the big leather chair beside the fireplace in the expansive living room. "You've been the apple of that girl's eye for going on two decades, and she has yet to leave. No matter how bad you hurt her."

Nausea follows a sinking sensation.

"I've never meant to. I swear I didn't know…not when anything could have come from it anyway. I mean, we all knew when she was a kid. But as an adult? How was this so obvious to everyone, but none of you assholes made fun of me about it until now?"

"Because it never seemed like you felt the same way. We did it enough when she was a teenager. It started to feel cruel. It wasn't funny anymore at some point. Not sure if anyone's ever told you this, Jasper, but you're hard to get a read on. You're moody and temperamental. Closed off. A little insecure at heart."

"Okay. Yes, I'm getting it. This is great for my self-confidence. Please, keep going." I prop my elbows on my knees and drop my head.

"You're also sensitive."

He's not wrong. I live in my head, and I feel things intensely. I always have.

"And scared," he adds, just to really drive the point home of how badly I'm fucking things up.

"Yeah. I am. I'm really fucking scared."

I hear Harvey's heavy footfalls as he crosses the room and flops down on the couch beside me. When he plants his hand in the middle of my back, the bridge of my nose stings. "Of what?"

"What if I make the wrong choice? What if I put it all on the line and it blows up in my face? What if she realizes I'm not worth it and leaves me? I… I'm paralyzed by all the what-ifs. This isn't just like, *What if I let a puck past?* Then I just lose the game. Life goes on. But this? I have a knack for fucking up the lives of people who love me and who I love back. It's my specialty."

"That's not true. You're looking at it wrong. I love you, and you've done nothing but make my life better."

A strangled noise lodges in my throat, and Harvey's hand moves up, squeezing my shoulder. I nod, still hanging my head.

"I don't know your parents from Adam, Jasper. But I've gotta say I don't want to. Anyone who could leave you behind? They don't love you the way you deserve. And I know Sloane would agree with that. That girl has never left you behind, not for a moment. No matter how unlovable you've been, she's loved you anyway. She's loved you when you didn't love her back and didn't ask for shit. I think all she's asking for is for you to love her back now. And you're telling me you already do but are too chickenshit to tell her. She's waited long enough, don't you think?"

"What am I supposed to do though? Beg her to choose me instead of her family? I know what it's like to lose your family. Even if they're assholes, you still want them around in some way. I don't want to be the one who makes that decision for her."

"You don't need to make a single decision for her—only for yourself. That girl has been choosing you for years. She's just sick of waiting around for you to choose her back. Can't say that I blame her. You're slow as molasses to figure things out. And now she's broken up with you. Anyone ever told you Sloane is the best you'll ever get?"

"She didn't break up with me. And, yes, Willa told me that today. You're all very thoughtful. Thank you for that."

"Are you two talking?"

I turn and glare at him, but deep down, my heart races. *Did she break up with me?* I really am an idiot.

"I mean, there's really only one question, Jasper." He sips his coffee and leaves me hanging. Old man has to get his kicks somehow.

Dick.

"What's the question?"

He shrugs like it's the most obvious thing in the world. "Would you make that gamble?"

"Over and over again."

I love hockey, but it's not even close to how I love Sloane. Two weeks off hockey compared to a few days without Sloane proved two things to me: I can live without hockey, but I can't live without Sloane.

He swats the back of my head lovingly. If that's even a thing. "Then tell her, you idiot."

A rapid knock at the door draws both our attention. Harvey slaps my knee. "I'll get that. You sit here and stew in your own stupidity while you muster up a plan to make this right."

I chuckle. Only Harvey could deliver an emotional pep talk and then mock me openly to make me laugh.

The hinges on the door creak, and I hear a voice I was not expecting. "Harvey."

"Cordelia?"

I'm up and walking toward the front door, rounding the corner just in time to see Sloane's mom lifting a Louis Vuitton suitcase as she says, "Any chance you have a spare room?" She looks down at her suitcase and then back up at Harvey. Her smile is watery. "I could really use a safe spot to get my bearings."

"Of course. I—"

"Oh," she breathes when she catches sight of me. "You're here."

I give her a nod, suddenly wishing I had my cap on to hide behind. "Mrs. Winthrop."

She stares at me for longer than is comfortable, and her eyes fill with tears. "Don't let him scare you off, Jasper." She pins me with her light-blue eyes, so similar to her daughter's. "Don't let him control you too. He's a master. He gets his claws into you, and suddenly you wake up in your fifties with nothing but a heaping pile of regret. The best thing I can do for her at this point is lead by example. I don't want that life for Sloane. I don't want *him* for Sloane. She's going to need you to be there for her when she breaks free of them."

"Them who?" I ask, alarm coursing through me as I put together what she's saying. What she's done.

I glance between Harvey and Cordelia. Harvey's eyes are latched onto his late wife's little sister with an intensity I've never seen before.

"Sterling. Robert. Men like them don't take well to being

slighted. They maneuver. They plan. This dinner won't just be a birthday celebration. It'll be a coup, and I can't be there for it. Can't watch her continue to get played by them."

My heart thrums in my chest, hard and heavy. "She won't be."

Her mom sighs and looks at me sadly. "Maybe not, but it won't stop them from trying."

I grab my keys from the front table and leave them both with a nod.

"Jasper!" Cordelia calls out to me right as I get to my driver's-side door. "The Frontier Steakhouse."

I almost laugh.

The place where it all started. I hate that fucking restaurant, yet I can't get there fast enough.

She's never left me behind, and I'm not leaving her behind either.

The only thought in my head as I make the hour-long drive back into the city is that Sloane needs me. She needs me to just *be* there with her.

And I love her.

37

Sloane

Mom: I'm sorry I can't be there.

Sloane: I really don't blame you. It won't be a long meal. I can tell you that much.

Mom: You inspire me, Sloane.

Sloane: Inspire you?

Mom: To care less what anyone thinks. To put myself first. To be stronger.

Sloane: I don't feel strong.

Mom: Oh, my darling. But you are. And I'll never regret sending you that text, because that day you learned just how strong you can be.

FROM WHERE I'M STANDING, I HAVE THE PERFECT VIEW OF Dad and Sterling sitting beside each other at a table by the window. They've got their heads together and smiles on their faces, like two little boys whispering in class.

Little boys.

That's precisely what they are. After the last couple months spent in the presence of real men, I'm seeing the difference clearer than ever. It has nothing to do with money or education or a person's public reputation. It has everything to do with what's inside.

Soul. Heart. Actions speaking louder than words.

These two assholes can say whatever the hell they want. I'm not falling for it anymore. I see right through it.

For too long, I was a soft, demure little dove. And then they burned me. Scorched me.

Turns out I'm a dragon and I'm fed the fuck up with boys and their bullshit.

My shoulders roll back as I lean against the outside wall of Cartier across the street from the Frontier.

I'm a little hungover today. Winter and I hit it off. Turns out we have more in common than I ever imagined. She's fun and totally down to drink too much cheap beer and lie on the floor with me.

I have her to thank for the power suit I'm wearing and also for the ride into the city. I also have her to look forward to as a neighbor in Chestnut Springs because once I'm done with this stupid fucking dinner, I'm heading straight back to that little house.

Where I belong. Where I feel like myself. I'll figure the rest out as I go—for myself.

And there's something freeing about having no rules.

After a lifetime of having a path and plan laid out before me, I'm going to do…whatever the hell I want.

I roll my shoulders one more time, check both ways across the four lanes of traffic, and step onto the street.

Even jaywalking feels good.

I give the host a flat smile, holding one hand up. "No, thanks. I know where I'm going." Without giving him a chance to answer, I march past, right toward the table by the window where two of the men I least want to see are seated.

I thought I'd be nervous, but I just feel…exhilarated.

"Dad, Sterling."

Their heads snap up as though they're surprised to see me. Usually, a staff member would guide me here, but that's exactly what I didn't want.

"Sloaney…" Sterling eyes me, head to toe. "You look very severe in that outfit."

I almost laugh. After months of me ignoring him, *that's* what he has to say.

"Thank you." I shoot him a sarcastic smile before moving to the chair beside the window, across from my dad. As far away from Sterling as possible.

Dad's eyes sweep over me, assessing me, and I wonder what he sees. I wonder if he can tell I've lifted the veil and see him more clearly than ever.

I don't *hate* him. I am indifferent toward him.

He used to tell me he wasn't angry, just disappointed with me. And that's how I feel about him now.

Deeply disappointed. Because I'll always love him. He's always been someone I've looked up to, and to find out that was all fabricated or not true to his character is disappointing. Knowing that another man in my life didn't love me *quite* enough to overcome his own shit stings.

But it stings less with my hair pulled back and nails painted bloodred and wearing a black pantsuit with shiny tuxedo lapels.

Winter was right. I feel ready to kick ass and take names.

"Happy birthday, Sloane," Robert says, lifting a glass of wine without offering me one.

I reach over and pour myself a big one. Another faux pas at a place like this is not waiting for the server—or to overpour the way I just did.

But I'm fucking done waiting around for these men to get their shit together, and I deserve a jug of wine for even being here.

"Thanks, Dad," I finally reply after leaving them both hanging with their glasses in the air while I poured. Clearly, neither of them is gentlemanly enough to offer.

Glasses clink, and we drink. I keep my eyes laser-focused on my dad and roll my lips together primly, tasting the wine. It's expensive, but I'd rather crush a Buddyz Best.

"When's Mom coming?" I glance around the restaurant, really putting on a show of it, but I know she isn't coming. She told me she isn't. Mom also told me she found that video on Dad's phone and sent it to me anonymously on my wedding day. I assume it was blackmail fodder.

It would seem she and I came to our senses right around the same time. It would seem Robert Winthrop has finally pushed us both too far.

"She's a little under the weather today. It's just the three of us tonight."

"Actually…" a voice I never expected to hear chimes in. My heart lurches in my chest, composure slipping for just a second. It feels like I'm moving in slow motion as I turn to see Jasper standing at the end of the table, looking heart-stopping in a perfectly tailored suit, eyes on me, smug grin on his lips. "It's going to be the four of us." He steps toward me with authority, leans down, and tips my chin up to him, eyes capturing mine with a look of ferocity. "Sunny, I'm sorry I'm late."

Late.

It's such a simple sentiment. But it warms me from the inside all the same.

He's here.

All I can manage is a firm nod, one he returns before pressing a bristled kiss to my forehead and taking a seat beside me.

My rock. My comfort. The boy with the sad eyes and the heart of gold.

I turn toward him. "You have a game." I glance down at the dainty Rolex on my wrist. "Right now."

"We made a promise in that truck, remember? I can't go without you again. Nothing is more important than being here with you." He palms my knee under the table and inclines his head toward my outfit. "You are stunning, by the way."

Nothing is more important than being here with you.

I swallow a couple of times, unable to tear my eyes from

the man before me. The promise. He's right. And I promised him too.

"Jasper…"

His hand squeezes reassuringly. "The answer is yes, Sloane."

My head tilts. "Yes, what?"

"I'll take that gamble. All day long. Every damn day."

My eyes sting, and I will away the wetness. I'm not going to cry here. I will not let my dad and Sterling be privy to this moment.

When I glance over at the two men, the fury is clear on their faces.

"You are not part of this conversation, Gervais." My dad glares at him like he might make him cower. But that power has slipped from between his fingers, right before his eyes.

Jasper leans back in his chair, smirks, and settles in. "You're right about something at least. I'm not here to contribute. I won't say a word. I'm just here to be with Sloane."

"You're overstepping," Sterling whines, practically vibrating with fury. "You don't belong here."

Jasper smiles at him, keeping his cool and poking at the men across from him in the process.

"Enough," I snap. "Was there something you both needed to say to me? Because I think I've made myself crystal clear. I told you"—I point at my dad—"that I would speak to you when I was ready." I shift my finger over to Sterling. "But I never want to speak to you again."

"Sloane, you need to get over your hurt feelings."

I arch a brow at Sterling. "You just don't get it, do you?

What you do with your dick doesn't hurt my feelings. What you did with your dick was merely a wake-up call. A wake-up call that I don't care about you even a little bit. I am indifferent. It's been easy to ignore you because I don't think about you *at all*."

The more I talk, the more Sterling matches the deep-red color of the wine in his glass. The more Jasper's fingers slide along the inside seam of my wide-leg pants, the more my confidence builds. Just having him here, next to me…

It's all I've ever wanted. We're so much better together than we are apart.

"That's only because you've been whoring around with this trailer trash."

Jasper's entire body goes taut beside me. My mouth pops open in shock at the venom in Sterling's words and tone. It might be the most passionate I've ever seen him over anything other than barrel-aged scotch and hunting exotic animals.

I'm about to say as much when Jasper jerks and Sterling's gasped squeal reaches my ears. An expression of alarm flashes across his features right as his face tips back and disappears backward in a splash of red wine and the loud clatter of the chair hitting the floor.

Sterling sputters as he struggles to right himself.

"Did you just—"

"Kick his fucking chair over?" Jasper provides, cutting off my dad's question. "Yes. Because you might be okay with him talking to your daughter that way, but I am not. Must have learned better manners in the trailer park."

My dad at least has the good sense to look a little cowed.

But me? I do what I always do in inappropriate situations.

I burst out laughing as I watch Sterling on all fours, awkwardly pushing himself to standing. Dress shirt stained with red wine. Hair all fucked. And not in a good way.

"You're dead, Gervais." He tries to sound tough, but everything about the man rings so damn hollow.

It makes me laugh harder.

We've made a spectacle, and I've got the goddamn giggles.

"Sloane, pull it together. People are watching," my dad snaps at me.

Tears well in my eyes, and I rub them, but the laughter won't stop coming.

Jasper leans down and whispers in my ear. "If it makes you laugh, I'll kick his ass while everyone watches."

I hear the amusement in his voice and wave a hand across my throat, silently begging Jasper to stop. Because now he's just egging me on.

Because he knows me.

He gets me.

"Sterling," I wheeze out. "I will never marry you. Like…" A giggle hits me, and I force it back down. This sentence is just so much more offensive to deliver while laughing. But I can't even muster any fucks to give about that. "Ever."

"And Dad…" I shake my head, laughter slowing. "I don't even know. The things you've said to me in the last few months?" I place a hand on Jasper's. "The way you treat the people I love? I'd like to think I can find it in myself to forgive you, but I'll have to do a little soul-searching to decide if that's true or if that's just me still being obedient. A little girl is supposed to love her dad, but he's supposed to love her back. Protect her at all costs. And if these last months have taught me anything, it's that you don't love me the way I've loved you. I deserve better."

I peek over at Jasper now, finding his eyes on me like they often are. But today they aren't sad. They're glowing with pride. They sizzle across my skin.

I look back at the two men across from me. "I'm done settling for less than I deserve. Sterling, fuck off forever. Dad, figure out how to deserve a relationship with me. Maybe one day we can talk."

The chair screeches back as I stand suddenly.

I reach for Jasper's hand, making an obvious show of doing it in front of them. Then I'm tugging him along, wanting out of this godforsaken restaurant once and for all.

As I brush against Sterling's arm on my way past, he grabs my bicep. "Where's the ring? I want it back."

I circle my arm abruptly, tugging away from him right as Jasper steps in close, looking like he's ready to murder Sterling for daring to put a hand on me.

"I lost it." I laugh again and wonder what is wrong with me. Why I have to laugh at the most inappropriate times. Right now I am truly unhinged.

But it's Jasper who really gets the last laugh when he leans in against my ex's ear and says, "I fucked that ring right off her finger."

I wish I could commission an artist to paint the

expression on Sterling's face when that blow lands. It would be money well spent.

Jasper guides me out of the restaurant. We take the exact path we took all those months ago. Except everything is so different now.

So up in the air.

So unplanned.

So...happy.

38

Jasper

Roman: Management and ownership are all on the same page. I relayed everything we talked about. I just wish I could be a fly on the wall when they tell this fucker to take a hike.

Jasper: Thanks, Coach.

Roman: I've always got your back, Jasper. Now go get the girl.

I shove that heavy wood door open, sucking in the frosty December air. It smells like snow and exhaust. And it tastes likes freedom.

"Never take me to that fucking restaurant again," I say, right as I turn to tug Sloane into me. Her lips are the same shade of red as her nails.

She's got a real femme fatale vibe going on, and I am so here for it.

She laughs, sounding giddy and looking all wide-eyed. "I can't believe I just said all that." One hand lands on her cheek. "I can't believe you told him you fucked the ring right off my finger!"

I laugh now too because that shit was satisfying. "Did you see his face?"

Sloane nods, biting at her lip, eyes twinkling from reflecting the headlights of the cars buzzing past. "You came for me," she says, tipping her chin up and gracing me with the prettiest fucking smile.

"Of course. I told you I never wanted to be without you, and I meant it."

"I wasn't sure—"

"I've been sick for days. I came to our house but didn't know what to say. I've tried to figure out a good reason for why I froze in the car the other night. A reason why I didn't use the words I really wanted to even though I could feel them right there at the tip of my tongue. But there is no excuse." I brush at her hair. "I've been hiding for so long, peeking out at you from under the brim of my hat, that I got comfortable there. I'm sorry that I'm late in so many ways. Not just to dinner but to figuring myself out. I was…"

For a moment, I glance away and swallow. "I was scared. Scared to need you this badly. Really fucking scared to lose you."

Her eyes flutter shut on a heavy sigh, and I cup her head, wanting her eyes back on me. "I know—"

"No, Sunny. I shouldn't be scared. You're the least scary thing in my life. You're not just tattooed on my skin. You're branded on my heart. Woven into the fiber of my being. The most constant and reassuring person in my life. When I close my eyes, I see you. When you're away from me, I dream about you. When I need someone to lean on, you are *always* there for me. God. You've loved me when I haven't even been able to love myself." My hands squeeze her cheeks, and tears seep out over them. But she's smiling up at me like I hung the moon.

"You've looked at me like *this* for so damn long. And I don't know when I started looking back, only that I did. Forcing myself to look away for so many years has been a special kind of torture. I've tortured myself for long enough. I'm done hiding, done missing out on this. On us."

A quiet sob leaps from her lips, and she presses her head into the center of my chest.

"Sloane, I won't go without you."

"You've never been without me, Jasper. Not since the first day I laid eyes on you."

My heart cracks at her admission, and she presses in closer. Like she knows she fits there. Like she knows she belongs there. Filling in all the cracks where I break.

I hold her tight and rest my cheek on the crown of her head.

"I'm sorry you're the only thing that's ever made me feel whole again. I'm sorry I've needed so much from you. Sunny, I'm sorry I'm so damn late. But thank you for waiting."

Her hand slides into my suit jacket, and she palms the

ballerina tattoo on my ribs. "You showed up right on time." She peeks up at me. "Have you been staying in one of the empty houses?"

My lips twitch. "Maybe."

"Is there a bed?"

I shrug. "An air mattress."

"Jasper!" She groans my name, but her voice is amused too.

"What? I don't like being away from you. In fact, I would have been earlier. But I had to pick up your birthday present."

"You bought me a birthday present?" Her eyes light.

"Of course I brought you a birthday present. What kind of asshole shows up to his girlfriend's birthday dinner without a gift?"

She quirks an eyebrow at me, and we both smile. "Girlfriend?"

"Of course."

Then from within my pocket, I press the button on the key fob, and the SUV behind me blinks to life with a soft beeping noise.

Sloane's gaze hits the white Volvo and then slices back to me. "You bought me a car?"

"Safest one I could find. They've done the crash tests and—"

"Jasper," she giggles my name. "I trust you. I'll take your word for it. I… I love it."

"I know you mostly walk everywhere in the city." I clear my throat, feeling suddenly bashful. "But I want you to have something safe for your commute."

"My commute, huh?" She's grinning now. It's infectious.

"Yeah. From our house in Chestnut Springs. You'll need a safe car to get into the city for work. And you need your freedom to go wherever you want. Do whatever you want."

At that, her eyes fill. She blinks, and a lone tear rolls down over her cheek.

"You just get me, you know that?" Her head wags gently. "You always have."

Everything aches—my heart, my throat, my chest—so I do the only thing that I can think of to make it hurt less. "I love you, Sloane Winthrop. I always have. I love you so damn hard I don't even know what to do with it. You're my person. And I think I'm yours too."

"You have *always* been my person," she chokes out. "I love you so much."

I don't pause. I don't think twice. I tilt her head up, and I kiss her.

In the middle of a busy street for the whole damn world to see while snow falls around us. In the exact spot she walked away from me once before.

But this time, it's us.

Together.

39

Sloane

Sloane: Get your asses to the rink!

Willa: I'm not playing hockey.

Summer: Why?

Willa: It's not safe. Hard ice. Sharp blades. A bunch of men trying to prove that they aren't past their primes. Fuck that noise. I'm going to sit on my ass and cheer for Luke.

Winter: I think show jumping is probably more dangerous. Medically speaking.

Sloane: Winter, are you coming?

Winter: Can't. I'm sick.

Willa: Yeah. Me too. I'm sick. *cough cough*

Summer: Well, you're all boring. I'm on Team Sloane! Merry Christmas! Let's fucking goooo!

I THOUGHT MY BEST CHRISTMASES CAME WHEN I WAS A child. When the magic was still alive and thrumming. But somehow this Christmas takes the cake. It takes all the cake. And all the magic is thrumming.

I woke up in Jasper's arms. In our perfect, cozy little house. The home we've slowly made together. We made love while snow fell outside the window before we even got out of bed. And then we hopped into one of our *very safe* SUVs and headed straight for Wishing Well Ranch.

My mom and Harvey met us at the door with welcoming hugs and kisses as they ushered us into the bustling ranch house. Everyone was there.

We've all been together all day long, and my heart has never felt fuller. Every time I get too far, Jasper reaches for me. I barely go for five minutes at a time without feeling him touch me in some way. Without him pressing a kiss to my hair for everyone to see. It's...well, it's magical.

Almost as magical as this new tradition. The first of many Christmas traditions I plan to make with Jasper.

Christmas shinny.

"I thought skating was supposed to be easy? You assholes all make it look so easy!" Rhett complains as he clomps around like Bambi on the ice, all long legs and awkward motions.

"Bad word, Uncle Rhett!" Luke, his six-year-old nephew, calls while skating speedy circles around his uncle.

Summer laughs before getting up off the log where she's been sitting with Willa. "I can help you, babe!" she calls as she skates effortlessly over to Rhett.

He rolls his eyes. "Seriously? You're good at this too?"

Summer just shrugs, acting all saucy as she winks at him. "I'm good at everything."

I laugh from where I'm leaning against Jasper's net, taking it all in. Soaking it all up.

"It's just proof that you're overachieving!" Jasper's voice draws my head up to the path that leads down to the ice. Cade laughs, each of them pulling a plastic sled loaded with snacks and thermoses filled with hot drinks. Harvey and my mom come after them, carrying blankets and even a couple of lawn chairs.

"You're overachieving too, Gervais!" Rhett shouts as Summer takes his hands, skating backward in an attempt to teach him how to skate.

Jasper shrugs, eyes finding mine almost instantly. "Yeah, the difference is I know it."

I shake my head at him because I don't feel like he's over-achieving at all. I feel like everything is *just* right.

We play the world's most ridiculous hockey game. Summer, my mom, Luke, and me against everyone else. People sub in and out willy-nilly. Cade constantly leaves the game to check on Willa and refill her hot chocolate. My mom and Harvey argue over whether she needs to wear a helmet. She says no; he says yes. Rhett falls on his ass multiple times. Everyone makes fun of him. Jasper stops every single shot on net and laughs at every person who tries to make a play against him.

Except Luke. Luke is the only one who scores any goals, and Jasper makes the biggest goofiest show of trying to stop him every time. Watching him with Luke is adorable. It makes my ovaries hurt.

I'm not sure I've ever seen Jasper smile so much.

I'm not sure I've ever been more attracted to him than I am at this moment.

I'm not sure I've ever loved him more than I do right now because, impossible as it seems, every day we spend together I just keep loving him harder.

"Coming for you, Gervais," I call as Summer passes me the puck.

"Bring it, honey. Show me what you got."

But instead of trying to score, I stop in front of him, spraying ice all over his pads. We're grinning at each other like crazy people as I pull off the beautifully painted helmet on his head, hooking my fingers through the metal bars as it dangles at my side.

"I need a kiss first," I say, trying to keep my expression neutral.

Because I know he'll never turn me down. I've learned that where Jasper Gervais is concerned, he'll do absolutely *anything* to keep me happy.

Including kissing me in the middle of a family hockey game just because I asked.

So I'm not surprised when his gloved hand comes to the side of my face and his mouth drops onto mine without a single moment of hesitation. I'm not surprised when I hear everyone hooting and hollering as we kiss on that little piece of ice in the middle of the ranch. I'm not surprised when he takes it a step further and slides his tongue into my mouth.

But I'm still a competitor. And I hate to lose. So I extend my stick and nudge the puck past Jasper's feet while he stands there kissing me senseless like I asked him to.

I hear Luke cheer. "Ahhhh! That was so gross. But Aunty Sloane scores! We win!"

Jasper chuckles against my lips with a gentle shake of his head. "Nice goal, Sunny."

"Thank you, Jas." I do a little curtsy. "Who knew you were so easily distracted?"

Our gazes lock, his irises bouncing between mine. "You've been distracting me for years. This is nothing new." But then his voice drops low and anticipation hums through my core when he murmurs, "But you've got my attention now."

My brow pinches, and I try not to blush as I smile up at him. He's even taller on his skates, towering above me. Frost-touched cheeks, sparkling midnight eyes, caramel hair flopped down over his forehead, looking so fucking handsome it hurts. "Oh yeah?"

His mouth drops to my ear. "Yes. Really feeling the spirit of giving this Christmas. And I've just decided I'm going to be giving it to you all night. Actually, maybe all afternoon..." His head snaps up, and he pulls me into his body as he calls out toward the side where everyone is sitting, "Game's over! Sloane and Summer's team wins. We're heading out."

I bark out a laugh, but he winks and reaches for his helmet, guiding me off the ice.

"Where are we going?"

"Home, Sunny. We're going home."

40

Sloane

Violet: Drink?

Sloane: No.

Violet: You need one.

Sloane: I'm too nervous to drink.

Violet: Yeah. You look pale. Need a little color in your cheeks.

Sloane: No one cares about the color in my cheeks tonight, Vi.

Violet: You'll look better on the news this way.

Sloane: What?

Violet: They have Buddyz Best!

I'M SO NERVOUS I FEEL LIKE I COULD PUKE. I'VE GOT MY elbows propped on my knees and my fingers tapping together in an anxious flutter.

"Girl, you give me anxiety just looking at you." Harvey's warm hand lands on my back.

"I've never been so nervous in my life."

"Never?" His brow quirks.

I suck my lips into my mouth and shake my head quickly. "Never."

"I mean, if tail babies can't make you nervous, then I'd have thought a Stanley Cup game would be a piece of cake."

"Harvey, good lord." I drop my head into my hands on a laugh. "Is the tail-baby thing ever going to stop being funny to you?"

He shrugs and grins down at the ice. "Probably not."

I want to pretend the joke isn't funny, but the truth is I'm so sick with nerves right now I could hurl all over my maroon Grizzlies jersey with *Gervais* emblazoned across the back.

It's the same one I bought all those months ago. It feels monumental somehow. *Lucky*.

And considering it's almost the final period of play in game six of the Stanley Cup Finals tonight, the Grizzlies are going to need all the luck they can get. It's their last chance to close the series out and win it all on home ice.

Their season has been nothing short of miraculous. They went on a hot streak just before Christmas and stuck with it. Those points catapulted them far enough into the standings that they made the playoffs.

Barely. But making it is making it.

They've fought long and hard. I know they're tired. Jasper is sore and ready for a break.

It's been a long, trying year, but it's also been the best year.

The playoffs.

A second Olympic gold medal in February.

And us.

Us. God, that still sounds so good to me. The "us" part of our life is so damn good. So damn easy. It feels so damn right.

Something about admitting it out loud, about really accepting it, has lifted a weight from Jasper. He's still quiet and introspective, but now he smiles.

Under the cover of dark, we crawl out onto the roof of our little house in Chestnut Springs and talk about life. Fears. Plans. Babies. We talk about everything because we always have.

"What you smiling about, Sloane?" Harvey nudges me, obviously watching me while I zone out and stare at the grizzly bear logo painted at center ice.

"I'm just…" I shrug, regarding the buzzing arena. "Happy. Even if they lose tonight. Everything feels…"

"You're both settled. Figured out what counts in life. It's the people. Not the things. Not the acclaim. The people."

"Yeah. Speaking of people. My mom still driving you insane?" She's been living at the house for six months now, and she and Harvey bicker like an old married couple. I really can't make heads or tails of it.

I'm not sure I want to.

"That woman," he mutters. "It's like after years of keeping her opinions to herself, she's just blurting them all out left, right, and center. It's an opinion surplus sale in that house. Buy one, get ten."

I snort a laugh before the row of people heading our way

catches my attention. Beau, home safe but still walking gingerly, leads the charge. He's followed by Rhett and Summer and Violet, who made the trip back just to take in this game.

A few seats down, Cade has his new baby girl, Emma, strapped to his chest in a carrier. He's all proud papa, eyes more on that little bundle than on the game. It does weird things to my ovaries watching him.

Willa is her usual playful self, sitting beside Luke and trying to show him how to toss popcorn up in the air and catch it with his mouth.

It just keeps hitting them both in the face.

No matter what, seeing everyone here to cheer Jasper on warms my heart. He needs this. Deserves this.

We're not up in the box. We've taken over almost an entire row of the stadium behind home net. Filled it with Eatons. Filled it with family.

Maybe not the family he was born into but the one that wanted him the most. The one that will do anything for him.

A buzzer sounds as Violet shoves a beer out in front of me and takes her seat. "Here. Drink it."

"I can't—"

She shimmies the plastic cup, making it dangerously close to spilling over. "You will. It's Buddyz Best. You love this shit."

I smirk down at the golden lager. It's true that I love this beer. But not because it tastes good. It's because I remember drinking it the night Jasper broke me out of that farce of a wedding. I remember drinking a pitcher of it while Jasper leaned over my back and taught me how to play pool.

The dog on the label makes me smile, and the memories it drums up make it taste fucking delicious.

I take a deep swig, and my nerves settle as I watch my man skate onto the ice from the bench. He glances up in our direction, and Beau waves the giant poster-board sign he and Rhett made in his direction.

I watched them make it. Like the children they are, they giggled while sprinkling sparkles over the glue they used to spell out the words.

It reads, *Jasper Gervais is my #1 stud!*

Jasper tugs his helmet on, probably rolling his eyes from behind the cage.

Rhett yells, "Marry me, Jasper!" right as Summer elbows him in the ribs. It wouldn't be an Eaton family outing without some type of insane shenanigans from the boys.

But once the timer starts, everyone settles into a tense silence. I should watch the game, but I spend huge stretches of time staring at Jasper in the net.

His incredible focus. The way he carries his body. The speed of his reflexes. He's not just good at hockey, he's a generational talent. He gives me chills.

And if I'm being totally honest, it riles me the hell up that he's so superior. I'm so attracted to that part of him. His passion and tireless commitment to being so good at his sport.

I admire that about him. We connect on that level. When we need to train, there are no hard feelings or whining about time spent apart. We both pursue our passions, and we're both better at what we do for having the other's support.

The crowd gets loud as the opposing team burns down

the ice toward Jasper's net. He squares off to face the attackers. Just by standing in the net, he blocks so many of their opportunities to score because of his height advantage.

Number 29 passes, and number 17 winds up, taking a hard, fast shot.

Not fast enough though. Jasper's gloved hand moves out in a blur and pockets the puck, making it look easy. I'm panting when he hands it back to the referee.

One hand on my chest, I take another sip of my beer and realize that I've nervously drained the entire thing.

The puck drops, and the clock keeps winding down. They're tied at one apiece. Jasper has played his heart out tonight.

I want this so badly for him. The big win. The crowning achievement. God, my body aches with how badly I want this for him.

Thirty seconds remain, and the crowd grows quiet. Overtime isn't a loss but isn't a win either. It means more time. More chances. More room for tired mistakes.

I can feel the anticipation. The entire arena is thick with it. You could cut it with a knife. Each second is like a drumbeat that reverberates through the stands.

The Gators take a shot and Jasper covers, but not long enough for them to blow the whistle.

And then…it happens.

Damon Hart flies down the ice, glancing over his shoulder with a smirk and a little wave at his goalie.

And there's the perfect gap.

Jasper drops the puck on the ice and sends it sailing

straight through that gap. Right onto the tape of his team-mate's stick.

I swear every single person collectively sucks in a deep breath of cold air.

The seconds wind down.

But there are no defenders. They let Damon skate right past them.

He taps the puck back and forth, dekeing left and right.

He fakes a shot.

Their goaltender falls for it and drops to make the save.

Damon takes the top corner, the hard rubber hitting the back of the netting with a whoosh that's heard through the entire building.

The buzzer sounds, and the arena *explodes*.

Music. Lights. Screaming. Confetti. Every single person erupts.

But I sit still, watching Jasper jump for joy. Stick and gloves flying, helmet tossed, he skates toward his team-mates with the biggest, most heartrending grin on his face as they pile onto him for the assist and Damon for the winning goal.

I want to remember this moment, this feeling, as clearly as I remember the first day I saw Jasper. Painfully handsome with sad eyes.

Today, when he turns and searches for me in the stands, he's different.

He's painfully handsome with happy eyes.

So happy that I want to see them up close. The colors. The way they swirl together. The fine lines beside them.

I want to feel his stubble on my cheeks and his heartbeat against my forehead when I drop my face against his chest.

I jog through the crowd, down those stairs to the gate at the end of the rink, and he's there.

Waiting for me.

Like he always has been.

I let him let pull me onto the ice, straight up into his arms.

"You fucking did it, baby!" I yell at him with absolutely no chill. My hands are in his sweaty hair, my legs around his waist, my eyes on his.

Right where they always have been.

"We fucking did it." His hands squeeze my ass, and he whispers all gravelly against my ear, "My years of training and your Stanley Cup Maker. The perfect combo."

I laugh like a crazy person and kiss his neck. There are cameras and media everywhere. Teammates and family. It's mayhem. But all I see is *him*. This moment. A good man who life dealt such an unfair hand, finally getting a win. *The* win.

"I love you, Jasper Gervais." I shake my head, tears leaking down my face as I marvel at the man before me. "I love you so damn much."

"I love you too, Sloane Winthrop," he says as he glances over my shoulder, back toward the entrance. "But do you know what I don't like?"

My heart races, and confusion blooms behind my brows. How could anyone not like something about this moment? This moment is…everything.

I barely notice when he reaches behind me.

I barely notice Beau's presence or the big shit-eating grin on his face.

I barely notice because in all his goaltending gear, in the middle of his Stanley Cup–winning celebration, my childhood crush is dropping to one knee right in front of me.

With a little velvet box in his hand.

"Do you know what I don't like?"

His eyes staring up at mine are so clear, so bright, so unapologetically joyful. I'm still confused, still having a hard time catching up with what's happening right now, even though it's so damn obvious.

"What?" I whisper, and I wouldn't think he could hear me, but he must.

Because he responds with "Your last name, Sunny. I really don't like your last name."

And with that, he flips the little box open to show me a ring. A ring I *like*. A ring I told him about while chugging trashy beer in the passenger seat of his SUV while wearing a wedding ring from another man.

It's a purple oval-cut sapphire, set horizontally into yellow gold. Surrounded on all edges. It's quirky. It's unique. It's one of a kind.

It's exact the ring I described to him all those months ago.

"Sloane Gervais sounds right, don't you think?" His head quirks, damp hair brushing over his forehead. He looks so boyish, all bashful and nervous.

I glance around now, realizing this moment is so much more than just us. It's the culmination of his life's work. "Jasper! You should be celebrating right now!" I blurt.

"Sunny, I will." He laughs, shaking his head at me like I'm amusing to him. "But I want to celebrate with my fiancée. Please, Sloane, let me marry you. Let me make you happy. I don't wanna be late with this too."

"Jas." I laugh, reaching forward and sliding my finger into the ring, hearing a roar of cheers behind us. "You are not late! I didn't see this coming at all."

The stone glitters under the bright lights as I flex and wiggle my finger.

"Yeah?" he asks, voice all warm and deep.

I peek back at him, kind of sad to look away from the ring now, and nod.

He laughs and scoops me up into his arms as he reaches full height again, making me squeal. "'Bout fuckin' time though, eh? You deserved me being early for something after all these years."

My fingers trail down over his rosy cheeks. "I love you, Jas."

"Sunny, tell me that's a yes."

"It's always been a yes, Jasper."

He whoops and twirls me before he kisses me stupid.

And just like that, the boy with the lanky limbs, the caramel hair, and the saddest eyes I've ever seen is mine.

Forever.

EPILOGUE

Jasper

Jasper: Meet me on the driveway.

Sloane: Yes, sir.

Jasper: Pocket that sentence for later when I strip you
down and make you crawl.

Sloane: YES, SIR.

"ARE YOU NERVOUS?" HARVEY EYES ME SPECULATIVELY AS I
wait for Sloane to come out of the house.

The sun is shining, and the snow is melting. It's one
of those perfect Chinook days in Chestnut Springs, warm
enough to make you want to wear a T-shirt because the heat
feels so damn good after a long winter.

It's our wedding day, but we aren't going traditional. We
spent last night together on the roof talking. The ceremony
is in the field, and the reception is in the house.

Before we get married, there's something I want to show her. So I guess I'm going to see her in her wedding dress too.

"No. Are you?"

He scoffs. "Why would I be nervous?"

"I don't know. You're getting old. Maybe you're worried about tripping and falling while you walk Sloane down the aisle."

To no one's surprise, Robert refused to come, so Harvey stepped up for Sloane. So steady and constant in his support. He really is one of the best.

"I'm an exceptional physical specimen, son. No tripping for this old fella yet."

It's my turn to laugh now. "Please tell me less about your physical capabilities."

"It's hereditary. I mean, look at you." He gestures at my wedding attire—brown corduroy blazer, bolo tie, hair only lightly styled, and boots rather than dress shoes.

"Harvey, I'm not so sure about your understanding of the word *hereditary*."

"Been raising cattle my entire life. I know the meaning. I know there's nature. And that there's nurture."

I roll my lips together and stare down at the gravel driveway beneath me for a beat before glancing back up at him as he continues. "Don't much care if I had a role in making you. I know in my heart I had a role in making you who you are today. And I'm damn proud of you, Jasper. Not sure I've told you that enough over the years."

"Thanks, Harv." My voice catches on his name.

"I'm not done," he announces, moving his weight

between his feet, like he's a little awkward about this conversation as well. "I… Well, I know you've struggled. I know you've struggled with what's in your heart. With feeling like you belong. And I'm just so dang happy that you found a place to belong with Sloane. But I also want you to know that you belong here. At the ranch with us."

I sniff and wipe at my nose. "What the fuck, Harvey. Are you trying to make me cry? Is this part of your nurture?"

He laughs but coughs roughly, clearing the emotion in his throat. "Yeah. I guess it is. But I wanted to give you this."

He yanks a white envelope out of his jacket pocket and hands it over to me. When I take it, he waves a hand in my direction and then wipes his nose. "Open it."

My throat is thick as I peel the paper open and pull the single sheet of paper out. I read it, but the words are…

"It's a deed," he says.

"I can see that."

"To your own quarter section. Over on the east side. Nice sunrises. I know you two like to sit on the roof talking until the sun comes up. Thought you'd build there eventually. Stay close. I don't know. Give your tail babies lots of space to roam." He wipes at his eyes, clearly trying to cover his emotion with the most overused joke he has. "All my kids got a quarter. And I feel like a real shmuck for not giving you one until now."

"Harvey, this is too much."

He waves a hand again before propping them both on his hips and peering out over the horizon. "Nah. Got more land than I know what to do with. Plus, you're my boy,

Jasper." He reaches out and grabs my shoulder now. "I want you here always."

I stare at the piece of paper, feeling like the little broken boy who showed up on this ranch that day all those years ago. He had no idea how much love he'd have one day. No idea that the people who really loved him would never leave him.

They're all right here.

And when I look up to see Sloane coming down the front steps of the big, sprawling ranch house, my heart stutters in my chest, and the tears in my eyes clear instantly. Everything I see is so clear with her in view.

"See you out there. Love you, Jasper," Harvey finishes, wrapping me in an aggressive hug.

"Love you too, Harvey," I choke out, and the man just stares back at me with watery eyes and a brusque nod of approval before striding away and doing the same to Sloane.

She hugs him back but keeps her eyes on me as she walks across the driveway. The wishing well is on her left, the house is behind her, and my ring is on her finger. She has on a loose dress that flows around her delicate ankles. Her hair is down, all soft as it frames her face. Ballet slippers are on her feet, and the expression on her face is relaxed. *Happy.*

This is the day she deserves.

The day we deserve.

Back where it all began.

"You look perfect," I murmur as she draws near.

"You look edible. Talk about teenage dream." Her eyes rake over me, and a smile touches her lips.

I hold the envelope up. "Did you know about this?"

She lifts a shoulder noncommittally. "A little birdie might have told me."

Her hands reach for me as soon as she's near enough, and I pocket the envelope before pulling her into me.

Into *our* hug. The one we've always done. Except now her hand reaches for her tattoo on my ribs every time.

"You ready?" My jacket muffles her voice.

"Not quite," I say, spinning her toward the ranch house and squeezing her back against my front.

I hold my left hand up in front of her and wiggle my fingers. The fresh lines of ink on my ring finger catch her attention, and she instantly grabs for it. "Got another tattoo for you this morning."

"Jasper…" Her voice trails off as her fingers brush over the dark ink. "That's…" Her hands tremble as she holds my hand with both of hers so reverently. "Permanent."

"So are we. I'm never going to take this ring off."

She nuzzles in closer against me, and I can feel her smile as her entire body presses back against mine. I fold my arm over her shoulder and link my fingers with hers.

Then I point to the window of the room that's always been hers. Right next to mine.

"Eighteen years ago, a little blond girl peeked at me out of that exact window. She stared at me that day, and I stared back. I didn't realize what it meant because we were just kids."

She hums softly, twining her fingers with my free hand. Wrapping herself up in me like I'm her favorite blanket. And I indulge her because wrapped around Sloane is my favorite place to be. "You saw me?"

I turn my head in, my lips dusting across her forehead. "Yeah. I saw you, Sloane. I noticed you too. Didn't know what made me look up there that day. Had no clue what it all meant."

"What did it mean?"

"That when it comes to you, I'm powerless."

BONUS SCENE

Harvey

CORDELIA STANDS, BLINKING AT ME. JASPER HAS JUST PRAC-tically flown to track down his cousin—his girlfriend? His… fuck, I don't know. The woman he loves.

And so I'm stuck here. Staring back at my late wife's little sister. One I haven't seen much of over the years since she got swept up in the glitz and glam of a very different lifestyle. When Isabelle died, so did my connection to her family. But I have to hand it to Cordelia, she made sure Sloane was out here getting to know her cousins every summer, whether the chump she was married to liked it or not.

"So…" I venture slowly. Assessing her as she stands before me. Chin tipped up, defiance practically wafting off her. "You look a little like a wild filly who finally turfed her shitty rider."

She blinks again, lips pursing slightly. "Thank you for that mental image, Harvey."

I grunt and rub a hand over my mouth, wishing I was better at choosing the right words sometimes. Then I step aside and gesture for her to come in. "You just gonna stand there?"

Now that stiff upper lip of hers wobbles, but she doesn't take another step. "I didn't know where else to go."

My chest aches for her. I've always known Robert was a fucking dick. I remember Isabelle crying at her sister's wedding as she sat in the pew watching her walk down the aisle. Other people smiled at her kindly, thinking they were happy tears.

I knew better.

She was devastated when her baby sister became a Winthrop.

"Cordy, it's fine." She tenses at my use of her nickname, like she hasn't heard it in years. "Here is a better place than most. It's just me and a lot of empty rooms. Every now and then a grandkid with foul mouth on him comes tearing through, followed by any number of the hooligans I've raised who all seem to come back."

She nods, eyes glittering as she looks around the house. The worn floorboards. The hunter green walls. The mule deer head hung over the stone fireplace.

"Listen, I know it's not what you're used to. But it's a place for family. And that's what you are. So, get in here." I tip my head to the side over my shoulder, tongue clicking against my cheek as I do.

She straightens, running a hand down over her prim, stiff-looking skirt. "Don't cluck at me like I'm a horse,

Harvey Eaton." She brushes past me with a venomous look that does nothing but make me smile. She never bit back at Robert like this, so I'll take her growling as a sign of her turning over a new leaf. "You may be family, but I'm not above kicking you in the balls like I did Robert."

Now it's my turn for some wide-eyed blinking. "*You* kicked Robert in the balls?"

She places her rolling suitcase at the bottom of the stairs, pushing the adjustable handle back down. "Yes. He tried to stand in my way when I went to leave, and it was self-defense."

"Don't need to dress it up as something it ain't, darlin'. You could tell me it was premeditated assault and I'd give you a high five for it."

Her lips quirk and she looks away, arms crossing over her chest. "He's really that bad, huh?"

I chuckle. "He's really that bad."

Her eyes are a storm when she turns them back on me. Nothing like Isabelle's clear, light, carefree blue.

Then she sniffs, straightens, and slips a cool mask back over her features. "Well, then. I'll freshen up and…I don't know. Figure out something to do with myself." With that, she turns and starts making her way up the stairs. Heels clacking against the wood as she goes.

Bag left at the bottom like she expects me to carry it up for her.

And goddamnit, I do.

"Morning, Cordy," I say over the rim of my coffee mug. Partly because I need my caffeine, and partly because I'm trying not to laugh.

The woman has walked down into the kitchen of a farmhouse. Set on a working cattle ranch. Wearing dress pants, a blouse, heels. Fucking pearls. Perfume. Her makeup is flawless. Her hair is swept back in an elegant twist.

She looks like she's going to work in the financial district or something.

"Hello, Harvey." She walks primly to the fridge and opens it up. All business.

"Planning on taking over the world in that power suit?"

She barely acknowledges my jibe. "This is what I always wear. Looking like a slob doesn't do anyone favors. Do you have any egg whites?"

I lean back in my chair, crossing a boot over my good knee. "I mean, I have eggs. Got chickens out back, too."

Her head shakes as she continues peering into the refrigerator like what she wants might magically appear from Narnia at the very back. "No. I mean, in a carton."

I snort. "Why would anyone put egg whites in a carton?"

Her body spins to face me. "Because it's convenient. And the whites are the healthiest part."

"Been eating the whole damn egg my entire life and I'm healthy as a horse."

She eyes me speculatively with a soft scoff. "You could be healthier."

"Remind me when you went to nursing school, Cordelia. And did you miss the unit on bedside manner?"

"I don't need to be a nurse to tell you that losing a few pounds might be good for you. Or to notice that you walk with a limp because of that old knee injury. Or that a big plate of bacon and eggs every morning"—her chin juts out at me with accusation—"probably isn't the best thing for your heart."

I work real hard at not rolling my eyes. Haven't had a woman in my house telling me what to do for coming up on thirty years. Cordelia Winthrop spends one dang night under my roof and she thinks she's got a read on me? I don't think so.

"I don't eat this *every* morning," I lie.

Her lips flatten into an unimpressed line, hands propping on her hips. "Bullshit."

"You look far too fancy to be talking like that." I chuckle, shoveling another forkful of buttery scrambled eggs into my mouth.

"Fuck that," she says on a sigh, turning to the stove and eyeing the pan where more eggs and bacon are waiting for her. "I'm so over watching my words when I really feel like cussing."

"Fuck that indeed." I chuckle again, getting a kick out of watching her dance around the space. She looks like a Porsche at a monster truck rally.

It's actually kind of endearing.

"Also, fuck you. I know you're lying about what you eat. And I know that Izzy would want me to look out for you if she were here."

Izzy. The nicknames those two had for each other. It

doesn't make me sad; I've had enough time to come to terms with the death of my wife. Or at least as much as you ever heal from that.

In fact, it's kind of refreshing to have someone around who knew her as well as I did. Someone who can mention her so casually. Like a fond memory rather than a painful reminder.

So, I laugh. Because she's right. Isabelle would have been on my ass about staying healthier than I am.

With a scant plate of scrambled eggs, Cordelia sits down across from me.

"Oh, would she now?"

I stifle a laugh as she *cuts* into her scrambled eggs with a goddamn fork and knife. Manicured nails propped against her cutlery like it's the finest filet mignon.

"She sure would. So get ready to be annoyed by me."

This time I really do laugh.

"I already am, Cordy. I already am."

~⁓

"What is this?" I pick at the white mush on my plate, wondering why it tastes so strange. It's been a month of living in the same damn house with Cordelia Winthrop. Enduring her caretaking, which she has taken on like it's her new full-time job. I don't even know what she did with her days before she left Robert. Lunched with her ladies? Planned fancy dinner parties?

Apparently now we hang out all day long, tidying things around the ranch. She repaints rooms in this old house that need a fresh coat of paint, wearing her ridiculous pearls while she does it. I snowplow the driveway. She still plans dinners, but they're for the entire family and she doesn't have a maid to help her.

Actually, she does. I've become her maid. Or her assistant. Or whatever you want to call it.

Can't lie, watching her light up with a table full of people warms my heart. Where Isabelle got this life—loud family dinners, muddy floors, inappropriate jokes—Cordelia got one that was cold and sterile. She's relaxed in her time out here—well, as much as someone as uptight as her can.

"It's white bean mash."

My nose wrinkles. "Why?"

"Why what?" She gives me this innocent wide-eyed look. But I've come to know better. She keeps trying to trick me into eating healthier.

It started with breakfast. Then she took over lunch. Now she's ruining dinner with her cholesterol management.

"Why would you mash beans up? I thought they were mashed potatoes."

"Exactly!" she says brightly, shimmying her shoulders back and smiling proudly at me.

And suddenly, I find myself not wanting to mock her mashed beans. It hits me. She looks happy and she looks *proud*. And for so many years around Robert, I watched her look beaten down. I watched her stand in the background. Hiding in the shadow of a man who thinks he's bigger than he is.

Making herself small for him. It's always irked me.

So if feeding me this fucking poison makes her smile like *that,* then I'll choke it back with a smile.

I take another mouthful, feeling the slippery bean husk separate from the mushy inside. "Is there butter in it?" I try not to choke on the words or the texture, instead focusing on the slightly golden tone her pale skin has taken on, the soft freckles dotting the bridge of her nose from time spent in the sun.

I'm not sure I've ever seen this woman with a freckle on her face in my life.

"Just olive oil!" Her hands are clasped in front of her chest and she stares at me expectantly. "I know how much you love your mashed potatoes. But I thought this was maybe a nice alternative."

I hide my grimace and swallow with a smile.

"It's delicious, Cordy. Thank you."

"Really?" She's flat-out grinning now, slightly leaned forward at the table, elbows propped up on the surface like all her prissy manners are being forgotten the more time she spends out here rediscovering herself.

"Yes." I say the word slowly. Cautiously. Eyes searching hers.

"You're a terrible liar, Harvey Eaton. Don't have a dishonest bone in your body, that's what Izzy used to tell me."

I smile at that. "Yeah?"

Cordelia nods, leaning back with a slightly faraway look on her face. "Yeah. She told me lots about you. About living here. The more time I spend in Chestnut Springs, the more I understand her. Why she left."

I just hum and take another bite of the terrible olive oil beans. *They're good for me.* And that's what I'll keep telling myself.

"I miss her." She says it so plainly. So matter-of-factly.

"Yeah. Same." I gently place my fork down on my plate and look across the big table at her sister. There are similarities. But I don't think you'd ever have seen them in public and automatically assumed they were sisters. "It's different than it used to be, though. It's nice having someone here who talks about her. Been trying to date. But it's weird."

"It's been long enough, Harv. No one would fault you for wanting that again."

I grunt my agreement, trying to decide how much I want to divulge, and then opting to lay it all out. "I think it's easier to feel kindred with a person when their partner was shitty, and their relationship ended poorly. But with a wife who died tragically during childbirth? There are no hard feelings between her and I. Seems like the women I meet don't like that. The thought that I might still love another woman, even if she isn't here, is a problem."

Cordelia watches me for a few beats before nodding carefully.

"I can see that. But really, any woman who isn't okay with you loving Izzy in the way that you do doesn't deserve a spot in your life. You've got a big enough heart for both as far as I can tell."

My chest thrums as her words sink in. She gets it. *She knows Izzy. She misses Izzy, just like me.*

I gape at her dramatically for a second. A second too

long, based on the way she glances down to check if she's spilled something on herself. "By god, Cordy. I think that might be the nicest thing you've ever said to me."

Her eyes roll then, and she dabs at her lips with a napkin to cover her smile. "Shut up and eat your fake mashed potatoes, Harvey."

~

"We're out of egg whites," she says from behind the fridge door.

It's been two months of Cordelia living in my house. Adding "throw cushions" to my old leather couches. Feeding me healthy shit. Making me ride a stationary bike she bought for me because apparently that's better for my knee. The only indulgence I'm allowed anymore is a snifter of whiskey with her on the porch swing a few times a week.

We sit at opposite corners of the bench, turn the heater on, share a blanket, and sip the amber liquid, relishing the burn and reminiscing about Isabelle.

We talk. We joke. We laugh. I'd be lying if I said I didn't enjoy her company.

And I'm starting to get the sense that Cordelia isn't ever leaving. Which is fine, because I might be sad if she did. Still, we don't talk about it—the future. We just *are*.

"We are not out of egg whites. There is a chicken coop full of eggs straight out the back door, Cordy. They even come in this fancy nature-made container that can be composted."

Yeah, I also compost now.

"Will you get them for me?" She turns pleading eyes on me and my stomach flips. I don't know when her dramatic facial expressions stopped annoying me and swapped over to making my stomach flip.

It's the most confounding development.

"It's been months. It's about time you learned how to collect eggs."

She bites at her bottom lip. A flash of wanting to bite that lip too pops up in my head. I push it away.

"I'm scared."

"Of the chickens?" I sound incredulous, and she immediately looks a little pissed off.

"Yes, Harvey. I didn't grow up on a farm. Have you seen that rooster? With the obscene-looking skin dangling from his chin? He chases people. And he's ugly. And I'm not taking my life in my hands to collect eggs."

I slap my knee as I push to stand from the dinner table. "Let's go, city girl," I announce, waving her along as I head toward the back door.

"Harvey. Wait! No!" I hear her calling to me as I head out the back door. But before long, I also hear her footsteps following. They're brisk. They just *sound* pissed off by the rhythm they make.

"What's that saying?" I call over my shoulder. "Teach a woman to collect her own eggs and she'll keep making you healthy breakfasts for the rest of your life?"

"That's not the saying," she snipes, falling into line behind me.

I turn back now and wink at her. "But it's true, isn't it?"

She huffs and rolls her eyes. Looking prim and pouty. And I find myself wanting to muss her up a bit. Make use of that puffed-out bottom lip.

I shake my head at myself as I unlatch the coop. *Get yourself together, old man. You're confused.*

Cordelia steps in behind me, and I feel her proximity. The heat of her body on an otherwise cold prairie day.

"Don't let them get me, Harvey." She steps up, fist curling around the back of my jacket, and I chuckle softly.

"The statistics for death by chickens are alarming these days. Growing so rapidly. A true epidemic."

"You want two bad knees, Eaton? I'll kick you." Her fist nudges against my back, electricity snapping between us as she does.

I've been so damn careful not to touch her lately. Ever since our eyes started catching and then staying there just a *little* too long. Ever since I found myself not worrying about if my knee fell wide and bumped against her beneath our blanket on the front porch swing.

Ever since, each time she bites her lip, I think about doing the same.

And *this*, this feeling is why. The rush of blood in my ears, the flutter in my chest. I feel like a little kid when she touches me. And I shouldn't. Or I think I shouldn't.

I don't even know anymore. I'm confused. Who else in the world could ever understand and adore Isabelle the way we both do? Miss her and cherish her the way we both do? It's like the thing that should keep us apart is really what's binding us together.

And yes, I'm very, *very* confused.

"Okay, so you just step up here. You can give her a pat." I run my hand over the hen's back. "Hi, Henny," I murmur.

"Her name is Henny?"

I chuckle. "All their names are Henny. I can't fuckin' tell them apart."

Her fingers soften on the back of my jacket and I carry on. "So then you just—"

Cordelia screams. It pierces the winter air. I catch sight of the angry rooster charging at us right as I turn to face her.

Which is when her fingers curl around the lapels of my jacket and she buries her face in my chest. Truly, the worst survival instincts in the world.

And yet, the notion that she feels safe with me, trusts me to protect her? It puts something inside of me that I haven't felt in a very long time.

I press her up against the wall, shielding her—from a goddamn rooster—with my body. "You get on outta here, you cranky motherfucker." I kick a leg out toward the rooster, making a *pssst* noise at him while Cordelia clings to me.

I swear the rooster gives me a dirty look, shakes his head, and then turns to strut away. Like he's still the toughest guy in here.

Turning to Cordelia, I slip a hand over the side of her head, smoothing her pale blond hair out of the way. Bits that came loose, threaded with gray, frame her dainty face. "You alright, Cordy?"

When she finally tips her head up to face me, there's an unfamiliar expression there. Her brows are drawn tight, but her eyes are a kaleidoscope. Twisting and flashing. Staying fixed on mine for far too long.

She licks her lips and my gaze drops.

"No, Harvey. I don't think I am."

I'm sucked in. I can feel her breath puffing against my cheeks, her fingers clutching tight. Tugging me closer until our faces are mere inches apart. Chickens cluck quietly in the background, but it's the sound of blood rushing through my veins in time with her quick breaths that strikes me.

Our gazes swap. When I look back at her eyes, she's got them fixed on my mouth.

I swallow, and the motion draws her gaze back up. "I'm sorry," she whispers. But she doesn't sound all that sorry.

And I don't want her to be.

"I'm the one who should be sorry." My voice is gravel. We're far too close.

"Why—"

I cut her question off when I press my lips to hers and swallow whatever words come next. My fingers stroke at her hair as I cup her smooth cheeks; she makes the sweetest little sounds against my mouth, her one palm flush over my pounding heart.

Maybe I shouldn't be kissing Cordelia Winthrop, but I also can't find it in myself to be sorry about it.

Because this? Kissing her?

It feels *right*.

RECKLESS
SNEAK PEEK

Winter

"I can't fathom why you feel the need to go work at that dingy little hospital in the country."

I used to think Rob was a nice guy.

Now, I know better.

"Well, Robert," I drawl, using his full name to piss him off as I shove a final sweater into my overfull suitcase. "I'm not sure if you're aware, but there are humans—real live ones—who live in the country who are also in need of medical attention."

I'm not sure why I'm packing so much for a single shift. When I'm in Chestnut Springs, I live in scrubs in the ER and in leggings in my hotel room at night.

"Thanks for clarifying, Winter." There's a biting tone to his voice that might make some people flinch. But not me. A dark part of me takes immense pride in the fact I know exactly how to piss off my husband. My lips twitch as I struggle to contain my satisfied smile.

"But why that hospital? Why Chestnut Springs? You're constantly taking off out there, and you don't even tell me you're leaving. Come to think of it"—he scrubs at his chin in an overly dramatic fashion while leaning up against the doorframe of my bedroom—"you never even considered my opinion on whether I would want my wife taking this job. This isn't a smart career move for you at all."

I used to think Rob was a good man.

Now, I've heard him whine like a child.

Nothing makes a man's masculinity shrivel up and die for me quite like complaining about a woman exercising her professional independence. He might as well stomp his foot and storm out like a tiny chauvinist toddler.

I reach for the zipper and start forcing it together against the bulging contents of my suitcase. "It's funny," I start, ensuring that I keep my tone cool and even. "It's almost like…you are the very last person I would ever consult about career choices."

With a huff of air, I finally slide the zipper into place and look down at the hard-shell case, propping my hands on my hips and letting a satisfied smile touch my lips.

"What the hell is that supposed to mean, Winter?"

The way he adds my name to the end of every sentence feels like he's trying to scold me.

Joke's on him. I won't be scolded.

He's blissfully unaware of what it takes to navigate the medical system as a young female doctor. If I let men as weak as Rob steamroll me on the regular, I wouldn't stand a chance.

And this career is the only thing I've ever had that's mine. So he can fuck all the way off.

Flipping one hand over, I gaze down at my neglected nails, trying to look bored by him. I'm wondering if I can find a good place for a manicure in Chestnut Springs when I reply, "Don't play stupid. It pairs so poorly with whining."

I find myself wondering why I'm still married at all. I know why I thought I was sticking it out. But now? Now, I just need to buck up and get it done. I glance back down at my suitcase, packed like I'm leaving for a long-ass time, and wonder if my subconscious knows something I don't.

Maybe that bitch is putting her foot down and breaking me out once and for all.

I'm not averse.

"You will not speak to your husband that way."

My eyes narrow on my cuticles as I struggle to bite down the rage bubbling inside of me. Hot molten lava simmering below the cool surface, just waiting to erupt all over the place.

But I've kept that at bay for years now. I will not let Dr. Rob Valentine be the one to make me erupt.

He's not worth the energy.

I shift my eyes to him across the room. My room, because when I told him in no uncertain terms that I wouldn't be sleeping in the same bed as him any longer, he directed me to the guest room rather than moving himself out—like the true gentleman he is.

Even though it was him.

He's the reason we are where we are.

And the worst part is I loved him once. He was all mine.

A safe place for me to land after growing up in what felt like some sort of domestic cold war.

I let my guard down with him. I fell so damn hard.

He broke my heart far worse than I'll ever let anyone know.

I don't respond to him. Instead, I grab the handle of my suitcase and shove past his lean frame, heading toward the front door of our sprawling ten-thousand-foot home.

I hear him following me. Dress shoes against marble. And, of course, he doesn't offer to carry my suitcase for me.

A wry smile twists my lips, and I shake my head at the thought that he'd bother to lift a finger for me. The hardest thing for me to accept with the implosion of my marriage is that I didn't see it coming. That I can be smart and accomplished and strategic in everything I do yet still allow this asshole to blindside me is just...offensive.

Being swindled this way irks me to no end.

I can feel the rage radiating off him as he seethes behind me. And I just carry on serenely, slipping my socked feet into a pair of tall leather boots and wrapping a long brown wool coat around myself.

"Seriously, Winter? You're not even going to dignify me with an answer?"

I methodically tie the coat belt around my waist, deciding I have zero desire to dignify him at all.

The problem is, Rob knows me well. We've been together for five years, which means he understands how to piss me off too.

His eyes trace over my face, taking on a vicious little slant.

Elsie Silver

"I liked you better with your hair lighter." His pointer finger sweeps over my head, judging the darker streaks topped with a warmer tone. He's always been obsessive about me having the silvery-blond hair, telling me how much he loves it. "This new look isn't appealing."

But the root touch-ups, the purple shampoo, and the deep conditioner were too much work for an exhausted resident, which is why I requested the stylist put in lowlights.

I blink a couple of times, like I can't quite believe he has the nerve to act like the way I color my hair is a personal slight to him.

Except I can. Because this year he took his mask off and showed me all the entitled ugliness underneath.

"That's funny. I liked you better when I thought you hadn't groomed my little sister and then fucked her over."

He scoffs. Scoffs. "That's not how it was. She was obsessed with me."

My nose wrinkles, smelling the bullshit wafting off him. "A much older doctor saves his underage patient's life. Uses his looks and power over her to get her eating out of his hand. Becomes a hero to her. Then, as soon as she turns eighteen, starts fucking her on the down-low like she's some sort of dirty secret. And when he meets her older, more appropriate sister, he drops her like a stone and marries the one who won't lose him his job for a medical license violation. Oh!"—my finger shoots up in the air—"except here's the kicker. He keeps contacting her anyway, hoping to sabotage her with boyfriends when she tries to move on, stringing her along, just because he can."

My anger swirls, but I'm the one stirring my pot by giving in to him at all.

His arms cross, and he glares at me. All golden coiffed hair, bright-blue eyes, and Ken-doll good looks. "You know I never loved her."

White-hot rage lances through me. Everything around me blurs as my eyes focus on the asshole I married. I try to keep my voice cool. Years of practicing this facade have carried me through the most heartrending of moments. I have this act down pat.

But today I struggle.

"You think you never loving her makes it better? That's my baby sister you're talking about. The one who almost died. And you fucked her around for years."

My words echo in the spacious foyer as we stare each other down.

"For what you've done to me? I am indifferent to you. For what you've done to her? I hate you. I wouldn't have touched you with a one-million-foot pole if I'd realized the type of man you really are. Fool me once, never again. That's the new saying, Rob."

With that, I tug my suitcase up and spin on my heel, flinging the door open so hard it smashes into the wall behind it. I hate how fired up I am. How out of control I feel. But I hold my chin up, press my shoulders down, and walk out of that house with all the placid, unaffected composure I can muster.

"Does that mean you're leaving me?"

How can someone so educated be so stupid? I almost

laugh. Instead, I flip him the finger over my shoulder and keep walking.

"You don't even like her!" he yells in a whiny tone that scrapes down my neck like nails on a chalkboard.

But I don't dignify his jabs with a single glance back. I just take satisfaction in knowing he's wrong.

That he's not as smart as he thinks he is.

Because I love my sister.

I just have a fucked-up way of showing it.

⁓

I hope I don't die now that I'm taking some control of my life back.

Chestnut Springs General Hospital is only an hour away from the house I live in, but it seems I'll never get there. I started taking shifts here a few months ago, so I could probably make the drive with my eyes closed, but today it's snowing hard enough that I'm white-knuckling the steering wheel.

I'm also still stewing over losing my cool.

Rob started that fight by saying he can't fathom why I'd want to work at this dingy hospital, and I didn't feel inclined to tell him the truth.

One, that working in a hospital where I'm not his wife and my mother's daughter is a relief. I can practice medicine and take pride in my work without having to contend with all the whispers and pitying glances. Without that shit hanging over my head.

Because everyone knows, but no one talks about it, and that approach to life is wearing on my sanity.

And two, because I've never wanted to be around my sister more than I do now. When she was sick, I used to sneak into the hospital and check on her, read her chart so I knew how she was doing even though I was still only in university. And now? Now, I look at my little sister and just see too many years missed.

I see a woman who lived in misery to save me a little of my own.

It would seem we're kindred that way.

She's happy now, engaged to a man whose hair is far too long but who loves her in a way that makes me green with envy. But I'm also happy for her—god knows she deserves a little peace. She left her law degree and secure job at our father's sports management firm in the rearview mirror to run a gym and live on a picturesque little country bumpkin ranch.

I admire her.

But I have no idea how to mend the rift between us. So I took a part-time position in the small town she's living in, hoping I might run into her organically.

I have this recurring story in my head, one that crops up all the time. I must be trying to manifest it or some shit.

In it, she's strolling down the sidewalk, and I bump straight into her as I exit the adorable little Parisian coffee shop on Main Street. She looks shocked to see me. I offer her a warm smile, and it isn't forced. Then I hike a thumb over my shoulder and say, "Hey, you, uh…wanna grab a coffee?" in a casual and charming way that will make her smile back at me.

Of course, I'd have to spend time somewhere other than the hospital or hotel for that to happen. But I keep slinking between the two safety zones, too scared and too embarrassed to face her.

"Fuck it," I mumble as I sniff and sit up taller, eyes laser focused on the road. "Siri, call Summer Hamilton."

The beat of silence that greets me is heavy, laden with years of anticipation.

"Calling Summer Hamilton," the robotic voice replies. The formality is a jab to the chest. Most sisters would have some cute nickname in their phone. Perhaps I'd call her Sum if we were friends. As it is now, I might as well include her middle name in the contact listing.

The phone rings. Once. Twice.

And then she's there. "Winter?" she asks breathlessly. My name isn't an accusation on her lips though. It's…hopeful.

"Hi," I say stupidly. Because no number of years of education or reading medical textbooks could prepare me for this conversation. Since everything blew up in the hospital that day, I've played out this conversation in my head a million times. I've lain awake at night preparing myself.

And it wasn't enough.

"Hi…are you…are you okay?"

I nod, while the bridge of my nose stings. I've been awful to Summer over the years, and her first inclination is to ask if I'm okay.

"Win?"

I suck in a deep breath of air. Win. Fuck. That nickname. She just falls into it so easily. I absently wonder how I'm named in her contacts. I always imagined it was EVIL HALF SISTER or something along those lines.

She's just so fucking nice. It almost makes me nauseous that someone could be this nice to me after everything that we've been through, after how cold I've been to her.

I don't deserve Summer. But I want to. And that comes with being honest.

"Not especially," I finally say, trying to cover the hitch in my voice by clearing my throat.

"Okay." I can imagine her nodding right now, rolling her lips together, mind whirring as she tries to solve this problem for me. That's just how she is. A fixer.

"Where are you? Do you need me to come and get you? Are you hurt?" She pauses. "Oh! Do you need legal help? I'm not practicing anymore, but I could—"

"Can I see you?" I blurt. And now it seems like it's her turn for stunned silence. "I'm on my way to Chestnut Springs already. I could...I don't know." A ragged sigh drags its way up my throat. "Buy you a coffee?" I finish lamely, glancing at the digital clock that shows it's already 6 p.m.

Her voice comes through the phone a little thick, a little soft. "I would love that. But we could do wine instead?"

A knot of tension unfurls in my chest, one I didn't even know was there until now. And now that I've noticed it, I can't help but feel like it's been there for years.

"Yeah." My fingers pulse on the steering wheel. "Yeah. Wine. Good."

I sound like a fucking cavewoman.

"We're having a family dinner at the main house tonight. There will be a bunch of people. I'd love if you came too."

My throat clogs uncharacteristically. This brand of kindness feels foreign after living in a sterile bubble with Rob and my mom for so long. This brand of forgiveness…I don't know how to react to it.

So I just roll with it. Seems like the least I can do.

"I'll be there. Can you send me the address?"

In my haste to get the hell out of the city, I ignored my gas tank for as long as I could. No doubt cutting it dangerously close. Which has only added to my anxiety the farther away I've gotten from that city limit.

So I give in and stop for gas in Chestnut Springs before hitting the sketchy back road my phone mapped out to the ranch.

As I stand here, freezing and wishing I'd worn more appropriate outdoor winter clothing, I let all the worry creep in through my carefully erected walls.

Worry over seeing Summer.

Worry over sitting down to dinner with a bunch of people who no doubt think I'm a heinous bitch.

Worry over the snow-packed roads. I've seen too many car accident traumas roll into the ER lately.

Worry over my career and what the hell I'm going to do—where I'm going to land.

Hilariously—albeit a dark kind of hilarious—I feel next to no concern over the thought of leaving Rob for good. I've strung that out for a long time. I've thought about it, looked at it from every angle.

Only a stupid person would stay married to Rob with nothing tying them to him.

And I'm a lot of things, but stupid isn't one of them.

I sigh a deep, heavy sigh and watch my breath puff out from between my lips into a smoky little cloud, more obvious under the neon lights that flood down over the gas bays. The tips of my fingers go from tingling to downright numb in a matter of seconds, where they're wrapped around the red plastic handle. I bounce on the spot and look up when I hear a bell jangle at the door of the gas station.

The man who walks out through the glass door is all swagger and broad shoulders. Dark hair, darker eyes, lashes that make the blond girl in me a little irritated. He's smirking down at the lotto ticket in his hand, like he thinks he's going to win.

I could tell him he's not going to win. That it's a waste of money. But I get the distinct impression that this is the type of man who doesn't care.

He's got unlaced boots, jeans stacked around the tops. A couple of long silver chains adorn his chest, disappearing under a plaid button-down that is open just a little too far, a heavy knit cardigan slung carelessly over the top.

He's sexy without even trying. He doesn't even seem cold. I bet he rolls out of bed after sleeping in yesterday's socks and just shoves them back in those worn leather boots.

I've stared at him so long, so thoroughly that the gas

pump makes a loud clanking noise as it bumps back into my palm, signaling the tank is full.

The noise of it draws his attention my way, and he turns the full force of his good looks on me. The square jaw dusted with the perfect amount of stubble, topped off with lips that are just wasted on a man. The way this man looks? It's absurd.

I drop my head quickly, fumbling with the pump to get it latched back in its holder. My tongue swipes at my lips.

I get the distinct sense that the man is watching me, but I don't glance up to see. There are a flutter in my chest and a heat in my cheeks, one I haven't felt for a very, very long time.

Because I was actually happily married. And now I'm...not. I think.

And *this* is the first man I've really let myself look at inappropriately. A man who can't bother to tie his shoes and plays the lotto.

"Ugh," I groan at myself as I approach my door, suddenly a lot less cold than I was before I saw him.

But as I'm about to slide into my seat, I look back over my shoulder at the man.

The one standing at his silver truck.

The one who's still looking at me with a knowing smirk on his face.

The one who runs a hand through his perfectly tousled hair and *winks* at me.

I'm in my car and out onto the dark road like a shot, getting away as quickly as possible.

Because the very last thing I need in my head is a man like *that*.

2

Theo

THE BLOND WOMAN STARED AT ME LIKE I WAS SOME SORT of alien. I had to stop and stare back because she was so fucking blatant.

I was ready to crack a joke about how objectified I felt by the way she was ogling me. But then she licked her lips once, blinked, and shot off. Which is a shame because I liked the way she gawked at me. I wasn't feeling objectified at all. If she'd looked me in the eye, all bets would have been off. I could have given her something to really stare at.

I didn't become a bull rider because I can't stand an audience. The show, the crowd, the recognition—I thrive on it. I was born into it. Gabriel Silva is arguably one of the most famous World Bull Riding Federation riders of all time.

And he isn't just my idol. He's my dad.

Was? I never know how to refer to him. He still feels very present to me even though he died so long ago.

As I swing up into my truck, I chuckle to myself. I know the stunning blond in the fancy Audi will cross my mind from time to time. Because there was something unusually wholesome about that interaction, like she was a teenager caught gawking and got embarrassed about it. I'd feel bad for her if I didn't feel so bad for myself that she ran off before I could get her number.

I hit the darkened road heading out to Wishing Well Ranch. I've come out here enough times over the years that I know where I'm going, whether it's dark or not. My mentor, Rhett Eaton, lives out here, and with my mom and sister living a province away, his family has become a little like my own over the holidays.

I'd usually head to Mom's place for Christmas, but she took a singles cruise with my little sister so they could both meet *Mister Right*, I think they called it.

And though I might be very, very single, I have zero desire to partake in that shit with my family.

Hard pass.

There are plenty of single buckle bunnies out on the WBRF circuit for me to pass the time with—boring as the endless series of mindless fucks have become—that don't require involving my mom.

Not to mention the whole boat thing freaks me out.

Put me on an angry bull? I'm fine.

Put me on a big boat with no land anywhere in sight? Hard pass. I saw an *Oprah* episode about people who go missing on those, and I'm too young and pretty to die.

Within a few minutes, there are red taillights ahead of me, and I'm gaining on them quickly. Really quickly.

"Come onnnn," I groan into the quiet cab of my truck as I tip my head back.

Yeah, it's snowing, but the roads are hard-packed and not icy. I finally catch up to the car and realize just how slowly they're going. Thirty kilometers an hour. In a fifty. And this isn't even a school zone.

It's when I get close enough that I realize it's the smoke show in the Audi. I should have guessed. The heeled boots and the long coat didn't scream country girl.

And neither does the way she drives a back road.

The signal light flicks left. The vehicle slows and then speeds up.

The signal light flashes right, and the car swerves a little.

Maybe she's lost? Or drunk? I sometimes zone out like she did staring at me when I've had a few too many.

Then I get close enough to see the light of her cell phone through the back window.

Perfect. Texting and driving. This chick is gonna kill herself. Or me.

Maybe if we shared a hospital room, I could get her number after all. Might be worth it.

When she slams the brakes, I startle and honk.

"Seriously!" I shout, my heart rate ratcheting up. I don't care how hot she is. She's a fucking terrible driver.

She shoots forward but slows again. I back off, not wanting to be too close to someone this erratic.

But dammit, I end up thinking of my mom or my sister lost on a back road. I go back to her being lost instead of driving like an asshole on purpose. A quick glance at my phone in its holster tells me reception is officially gone on this stretch, so she can't possibly be texting anyone.

I flash my high beams, thinking I can help if she pulls over.

I immediately feel like a serial killer.

No woman in her right mind would pull over on a dark road to talk to a strange man who flashed his high beams at her.

So I settle in, crank my Chris Stapleton, and let my eyes wander out over the snow-covered fields. All crisp and white, reflecting the light of the moon, they make it seem not so dark anymore. Before long, I'm approaching the turnoff into Wishing Well Ranch, which means I can finally bid my terrible driving temptress farewell.

Except she signals. And turns into the ranch.

My mind whirs with what that might mean. She's definitely going to think I'm stalking her. And if we're both heading to the same place, she's someone I know in a roundabout way.

Once the lit house comes into view, her car accelerates right to the front porch. She hits the brakes and flies out of her car, slamming the door and storming in my direction before I can even get out of my truck.

When I make it out, I hear, "Are you fucking insane?"

Okay. She's mad. And she doesn't sound drunk at all. She's got her keys wedged between her fingers like claws, and I instantly like this girl.

No preamble. Just comes out swinging. She's tiny and ferocious. I feel like Peter Pan getting reamed by Tinkerbell.

"Easy, Tink." I offer her a smile and lift my hands in surrender, not wanting to make her feel threatened.

"Tink?" Her voice goes even louder.

I wave a hand over her. "Yeah, you've got this whole angry little Tinkerbell vibe happening. I dig it." I let my gaze trace her body for only a moment, not wanting to border on leering. But hey, fair is fair after the way she gawked at the gas station.

"You're fucking nuts, you know that?" She starts back in. "You drive like an asshole behind me for a solid ten minutes, and now you follow me here? To…to…check me out and compare me to a Disney pixie?" Her arms flap angrily, and her dainty face twists up in fury. A look like that could incinerate a man on the spot.

But not me.

I shouldn't prod her. I know I shouldn't. But I feel like a kid with a crush who mocks the girl he likes to get her attention.

And I like the way this one fires back.

I want more.

"I think she's actually a fairy. And for the record, driving twenty below the speed limit is also dangerous and could kill someone. Mostly me. From boredom," I joke.

Her eyes widen almost comically, a sure sign that I failed to lighten the mood at all. "It's dark and snowy! I don't know the area. There could be wildlife! Driving slowly is safe so long as a back-forty hillbilly isn't riding my ass in his small-dick truck, flashing his high beams at me."

My lips clamp down against each other.

Fuck.

I really like this girl.

I should stop. I should walk away. I should channel my maturity and not flirt with her by infuriating her.

But I've always been a little reckless.

"I hear that if you want your ass ridden, a small dick is the way to go. So maybe I'm your guy."

My dick isn't small. But I'm happy to make sacrifices to land a good joke. Only a small-dicked dude would miss this opportunity.

I shouldn't have said it, but the pure shock that paints her pretty features makes it all worth it. She's so fired up; I just can't help myself. Play with fire and I'll be there to pour gasoline on it for you.

Her hand shoots up between us. "I'm married, you fucking pig. Now leave." Her hand flips out firmly, pointing down the driveway.

Married. I just shrug. "Married for now, maybe."

I'm persistent. And this girl wasn't staring at me like a married woman. Not a happily married one anyway.

It's Rhett's voice that draws our attention to the sprawling wrap-around porch attached to the huge ranch house. "Yeah, don't worry, Winter. We're gonna free you from that husband and bury him in the back field. It'll be like that Dixie Chicks song. Rob is the new Earl."

Winter.

Winter, as in Summer's sister? Fuck, that's a stupid combination of names for two sisters. They should hate their parents instead of each other, if you ask me.

I glance back at the woman before me, about six feet

away. Everyone has described her as cold and distant. A real ice queen.

I've heard the stories. The drama. They've made her sound like some sort of criminal mastermind. But all I see is a firecracker who needs my help to work out some aggression.

And I wouldn't be mad at helping her with that. Not even a little. I'm philanthropic that way.

Winter rubs her temples like she has a headache. I consider offering her an aspirin from my truck or an orgasm. I hear those help too.

"You're lucky you make my little sister so happy, Eaton," she says, sounding utterly exhausted.

Rhett hums good-naturedly, his eyes taking on that melty, drugged look he gets when people so much as mention Summer. But he doesn't address that; instead, he says, "Theo's just a baby though. You can't corrupt him, Winter."

I roll my eyes. "I'm not a baby. I'm twenty-six."

Rhett scoffs. "No, you aren't. You're twenty-two."

Good god. Does he think he knows my age better than I do?

"Dude. I was twenty-two when I first met you on the circuit. I've gotten older. You're doing the same thing my mom does with her pets. They hit a certain age, and then she says that they're that same age until one day they just die."

He chuckles. "Well, I'll be. You're like that store with the skimpy dresses. Forever 22."

I prop my hands on my hips and sigh with a bemused twist to my mouth. "Yeah. You're definitely getting old. That store is called Forever 21."

Rhett just waves me off. "Whatever. I only know about the skimpy dresses."

"Are you two done? I need a drink if I'm going to stay here all night," Winter cuts in, clearly irritated by the route our conversation has taken. Though Rhett's interruption did successfully put a stop to our little spat.

Sadly. I was enjoying sparring with her. She can hold her own in a way I haven't encountered in any of my relationships.

If that's even what you could call them.

"Ah, yes, Winter, meet my protégé Theo Silva. Theo, meet Dr. Winter Hamilton, my future sister-in-la—"

"Winter Valentine," she interrupts him with a stiff correction.

"For now," I add, winking at her. Because now that I know who she is, I don't feel so bad about making my play. I know who her husband is. And I already know I don't give a fuck about that guy.

I already know Winter can do better.

And I'm a lot better, whether she realizes it yet or not.

She gives me the most dramatic eye roll and walks in my direction. I stick my hand out—because Mama raised a gentleman—but she just walks past, glaring at me with eyes bright blue like the bottom of a flame. I turn my head to hold her gaze as she draws even with me, shoulder to shoulder.

She doesn't take my hand though. So I roll with it, swiping my hand through my hair with a wink.

The same wink I gave her at the gas station.

Our little secret.

"Call your dog off, Eaton." She keeps walking, only addressing Rhett, like I'm not even here.

But goddamn, I love a challenge.

I turn with a loud "Woof!" as I watch her petite frame slip into the bright light of the warm, bustling house.

Rhett is laughing. At me. Not with me. "You're an idiot, Theo."

I shake my head. "Dude. I think I'm in love with your sister-in-law. She's so fiery."

Now it's Rhett shaking his head, like he knows something I don't. And I follow him into the house because I want to know more.

I want to know more about Winter Valentine.

Like when that divorce is happening.

ACKNOWLEDGMENTS

Younger Elsie dated some hockey players. But none were a Jasper Gervais. And I really feel like I righted some wrongs in this world by creating him. It's just proof that book boyfriends are often a superior breed of man because, to me, Jasper is perfect.

In all seriousness, I hope you loved him and Sloane as much as I do. Because these two characters really got their hooks into me. I felt every feeling and every heartache, all the longing—I felt all the love. It wasn't an easy book to write. But it was consuming. I'm not sure I've ever had such a visceral experience writing a book, so this story will forever be special for me.

To my readers, thank you. You continue to blow me away. Where would I be without you? Your excitement is infectious, and your passion is inspiring. I love writing stories for you. Knowing there are people in the world who are so invested in the things I make up in my head is truly humbling.

To my husband and son, thank you for giving me the space to be creative—to be my own person. To disappear into other worlds. To work until I can't see straight just to hit a deadline. I don't think I could do this without my two boys being as proud of me as the two of you are. I am beyond blessed to have you both.

To my parents, remember when my grade ten English teacher told me I was a bad writer? Maybe he was trying to inspire me.

To my assistant Krista, they say that food, water, air, and shelter are the basic human needs. (I googled it, okay?) But "they" are wrong. I'd trade shelter for having you to work with.

To my Spicy Sprint Sluts, love your faces.

To Catherine, #immunitynecklacesforever.

To my beta readers Júlia, Amy, Trinity, Leticia, Josette, and Krista, thank you for helping me make this book the best it could be. Your notes make me laugh, and your feedback makes me a better writer. I'd be lost without you.

To my editor Paula, if I'm the butter, you're the bread. We go so well together.

To my cover designers, thank you for tolerating me and my incessant questions/ideas for covers and graphics. The packaging on this series is beyond beautiful, and I have you to thank for that.

Finally, to my ARC readers and street team members, THANK YOU. So many of you have been with me since the

Elsie Silver

very beginning of this wild ride. And now so many of you are new. Supporting an author in this way might not feel like a big deal to you, but it's a *huge* deal to me. Every post, every TikTok, every review literally changes my life. I don't know that I'll ever be able to repay your kindness, but I will do my best to pay it forward in whatever way I can.

Happy reading, friends.

ABOUT THE AUTHOR

Elsie Silver is a Canadian author of sassy, sexy small-town romance who loves good book boyfriends and the strong heroines who bring them to their knees. She lives just outside Vancouver, British Columbia, with her husband, son, and three dogs and has been voraciously reading romance books since before she was probably supposed to.

She loves cooking and trying new foods, traveling, and spending time with her boys—especially outdoors. Elsie has also become a big fan of her quiet 5 a.m. mornings, which is when most of her writing happens. It's during this time that she can sip a cup of hot coffee and dream up a fictional world full of romantic stories to share with her readers.

Website: elsiesilver.com